ULTIMATE TEST

Hughes leveled off the F-104 Starfighter at 60,000 feet, took a deep gulp of oxygen, and then he saw it—the long white trail of fire and smoke rising out of the morning clouds.

At the head of the blazing cyclone was the unmanned F-98 Tomarc missile, looking black and ominous. He watched with awe as the missile reached 60,000 feet and effortlessly turned and streaked out over the Pacific.

Suddenly everything that Hughes had endured in the last ten years—all the flight testing, the tragedies, the loss of friends, the combat in Korea—was at stake. Had it all been in vain? Was the unmanned Tomarc the wave of the future? Would it make pilots like him obsolete?

It was up to him to find out. He slammed the throttles forward. Instantly he felt the resounding kick as the F-104's powerful engine hurtled him through the sound barrier in pursuit of the Tomarc. The race was on. . . .

Storm Birds #3

THE GATHERING STORM

BRIAN KELLEHER

A SIGNET BOOK

NEW AMERICAN LIBRARY

A DIVISION OF PENGUIN BOOKS USA INC.

PUBLISHER'S NOTE

This book is a work of fiction. Names, characters, places, and incidents either are the product of the author's imagination or are used fictitiously, and any resemblance to actual persons, living or dead, events, or locales is entirely coincidental.

SIGNET TRADEMARK REG. U.S. PAT. OFF. AND FOREIGN COUNTRIES
REGISTERED TRADEMARK—MARCA REGISTRADA
HECHO EN DRESDEN, TN, U.S.A.

SIGNET, SIGNET CLASSIC, MENTOR, ONYX, PLUME, MERIDIAN and NAL BOOKS are published by New American Library, a division of Penguin Books USA Inc., 1633 Broadway, New York, New York 10019

First Printing, December, 1989

1 2 3 4 5 6 7 8 9

PRINTED IN THE UNITED STATES OF AMERICA

For my brothers,
Jimmy, Chris, and Joe

Prologue

THE ONLY ILLUMINATION IN the darkened compartment was coming from a fading cigarette lighter. As its wick burned down and its butane slowly ran out, the shadows its flame cast were dull, red, and grotesque.

"What the hell is that? A king or a queen?"

"It's the king of hearts."

"Are you sure?"

"Pick it up and look at it if you don't believe me."

"I thought picking up was against the rules."

"It is. But you've always been a cheating SOB, why would you change now?"

"Here he comes. . . ."

"Damn! Hide the cards."

"You take half and I'll take half."

"Quick, douse the lighter!"

"*Ouch!* The frigging thing is hot!"

"He's here. . . ."

Suddenly the only door in the now pitch-black cabin opened, letting a shaft of dim light from the passageway sneak inside.

"Jesus, shut that door! My eyes . . ."

"*Ow!* My eyes are burning. . . ."

"I'm blind!"

Walking with a pronounced limp, the figure on the other side of the door quickly slipped into the cabin, balancing five trays of food as he did so.

"I smell a lighter in here," he said.

"It's your imagination."

"It's diesel fumes coming up from the engine room."

7

"Bullshit. There hasn't been diesel fuel in that engine room in years. That's a lighter I smell."

"We don't smell anything."

"If you guys had a lighter going in here there'll be big trouble."

"Aw, stop your jabbering and give us our chow."

"Come over here and get it."

"God, what the hell is it? It smells terrible."

"It's eel. Someone caught a big one today."

"*Eel?* I ain't eating no eel. I want real food."

"Me too."

"And me."

"Ditto."

"*Double* ditto."

"God, will you guys cool it? I'm not your fucking butler and I'm not the fucking cook. And I don't give a damn whether the five of you eat it or not."

"Where's my pen and paper?"

"I told you a hundred times, you ain't getting any pen and paper."

"But I want to write a letter back home."

"*Forget it*, will you? You know there are no letters going out from here."

"But I want to write my congressman. Tell him about all this eel crap . . ."

"That's it. I've had it with you guys. The five of you can starve for all I care."

"We're too valuable to starve. That's what your boss keeps telling us."

"Well if he finds out you guys had a lighter going in here, he'll probably change his mind on that."

"Will you relax? What would we need a lighter for? We're supposed to be able to see in the dark, remember?"

"That's it. I'm leaving."

"Good riddance . . ."

"Just one more thing."

"What?"

"Can you tell us who the hell is winning this war?"

Part One

Doryoku

1

Over North Korea
Late November 1950

THE FLIGHT OF FOUR U.S. Air Force B-29s known as "Buster Force" had just passed over the eastern coast of North Korea when the squadron of Red Chinese MiGs suddenly appeared.

"Bogies at eleven o'clock!" the rear gunner aboard the lead B-29, "Buster Force One," screamed into his microphone.

An instant later, the bomber's intercom was crackling with the alarmed voices of its crew.

"Unlock the gun! . . . unlock the gun!"

"Ammo! Ammo!"

"We need more power back here!"

"Christ—the sky is full of them!"

The attack came as a terrible surprise. Buster Force had just completed a hazardous nighttime bombing raid over the northernmost reaches of North Korea and was heading for the safety of its home base in Japan. After seeing the coast of North Korea pass below them, everyone on board the big, four-prop Superfortresses had finally started to relax, believing the most difficult part of the mission was over.

Then the dozen MiG-15s suddenly appeared overhead, high above them in the predawn skies.

Now the enemy jets were peeling off in groups of three and screaming down on the B-29s, their cannons blazing.

Immediately the pilot of Buster Force One keyed in his microphone.

"Everyone remain at your stations," he called to his crew. "And knock off that unnecessary chatter!"

Quickly switching his radio set from internal to full

11

broadcast, the pilot called over to the other three B-29s
in his flight.

"Buster Force, this is Buster Force leader," he said,
trying to keep his own voice as calm as possible. "We are
turning to escape route Bravo—now. . . ."

At that moment, all radio silence between the bombers
was broken. Buster Force leader called out further instructions to the other B-29 pilots and, following his
orders, the bombers dove to a lower altitude in a desperate effort to shake the MiGs.

But everyone aboard the four B-29s knew the situation
was already hopeless.

"More bogies coming in at ten!"

"I got two—no, *three* of them right on our tail!"

"There are too many of them!"

A second wave of MiGs roared in—this time six jets in
staggered echelon. Sticking to their usual tactic of attacking one enemy aircraft at a time, the Red Chinese pilots
selected the second-in-line bomber, Buster Force Two,
as their victim. The big Superfortress's port wing and tail
sections were instantly shredded by the MiGs' initial
.50- caliber and 30mm-cannon fusillade. Then one of its
propellers was blown off, causing the B-29 to lose speed
and drop out of formation.

Three more MiGs streaked by, their pilots pouring
frenzied cannonfire into the helpless B-29's vulnerable
wing fuel tanks. Another pair roared in and concentrated
their fire on the airplane's tail section. Finally, a trailing
MiG pilot applied the *coup de grace*, blasting the mor-
tally wounded airplane's flight deck, instantly killing the
aircraft's two pilots.

The crippled B-29 flew along eerily for several seconds, its entire left side being eaten up by flames. Then it
exploded. The port wing completely disintegrated, and a
large chunk of the tail section simply fell off. What was
left flipped over and began the long plunge down.

No parachutes were spotted.

The MiGs quickly regrouped, the taste of blood en-
boldening the Chinese pilots to change their tactics. Split-
ting into three echelons of four, each group went after
one of the remaining bombers.

Buster Force One was immediately riddled with cannonfire, which killed the flight engineer and wounded several others. The B-29 to the right and below—Buster Force Three—had half of one engine shot right off its wing. Buster Force Four, trailing far behind, lost its co-pilot and navigator when a cannon shell exploded on its flight deck. All the while, the gunners on the B-29s were shooting back at the speedy MiGs but to no avail.

Still the Buster Force flight leader pressed his pilots to stay together, knowing that that was their only hope to hold off the swarming MiGs. But when he saw the Chinese pilots regroup for a third attack, he knew the fate of the remaining B-29s was probably sealed.

It was almost as if the men of Buster Force had been cursed from the beginning.

A total of six air crews had commenced training in Japan three weeks before—all of the men volunteers for the treacherous nighttime mission. The first night up, two of their B-29s collided in midair, killing all those on board. The remaining crews carried on, flying three practice missions a night for two weeks before learning that their target would be a pair of bridges that spanned the Yalu River, the waterway that served as the border between Red China and North Korea. The bridges linked the Manchurian city of Antung with North Korea, and they were being used by the Red Chinese twenty-four hours a day to transport men, heavy equipment, and weapons into the battle zone.

This flow had to be stopped.

The problem was that a large MiG base was also located at Antung, making a successful daylight B-29 raid on the bridges almost impossible. After much hand-wringing, the Air Force command determined that the target had to be hit at night, and Buster Force was born.

But even at night, the mission to bomb the Yalu bridges would be perilous. At least a dozen rare, radar-equipped, night-flying MiGs were also thought to be stationed at Antung, and should they be scrambled, the four lumbering B-29s of Buster Force would present easy pickings for them.

To counter this possibility, Buster Force was to have linked up with a fighter escort before heading in over the target. But once again, Buster Force met with bad luck: As was the case so often in the Korean theater, bad weather at the USAF base at Kimpo, South Korea, had at first delayed and then finally prevented the escorts from taking off. Buster Force circled at the prearranged rendezvous spot for two hours before realizing that no escorts were coming.

Yet the flight leader of Buster Force knew he could not scrap the mission. His commanders had successfully impressed upon him that, at this point in the Korean conflict, stopping the flow of war materials over the Yalu bridges was a number-one priority, no matter what losses in men and airplanes the Americans might incur.

So he ordered Buster Force to proceed over the target alone.

Ironically, such a desperate mission would not have been necessary just a month before. At that time, UN forces had chased the North Koreans right up to their Chinese border, and the five-month conflict seemed to be nearing an end. But then came the surprise onslaught of more than a million Red Chinese in early November. The United Nations forces had been in retreat ever since.

With the Chinese entry into the war came the MiGs, and since their first appearance, the small and quick Soviet-built jet fighters had become surprisingly invincible. Their pilots easily handled American prop-driven fighters such as the Mustangs and Corsairs. They also represented more than a match for the Air Force's sluggish jet fighters, including the F-80 Shooting Star, six of which were supposed to have escorted Buster Force.

The bombing raid itself had gone surprisingly well. Despite encountering crosswinds of nearly a hundred miles an hour over the target area, the four B-29s of Buster Force dropped 80,000 pounds of explosives close enough to the bridges to cause substantial damage.

By that time, however, their principal enemy had become the clock. The whole idea had been to bomb the target in darkness and thus elude the swarms of "Dawn Patrol" MiGs that appeared over the Yalu every day just before first light. But for the third time, the men of Buster Force had run up against bad luck: Because of the two hours wasted in waiting for the escorts and the worse-than-usual crosswinds on their bombing approach, Buster Force finally bombed the target at 0455 hours—exactly three hours behind schedule.

It was a half-hour later, with the sun just rising, that the squadron of MiGs attacked.

The survivors of the mission would never forget what happened next. . . .

"Sir, I think our fighter escort have just arrived!" the Buster Force flight leader heard his rear gunner yell over the cabin intercom.

Already overworked as he attempted to lead the three bombers away from the MiGs, the pilot thought he was hearing things. He quickly called back to the gunner to report what he saw.

"I got five jet tailpipes coming out of the south," the gunner replied, "moving really fast—and I mean *fast!*"

"Christ, are they running with red taillights?" the pilot yelled back, knowing that Allied planes carried red taillights while the Chinese flew with green.

"Affirmative," came the gunner's hopeful reply. "Red taillights for sure. They are engaging the trailing MiGs right now!"

"Goddamn, can we be this lucky?" the co-pilot yelled over to the flight leader.

"Let's not stick around to find out," the pilot hastily replied.

The flight leader ordered the other B-29s to level off and run south-southeast at full power. At this heading, it was the B-29 rear gunners who had the best sight of the developing dogfight.

At first they saw little more than two sets of red and green lights streaking toward each other through the emerging daylight. Then, to the astonishment of the gunners, two of the unidentified jets broke off and rose to meet a wave of diving MiGs—just a pair against at least half a dozen. Within seconds, swirling patterns of bright

exhaust and streams of gunfire criss-crossed the dawn sky
as the furious battle between the opposing fighters erupted.

"Our guys are really mixing it up with them, sir!"
Buster Force One's rear gunner called ahead to the flight
leader.

"They're right in the middle of all them . . . They're
scattering them. . . . *Jesus!* These airplanes are moving
like . . . like they're rocketships or something!"

The pilot of Buster Force One would have attributed
his gunner's last comment to the excitement of the moment if he hadn't heard similar accounts being screamed
over the radio from men in the other B-29s.

"God! Look at our guys go!" several airmen seemed to
yell at once.

"How can anything go that fast!" another hollered.

The pilot of Buster Force Three had taken a quick
look over his shoulder just as one of the mystery jets
streaked by. He was astonished to see that in addition to
the standard jet-exhaust flame coming from its tail, two
long trails of powerful flame were sprouting from the
fighter's belly.

"Good God!" the veteran pilot called out, bewildered.
"These things are *unbelievable*!"

"What kind of aircraft are they?" the pilot of Buster
Force One radioed back to his gunner. "Air Force or
Navy?"

"No way of telling, sir," the gunner replied, his voice
jumpy with excitement. "It's still too dark. They're not
F-80s or F-84s. That's for *damn* sure. I've just never seen
anything like this. They've got to be secret weapons of
some kind. . . ."

All the while, the B-29s were gradually pulling away
from the action while the mystery jets brazenly took on
the superior force of MiGs. First one, then two explosions ripped through the sky—both of them MiGs destroyed by the fierce machine-gun barrages from the
strange airplanes. Some of the B-29 airmen saw one of
the red-tailed "rocketships" accelerate head-on into three
MiGs with its guns blazing, causing two to veer off while
destroying the third. Others watched in amazement as
another of the strange jets forced two MiGs down into a

gut-wrenching power dive from which one of the enemy airplanes could not recover. It slammed into one of the low hills that dotted the North Korean shoreline, exploding on impact and instantly killing its pilot.

The battle went full force for five long minutes, all to a chorus of astonishment from the handful of men in the B-29s who could see the surprisingly one-sided aerial action. By later accounts, at least five of the MiGs were shot down.

Then, as suddenly as it had started, it was over. The MiGs broke off the attack and fled northward, just as the first rays of bright sunlight broke through on the horizon. Just like that, the rest of Buster Force had been saved.

"Talk about the fucking cavalry arriving just in time!" the flight leader said, with a whistle of relief.

"I will personally give up a week's pay to get all those fighter jocks shitfaced," the co-pilot agreed. "Whoever the hell they are!"

"I'll give *twice* that just to see what kind of buggies they're flying," the pilot replied.

So it was with some surprise that they heard their tail gunner call out: "They're leaving, sir. . . . Our fighters are bugging out! . . ."

The lead pilot twisted in his seat just in time to see the five distinctive tail flames of the mysterious jets form up and depart the area.

"Where the hell are they going?" he wondered aloud. It was standard procedure for accompanying fighters to escort the bombers back to their base of origin, especially after seeing action. This way the proper paperwork and debriefing could be carried out—and, more important, the bomber pilots could show their gratitude by treating the fighter jocks at the base officers' club.

But just as mysteriously as they had arrived, the five strange airplanes roared off, flying to the southwest, leaving the trio of battered B-29s to limp back to their base alone.

2

Yokota Air Base, Japan

THE JOB OF DEBRIEFING the survivors of Buster Force fell to Captain Eddie Dorp, a young USAF intelligence officer who had been in Japan for only two weeks.

It had started out to be a fairly routine job for Dorp. Initial reports indicated that Buster Force's targets had been hit hard, and this would bode well for the Air Force's night-bombing advocates. Plus, Dorp knew his superiors would be very interested in learning more about the MiGs that had attacked the B-29s.

It was only after speaking with several of the airmen—the Buster Force flight leader and his co-pilot, especially—did Dorp realize that quite a few unusual things had happened during the mission.

So many crew members of Buster Force were injured during the flight and in the crash landings that followed that the postmission debriefing had to take place in Yokota's base hospital. Still, despite their injuries, the bomber crews were quick to heap praises on the fighter pilots who had arrived in the nick of time to save them from certain disaster.

But Dorp was puzzled by the reports of the mysterious fighters: His documentation of the Buster Force flight indicated that no escorts had accompanied the bombers on their mission; those originally assigned had been grounded at the Kimpo air base by the highly unpredictable Korean weather.

Intrigued by their story, Dorp asked the survivors who had seen them to describe the mystery jets as best they could, hoping he could glean from the information the base, unit, and squadron of the heroic fighter pilots. As it turned out, getting the men of Buster Force to identify the fighters proved at first difficult and, eventually, impossible. Because of the less than ideal nighttime conditions, the airmen could only hazard a guess as to what type of airplanes were involved. A few of the men assumed they were souped-up F-84s. Several others believed they were actually a new type of carrier-based jet, though a quick check by Dorp with the U.S. Navy's Task Force 77 command confirmed that no Navy aircraft were on escort duty the night in question.

Most of the B-29 crewmen insisted that their airborne saviors were flying a new kind of airplane, a secret weapon that was somehow powered by rockets as well as jet engines. When Dorp asked the men to sketch what they had seen on a pad of paper, most of the eyewitnesses drew a kind of rocketship.

It was the rear gunner aboard *Buster Force One* who provided the most detailed, and therefore most baffling, description of the five mystery planes. Even though he saw them no closer than an eighth of a mile away in the darkness, he claimed that besides using some kind of rocket power, the strange airplanes were painted all black and carried a row of five red navigation lights on their tails, four more than the usual number.

Dorp did a quick check of all the Allied groups in the Korean theater and found that no unit's aircraft fit this description. . . .

Dorp hand-wrote a quick report on Buster Force's strange encounter and, with the crewmen's drawings in hand, ran across the windy tarmac at Yokota to the office of USAF Lt. Colonel Douglas Harvey, his commanding officer.

Harvey was a strange bird; Dorp had been warned about the man's peccadilloes even before he'd shipped out from the states. In 1948 the old Army Air Corps was branched off to create a new military service, the U.S. Air Force. A thirty-year career Army officer at the time, Harvey had been swept up in the changeover, and from all reports, he hadn't gone peacefully. Like many long-time Army Air officers of the time, he believed that the job of air support and air defense belonged solely to the

Army, an institution that had been around for some 170 years. He had no use for the young lions who had pushed for the third service, no use for their gaudy blue uniforms or their insistence on wearing silver buttons and wings.

But the military was his career, so Harvey grudgingly put on his Air Force blues and, in 1949, was given charge of an aerial recon and intelligence unit, based at Yokohama, Japan. When the Korean conflict broke out, Harvey and his group were moved to Yokota, where the first B-29s to be used in the war were based. He made a lasting impression right away: The first night in the new digs, Harvey showed up in the base officers' club, stinking drunk and wearing his old Army uniform. He lectured the astonished patrons for twenty minutes on the evils of the Air Force and why the third service should revert back to the old Army Air Corps. Finally, two sympathetic colleagues led him away and put him to bed.

Since that night, he was known to all as "Hard-Ass" Harvey.

Now Dorp was sitting in Harvey's office, staring at the dozens of pictures of old Army aircraft hanging on the walls, while the man himself read over his hastily prepared report.

"These reports are supposed to be typed, in triplicate, Captain," was the senior officer's first reaction. "Do you have an explanation as to why this one is handwritten—in pencil, yet?"

Dorp cleared his throat. "Well, I thought you'd want to know the rather unusual goings-on with Buster Force right away, sir," he answered.

Harvey looked up at him through his intimidating bifocals. The colonel was a large man, with black-gray hair and a head like a pumpkin. His face seemed melded into a permanent sneer.

"This is a question of typing, Captain," he said. "I'm not interested in any report that is not properly prepared."

"But sir," Dorp protested, "some very strange things happened to those B-29s out there. Not only were they hit by MiGs, they were saved by some rather unusual airplanes from a unit that I can't find. . . ."

Harvey took off his glasses and began to suck on his thumb knuckle.

"Captain, this is a perfect example of why we are doing so badly in this war," he said stonily. "People feeling they can just go off and do whatever the hell they want, ignoring procedures, ignoring regulations. Now, I was in the U.S. Army for thirty years, and never, *ever*, did anyone hand-write a debriefing report in pencil. And while I realize that all you young officers here in this Air Force would just as soon do things your own slipshod way, I will remind you that I am still in charge of this unit. And as long as I am, every report—whether it concerns a flat tire on a B-29 or the Second Coming of Our Lord—will be typed, in triplicate, before crossing my desk.

"Is that clear?"

Dorp was astonished. "But what about these strange airplanes, sir?" he asked.

"Forget about them," Harvey roared. "And don't put a word about them in your properly typed report. That's an order. We have a war to fight and can't waste time chasing rumors being spread by a bunch of battle-fatigued airmen."

With that, the senior officer flung the handwritten report across his desk at Dorp.

"You're dismissed, Captain," he said, putting his glasses back on. "And take these children's drawings with you."

3

Sinanju, North Korea
Two Days Later

THE AMERICAN POW HAD staggered into the U.S. Marines' defensive perimeter near Sinanju shortly after midnight, bleeding from wounds to his right ear and shoulder.

He had been shot—mistakenly, by U.S. Army troops —as he approached their outpost two miles north of the Marine position. Already suffering from frostbite and shock, the wounded POW had nevertheless managed to stumble the two miles to the Marine outpost, screaming out his name and serial number as he went.

The Marine guards who first spotted him nearly shot him as well. Their first reaction was understandable. The wounded man was wearing a quilted suit and cap and mustard-colored cloth boots—the standard uniform of the Red Chinese People's Liberation Army. Wearing such an outfit was reason enough to get fired upon by UN troops in the Sinanju area: As in most of the battle zones between the communists and the UN soldiers in occupied North Korea, the lines around Sinanju were often confused, fluid, and subject to change by the hour.

But the man had actually escaped from his Red Chinese captors—or so he claimed. The Marine intelligence officer who questioned him the next morning as he lay in the camp's hospital tent was very skeptical at first. Escaped POWs were rare in the Korean conflict. The Red Chinese usually force-marched their prisoners up to the Manchurian border immediately upon capture. Those surviving the grueling trek were locked up in camps close to the Yalu River. Anyone who managed to get out of a communist prison camp faced the long, cold, and virtually impossible task of making his way back through miles of enemy-held territory.

Yet this POW, a U.S. Army sergeant named Baker, had a different story—one so odd the Marines suspected he had actually been brainwashed and intentionally sent back across the lines by the Red Chinese. It wouldn't have been the first time such a ploy had been tried by the communists.

After treating his wounds and questioning him at length, the Marines transported Baker back to their divisional headquarters near Chungju. From there he was secretly flown to Yokota, where the case was turned over to Hard-Ass Harvey's Air Force intelligence unit.

"He says he was captured nine days ago," the Marine

lieutenant who had accompanied Baker to Yokota told Eddie Dorp. "Claims he was held most of that time with seven other Americans up near Sonchon . . ."

Dorp ran his hand through his close-cropped hair. It was cold inside his converted barracks office despite the three iron stoves working overtime to warm the shelter. Before he'd shipped in, he had been under the impression that Japan and Korea had a tropical environment all year round. It was a common mistake.

"The fact that this guy was wearing a Chinese uniform doesn't bother us that much," the Marine officer told him. "We've had reports of the Reds giving their extra clothing to our POWs. And it's not so unusual that they didn't march him and the others up to the Yalu camps right away. The fighting's been heavy all around Sonchon. The Reds were probably staying put to save their own behinds."

The Marine's face creased in worry at this point. "But it's this damn airplane-crash story that sounds screwy to me," he continued. "On the one hand, I can't imagine a guy like that making it up. On the other, I can't imagine the Reds making it up either."

Dorp lit a cigarette and offered one to the Marine.

"He should be awake by now," the lieutenant said, taking a drag of the butt and checking his watch. "Are you ready to question him?"

Dorp nodded. "I sure am," he said.

Both men walked across Yokota's chilly wind-swept tarmac to the base hospital. Upon entering, they went through an unmarked door and down a stairway that led to the basement of the building, an area off-limits to most base personnel. Passing by three sets of sentries, they reached a darkened corridor with a single room at the end.

"This will be the fifth time he's told the story," the Marine lieutenant said as they paused at the room's heavy metal door. "So far, it's been the same, every time."

"Time to lean on him?" Dorp asked.

The lieutenant nodded. "Maybe a little," he replied.

They entered the room to find Sergeant Baker sitting

in a wooden chair next to his bunk. Other than a wash
basin, a table, and a lamp, the room was bare.

The Marine introduced Dorp by rank only, then said,
"Sergeant, let's go over your story once again."

Baker's eyes instantly misted over.

"How many times do I have to go through this?" he
asked. "Why am I being treated like a prisoner?"

"This will be the last time," Dorp said quickly. "I
guarantee you that."

Baker shook his head dejectedly and rubbed his bandaged shoulder.

"That's what everyone keeps telling me," he mumbled.

Dorp gave Baker a cigarette and lit it for him.

"Okay, pal," he said. "Once more, from the beginning . . ."

"The day I escaped started out just like the other nine
days they had me," Baker began, his voice worn out and
raspy.

"Me and seven other GIs had been captured near the
Sonchon bridge. The Chinese put us all together in this
shitty little shed. It didn't have any heat or a stove, so we
all used to sit close together in the corner, trying to stay
warm. We could hear the artillery and air bombs going
off near us, and sometimes it sounded like the fighting
was right outside. We thought we were going to get
killed in the crossfire or by one of our own bombs.

"The Reds ignored us most of the time, except for this
one asshole officer who would come around in the middle of the night and scream at us in Chinese for no
reason. The only other time we saw them was at noon,
when two or three soldiers would give us a couple pots of
hot water and a few handfuls of sorghum or millet. This
is all we had to eat each day.

"On my ninth night, this Chinese captain we'd never
seen before walked in just as we was all huddling down
to go to sleep. He picked out four of us and made us go
outside, where he had a bunch of Chinese privates waiting. They handed us some Chinese Army uniforms and
boots and told us to put them on. Then they put us in the
back of this beat-up truck and tied us all together. An-

other truck came up—it was carrying another bunch of Chinese soldiers—and off we went.

"We drove for miles. We went over hills, through ravines, by bombed-out villages. At one point, I thought we were actually going in circles, because some of the terrain began to look mighty familiar. At other times, I wasn't so sure.

"Finally, after about three hours, we stopped on the edge of this big field. It was surrounded by trees on three sides, and there was a bunch of small mountains on the other. I'm sure we were near the sea, because I could hear the sounds of waves breaking off in the distance and there was a smell of salt in the air.

"We was hauled off the truck and untied. Then they ordered us to march into the field. I darn near shit my britches when I heard the Chinese soldiers loading rounds into their rifle chambers. I started saying the Act of Contrition, right out loud—I was sure they were going to execute us.

"But when we reached the middle of the field, the Chinese captain ordered everyone—us and his soldiers—to sit down in a circle. It was frigging cold and the field was covered with snow, but those Red soldiers did just as he told them to do and they made us sit in the snow with them.

"Then the officer started rattling off long sentences in Chinese. He was talking to us like we understood it or something. He kept pointing to us and then to the sky or the stars or something overhead. We finally figured out that he wanted us to look up in the sky for something.

"At that point we would have done anything if we thought it was going to save our lives. So we all start looking up into the sky and making like we was really interested. Once this officer saw that his message had got through to us, he sits his ass right down in the snow too and he starts staring up into the sky.

"It was a really cold night. There was no moon, no clouds or anything. But I can still see that Red officer. His eyes were wide as doughnuts, looking up there, over there, behind him. It was like he was expecting something to happen. By this time I remember thinking that this guy was a little weird—maybe shell-shocked or something. He was just acting pretty strange.

"We sat there for at least three hours. Thank god they had given us the Chinese uniforms, because we would have freezed to death in our own raggy stuff. But it was still *damned* cold. We spent the whole time looking up at the sky, rubbing our arms, blowing hot air into our hands, and not saying a word. We was near frostbite but we was also damn happy to be still alive. At one point, I even started picking out a few constellations that I knew. Later on I tried to count the brightest stars.

"Then something really strange happened. . . ."

At this point Baker asked Dorp for another cigarette. The young Air Force officer lit one for the man, then one for himself.

"Go on," he finally said to Baker.

"Well, it was just about a half-hour before sunrise," the POW continued, his voice getting shaky and nervous. "Suddenly, something big and red streaks over our heads. It scared the hell out of us! At first I thought it was an illuminating shell, the kind the Chinese use at night. But I knew it was moving too high and too fast for that.

"It took me a few seconds to realize that this thing was an airplane. It was a very strange one, though. It was really moving and it was trailing a long bunch of fire behind it.

"It disappeared off to the east, but then it came back and started to circle very high right above us. It was still pretty dark at this time, but I could see a little more than an outline of it. It wasn't like any airplane I've seen since being in Korea. It was painted black or in some dark color and it had no markings. I couldn't tell what country it belonged to."

"Did it have a propeller?" Dorp asked.

"No, not at all," Baker replied quickly. "It was a jet—no doubt about that. We could hear its engine. And every once in a while, this long streak of fire would just *explode* from underneath it. Man, when that happened, it would shoot that baby right across the sky."

Dorp felt a shiver run through him. He had heard this kind of description before.

"We watched this thing for about a minute," Baker went on. "Then all hell broke loose. A bunch of airplanes suddenly came out of the north. They was moving fast— and I mean *fast*! They were jets, too. We could see they was painted silver with rows of green lights on their wingtips. We figured they're probably them MiGs we'd all heard so much about. Anyway, they went right for this guy that was circling, firing all their guns at once."

"What were the Chinese soldiers doing at this point?" Dorp asked.

"They were getting *very* worked up," Baker said. "Hysterical, even. They were on their feet and jabbering at each other, all the while pointing toward the airplanes. And the officer was really going nuts!"

Baker cleared his throat and took a long drag of his cigarette. "Then, no sooner had these silver-and-green guys showed up, when four more of the other black airplanes came out of nowhere. It was really weird. One moment there was nothing; then the next second—*boom!* —they were just there. It was like a movie. It looked like they just came out of thin air."

Dorp glanced at the Marine, who rolled his eyes. "Go on," he said.

"Well, now there was a real rumble," Baker said, his eyes going wide again with excitement. "Man, these guys were shooting everything they had at each other. Sometimes they would swoop down low and we'd get a good look at them. It was louder than a thunderstorm, and the sky was just filled with fire and smoke. I guess it went on for ten minutes or more. We just couldn't believe we were watching it. . . .

"One of the silver airplanes was hit, and he crashed right into the side of the mountain off to our west. Then another silver guy got it. He took off with a fire coming out his ass end, really banged up. Then a third silver guy just blew up."

"Sounds like the MiGs were getting the worst of it," Dorp said.

"That they were, sir," Baker replied. "And each time

one of them bought it, the Chinese looked like their granny had just died."

Both Dorp and the Marine paused to light cigarettes as Baker took a few moments to collect his thoughts.

"It was right at the end of the battle," he began again, choosing his words carefully. "The sun was almost up and it almost seemed like . . . well, like none of these flyboys wanted to be caught in the daylight. We could see them breaking away from each other. They were disengaging. But all of sudden, two of them—a dark one and a silver—just smashed right into each other. Head-on. *Blam!* Right above us.

"The silver jet blew up. In an instant. What was left started spinning and smoking, throwing fire everywhere. That's when I realized that damn thing was going to drop right on top of us. It looked like the sky was falling in. It was awful. . . ."

"What did you do?" the Marine asked.

"*I ran*, sir," Baker replied anxiously. "I ran faster than I'd ever run before. That thing was coming down like fire and brimstone, and it looked like it was going to drop right on top of my head. So I took off—ran like crazy towards the woods. . . ."

"And the others?"

Baker's next breath caught in his throat. He was now having difficulty speaking. "They just . . . *stood there*, sir," he said, almost in a gasp. "They stood there and that thing came down and . . . and it *killed* them all. Crushed them. It was like they was spooked. Frozen. They couldn't move—almost like they was *hypnotized*. . . ."

Baker broke down completely at this point, his eyes watering, his tongue going thick. Dorp poured a cup of water and handed it to him. Instead of drinking it, Baker simply threw it onto his face.

"Keep going, Sergeant," the Marine said. "You're almost through . . ."

Baker shook his head and dabbed his teary eyes with his shirt-sleeves.

"They were all dead, sir," he said. "Gone. Crushed by that wreck. I could see the bodies burning. I could *smell* the flesh. It was awful. I didn't know any of the other

Americans—they weren't like my buddies or anything. And I didn't think I'd give a damn about the Chinese. But this has really bothered me, sir. Something went funny in my head—it was just so damned strange! Like we had taken a night off from the war. And we witness this weird air battle. Then, next thing I know, they're all dead. . . . And I'm the only one left. . . ."

"What about the other airplane?" the major asked. "What happened to it?"

Baker caught his breath and coughed heavily a few times.

"I was just by the treeline at this point, sir," he continued, sobbing. "I was hugging a tree like it was my mama. Then I saw the other airplane was trying to stay up, but it couldn't. It was on fire and it looked like a good part of one wing was gone. It started to come down, almost like the pilot was trying to make a landing. He came in kind of level. Even put his wheels down . . ."

"And?"

"Well, he plowed in, sir," Baker said. "Tore up about an eighth of a mile, I'd say. Left a string of little fires and had stuff ripping off him. The airplane was covered in flames by the time it came to a stop. It was so hot it made the snow all around him sizzle and steam up. I couldn't believe it when I saw the canopy open and the guy actually crawl out. . . ."

Both Dorp and the Marine officer shot nervous glances at each other.

"Didn't you try to help him?" Dorp asked.

Baker hung his head and covered his face with his hands.

"I wanted to, sir," he said, sobbing again, "I *really did*. But I just couldn't move. . . . He came right toward me. God, I can still see him! He was dressed all in black and had a weird helmet on—almost like a spaceman. He was hurt bad, but I could see he was trying like hell to get away from that airplane."

"And then what happened?"

Tears were streaming down Baker's face at this point.

'Like I told everyone before," he said, "he fell about twenty feet in front of me. Yelled out something, then that was it. I finally worked up the guts to crawl over to him, and when I did I saw that he was dead."

"Was he an American?" Dorp asked.

"He was a white man, sir," Baker replied, wiping his runny nose on his sleeve. "His eyes were turned up into his head and there was a lot of black stuff coming out of his mouth. Almost like black paint.

"I tried to drag him into the woods, but that's when the other unmarked airplanes came back."

"And what did they do?"

"They blasted his airplane, sir," Baker said, shaking his head in disbelief. "Machine guns. A few bombs. They blasted the hell out of it—his own guys! Kept doing it until nothing was left."

Dorp, too, was shaking his head by this time.

"I just got the hell out of there then," Baker said without any prodding. "I was all mixed up. I couldn't figure out why his own guys would bomb his plane like that, but I didn't want to stick around and find out, either. I thought for sure the Reds would be coming at any minute. I ran about a mile, then I hid in the woods during the day. I only moved at night. Tried to keep going south. I finally reached our lines, and then I got shot and I guess you know the rest."

Baker wiped his eyes and looked up at the officers.

"You believe me, don't you?" he asked them, desperately.

Neither man answered him. Instead, Dorp retrieved a small envelope from his jacket pocket.

"Okay, Sergeant, I'm going to show you some pictures of airplanes," he said. "I want you to tell me if any of them look like the black airplane you saw crash that night."

Baker wiped his eyes and mouth with his sleeve and looked at the first picture Dorp was holding. It was of an F-80 Shooting Star.

"Nope, that's not one of them," Baker said.

Next he showed him a photo of an F-84 Thunderjet.

"No sir," Baker said. "I've seen those kinds of jets flying around."

Next came photos of a Navy Panther jet and a Marine Skyknight. Once again, Baker shook his head.

Dorp then showed him the last photo in the pack.

"That's it!" Baker said, unconsciously taking the photo from Dorp. "So they really *do* exist! . . . What kind of airplane is it?"

Dorp and the Marine were silent for a long moment, then Dorp gave Baker a brotherly pat on the shoulder.

"Get some rest, Sergeant," he said.

4

Over North Korea
Late November 1950

THE ESCORT CARRIER USS *Cape Esperance* had just crossed the international date line when the message from the U.S. Far East Air Force came in.

The ship's captain was on the bridge when the sealed teletype was hand-delivered to him by the communications officer's mate, but he ignored the message at first. He had other things to attend to.

The sea was particularly rough this day, by far the worst of the past four days. The small "jeep" carrier—a dwarf compared to superior flattops like the *Lexington* or the *Valley Forge*—was being tossed around a fair bit by the high waves, ones that occasionally swelled to twenty or even thirty feet.

The captain wasn't concerned so much about his vessel itself: The ride was uncomfortable, but the ship's structure was by no means in any danger. Nor did he worry about his crew: They were all veterans, and they could handle the rough seas. No, his major concern was for his cargo. A veteran of World War II and more than twenty-five years at sea, the captain knew the rough conditions were taking a silent toll on the top-secret freight that was locked up and lashed below decks.

*   *   *

Another ten minutes passed while the captain attended to the necessities of sailing a pitching ship through rough seas. Finally he ripped open the communique from USFEAF.

Any assumption that the message would be just another piece of normal communications traffic quickly vanished. In fact, the captain had to read the short message several times over in an effort to make some sense of it.

In the end, he couldn't—the message made no sense. He checked with his communications officer to make sure the communique had been decoded correctly. It had been. He briefly considered that the message might be a practical joke—perhaps one of his old sea friends was tweaking his nose. But once again, the captain quickly discounted the idea: Sending unauthorized coded messages during wartime was a gag that could land the comedian in Leavenworth facing life at hard labor.

Finally he knew he needed help in deciphering the strange communique. Leaving command of the bridge to the steering crew, the captain called down to his executive officer and requested that he meet him in his quarters in five minutes.

The XO knew something was up the second he walked into the captain's cabin and saw the worried look on the senior officer's face.

"Have a seat," the captain told him, pouring them both a cup of coffee.

"Trouble, sir?" the XO asked.

"Maybe," was the captain's quick reply.

The senior officer paused in thought for a moment, then continued.

"I know I'm breaking a few regulations here," he began, "but something's come up and, frankly, I need your help in figuring it out."

"I hope I can be of assistance, sir," the XO replied.

The captain frowned and took a sip of coffee.

"Do you have any idea what we are carrying in the hold of this ship?" he asked the XO point-blank.

The XO quickly shook his head. "It's classified," he

said. "As I understand it, only you and the Air Force guys on board know the contents. . . ."

The captain smiled, momentarily cheered in the knowledge that his XO was a damn good one.

"Okay, that's the company line," the captain told him. "Now, off the record, do you know what we are carrying?"

The XO took a moment before answering. There had been so many precautions when the ship took on the classified cargo in San Diego that Sherlock Holmes himself would have had a hard time figuring out just what was locked away in the carrier's hold. The crew had been kept in quarters for nearly eighteen hours as the special team of Air Force workers on-loaded the secret cargo, and since then, no one but these specialists and the captain had been allowed anywhere near the sealed-off flight compartment.

Still, the XO had a good idea what they were carrying.

"I believe they are new jets, sir," the XO answered truthfully. "At least that's what the poop on ship says. . . ."

Again the captain smiled, albeit it briefly. "Well, the poop is accurate," he said, lighting a cigarette. "And that's the sign of a good ship and crew."

He took a long drag on his cigarette and turned serious again.

"Now, here's where I break my first regulation," he said. "In the hold of this ship are fourteen F-86A Sabre jets—the Air Force's newest combat airplane. They were ordered to Korea by the Joint Chiefs a week after the Red Chinese intervention, even though they are so new that not all the bugs have been worked out of them."

"Sounds like a drastic step, sir," the XO said.

"It is," the captain confirmed. "But something had to be done to counter the Chinese MiGs. Those sonsofbitches are faster and more powerful than the F-80s and F-84s the Air Force already has operating in the theater. The Air Force is hoping the F-86s might be the answer."

"Can they do it, sir?"

"No one knows," the captain replied frankly. "Some think the Sabre can match the MiG in speed and maybe handle better under certain conditions. But a lot of peo-

ple think they can't. Still, none of this will be known for
sure until both airplanes actually face each other in combat. Once that's happened, we'll know just who will be
controlling the skies over Korea."

"You don't seem convinced the Sabre can do the job,
sir," the XO said.

"I'm not," the captain replied. "But I sure as hell ain't
going to broadcast it. The facts are that the MiG *can*
climb faster and fly higher than the Sabre. Plus it can
outshoot the Sabre because it carries two cannons in the
nose, while the F-86 only has six .50-caliber machine
guns."

The XO had to think about that for a moment.

"But six guns to two sounds like an advantage for the
Sabres," he said.

"That's what everyone thinks—at first," the captain
said. "But actually it's probably the most overwhelming
factor in favor of the Reds. Look at it this way: A
cannon shot packs more punch than a machine-gun round,
right? More punch means less firing time for the MiG
pilot. Less firing time means quicker kills: A MiG pilot
only has to keep the Sabre in his sights long enough for a
short burst from his cannons. . . ."

The XO was now nodding in agreement. "Meanwhile
the F-86 pilot will have to stick to the MiG's tail like glue
in order to pump out enough machine-gun rounds to
inflict damage," he said.

"Exactly," the captain replied. "But there's more: The
MiG pilots have already had a month's head start in
seeing what their planes could do. That's a frigging eternity of experience under actual combat conditions, especially in this brave new world of jet-against-jet dogfighting.

"When those Sabre pilots finally go into combat, it will
be their first day of school and they're going to have to
learn fast. *Damn* fast."

The XO had no trouble understanding why the captain
had kept all this to himself. These were desperate days
for the UN forces in Korea and paranoid ones back in
America. Any questioning of policy could land an officer
into an unemployment line—or, worse, before one of the

many Red-baiting congressional committees hunting down disloyal Americans in the U.S.

Still, he wondered why the captain was telling it all to him now.

"Sounds like things are desperate over there," the XO said.

"Worse than even the newspapers are letting on," the senior officer replied grimly. "But all is not lost yet. In fact, I think everyone is overlooking the *real* key to the success or failure of this gamble—something I can only describe as 'the human factor.'"

"I guess I don't understand," the XO admitted.

The captain took a long sip of coffee and lit another cigarette. "It's simple, really," he said. "I think that in the end, it will be the *talent* of the men flying the machines that will determine the outcome—and not the machines themselves."

"You mean that our pilots are better than theirs?" the XO asked.

"We'd better hope so," the captain replied.

The senior officer went on to explain that the ship's classified destination was actually Kisarazu, Japan, where the Sabres would be off-loaded and readied to go into action against the Red Chinese. But again, the captain warned that there'd be problems. He told the XO that even now, just a week into the two-week trip, the salt air and rough travel was wreaking havoc with the Sabres' engines, electronics, and various moving surfaces. As sailors, both knew that nothing was as corrosive as salt; on a ship, living with it was a way of life. But the Air Force jets weren't sealed up like Navy carrier aircraft, and now the salt was taking a toll. The captain revealed that he had made an extensive inspection of the Sabres that morning and calculated that they faced a minimum of two weeks of repair before they could ever hope to go into combat.

"I had no idea things were this bad, sir," the XO finally told him.

"They might have just gotten worse," the captain said. "Which is why I asked you here in the first place."

Reaching into his shirt pocket, the captain pulled out

the strange message he'd received from the Far East Air Force.

"Now, knowing what you know," he said, handing the communique to the second-in-command, "tell me if you can make any sense out of this. . . ."

The XO read the message over quickly, stopped, screwed up his face in bafflement, then read it again.

"This has got to be a joke," he finally said. "Someone's pulling our leg. . . ."

The captain frowned and shook his head. "I don't know anyone that stupid," he said. "At least not on our side."

The XO quickly shook his head. "But it can't possibly be the Chinese or the North Koreans," he said, rereading the bizarre missive a third time. "I can't believe they would have this . . . well, this sense of humor."

"The Russians, maybe?" the captain offered.

The XO thought this over for a moment. "Trying to get some intelligence?" he wondered aloud.

The captain could only shrug. He took the message and read it aloud: *"Confirm you have not sea-launched any aircraft."*

The senior officer shook his head. "Now, tell me, what the hell does it mean?"

The XO had no idea. "As we don't have any other aircraft aboard, I assume they are referring to the Sabres."

"They would have to be," the captain replied. "Why else would the Air Force be calling us?"

"Could it be a loyalty test?" the XO asked.

The captain blew his nose in disgust. "Well, if it is, then I take it as an insult to our intelligence."

"Likewise, sir," the XO said. "I mean, sea-launching? Those jets?"

"*Any* jet," the captain added. "What the hell do they think we're driving here? The *Enterprise*?"

The thought of one of the Sabres taking off from the deck of the *Cape Esperance* was absurd: The carrier didn't have the powerful system of steam catapults needed to launch a jet. And even if it did, the Sabres were strictly land-based aircraft: They had neither the reinforced undercarriage needed for carrier take-offs nor the ass-end arresting hook essential for carrier landings.

"It's just so screwy, sir," the XO said. "What could possibly be behind it?"

"I just don't know," the captain replied. "And I guess I feel better that you think the same way. But I will bet you a bottle of Scotch that the Air Force has screwed up royally and that this is one of the grandest efforts at ass-covering since Monty tried for Antwerp."

The XO shook his head. "That's one bet I *won't* take, sir," he said.

5

Yokota Air Base, Japan

THE DECODED REPLY FROM the USS *Cape Esperance* was sitting on Hard-Ass Harvey's desk two hours later.

It read simply: *"We have no capability for sea-launching aircraft in question."*

Harvey's pumpkin-shaped head was flushed with anger —so much so, he was having a tough time even speaking.

"I still cannot believe that you went ahead and did such a foolish thing, Captain," he raged across the desk to Dorp, his words coming out in a series of spits and sputters. "Especially after I told you—no, *ordered* you—to give up this asinine wild goose chase."

It was Dorp who had sent the peculiar message to the *Cape Esperance*, an act that, although within his authorization to do, had nevertheless infuriated Harvey.

"How could you have initiated this incredible blunder?" Hard-Ass continued to spit. "How do you even know that this carrier captain can be trusted?"

Dorp was momentarily bewildered. "Trusted, sir?"

"Is he a loyal American, Captain?" Harvey snapped.

Dorp involuntarily sighed. By using the "loyal American" code words, Harvey was actually asking him whether the Navy officer was a "hidden communist," like the ones that the various congressional committees back in Washington seemed to be finding under every other bed these days.

"I checked his dossier thoroughly before sending the message, sir," Dorp half lied. "His record is outstanding, both in action in the Pacific and during peacetime."

Harvey pointed his finger directly at Dorp, momentarily startling him. "That proves *nothing,*" he said angrily. "Our State Department is filled with communists and they probably all have outstanding records, too! Don't you forget that."

In the midst of Harvey's paranoia and anger, Dorp knew that they were actually avoiding the real issue at hand, the gist of which was contained in the precisely typed report that was now sitting unopened and unread on Harvey's desk. It had taken Dorp the last eighteen hours to fully prepare the document (in triplicate), and he had done little else in that time but concentrate on what he considered to be the facts of the case. Dorp's immediate recommendation was for a recon patrol to be sent to the small isolated valley on the western coast of the Korean peninsula, a place called Tsing Buk, where Baker claimed he saw the strange aerial battle. Dorp's conclusion, written with as much eloquence as he could muster, was that evidence found at Tsing Buk could prove that the story told by Baker and the strange encounter by Buster Force were linked.

The key to Dorp's opinion turned on one outstanding fact: The airplane that Baker had identified in the photo was an F-86 Sabre jet. Follow-up interviews with some of the Buster Force crewmen convinced Dorp that they too had seen Sabres in the night sky over North Korea, though for some reason they still insisted the airplanes were extremely modified to look and perform like rocketships. In fact, many of their crude drawings from the first debriefing resembled souped-up Sabres.

The problem was that there wasn't supposed to be a

Sabre jet anywhere within a thousand miles of the war zone. . . .

It was for this reason that Dorp sent the odd message to the *Cape Esperance*. He was cleared to know that the flattop was carrying America's first squadron of F-86s to the war, and as part of his thesis that something was not as it should be, he thought it only prudent to check on the condition of the Sabres nearest to Korea, no matter how dumb it might have seemed to the Navy. In fact, he actually thought Harvey would have praised him in his attempt to cover all the bases.

He couldn't have been more wrong.

Harvey wet the end of his pencil with his tongue and made a notation in a mysterious little black book.

"You realize I have no choice, Captain Dorp, but to report all this to Tokyo Intelligence Command at once," he said, scribbling furiously. "And besides detailing what I consider your overwhelming lack of judgment, I will also have to indicate that you believe this carrier captain can be trusted, that his loyalty is beyond question. Should it turn out that he is not a loyal American, you, too, will bear the consequences, I'm afraid. . . ."

Dorp nodded unenthusiastically. "I understand, sir."

For the next ten minutes, Dorp watched nervously as Harvey scribbled away in his notebook, the senior officer smearing him beyond all hopes of rehabilitation, he supposed. But in a way, Dorp did not much care what Harvey was writing about him. He was fairly sure that something *somewhere* was out of kilter, and he was determined to uncover it. He knew that figuring out how someone was able to fly a bunch of unauthorized F-86 Sabre jets around Korea was a challenge—never mind ones that witnesses swear were unmarked, painted all black, and acted like "rocketships."

And in his naïveté, Dorp had actually thought his commanding officer would want to get to the bottom of it, too. Yet Harvey insisted on nipping at Dorp around the edges. The blustery senior officer appeared to be more concerned with things like Dorp's indiscretion in sending the radio message or the neatness of the typing of the first page of Dorp's detailed report than what was contained within it.

"Do you have anything else to say for yourself, Captain?" Harvey asked him after what seemed like an eternity of scribbling.

Dorp let out a long, low exasperated breath. He was certain at this point that Harvey would never read his report.

"Sir, all I know is that, corroborating the Buster Force story, we've got a POW who says he saw these same unidentified jets mixing it up with some MiGs," he said, as if he were reading from an overly memorized script. "And that those jets appear to be Sabres—"

Harvey banged the desk with his fist. "But this POW might be shell-shocked!" he yelled. "He might have been brainwashed or drugged."

"How about the B-29 crewmen, sir?" Dorp retaliated.

"A more genuine case of battle fatigue I have never witnessed," Harvey shot back.

Now it was Dorp who was turning red—this time with frustration.

"Perhaps if I could talk to the B-29 guys again, sir," he said.

"That would be impossible, Captain," Harvey replied smugly. "All of them have been shipped back to the states, just like that POW."

Dorp was astounded. "Shipped home?" he said. "Why?"

"For further examination, of course," Harvey said. "*Psychiatric* examination, which is exactly what I have arranged for you."

Dorp felt like someone had just punched him in the stomach.

"Captain," Harvey said dramatically, "you are to report to the base hospital and see a Doctor Spitz immediately."

It was a dreary walk from Harvey's office to the base hospital. Dorp knew that once it was entered onto his service record that he had been sent to see a psychologist, all hope of advancement was probably gone.

He finally arrived and was shown to an office by a

nurse who made sure she stayed at least an arm's length away from him. There were two chairs and a bare desk inside the room and virtually nothing else.

Thank God there's no couch, Dorp thought.

He waited there for twenty minutes until a small, ratty man walked in and introduced himself as Doctor Spitz, psychologist for the Yokota base. Up to that point, Dorp hadn't realized the base even had a resident shrink.

The doctor was carrying several folders under his arm, along with Dorp's massive triplicate report to Harvey. He set down all the documentation on the desk and retrieved a small notebook from his pocket.

"Are you comfortable, Captain?" he asked, with just the barest hint of a European accent coming through. "If so, let us begin."

They spent the first ten minutes going over Dorp's family medical history. Then Spitz got down to the matter at hand.

Reading from Dorp's report to Harvey, the doctor clucked his teeth several times, then looked at the young officer.

"Captain, it is not normal behavior for a junior officer to insist on pursuing matters in total disregard of their superior's orders," he told him. "Do you understand that?"

Dorp could only stare at the floor. "Yes, sir."

"And do you also realize that in wartime, it is impossible for every man to pursue his own agenda?" Spitz continued. "That we must be united in our purpose, our efforts to defeat the enemy?"

"I realize that, sir," Dorp said. "I thought I was just doing my job."

Spitz let out a rather unprofessional chuckle. "Captain, chasing outrageous rumors is hardly your job," he said. "I'm certain that for a man of your young age to ascend to the rank of captain in such a short time indicates some high level of intelligence and judgment. But it appears that you have been consumed by these strange stories of 'ghost airplanes.' And in your obsession, you have let more important duties fall by the wayside."

Dorp was about to say something, but he held back at the last instant.

"Look at yourself, Captain," Spitz went on. "You're disheveled, in obvious need of sleep, and I'll bet you haven't had a square meal in two days. Can't you see that you have set yourself up, so to speak, to reach irrational conclusions?"

Once again, Dorp felt like someone had just hit him in the stomach. Was the shrink starting to make sense?

A strange, almost fatherly smile spread across the doctor's face.

"Captain, let me tell you something," he said, his voice rising an octave, up to the level of maiden aunt. "In the stress of wartime, people see all kinds of strange things. I can't tell you how many reports I come across very much like the ones you've documented here. If we were to analyze every single one of them, there'd be no time left over to fight the enemy.

"When one is living under the pressures of war, whether it be in combat or in the rear areas, they want to believe that they are fighting on the right side. They want proof—proof that something almost magical is on their side. It's a justification for what they are doing, which is trying to kill as many human beings on the other side as possible. Look at history and all the religious wars, like the Crusades, for example. These people believed they were acting under orders from the Almighty Himself. 'Slay the infidels!' so sayeth the Lord. How can one go wrong with such an impression? How can one question it?

"There are many documented cases of soldiers seeing angels in the midst of battle, heavenly warriors sent by God to help them slay their enemies. Battle reports from World War I are especially ripe with such tales. But the strange thing is that these reports come from *both* sides. Both sides have to think they are right in their cause. Hell, the Reds probably see the face of Lenin or Marx hovering over the battlefield. There's no doubt that they suffer the same kind of battlefield stresses as we do. All soldiers are the same in the end.

"But you see, in order to reinforce this idea, a soldier's mind can begin to play tricks on him. He sees things that are not there. And when large groups of men see these things, it becomes a form of mass hysteria."

"And that's what you believe the POW and the men in Buster Force were seeing?" Dorp asked sheepishly. "Some kind of hallucinations?"

Spitz nodded and retained his smile. "The human brain is a very complicated thing, Captain," he said. "It can make you convince yourself of things that aren't really true. It can make you do things that you would not normally do."

At that point, Spitz pulled out a sheaf of papers from his folder and began shaking them. Dorp looked closer and realized they were the drawings he had had the Buster Force crewmen do for him.

"I mean, Captain," Spitz went on, "look at what you included in your report. These look like pictures drawn by schoolchildren. Now I ask you: Is that how an officer in the United States Air Force should be acting?"

Dorp felt his head start to do a slow spin. *So this is what it's like to go crazy,* he thought.

"You took two pieces of evidence," Spitz continued. "One from a POW who was most likely brainwashed and one from a group of men who had been training night and day for weeks to fly a very hazardous mission. For the POW, his story of these strange airplanes was his denial of what had probably *really* happened to him. In my opinion, he most likely *was* brainwashed yet was able to escape from his captors somehow. However, I'm sure he knew that as a result of his actions, his comrades would be killed by the Chinese. But you see, his mind couldn't handle the guilt of something like that, so it made up this incredible story.

"The same holds true for the men aboard the B-29s. They were on what amounted to a suicide mission. I'm sure every one of them had convinced himself—subconsciously, at least—that he was going to die. When they didn't, their minds had to provide an explanation. Thus, we get this story about strange airplanes appearing out of nowhere, saving them like the cavalry or something.

"And you, Captain, wanted to believe all this as rationalization that *you* were on the right side in this war. That what you were doing was correct—morally and ethically. You quite simply wanted to believe that God was in your corner and that he was sending supernatural help to our side. It's a perfectly human response, especially for a Roman Catholic like yourself."

Dorp was completely shattered. He had visions of himself sitting in a veterans' hospital psycho ward somewhere, making potholders, oatmeal drooling down the sides of his mouth.

Spitz scribbled something in his notebook, then closed it with a dramatic flair.

"These mystery airplanes of yours just don't exist, Captain," Spitz said, tossing the triplicate report into the wastebasket. "And I think it's time that you came around to realizing that. Don't you?"

6

THE TWO CIVILIAN AIRCRAFT mechanics adjusted their oxygen masks, then entered the darkened chamber.

One man was holding a powerful lantern, the other a clipboard and pencil. The inside of the chamber was so smoky they had a hard time seeing their hands in front of them. The dim bulbs hanging from the high ceiling did more harm than good, and the irregular rocking of the ship didn't help either. Packed as they were in their bulky overalls, boots, and safety helmets, it seemed like everything was combining to upset their equilibrium.

Still they pressed on, gingerly walking across the grease-slicked metal surface, feeling their way around the various support mechanisms, trying not to trip on the gaggle of cables, electrical wires, and fuel hoses that criss-crossed the compartment floor.

Finally they reached Aircraft #1. The man with the lantern focused its powerful beam on the nose of the airplane while the man with the clipboard began a meticulous examination of the aircraft's metal skin.

"Here's one . . ." he called out, his voice, though muffled by his oxygen mask, just loud enough for his partner to hear. "Here's another. . . ."

The lightman directed the beam toward his colleague's pointing finger and immediately saw the two holes in the aircraft's fuselage.

"Cannon?" the lightman asked.

His partner ran his finger along the perforations and nodded. "Definitely," he replied. "I'd say it was a thirty millimeter."

The man with the clipboard, known as "the counter" in this procedure, quickly measured the holes with a wooden ruler and scribbled two notations on his page. Then he indicated to the lightman to move on.

"Two more," the counter called out, finding another pair of holes just inches in front of the leading tip of the airplane's canopy. "Just missed the battery . . ."

Again he made two more notations, then moved on.

They found two chips taken out of the canopy glass close to the aircraft's radio-compass loop antenna and a single hole midway up on the starboard side's automatic wing slat. There was another nick taken out of the midfuselage airbrake and a relatively large hole back on the right-side horizontal tail.

"Looks like one pass," the counter yelled to his partner, totaling up the number of holes. "I'd say he tried to ice him with a quick burst of his thirty, and this guy was just too slippery."

The lightman nodded and nimbly sidestepped one of the two still-smoldering rocket bottles that was attached to the airplane's underbelly. The fumes from the bottles—technically known as Rocket-Assisted Take-Off bottles, or simply RATO bottles—were poisonous, and even the small amounts that continued to leak out of the containers well after they'd been expended was enough to make a person extremely ill. This, in combination with the leftover jet exhaust fumes, was why the compartment was so smoky. It was also why the mechanics were wearing oxygen masks.

When used during takeoff, the RATO bottles gave the pilot and his airplane the extra kick needed to become airborne from a shortened runway. The brief flash of fire and smoke made a RATO-equipped airplane look like a spaceship ascending into the heavens. Under normal operating circumstances, the bottles were jettisoned once the airplane was safely airborne, usually only a matter of ten seconds or so. But both mechanics knew these airplanes were not operating under "normal" conditions and that the whole operation could be jeopardized if the wrong person found just one depleted RATO bottle floating in the water somewhere nearby. Thus the pilots had been told to keep the bottles attached after they'd been used up.

The counter rested his hand against one of the bottles for a few moments. "Still pretty hot," he said.

"You think he used it . . . up there?" the lightman asked.

The counter shrugged and looked at the notation he'd made on his board. "The damn thing is still warm and the plane's been down almost an hour. What do you think?"

The lightman could only shake his head. "If they're playing around with the rocket-assist during the missions, it could really screw up the numbers," he said. "Not to mention it being a very fucking dangerous thing to do."

"These hero flyboys don't give a damn about that," the counter replied, examining the airplane's second RATO bottle and finding it hot, too. "Or about the numbers. They're too busy looking for medals."

The lightman could only nod in agreement. "You got that right," he said.

With that, the two men moved on to Aircraft #2.

7

IT WAS SO DARK inside the compartment that it was hard to see the paper in the fading light of the cigarette lighter. Therefore it was impossible to check if all the spelling in the letter was correct or whether the writing was even decipherable.

"How much are you going to pay him?"

"All I got—fifteen hundred."

"He'll take it."

"He'd better."

"Here he comes now."

"Kill the lighter."

"*Ouch!* You son of a bitch . . ."

The door to the pitch-black compartment opened and the man with the limp hobbled in.

"Chow time."

"That better not be eel."

"Quit your yapping. They're scrambled eggs."

"Powdered?"

"What the hell do you think?"

"How much you getting paid for this, Gump?"

"Not enough. So just shut up and take your eggs, will you? I can't see a damn thing!"

"Want to make about a half year's pay "

"Sure, sure. Who do I have to murder?"

"No one. Just mail this."

"What? What are you giving me?"

"It's a letter. I want you to arrange for it to be mailed."

"*Are you crazy?*"

"No. Just rich. Give it to the supply pilot. Here's

fifteen hundred bucks. Pay him whatever you think it takes, you keep the rest."

"You guys *are* insane. How did you even write this? Do I smell a lighter in here?"

"Are you married, Gump?"

"Ha! Who'd marry someone like me?"

"When's the last time you had piece of tail?"

"Can't remember that far back."

"Well, you got enough money there to get yourself laid about a hundred times in Tokyo. Just pay the seaplane pilot enough so he does his job."

"You guys are touched. Your brains are whacked because you've been in the dark too long."

"Don't start, Gump. Remember, we can see you. But you can't see us. Now, take the money and do what I told you."

"But we could all get in a lot of trouble for this."

"Not if I keep your mouth shut, we won't."

8

Antung, Manchuria

COLONEL PEI DEN WENG, deputy commander and intelligence officer of the People's Liberation Army's 4th Air Defense Squadron, placed the sealed packet of photos on his commanding officer's desk.

"Would you like a drink, Colonel?" the officer, a Caucasian known to Pei only as "Comrade Tusk," asked. "Rice wine? Vodka, perhaps?"

Pei shook his head no. "Thank you for asking," he said in a curt, perfunctory style. "As an officer of the People's Army, I cannot drink."

Comrade Tusk shrugged twice, poured himself half a glass of vodka, and drained it in one gulp.

"So, what is the purpose of your visit, Colonel?" he asked Pei in French, their only common language.

"It concerns those unusual reports we've been getting about the Americans flying a new secret fighter," Pei replied, his voice betraying a tinge of nervousness. "We have new details that some were encountered recently during an attack by our MiGs on a force of B-29s that had bombed the Yalu bridges; and again, early this morning, more were reported up around Wonson."

A look of only the mildest surprise came across Comrade Tusk's face.

"I thought we had decided these rumors of a new American fighter already deployed in the field were just that, Colonel," he said. "Simply *on-dit*. Idle gossip among the troops of little worth investigating."

"I am still of that mind, sir," Pei replied, "However, our pilots did take some rather intriguing photos during the action against those B-29s."

He pointed to the package he'd placed on Tusk's desk, but the other man seemed to want to ignore it.

"Do you have anything conclusive, Colonel?" Tusk asked. "I'm extremely busy at the moment."

Pei paused to consider his answer. "I believe that is a matter of interpretation, Comrade," he said finally. "Some people see conclusions where others don't."

Tusk smiled and began picking lint off his uniform. "Well, isn't that true in all of life, Colonel?" he asked harmoniously. "Don't you find that many times people—"

"*Comrade,*" Pei said suddenly, louder than he intended, "I do not mean to be disrespectful, but we may have an important situation here. I do not believe that this is the time to speak of philosophy."

Tusk was momentariliy taken aback by Pei's outburst.

"But you *are* being disrespectful, Colonel," he shot back, abandoning for the moment the task of nit-picking his uniform. "Do you think this is all I have to attend to? What would happen here—at this base, to your airplanes— should I make the mistake of devoting all my time to your little puzzles?"

Pei felt his temples begin to ache. He hadn't slept much in the past three days.

"Many pardons, Comrade," he replied, trying to calm his voice. "But at the very least you must conclude that we may be faced with a baffling riddle. If the Americans have already secretly deployed new fighters in the battle, it will have an effect on whether we are to be ultimately successful."

Tusk angrily tapped a finger on his desk. "I'll make the decision as to what will be needed for our 'ultimate' success, Colonel," he growled at Pei in French. "We know that the Americans are transporting some of their new Sabre jets to Japan. But that shipment is still weeks away from landing, and then there will undoubtedly be a period of training for the pilots. By that time, we will have solidified our control of the air over the entire peninsula and those Sabres will be practically useless. That is, Colonel, if your men perform their duty properly."

Pei cast his eyes downward. He was soundly humiliated.

"Yes, Comrade," he replied quietly.

Tusk smiled, then picked up the package and ripped it open. He unceremoniously dumped its contents—more than two dozen 8×10 photographs—onto his desk and began rummaging through them.

"All I see are underdeveloped photos," he said.

"They were correctly developed, sir," Pei replied quickly. "They were taken in dim light during this encounter with the B-29s. Our pilots were in the midst of combat and had little time to take clear shots."

Pei retrieved five of the most important shots and spread them in front of Tusk.

"See here," he said, pointing to the vague, murky shapes of each of the photos. "And here. And again here. They look like Sabres, but we have not seen enemy aircraft of this design in the theater before."

Tusk squinted dramatically, pretending that he couldn't make out the silhouettes in the photos. "Where?" he snapped. "I see nothing."

"Right there, Comrade," Pei said, stuttering slightly as

his tongue became wrapped up in the little-used French. "You can see the swept-wing design. . . ."

Tusk retrieved a magnifying glass from his otherwise empty desk drawer and studied the pattern next to Pei's finger.

"But this looks like nothing more than a bad photograph of one of our own airplanes," he said testily.

Pei shook his head. "No, Comrade," he said, outlining the shape on the grainy photo. "See the difference in the tail section? This airplane rides with a midposition stabilizer, just like a Sabre."

Tusk looked more closely. "Colonel, these photos are of such poor quality, I can't tell the front from the rear."

With that, he brusquely pushed the majority of the pictures away from him, causing some to fall to the floor.

Pei was aghast.

"Please don't think I am being disrespectful, Comrade," the Chinese officer said, not bothering to conceal the anger in his voice. "But these photos are very important."

"They are nothing but a bunch of fuzzy pictures!" Tusk exploded. "And they are hardly of new American jets."

"But Comrade," Pei almost pleaded, "I think this whole matter is worth further investigation."

Tusk looked him straight in the eye and was silent for several long moments. "What are you suggesting, Colonel?" he finally asked.

Pei took a deep breath. "Some of our ground commanders report a similar action between unidentified aircraft over a valley called Tsing Buk," he said. "I believe that a reconnaissance of the area may lead to further evidence of—"

"Stop right there!" Tusk interrupted. "Now I have heard enough of all this, Colonel. We have more important things to do than to be chasing spirits."

"But Comrade," Pei began to protest.

"Colonel Pei," Tusk growled, his face twisted in cool anger. "I am ordering you to end this nonsense at once. Forget about these rumors and get on to your more important regular duties. Do you understand?"

Pei nodded. He had never seen the mysterious Comrade Tusk so upset. Suitably humbled, he saluted and left the room.

Once the door was closed, Tusk chuckled, put his feet up on his desk, and went back to casually picking loose threads from his uniform.

9

Mokpo Island, Off the Coast of South Korea

HIS NAME WAS CHOJI Harakitsu and this morning, like every other morning for the past five years, he was awakened by the crashing of the waves at the bottom of the cliff.

As always, he was startled by these first sounds of the day—the waves smashing against the rocks sounded so much like gunfire and the fog around his hut looked so much like smoke, that Choji almost always thought for a moment that he was in the midst of battle once again. But then his eyes would open and his mind would clear and he would realize that it was just the waves and the rocks and the ever-present fog, conspiring to frighten him again.

The crude hut at the top of the cliff was his home. The rusting wood stove, the dilapidated water barrel, his meager tool box, and the leaky oil lantern inside made up most of his worldly possessions. Only the cracked handheld telescope resting in the corner looked too ornate for the shack and then just barely.

He stretched, but not too much, and finally rolled off his sleeping mat. Immediately he pulled himself up into a kneeling position and said a prayer to his Emperor. Then he arose and retrieved a fish ball and a cup of rice from the mouth of the wood stove—soggy remnants of his

meal the night before. After another short prayer, he ate
the meager breakfast, washing it down with a handful of
water from the barrel.

Once finished, he removed his ragged sleeping gown
and splashed the rest of his wrinkled body with the cold,
dirty water, drying himself by spinning around until he
was dizzy. He could not shave today—his only remaining
razor was turning dull, so he was rationing its use to just
once a week. Still, he knew it would not last more than
another two months. He imagined that in a year's time
he would have a full beard and hair down to his waist,
and this thought disturbed him.

But perhaps this would not happen, he reasoned in the
next moment. Perhaps the war would be finished by then
and he could return home once again, victorious and
clean-shaven.

Suddenly, he remembered a particularly vivid dream
he had had that night. He was peering through the jagged square opening that passed as the hut's only window,
and off in the distance he had seen first one, then another bright flare of light pierce through the foggy night.
There had also been a loud noise accompanying the fire
in this sky.

Had it been a dream at all? He shook his head. He felt
too feeble to recall whether he had dreamed the vision or
whether it had actually happened. Then, just as every
morning, more questions began to flood his head. *Would
he see any enemy ships today? Would he see any enemy
airplanes? Would the opportunity to redeem his soul be
offered before the day's sunset?*

He shook away the persistent questions, knowing the
answers would not come easily. He knelt for a third
prayer, beating himself on the chest ten times before
finishing. Only then did he arise and, performing a ritual
he'd followed every day for the past five years, climb into
his brown-and-gray uniform of the Japanese Naval Air
Force.

10

Tsing Buk Valley, South Korea

COLONEL PEI HAD NEVER carried a real rifle before—not in his basic Army training, not during the war against the Japanese, not as part of his village militia. There had never seemed to be enough weapons to go around in those days. Now, if anything, there were more than enough.

At that moment, he and fifty hand-picked PLA soldiers were climbing up the steep slopes of a mountain that bordered the narrow seaside valley called Tsing Buk. Located on the far western edge of the Korean peninsula, it was here that a handful of Chinese unit commanders had reported seeing some kind of mysterious and spectacular aerial action for several nights running. One had claimed that the two opposing forces were comprised of MiGs on one side and unmarked, unknown enemy airplanes on the other. Another PLA commander had reported that two or three MiGs had been shot down during one of these alleged battles.

Next to the blurry photos, the reports of aerial actions over Tsing Buk formed the most tangible aspect of Pei's investigation into the *houng jung quay mut*—the "strange things in the sky"—that may or may not have to do with a new type of American fighter jet.

Still Pei was suspicious. Comrade Tusk had at first so adamantly berated his idea for the recon patrol that the Chinese officer thought he was going to be demoted or, worse, sent home in disgrace. But then, no more than eight hours after their unpleasant meeting on the subject, Tusk had done an amazing about-face and approved the mission, calling it "necessary" and "important." The only caveat was that the mission had to be conducted in secret, under the cover of darkness.

The odd thing was that now it was Pei himself who was beginning to think the trip to Tsing Buk would prove to be an exercise in frustration. In the time spent preparing for the mission, the Chinese officer found that he was beginning to doubt that anything had ever happened over the valley. He had spent many hours looking into the field commanders' reports, trying to track down the MiGs that were supposedly involved in the battles above Tsing Buk, and he had come up empty. All actions from all Chinese air units operating in the area were meticulously documented, and nowhere had anyone mentioned any aerial battles over Tsing Buk.

Pei knew any army in the field was rife with rumors, legends, and exaggerated tales of either cowardice or glory. The People's Liberation Army was no different. But long before, his first cadre leader had told him that a soldier in the People's Liberation Army should be prepared to make any sacrifice to further the Revolution. Just the day before, Comrade Tusk had told him the same thing. It was for this reason, he kept telling himself, that he, a senior air force officer and a pilot, was slogging up the side of the small mountain, rifle in hand, his feet and fingers freezing in the bitter cold, with a patrol of fifty men behind him.

They had been deposited on an isolated beach by two camouflaged junks shortly after sunset and had been trudging along now for nearly three hours, climbing over jagged rocks, through narrow gulleys filled with deep snow, and across ice-covered streams. It was a frigid, back-breaking route, but they had little choice. The only road leading into the valley was at its northeastern edge and this was in the hands of the enemy.

So they climbed and stumbled and silently cursed the dark and the freezing drizzle that rained down on them nonstop. Through it all, Pei found himself thinking that, rumors or not, there probably weren't many places in the middle of a war zone that were as remote as Tsing Buk.

*   *   *

They found the wreckage of the first MiG shortly after midnight.

Pei was startled when his advance scouts came scrambling back to the main group, out of breath and excited, to tell him there were pieces of wreckage strewn about the other side of the rise. He couldn't believe he had been this lucky. The reports of the MiGs being downed in the valley had been sketchy, to say the least. For them to virtually stumble across one wreck, in the middle of the night, was at the very least extremely fortunate. Pei would have taken it as a good omen if he hadn't dreamed up so many misgivings about the whole mission in the first place.

When the rest of the patrol had reached the wreckage, Pei instructed half of them to spread out and set up a defensive perimeter around the area; the other half was given the task of gathering any pieces that could be carried to a central point.

Their preliminary search for the pilot's body proved fruitless but, working with two MiG aircraft mechanics who were included in the patrol, Pei was able to examine the larger parts of the airplane's wreckage. It was undoubtedly a MiG-15, and judging by what was left of its engines, its cannons, and its cockpit instrumentation, it had been a newer model, more advanced than anything Pei or the two mechanics had seen.

But these facts alone did not make it part of the whole *houng jung quay mut* puzzle. New models of the MiG-15 were being absorbed into the Chinese Air Force every day, some of them being flown from manufacturing plants in the Soviet Union to bases near the Yalu and then directly into combat. Others were even being delivered to secret bases within the westernmost portion of the Soviet Union itself and being flown by communist pilots from there. Pei knew this airplane could simply be one of those recent additions, a plane that had developed engine trouble or whatever and simply crashed in the valley.

After spending an hour picking over the wreckage, Pei left a dozen men to guard the site. Then he led the rest of the unit into Tsing Buk itself.

No sooner had they reached the valley floor when the first four men in his column were cut down by gunfire.

USAF Captain Eddie Dorp was scared shitless.

He had never been in combat before. Never even been close to it. But now he and a special recon unit of the U.S. Army Rangers were going tooth and nail with a larger, still unseen, hostile force right in the middle of the Tsing Buk valley.

The mission had gone well up to that point. When they had first set out from Yokota, Dorp's spirits were particularly high. For the first time in days, he didn't feel like he was going insane, a change in attitude that he owed to Hard-Ass himself. Something had happened to the commanding officer's thinking shortly after Dorp had seen Dr. Spitz, the Yokota base shrink. The following day, in fact, Harvey had summoned Dorp back to his office and, along with Spitz, recommended that he go ahead and conduct the recon patrol of Tsing Buk, if only to prove to himself that nothing was there. Spitz had described it as a kind of "combat therapy."

Harvey had even found the Ranger recon unit to take on the mission—the fourteen-man group from the old Okinawa occupation force was made available to him on a day's notice. Things got better when Dorp learned that the single roadway leading into Tsing Buk was in the hands of the Australian Army. The original plan had called for only eight men—Dorp and seven Rangers—to be ferried in aboard helicopters, aircraft that very few people trusted, Dorp included. But with the important roadway in friendly hands, trucks could replace helicopters as the means of transport. Plus all fourteen men of the Ranger force could take part in the mission. To Dorp's mind, more was better.

They had found some scant evidence on the valley floor about an hour before the shooting started. Actually Dorp didn't believe they were looking at the remains of an airplane. All he could see in the darkness was a large black hole in the frozen-over ground surrounded by some exposed, burnt grass and pieces of charred metal. One of the Rangers—an expert in demolition—said he thought it was more likely the remains of a truck or a jeep. Another theorized the crater could have been caused by naval gunfire, the blackened, twisted metal being the remains of a large shell.

Dorp left five of the Rangers behind to scour the area, then he pressed on with the remaining soldiers to the middle of the small valley where Baker, the POW, had said he saw a second airplane come down. By this time, the miserable weather was rapidly clearing off, to the extent that many stars were becoming visible.

Just minutes after spotting another crater—this one larger and filled with pieces of authentic wreckage and more than a few charred bones—the Rangers detected an unknown force coming down off the mountain and heading right for them. The Rangers' point man, a sharp-eyed Cherokee Indian, eventually identified the group as being Chinese soldiers, about two dozen strong. When they got within fifty feet of the Rangers' hidden position, the Army commander had no choice but to order his men to open fire.

"What now?" Dorp shakily asked the Rangers' top man, a major named Stephani, as bullets whizzed mere inches above their heads.

Displaying commendable coolness under fire, Stephani took a long look around him, considered all the options, then said, "I suggest we get the hell out of here."

It was a decision Dorp would not argue against. He had no idea what the Red Chinese troops were doing in the supposedly deserted valley—and it wasn't part of the mission's objective to stick around and find out. So when Stephani told his men to start withdrawing in threes and suggested that Dorp fall back with the first group, the Air Force intelligence officer readily agreed.

Accompanied by the unit's second radioman and another private who had been wounded in the arm, Dorp crawled through the snow for the next ten minutes, gradually gaining more courage as he realized that with each movement, he was getting that much farther away from the shooting.

They reached a small ice-covered gulley that Dorp

figured was the halfway point between the gun battle and the Rangers left behind at the crater. At this point he took his first unadulterated deep breath since the fighting broke out.

"Almost there, boys," he called out to the two Rangers, more for his own encouragement than anything else.

That's when he heard the thunder.

The sky was almost entirely clear of clouds by now, so that when he twisted over onto his back, he saw the four sets of bright lights off to the north right away. Suddenly all the firing stopped—on both sides—evidence that the Reds had also spotted the oncoming aircraft.

Dorp's first thought was that the four approaching airplanes were American—to his knowledge, the MiGs never ventured out in small groups, nor did they engage in ground-attack missions.

As he watched, the four jets broke off and came screaming in low over the valley. Suddenly the first plane in line opened up with a fierce barrage from its nose guns, its shells exploding back near the line separating the other Rangers from the Red Chinese.

"Did your honcho call in air support?" he whispered urgently to the radioman.

"Are you kidding?" the radioman said. "The Air Force doesn't get up this early!"

Dorp chose not to answer the insult from the lowly enlisted man. At that moment he was watching the second and third planes mimic their leader's maneuver. Both swooped down low and began shooting up the territory about an eighth of a mile away.

Who the hell did these airplanes belong to? It was still too dark to tell. Could they be F-80s that had just happened along? he thought, still clinging to the hope that the fighters were American and that somehow they would get him and the others out of the tight jam.

But then he checked his watch. It was 0500, with about another thirty minutes before dawn. He felt something in his stomach drop: No F-80 pilot *would* be flying this early in the morning. The only night-support missions were flown by B-26s or F-82 Twin Mustangs, both prop-driven aircraft. The airplanes above him were definitely jets.

"Call your CO and find out what's happened up there," he told the radioman.

The man did as told, listened for a few seconds, and then turned back to Dorp. "Christ, he says those airplanes are shooting on off-line coordinates."

"What the hell does that mean?" Dorp asked.

The radioman and the wounded Ranger had already started crawling away. "It means they're hitting anything that moves," the radioman growled back at him.

"On purpose?" Dorp cried out, terrified at the first thought that had entered his mind.

Both Rangers stopped and looked back at him strangely.

"What the hell are you talking about?" the radioman yelled back at him. "Do you think those flyboys can see in the dark?"

Feeling foolish and naive, Dorp rolled back over in the snow and began crawling again. Suddenly he felt very, very cold.

It was Stephani's Cherokee scout who first heard the second set of jets.

Despite the fact that both the American Rangers and the Red Chinese soldiers just a few feet away were being strafed mercilessly by the unmarked airplanes, the Cherokee had been able to somehow tune his ears over the roar to a different sound approaching from the west. Dodging the shells that were exploding all around him, he quickly scrambled over to Stephani and pointed to the mountains about ten miles west of their position. It took the Ranger commander a few moments, but then, in the gradually brightening sky, he did see four more aircraft approaching, each one flying with bright red navigational lights on their tails.

The four newly arrived aircraft thundered over their position in a blatant attempt to make their presence known to the attacking jets. Suddenly, the first four airplanes pulled up from their shooting runs and turned toward the interlopers. Within half a minute, a spectacular, swirling dogfight was in progress.

A quarter-mile back, the unit's second radioman answered Stephani's call.

"Tell that flyboy to get his mug out of the snow and ID what the hell is going on up here," Dorp heard Stephani's voice crackle over the field set.

Dorp dared to turn back toward the noise and discovered for the first time that four more airplanes had arrived.

He saw the two sets of lights and then he punched himself in the head.

"Jesus Christ!" he yelled out, so loud the other Rangers stopped crawling and looked back at him. "How could I have been so stupid?"

"Don't ask us!" one of them yelled back.

But Dorp didn't hear him. He was too busy looking at the lights streaking through the predawn sky.

Suddenly he knew that the POW Baker and the men of Buster Force hadn't been seeing things after all.

11

Yokota Air Base, Japan

WHEN CAPTAIN EDDIE DORP woke up, he found his hands were bandaged up to his elbows and his legs wrapped up to his knees.

Still he was able to scratch the persistent itch on his nose that had roused him from his long slumber. Blinking his eyes rapidly in an effort to clear them, he soon realized that he was in a hospital bed, in a near-empty room with no windows. The place looked like a basement, smelled like a basement, and, judging by the small masses of mildew clinging to the walls, probably *was* a basement.

It was all coming back to him now: The mission to Tsing Buk. The gunfight with the Red Chinese troops. His long crawl back to the Rangers' rear line. The strafing airplanes. The dogfight. It got a little fuzzy after that.

He vaguely remembered the Rangers' medic forcing his hands and bare feet into a bucket of hot water and then his long, painful plunge into unconsciousness. And somewhere in there, he had taken a helicopter ride.

Off in the distance, he heard a pair of jets take off, part of the distinctly familiar hum that told him he was back at Yokota. Then he looked at his bandaged hands and feet again and correctly theorized that he was being treated for frostbite.

What bothered him was why he was in such a "private" room.

A nurse entered a short time later, took his temperature, and felt his pulse. She was pretty and smiling, but whenever he started to ask a question, she sweetly put her hand over his mouth. Dorp got the message right away.

She ended the examination by giving him an injection in the butt. He felt embarrassed at first when she had him flip over in order to expose himself, but she didn't seem to mind. After sticking him twice, she patted his head, smiled, and left the room.

Dorp was starting to drift off to sleep again when the door opened and three men walked in.

Two were wearing Army Ranger uniforms. The third man was none other than Hard-Ass himself.

"How are you feeling, Captain?" one of the Rangers asked.

Dorp could only raise his bandaged appendages and manage a shrug.

"The doctors tell us that you'll be all right," Hard-Ass told him. "They were able to save all your fingers and toes. . . ."

Dorp felt a chill run through him. He didn't think his injuries had been that serious.

"You guys had quite a party out there," the other Ranger, a major, told him, as all three men pulled up chairs close to the bed. "Do you remember any of it?"

Dorp shrugged again. "Got real cold," was all he could say.

"How about the dogfight?" the other Ranger asked. "Did you get look at that?"

Dorp nodded immediately. "Saw it all," he said. "It was the guys we were looking for."

"Speak carefully, Captain," Harvey inserted at this point, causing the Rangers to shift uneasily in their chairs.

Dorp almost laughed. "I saw what I saw, sir," he said, the statement making more sense to him than the three others. "And I don't care who hears it, sir. At least I know I'm not crazy. . . ."

"We're glad to hear that, Captain," the senior Ranger said, lighting a cigarette for him and placing it in his mouth. "We lost six men out there and we want to know why. So, tell us what you saw."

Dorp ran through the whole story, from finding the suspected wrecks to encountering the Red Chinese troops, to the enemy jets' strafing attack to the sudden swirling air battle that raged above them for ten full minutes.

"I didn't see anyone get hit on either side," he said. "But I got a damn good look at the airplanes. They were unmarked, painted all black. But they were definitely F-86s. Sabre jets. No doubt about it."

"Captain!" Harvey nearly shouted. "Be still!"

Dorp thought he could feel a slight painkiller moving through his system. The familiar dull headache he always experienced in Harvey's presence was now, happily, nowhere to be found.

"I'm telling you what I saw, sir," he said. "These 'unauthorized' planes we've been looking for—I saw them. And they were Sabres."

The two Rangers glanced at Harvey, then turned back to Dorp.

"Well, Captain," the junior Ranger officer said, "according to the Air Force, there ain't no Sabres in Korea. Not yet, anyway. We were just briefed that they're still more than a week away on a jeep carrier named the—"

"The *Cape Esperance*," Dorp interrupted, finishing the officer's sentence for him. "I know all that. But what I'm telling you is that those were Sabres over Tsing Buk."

One of the Rangers produced a photograph from his

briefcase and held it up to Dorp's face. It was a picture
of an F-84 Thunderjet.

"Could this be what you saw, Captain?" the senior
jarhead officer asked.

Dorp shook his head. He never thought he'd be on the
receiving end of this show-and-tell exercise.

"No sir," he said confidently, choosing to play along.
"That's an F-84 . . ."

"How about this?" the Ranger asked, showing him
another photo.

"No sir," Dorp chimed again, now sure that some kind
of drug was making its way through his veins. "That's an
F-9F Panther. Navy jet. Carrier-launched . . ."

Once again the Rangers looked back toward Harvey.
The Air Force officer's face had turned ashen.

The senior Ranger finally held up a photo of a Sabre.

"That's it!" Dorp exclaimed. His mood was bordering
on euphoric. "Those are the babies I saw. Put on a hell
of a show. Now I know what Baker was talking about."

"How so?" the senior Ranger asked.

Dorp went into a more detailed account of the dogfight he'd witnessed, giving the Sabres the lion-sized share
of the heroics, especially when they first arrived and
distracted the strafing airplanes, which he now knew
were probably MiGs.

"If it hadn't been for those Sabres, I think the MiGs
would have gotten us all," he concluded, after the Ranger
had taken the expended cigarette from his mouth.

"Do you know that those MiGs killed eleven of their
own men?" the junior Ranger officer asked him.

Dorp could only shake his head. "On purpose?" he
found himself asking again.

None of the officers answered him. Instead, on a signal
from the senior Ranger, the trio moved to the far corner
of the room and held a short discussion. When it broke
up, the two Rangers left, leaving only Hard-Ass in the
room with him.

"Once again, you have disappointed me, Captain,"
Harvey said, hovering over Dorp's bed like a vulture
waiting to feed. "Despite what you told those officers,
we both know that those Sabres don't exist. Isn't that so?"

Dorp could only weakly shake his head. Suddenly he felt the beginnings of a familiar headache returning. At the same time, the formerly pleasant drugged feeling gave way to a painful sort of sluggishness.

"Did you hear me, Captain?" Harvey was saying, though his voice seemed to dissolve into an echo as Dorp began to fade away. "Those Sabres do not exist. . . ."

12

COMRADE TUSK WAS SHINING the brass buttons on his latest uniform when Colonel Pei was shown in.

"You've been hurt, Colonel?" Tusk asked, just barely looking up at the man.

Pei unconsciously rubbed his heavily bandaged shoulder. He had just come from the base hospital, ignoring the doctor's advice that he stay in bed for at least three days.

"I saw them," he told Tusk sternly.

"Saw who?" Tusk asked nonchalantly, not pausing a moment from his polishing job.

"*Houng jung quay mut,*" Pei burst out, for the moment abandoning French for his native language. "I saw them. Four American jets. They fought with four airplanes from our side."

Tusk continued to shine his buttons as he looked up at Pei.

"When did you see these things?" he asked. "During your recon mission? Or while you were recovering under sedation?"

"During the mission," Pei replied, resentment and exasperation coming through equally in his slurred French. "There was a battle, above Tsing Buk. It was the same time as the others said. Sabres. MiGs. They fought right over our heads!"

"How strange that you would be so lucky, Colonel," Tusk said finally. "These ghost airplanes of yours showing up on the same night you happen to be on the ground."

"We also found some wreckage, sir," Pei went on. "Of a new MiG model. One neither I nor the mechanics who accompanied me had seen before."

Once again, Tusk appeared unimpressed.

"Is that so?" he asked. "Did you bring back pieces of this wreckage?"

Pei hung his head. "No, sir," he said humbly. "We were forced to withdraw sooner than we had hoped."

"Why was that, Colonel?"

At this point, Pei felt his temper getting the best of him. He was sure that Tusk knew of the gun battle.

"We ran into an enemy force patrolling on the floor of the valley," he said bitterly. "We exchanged fire. Several of my men were killed."

"And that's how you were wounded?" Tusk asked nonchalantly.

"No," Pei answered through gritted teeth. "I received my wounds when four of our own airplanes came down on us and strafed us."

At this point Tusk actually had to stifle a yawn.

"Our airplanes, Colonel?" he said. "Really? I've never known any of our pilots to take on a ground-attack mission. Isn't there a chance that you may have been mistaken? Perhaps it was these American 'mystery' airplanes who shot at you."

"No!" Pei said again, this time louder. "They were *our* planes. MiGs. They came right down on us. Without warning. Six more of my men were killed, many others wounded. We had to bring them back, and that's why we couldn't—"

"Retrieve any parts?" Tusk concluded the sentence for him.

Pei nodded. "But these MiGs, sir, acted very strangely," he said quickly. "If I didn't know better, I would have to say they were intentionally . . ."

Tusk held up his hand, indicating that Pei be silent. Then he calmly poured himself a glass of vodka and downed it.

"Be very prudent in what you say, Colonel Pei," he said, smacking his lips. "You never know who may be listening."

Pei felt his heart freeze. Suddenly he clamped his teeth together, battling himself to remain still.

"Colonel, this time I really am disappointed with you," Tusk said after a long, dreadful silence. "You'll recall that I was against this mission in the first place. However, because of my respect for you as an officer, I authorized it. Now you have displayed actions that are decidedly not those of a committed socialist.

"You are making wild accusations that have no foundations. And it's obvious that your first taste of battle didn't agree with you."

Tusk poured another shot of vodka and just as quickly downed it.

"Now, Colonel," he went on, "wouldn't you agree that bringing back parts of your so-called wreckage would have been more important to our cause then the return of your wounded men?"

Pei didn't answer.

"Don't you realize that the wounded soldiers you brought back will probably not contribute any more to the battle?" Tusk continued. "And as such they are worthless to us. No . . . more than worthless, because now they will eat food that our healthy men should be receiving. They will get medicine and care that our front-line *fighting* troops are more deserving of.

"You have made a grave error, Colonel. For all your trouble, I think you have failed rather miserably in what you set out to do. Don't you agree?"

Pei cleared his throat and found himself staring at the floorboards.

"I saw the airplanes, sir," he said slowly. "The American airplanes we've been searching for. They're Sabres. They are already here and they are equipped with many secret weapons. Believe me, sir, they move through the night like demons. Faster than anything we could possibly have. They were reported in the same general vicinity again early this morning. If I am able to take my aircraft aloft within the next few nights, I will fly to the area. I will take photos of the Americans' new fighter and I will follow them. Then, at last, this puzzle will be solved."

Tusk shook his head. "War is not about solving puzzles, Colonel," he said. "War is about killing the enemy. I am getting fed up with your obsession about these *houng jung quay mut*. I even doubt whether you still have the capacity to fly again."

The last comment stung Pei in his heart.

"Report to your barracks, Colonel," Tusk said, returning to his button polishing. "Await my orders there."

13

THE SA-6 USAF ALBATROSS came in for a shaky, splashy landing.

Its civilian pilot, a veteran of air-sea rescue during the war in the Pacific, still had a hard time setting the big amphibious craft down on the rough, fog-shrouded sea. He killed the two engines immediately and breathed a little easier when the big floatplane finally came to a stop.

"They don't pay me enough . . ." he murmured, turning to his co-pilot/navigator. "How'd we do?"

The co-pilot shrugged and checked his map. They had had a bitch of a time finding what they thought were the correct coordinates. Now, with the fog and the rough and rolling sea, it was almost impossible for them to see any landmarks that would indicate they had landed near their objective.

"Hard to tell," the co-pilot said finally. "A radio beacon would have helped."

The pilot began to say something but instantly thought

better of it. He had met the co-pilot for the first time just a few hours before and thus he wasn't exactly sure how extensively the man had been briefed.

For instance, did he know that they had just flown into a section of the Yellow Sea that had the worst weather per square mile of any other point on the civilized globe except for the Cape of Good Hope? Did he know that the climatic conditions here were so unpredictable that the enemy avoided the area even during the best of weather? Did he know that the last Albatross to make this run had been lost—without a trace—somewhere very close to their present position?

"I don't think even a radio beacon could have made a difference in this soup," the pilot said instead. "We just got to believe our calculations were right and we're down somewhere close to the mark."

They sat there and bobbed around for a full hour, on the one hand not able to confirm their position, on the other not daring to use a radio. This mission had to be done in strict radio silence.

Another half-hour went by. The fog got thicker and it started to rain. Judging by the spray coming from the top of the waves, the pilot determined that the wind was coming in at thirty knots or more. Should it increase to forty knots, he would be forced to make the difficult decision of abandoning the mission and taking off. But before doing so, they would have to toss out the half-ton of crucial supplies stored in the back of the seaplane.

Thirty more minutes went by. Then, just as they were finishing the last of their thermos coffee, a pair of green flares streaked up through the gloom. A moment later they saw a landing barge plowing through the rough waters, coming toward them.

"*Ha-lay-loo-ya!*" the pilot yelled, unwrapping his seat harness and slapping the co-pilot on his shoulder. "Let's get that stuff unpacked before we go under!"

The first of the two dozen crates in the back of the Albatross were untethered by the time the landing barge had pulled up alongside the seaplane.

The pilot swung the cargo hatchway open just as a

small rogue wave came by. It crashed against the side of the plane and soaked him completely. The pilot didn't care. All he wanted to do was pass out the cargo to the men in the landing craft, take on the parcels they had for him, and then get the hell out of there.

He grabbed the heavy hemp line thrown to him by one of the three men on the boat and, with the help of his co-pilot, fastened the line to a packing boot on the plane's floor. Thus secured, two of the three men from the boat climbed inside the Albatross.

One of them was wearing a well-worn cowboy hat and the seaplane pilot recognized him as the same guy who'd met the Albatross once before. He was small, fairly hunched over, and looked a little too old to be wrapped up in this kind of work. He also walked with a pronounced limp.

"Want a look at the packing list?" the seaplane pilot asked him, holding up the sealed document that he was under orders not to open under any circumstances.

"Screw it," the man in the cowboy hat replied, taking the list and shoving it under his heavy jacket. "We're running late."

They worked until breathless for the next twenty minutes, lifting the heavy boxes out of the seaplane and down into the bobbing landing craft. The Albatross pilots had no idea what was in the crates—that is, until one of them accidentally opened.

Actually, only the cover was disturbed, and then just slightly. But it was enough for the seaplane pilot to see that at least one of the heavy three-foot-by-three-foot wooden boxes was packed with stacks of small gold ingots.

There were a few moments of uncomfortable silence after the man in the cowboy hat realized what the pilot had seen. But then he just shrugged, tipped his Stetson, and passed the resealed box down to his cohort in the landing craft.

"No big deal," he said.

At that point, the seaplane captain sent his co-pilot ahead to begin preparations for starting their engines. The weather was getting worse, and the sooner the Albatross got airborne the better.

Meanwhile four similar wooden boxes—these painted black—were then passed up from the barge to the seaplane pilot."

"You know what to do with these?" the cowboy asked the pilot.

The seaplane commander nodded. "Express to Yokota."

The pilot was about to help the cowboy out of the plane and back into the landing barge when the man turned and took a step closer to him.

"Got a favor to ask of you," the older man said.

He pulled an envelope from his jacket and pressed it into the hand of the seaplane pilot.

"Mail this for me, will you?" he asked.

The pilot was horrified.

"Are you nuts?" he nervously said to the cowboy. "They'd shoot me if they found out I was . . ."

The cowboy reached out and put his finger to the man's mouth. With his other hand, he retrieved a small brown packet from his pants pocket.

"There's five hundred American dollars in here," he said, putting the packet inside the pilot's coat. "And there's nothing in that letter that will screw up this operation. Just mail the fucking thing, keep your mouth shut, and the fiver is yours."

With that the cowboy literally jumped out of the hatchway and down into the landing craft, trying to steel his bad leg against the rocking motion of the boat.

The seaplane pilot was speechless. Looking down at the cowboy, he saw the man give him the thumbs-up sign. Then he flashed a quick toothy grin and yelled to his colleague at the controls of the boat. With that, the landing craft quickly pulled away.

In the next instant, the seaplane captain heard the Albatross's two big engines start to whine, indicating they were just moments away from start-up. He took the packet from his coat and peered inside. Sure enough, it contained a stack of wrinkled, soiled twenty-dollar bills. It was more money than he'd seen in one place in a long time.

He took a few seconds to run his thumb through the bills, wondering what the hell he should do. When he looked up, the landing craft had already disappeared into the fog.

Ten minutes later, the Albatross was plowing through the rough seas, both men yanking back on its steering yoke, straining to put the big seaplane into the air.

"Jesus, we're not going to make it!" the co-pilot yelled. "Waves are too damned high!"

Their mutual alarm caused them to pull even harder on the controls, and slowly, painfully, the Albatross became airborne. But not without some mortal damage to its port wing. The float on that side had ripped off in the tumultuous takeoff, tearing a large gash in the seaplane's wing-contained fuel tank.

In just a few seconds, the Albatross had lost over half the fuel it needed to return safely to its base.

From a cliff not far away, the Japanese officer named Choji Harakitsu watched through his telescope as the Albatross staggered into the air and vanished into the fog to the east.

Once it was gone, he picked up the piece of slate he always kept next to the telescope and excitedly scratched a message onto it with a crude piece of sea chalk.

"This is the third time I have seen this enemy seaplane in three weeks," he wrote. "I think they are looking for me. . . ."

14

EDDIE DORP COULDN'T BELIEVE he was actually going home.

Yet here he was, happily sitting in a wheelchair, his hands and feet still bandaged and his bloodstream positively bubbling with painkillers, watching the pretty airline stewardess check his ticket and baggage.

"Wounded in combat, soldier?" she asked him sweetly, lightly touching his shoulder with her soft fingertips.

"Secret mission," Eddie replied. "Can't say anything about it."

Her eyes went wide with excitement. "Don't tell me you're a spy or something," she said.

"Okay," Eddie replied, taking his cue perfectly. "I won't."

She laughed and he laughed, and then she began pushing him down the corridor toward the waiting TWA Super Constellation.

Tokyo International was typically chaotic this morning. Everywhere Eddie looked he could see American military types walking about, as well as many American wives and kids, too. Eddie knew these were the families of pilots lucky enough to be involved in Korea's so-called Bankers' War.

Based at airfields in Japan itself, these pilots took off in their F-80s and F-84s in the late morning, flew over to Korea, carried out their missions and returned just in time to be with the wife and kids for supper. The reason the wife and kids were there in the first place was a story in itself. In the years following the end of the war with Japan, the military had a hard time keeping veteran pilots in the service. In an effort to keep these experienced fliers happy, the Air Force had carted their families over from the states and put them up in base housing projects. When the hostilities in Korea had broken out, no one could think of a good enough reason to send all the dependents back home. So the pilots became involved in the war only between the hours of nine and five—a bankers' work day back home—and were thus spared the trials of being based in Korea itself.

It was an uneven, unfair system, but at that moment Eddie couldn't have cared less. He couldn't imagine anything so petty bothering him in the slightest anymore.

It didn't bother him that his hands and feet were wrapped in a mile or so of bandages—just a slight case of frostbite, Mrs. Dorp; all the toes and fingers were saved.

Nor did it bother him that twenty-four hours before he had convinced himself that Hard-Ass Harvey and Dr. Spitz had set him up during his mission to Tsing Buk—hoping he'd be killed on the mission, just to get him out of the way. "Postcombat trauma" is what Spitz called it after Dorp had confronted him with the charges, a malady that would disappear in time with the help of a large bottle of codeine painkillers.

It didn't even bother Eddie to know that the black airplanes he'd seen above the valley that night had been Sabres—ones that *did* look like rocketships at times.

No, nothing could rattle Eddie Dorp now. Because just like Baker the POW and all the guys who'd survived Buster Flight, and even all the Rangers who'd made it out of Tsing Buk, he was going home. The closer the stewardess pushed him toward the departing gate, the more he could actually smell the air back in Concord, New Hampshire. The pine, the streams, the mountains, the lakes. Fishing. Cooking. Drinking. Girls. Baseball. It all awaited him, along with an honorable discharge and a full-disability pension for life. And all for signing a report stating that he never saw or even heard of any mysterious "unauthorized" jets that were painted black, flew without national markings with a lot of red navigational lights on their tails, and sometimes looked like rocketships.

"Thank you, Hard-Ass," he laughed to himself as the stewardess loaded him onto the airplane. "Thank you, Uncle Sam."

15

Dear Molly:

This is either the ninth or the tenth letter I have written to you since 14 November. I've lost count and it bothers me that you might not even be getting them.

I'm sure you know that I'm taking a big risk even trying

to write to you, but I guess I just don't understand you women. When I got mustered home earlier this month, I would have bet the world that I was going to be stationed there at Mescalero for the rest of the war. Of course, at that time we all thought this damn thing would be over and soon!

But it isn't and it broke my heart to only see you for a few hours and then get the call that I was heading back here again. I hate this place. I hate the people here and I don't even know what the hell we are fighting the Chinese for. I know they are commies but they were our allies just a few years ago.

I know the world is turning upside down and I have a feeling that I wouldn't be saying these things if I didn't miss you so much. I'm mixed up over how you feel. I'm mixed up over how I feel. You say you want to be your own person but I guess I don't understand what that means.

All I can tell you is that I want to marry you and I want to talk to you and that I hope this letter somehow makes it to you.

Love, Gil.

The officer knew the letter hadn't been written by either of the two pilots killed in the Albatross crash—neither were military officers and neither of their names were Gil. He *did* know that whoever wrote the letter was an American, though—it was painfully obvious from the sentence structure.

The British officer looked out onto the wreckage of the Albatross, still burning beside the jetty of jagged rocks about fifty feet away. His squad of sailors were vainly trying to douse the wreck with puny cans of fire retardant, but he knew the blaze would just as quickly burn itself out.

What a damn twist, he thought. The seaplane's pilot had attempted to land the craft with two dead engines and one wing afire, and in another few seconds he might have made it. The jetty was the only obstacle in the twenty miles of coastline stretching on either side of the remote British-run UN coastal patrol base, and the Albatross pilot had been unlucky enough to smash right into it. The impact was so great it had nearly split the big seaplane in two, and its contents were scattered all over the jetty rocks and the beach surrounding them.

The bodies of the crewmen were recovered from the water shortly after the crash, both burned beyond recognition. As their clothes had been burned away too, no ID could be found on either man, and they had not been wearing dog tags. The only thing so far recovered was the handful of green paper scraps—pieces of American dollar bills, perhaps—found in the seared boot of one of the victims.

The British officer reread the letter once again, then carefully folded it along its original creases. His first thought was to turn it over to his superiors: Maybe it would help them determine what this mysterious Albatross and its two civilian pilots were doing flying over one of the most isolated sections of the Korean coastline in such bad weather.

But something in his gut told him this was not the thing to do. He was certain that the letter wasn't a piece of official correspondence. It was a love letter—written from the heart but at this point of little value. Almost unconsciously, he tore the letter into a dozen pieces and threw them up into the wind.

The British officer then rejoined the others on the jetty. The skeleton of the seaplane was still engulfed in flames, but their intensity was diminishing by the second. Off to one side, four of his men were retrieving pieces of debris from the waterline. Already they had snagged several lifejackets, a length of packing rope, and an empty coffee thermos, but they were still trying to capture one of the thousands of small red pieces of paper that were floating farther out from shore.

Frustrated by his crew's half-hearted attempts with their grappling poles, the officer finally waded waistdeep into the water himself and grabbed one of the red-inked scraps.

He immediately shook his head in disbelief.

"This can't be . . ." he said aloud to himself.

He grabbed another and found it was just like the first. More floated by, and he examined these too. Then, just beyond his reach, he spotted a half-submerged black box that had a long line of red notes streaming out of it.

It was money—but not just any money. Astonished, he looked back toward the burning airplane, baffled as to why the Albatross had been carrying a fortune in Russian rubles when it crashed. . . .

16

Mokpo Island

CHOJI SPENT THE REST of the day and most of the next night poised at the peak of the cliff, looking for the seaplane, his small, standard-issue Akizu 4w3 rifle in his hands and a box containing seven bullets—the extent of his rifle ammunition—at his side.

But no one came. No American soldiers scaled the cliffs, no American airplanes bombed his position. And the seaplane never returned. Several times he thought he saw glimpses of a large ship enveloped in fog way off in the distance, but like the flashes he might have seen that night, he couldn't be sure. By midnight he knew he had to get back into his hut to get warm, as his fingers and toes were already beginning to stiffen. With the tears freezing as soon as they touched his cheek, he packed up his weapon and ammunition and hobbled back to the shack.

Why was it like this? he thought sadly, bowing before the fading picture of his Emperor. *When will it end?*

He gathered up a handful of sticky, cold rice and forced it into his mouth. Two days from now he had his chores to do; he hoped no attack came then. Two miles away, down off the cliff, was a cave in which he stored the remains of the supplies he had salvaged five years before from a prewar shipwreck: ten twenty-pound bags of rice, two barrels of lamp oil, and two barrels of lubricating oil. Deeper in the cave, where it was especially cool, was a crate of TNT packed in straw and sand and two forty-gallon sealed tanks of siphoned-off aviation gasoline.

When the time came he would make his weekly trek down to the cavern, take his ration of rice and lamp oil, and check to make sure the aviation fuel was not spoiled and that the TNT was still sufficiently dry. Then he would venture down to the beach and set his small net into one of the tidal pools and attempt to catch a school of minnows or possibly a large sea fish.

And as always, he would look for an eel.

He had seen one several years before and nearly drowned trying to catch it. Later he had dreamed that the eel had come to him as a sign from his Emperor and that when he saw it again, his world would change.

Now Choji lay back on his mat and huddled beneath his coarse army blanket. Yes, he had many things to do, so he hoped sleep would come quickly. Closing his eyes, he wondered if he would dream about the eel again that night.

17

THE FOUR PILOTS HUDDLED around the practically bare table were all members of the super-secret 39th Air Wing of the USAF's Special Weapons Command.

At the moment, the four men—USAF Captain Gil Hughes, USAF Major Gabe Evers, U.S. Navy Lieutenant Commander Jack Kenneally, and USAF Captain Chas Spencer—were intently eyeing a cigarette lighter flicker away in front of them. As they watched, the flame from the lighter suddenly flared up in a distinct blue plume. Then after a few seconds of sparkling, it finally went out for good, plunging the cabin into total darkness.

"Well, that's that," Hughes said, his image fading from the others' sight. "It'll be like a coal mine in here from now on."

"And it was Ernst's lighter, too," Spencer said, his voice now just a series of vibrations coming out of the darkness. "The poor bastard. I wonder if they ever found his body down there."

"Wouldn't be much left if Ernst was a good Boy Scout and chewed the pill like he was supposed to," Evers said. "That stuff goes right through you—burns your skin off, disintegrates your bones. They say you're dust in a matter of a day and a half."

A forlorn silence enveloped the cabin, each man wondering if their fate would be the same as their late colleague, Captain Sam Ernst, who had been lost in action several nights before.

It was Hughes who broke the gloomy quiet.

"I don't know about you guys, but I'm getting a little fed up with this whole thing," he said, his anger coming through loud and clear in the darkness. "I mean, I know it's your basic top-secret crap, but . . ."

"Well, I'm finally glad to hear someone else say that," Kenneally replied.

"Same here," Spencer added.

The truth was, Hughes was getting suspicious. They had been cooped up in the cabin for nearly a week; the only time they spent outside the compartment was when they were strapped into the cockpit of the airplanes, and that was only at night. As it was, none of them had seen the sun in six days—their imposed darkness being part of an experiment conducted by their mission commanders in improving night vision for pilots. Or so they claimed. It was also a convenient way to prevent the pilots from getting a close look at anything around the secret base.

Not seeing the light of day was just one of many strange aspects of the operation. Hughes knew that in any covert mission, some things had to be expected. The fact that their aircraft carried no national markings whatsoever was typical, as was their flying being restricted to the hours between three in the morning and dawn. Even the bizarre circumstances surrounding the location of their secret base were understandable to a point—all four of them had been stationed at a super-secret air base in New Mexico before the war and were used to living under a tight cloak of security.

But it was the issuing of the suicide pills that was a little too spooky for Hughes and the others. The capsules, filled with some unknown but highly lethal poison, were to be chewed if the pilots were shot down and their capture imminent. Along the same lines, the surviving pilots were under orders to destroy any of the aircraft that landed anywhere other than at the secret base—again to prevent them from falling into the hands of the enemy.

It had been just these circumstances they'd faced the night Ernst went down after colliding with a MiG over Tsing Buk. Once they saw that his airplane had not been completely destroyed on impact, they had no choice but to strafe it until it was.

To Hughes's mind, things had gone from bad to worse ever since.

"That mission the other night has been really giving me the creeps," he continued. "I don't think they were too happy we went back over Tsing Buk."

"Why not?" Kenneally asked. "Just because we caught our little Red friends frying a ground target for the first time in their careers?"

"They *told* us to shoot down MiGs just about anywhere we could find them," Spencer added. "We just happened to find them over Tsing Buk again. . . ."

"Well, I just got the feeling that we weren't invited to that particular party," Hughes answered. "I mean, those MiGs were strafing in a pretty way-out pattern. Anyone within seventy-five yards was going to get hit, no matter whose side they were on."

"Well, that's just the commie way of thinking for you," Kenneally said. "It's okay if we kill fifty of ours just as long as we kill one or two of you in the process."

"But we don't even know if anyone *was* down there," Evers said. "What those MiGs were doing to who really isn't our concern. We chased the bastards back to China, so our job was done."

"Still, there was something weird about it," Hughes said. "I could tell at the debriefing. I saw a lot of jaws drop when we told them we went back over Tsing Buk."

"I noticed it too," Spencer said. "It was just like when we screwed up and told them we took on those MiGs who were chewing up those B-29s. . . ."

"Don't sweat it," Evers said with his usual swagger. "They got over that as soon as we convinced them no one got a good make on us. You know—we came, we saw, we kicked the shit out of the bad guys. After all, we are up there looking for targets of opportunity—most of the time, anyway."

"I'm just getting a bad feeling about this whole thing," Hughes said. "I mean, we've all dealt with covert types before, but these guys just seem a little *too* wacko."

"Hey, they're Spooks," Evers replied. "What do you want? They're *all* nuts. We should all know that better than anyone else.

"Look, we're doing what they hired us for. We're getting paid more money than a carload of generals and, besides that cruddy eel, we're eating good. What's to complain about?"

"You mean you don't mind being locked up—in complete darkness?" Hughes asked.

"Hell no. I like it," Evers replied, half seriously. "My older brothers used to lock me in a closet for hours—days, even."

"Why am I not surprised to hear that?" Kenneally said.

"Besides," Evers went on. "We can't do much about anything cooped up in here."

"We can fly off and not come back," Spencer offered.

"And risk blowing a top-secret operation, not to mention a desertion charge?" Evers replied. "Not me. They hang you for that kind of thing.

"Face it, guys: We're stuck here either until the war is over or until they're through with us."

Spencer let out a morbid laugh. "I wonder what will come first?" he asked.

Just then there was a knock on the door.

"Time to get cracking," the man named Gump called into the room. "Briefing in five minutes. Takeoff in fifteen . . ."

18

HUGHES STRAPPED ON HIS oxygen mask and took a long, deep breath. He felt a familiar jolt run through him, the usual momentary, pleasant side-effect derived from sucking in the pure air.

Nothing like a blast of the big O to juice a fellow up, he thought as he took another deep gulp and closed his eyes, letting his body adapt to the artificial atmosphere.

He was sitting in the cockpit of his battered F-86, the Sabre officially known as Aircraft #1. At that moment, everything around him was pitch black, so much so that he had to snap on the cockpit's small utility light in order to do a quick scan of his flight instruments. Fuel load, gyro, radio compass, magnetic compass—everything seemed okay. Battery-starter light was on. Engine master switch was on. Clock was set at 0415 hours.

Suddenly he felt the entire airplane shudder as the huge flight elevator began to move. The F-86 was slowly raised out of the darkened compartment and up into the gloomy predawn fog. At this point he closed the canopy and adjusted his flight helmet.

Here we go again, he thought.

Once the elevator had stopped, a ten-man crew of mechanics and launch personnel pushed and pulled the F-86, jockeying it around for takeoff. Another F-86, this one being flown by Evers, was already in position, its external power units plugged in and providing the electricity needed to start its engine.

Meanwhile, Hughes's aircraft was turned so that its nose was pointing in the proper direction. An external power unit was quickly hooked on, and he felt the electricity start to surge into the jet. A brisk signal from the deck officer told him it was time to fire up his engine.

Hughes took another deep breath, but this time he was rewarded with nothing more than a familiar twinge of pain in his back. He closed his eyes and waited for it to subside. Then he began the start-up procedure.

Punching in the ignition circuit-breaker, he clicked the engine master switch back to ON. Next he moved his throttle lever forward and waited for the low-fuel-pressure warning light to go out. This done, he held the battery-starter switch in the STARTER position, counted to three, then moved the switch to BATTERY.

He felt the Sabre's powerful J-47 turbojet engine instantly burst to life. Suddenly the whole jet was shaking like a bronco. Even without turning his head, Hughes could clearly see the reflection of his tail flame on his canopy glass as it lit up the dark mist around him.

Working quickly, he advanced his throttle to the idle position and watched as the RPM rate increased. When it reached the magic 30-percent mark, he disengaged the starter button.

At last, the 5970-pound-thrust engine was running on its own.

He watched as the engine idling speed increased to 36 percent. A quick check of his all-important jet-pipe temperature told him it was well below the danger point of 1004F. At that point, he gave the signal for the deck crew to disconnect the external power sources.

A second later, he heard the radiophones in his crash helmet crackle and the disembodied voice of the deck launch officer come on.

"All right," it drawled. "Let's have your hydraulic pressure."

"Three thousand pounds per—"

"Harness belt tightened?"

"Roger," Hughes replied.

"Trim?"

"Set for takeoff."

"Fuel?"

"Check."

"Gyros erected?"

"Check."

"Switches?"

Hughes did a quick scan of his instruments, then called out, "Generator is on. Engine master is on. Instrument power is normal. Oxygen is on and normal. Bomb-release selector switch is on auto. Gunsight is on. All other armament switches are off."

"Okay, cowboy," the launch officer replied. "You passed the audition. Take off on my signal. Over."

At that moment Hughes heard a blast of power come from Evers's F-86 right next to him. Suddenly the tail of Evers's Sabre erupted in flame and, not an instant later, the two RATO projections from the Sabre's belly exploded to life. In less than a heartbeat, the F-86 was roaring away from him.

"Go, Gabe," Hughes silently urged his friend. "Pull it up . . ."

Just at that moment, he saw the nose end of the Sabre lift off. Suddenly the whole airplane was up and climbing into the night, the awesome flare from its underside blinding out all traces of the aircraft above.

Then, just as quickly, the aircraft was gone—vanishing into the night and mist like a ghost. To anyone seeing it for the first time, it would have seemed like the Sabre had simply disappeared.

19

Over North Korea

IT WAS 0435 HOURS when Hughes and Evers reached the attack coordinate, a point just off the western coast of Korea and forty-five miles from the communist capital of Pyongyang. They closed into a tight two-ship formation and steered into a long, wide-out circling pattern. Once again, the wait had begun.

The flight to the designated area had been uneventful, as was their back-breaking, rocket-assisted takeoff, their fourth in five days. Shortly after launch, they'd been forced to climb to 42,000 feet in order to avoid some typically dismal Korean weather, then they diverted west to miss being seen by a C-47 cargo plane making its way toward Seoul.

They circled the coordinate for ten minutes before the force of MiGs showed up, as advertised. They were flying down around 35,000 feet and cruising at 500 mph— just as the briefing intelligence had said they would be. Hughes counted eighteen airplanes in all—definitely a squadron sweep formed into six three-unit echelons. This, too, was just as the secret operation's intelligence officer had predicted. As Hughes and Evers watched unseen from above, the enemy airplanes turned out to the west, over the ocean—again, just as the pre-mission information had said they would.

Hughes shook his head in a combination of disbelief and admiration. One of the strangest aspects of the secret Sabre operation was the intelligence on the MiG operations that the Spooks seemed to have at their fingertips. It was always amazingly accurate. Almost *too* accurate.

Evers pulled alongside Hughes's airplane and wagged his wings. Hughes knew this was the signal to begin communication on how best to attack the large MiG formation. They couldn't talk to each other, of course— the Sabres had no radio sets. These were yanked out even before the Spooks had managed to sneak them aboard the secret base.

But Hughes and Evers didn't need radios. They communicated by a system devised by Evers months before—ironically, while they were flying yet another covert mission. The system was simply Morse code dots and dashes—the transmitter was their cockpit lights.

It only took a few seconds for Evers to communicate that he would go in on the MiGs first and that Hughes should "cover his ass." Hughes blinked back a "roger," then checked to make sure his guns were in working order.

By this time the force of MiGs had completed their short turn to the west and were now turning again, this time to the north. Because the Sabres were riding so high in the night sky, the MiG pilots had no idea what was about to befall them.

So what else is new? Hughes thought.

With that in mind, he watched as Evers dropped the nose of his Sabre and booted its throttle. Hughes did the same a split second later, gulping his oxygen like a madman in anticipation of the impending combat. Somewhere behind them, maybe five minutes away, were Kenneally and Spencer. If everything went right, they would arrive just in time to deliver the second half of the preplanned one-two punch.

Less than ten seconds later, Evers was lining up the trailing MiG in the last echelon of the enemy formation; Hughes was aiming at the wingman. Even in the moments before he squeezed his gun trigger, Hughes had a begrudging respect for the Spooks' training: He *could* see better at night—or at least in the minutes of darkness just before daybreak. Peering down at the MiG, it was almost as if the enemy fighter were running with its headlights on.

An instant later, he saw Evers's nose light up like a string of fireworks, its six machine guns ripping into the tail and rear fuselage of his targeted MiG. Hughes immediately fired his own guns at his target, with the same result. Pieces of the MiG's tail came flying off two seconds later, so close that Hughes had to do a quick bank to the right to avoid being hit by the debris.

Startled, both MiG pilots turned and dove, Evers and Hughes right on their tails. Hughes walked another long burst right up the MiG's midsection, culminating in a small explosion just aft of the jet's canopy. That's when He broke off and pulled the Sabre to the right. His bullets had found the enemy's main fuel tank and perforated it. He knew from experience that it would take only a matter of seconds for the leaking fuel to wash over the jet's turbine and ignite. Sure enough, no sooner had he cleared the enemy's tail than the MiG blew up in a spectacular explosion.

Evers was making slightly longer work of his quarry, pumping the MiG with short bursts as the obviously more-experienced Red pilot tried desperately to get away.

But his maneuvering was in vain. Evers pushed his throttle ahead slightly, causing his guns to fire directly into the MiG's cockpit. One last burst and the enemy pilot was killed instantly. The MiG flipped over on its back and started the long plunge to the sea below.

By this time, the sixteen remaining enemy fighters had already commenced their escape. In the short time that the clandestine war between the MiGs and the Sabres had been waged, both sides had quickly learned that the

MiG had several advantages. One was its faster climb rate. Another was its ability to fly higher than the Sabre, and that's where the surviving MiGs were heading, up to the higher altitudes.

The Reds' safe haven was at 50,000 feet—a few thousand feet higher than the prudent operating altitude of a standard armed-up Sabre. But the Black Sabres were anything but standard issue for at least one reason: the rocket-assist bottles.

Hughes and Evers quickly regrouped and, without any problem, spotted the rest of the MiG squadron 15,000 feet above and about five miles north of them. As usual, the MiGs were scurrying home: Since the one-sided pre-dawn slaughters over the Yalu and Tsing Buk Valley, the Red pilots, they being part of a secret thirty-airplane unit, had become very reluctant to turn and fight the Sabres. And the lightning-quick downing of their two comrades had made this flight a particularly squeamish bunch.

Still the Black Sabres pressed the fight.

Hughes looked over at Evers, who was madly blinking his cockpit light. But Hughes didn't need to interpret the dots and dashes. He knew immediately what Evers had in mind.

Reaching for a rather inconspicuous device on his left-side control panel known as the Bomb-Rocket-Tank jettison button, Hughes counted to three, then pushed.

Suddenly the Sabre jet was thrown forward with such force that his spine felt as if it were going to break in two. He had ignited what was left in his RATO bottles, and the extra kick—in combination with his pulling out of the high-gravity dive and booting the engine throttles to max—made the Sabre rocket forward like a bullet. In fact, Hughes was going so fast that Evers's airplane looked like nothing more than a gray blur right off his starboard wing.

Pressed back against his seat by the increased g-forces, Hughes was still able to keep the fleeing MiGs in sight. They were just passing through the 40,000-foot mark, their own RD-45F, 6000-pound-thrust engines screaming to reach the magic 50,000-foot mark.

But as superior as the MiG's climbing rate was, it wasn't fast enough to outrun the rocket-assist Sabres.

Hughes and Evers immediately picked out two more targets and, in a bold up-from-below maneuver, streaked underneath the fleeing MiGs. If there was any drawback with the maverick rocket-assist procedure it was that the Sabre might be going *too* fast when it came time to press the attack. So at just the right moment, Hughes and Evers switched off their RATO bottles, applied their air brakes, and let the deteriorating velocity of the unorthodox ascent work for them.

As if on cue, both Sabre pilots opened up on their targets, the combined drag of gravity and the now-depleted RATO bottles serving to slow the Sabres down just enough to get a long, solid burst into the MiGs' underbellies. This time, Evers's target blew up first as he laid a concentrated stream of .50-caliber bullets into the MiG's wings and undercarriage. The resulting explosion nearly clipped Evers's own wing, and the American pilot was forced to spin out in order to avoid critical damage.

Although Hughes was pouring on the big fifties himself, he coolly took a split second to watch his partner's crazy escape pattern.

"Typical," he whispered as he watched Evers's Sabre plunge nose over tail.

A moment later, Hughes's target was destroyed. His machine guns had ripped into the MiG's tailfin in mainspar, severing its elevator trim tabs and rudder. The MiG instantly went haywire, spinning and twisting as the pilot lost all control. Soon it simply pointed straight down and fell, trailing a long plume of red and gray smoke behind it.

At this point, the fourteen remaining MiGs scattered. Some chose to continue their desperate climb up to 50,000 feet; others decided to bank off and head back toward the Korean mainland, where at least they would have a chance to eject, should it come to that.

A few, possibly the more experienced pilots, elected to dive, thinking that perhaps the two attacking Black Sabres wouldn't expect them to retreat to the muddy air below.

That's where Kenneally and Spencer came in.

Following the dogfight from their vantage point several

miles behind, neither pilot had any problem locating the three MiGs that decided to chance escape at the lower altitudes. Following a quick conversation via their blinking cockpit lights, both Sabre pilots relit their own RATO bottles simultaneously.

Cruising high above, Hughes and Evers had regrouped and now watched as their colleagues streaked wildly below them, the long twin fires of the RATO bottles lighting up the early morning sky. Spencer and Kenneally made short work of two of the low-flying MiGs—one rocket-assisted pass was all it took. Two corresponding splashes in the Yellow Sea seconds later confirmed the kills.

A minute later, the four Black Sabres had grouped into a finger-four formation and turned south, heading back to their secret base before the sun came up.

20

THE TELEPHONE INSIDE THE control tower at Kimpo Air Base rang five times before anyone picked it up.

"Tower!" the Air Force air-traffic control officer answered harshly, upset that someone would ring him in the middle of the night.

The voice at the other end was faint and staticky.

"This is Forward Observation Base Number Two," the voice said. "We got a Bed Check Charlie heading your way."

"Christ!" the tower officer cursed. "Not again."

He grabbed a pencil and paper and began writing. "Okay, let's have it," he said.

"We are at position six-niner-seven," the caller told him. "He buzzed us for a few minutes. Came in so low we thought he was going to plow right in. But he's coming right toward you now, so you guys better get ready."

The tower officer quickly noted the time. It was just two minutes after midnight.

"Did you get a make on the aircraft?" he asked.

"It's a Pooper Deuce," came the reply. "He didn't shoot at us and he looks to be flying pretty light."

The tower officer gruffly thanked the man and hung up.

"Goddamn it," he cursed to himself. "Why do these guys always show up on my shift?"

The Kimpo Air Base had been plagued by Bed Check Charlies for almost the entire war. The enemy pilots got their name because, in most cases, their mission was only to fly over allied military installations in the middle of the night, creating enough noise to wake everyone on the base and therefore deprive them of a good night's sleep. Sometimes the Red pilot would just make several sweeps over the air base, intentionally running his engine loud and heavy. Other times he would drop fireworks or even authentic ordnance.

As crude as the tactic sounded, it was very effective in spooking everyone at the afflicted base and was practically unstoppable. One of the reasons for this was the airplane the Bed Checks flew. It was a PO-2, an antique Russian-built biplane that had served as a trainer before World War II. Slow, noisy, and built of little more than wire, wood, and canvas, the PO-2— nicknamed the "Pooper Deuce"—was perfect for the night harassment raids. It could easily fly low enough to sail under the UN radar net, and it was so slow that many of the aircraft in the allies' high-speed airborne arsenal couldn't decelerate enough to shoot at it.

It was, however, a rare occasion for the Kimpo tower to get an advanced warning that a Bed Check was on its way. The call from the forward-observation post gave the tower officer enough time to formulate a strategy. But, as always, he was faced with a dilemma: What was better, the sickness or the cure?

The tower officer knew he could scramble a couple of

airplanes—F-80s or even two of the F-82 Twin Mustang
night-fighters assigned to the base—and have them intercept the PO-2. Trouble was, the pilots would probably
do more harm—to themselves—than good. Everyone knew
the story of the F-80 pilot who, in an attempt to shoot
down a Bed Check, slowed his speed so much that his
engine stalled. The pilot was killed when his canopy
failed to blow off while he was ejecting. Another pilot,
flying an F-84, tried the same thing and wound up flying
right into the Pooper Deuce, killing himself and the Red
pilot.

Not wanting to complete the trilogy, the Kimpo tower
officer decided against scrambling any airplanes. Instead, he alerted the base's antiaircraft-battery officer
and told him to expect a Bed Check within the next ten
minutes.

The Marine antiaircraft unit charged with protecting
the base leaped to the job with relish.

Unlike the grouchy tower officer, the Marines welcomed the opportunity to shoot at the enemy, especially
if he happened to be a hated North Korean. Mustering
out in their combat gear, under the guidance of a Reserve lieutenant, the Marines quickly unlocked their AA
guns and loaded them up. This done, the lieutenant
himself piled four of his best marksmen into the company
jeep and sped toward Runway 3A, which was located at
the far end of the base. Judging from the information
given to him by the tower officer, and assuming the Red
pilot stuck to his last reported heading, it was here they
would first spot the PO-2.

They didn't have to wait long. No sooner had the
Marines arrived and doused the jeep's headlights when
they heard the unmistakable racket of the biplane's engine approaching them from the north.

"We're going to get this bastard," the lieutenant growled
to his anxious men. "If he's low enough, we'll open up
on him with everything."

"Everything" included the M-60 heavy machine gun
that was mounted in the back of the jeep. The three

other enlisted Marines were armed with World War II-vintage Thompson machine guns, and the lieutenant was packing a Browning automatic rifle.

"There he is," one of the soldiers called out in an urgent whisper. "See him?"

The lieutenant peered out into the darkness and, sure enough, over a line of trees about half a mile away he could see the exhaust flashes of the biplane's ancient engine. Right away he noticed the PO-2 was flying extremely low and slow.

"Get ready," the officer told his men. "On my call."

The Marines patiently waited for the noisy airplane to draw closer. All the while it appeared to slow down even more.

"Hold it," the lieutenant cautioned, even as he raised the heavy BAR to his shoulder. "Get a good bead on the bastard. . . ."

The biplane came on, dipping and twisting and losing altitude by the second, presenting a perfect target for the waiting Marines.

"Okay, on three . . ." the lieutenant called out, estimating the PO-2 was only about a hundred yards from their position. "One . . . two . . . three . . . *fire!*"

All five Marines opened up at once, the noise of their combined fusillade being sufficiently loud enough to wake as many people at the base as any Bed Check Charlie could hope for. Instantly hundreds of bullets ripped into the canvas-covered biplane as it came right toward them, no more than twenty-five feet off the tarmac.

"Keep shooting!" the lieutenant yelled, trying to be heard over the racket of the gunfire and the noise of the PO-2's engine as the biplane passed so low right over their heads that all five soldiers involuntarily ducked.

The stream of bullets followed the biplane as it got lower still, its wings and fuselage now tattered and smoking.

"It's on fire!" one of the Marines yelled jubilantly. "He's going to crash!"

But the lieutenant knew better. The airplane was crippled and flames were streaking out of its tail. But it wasn't crashing.

It was trying to land.

The tower officer was one of the first people to reach the burning PO-2 after it had skidded to a fiery halt on the runway.

He stopped about ten feet from it and watched as the terrified pilot tried to pull himself out of the burning cockpit. In an instant the tower officer knew the Red couldn't get out on his own. His mind flashed two options: Do nothing and watch a human get cooked alive, or rescue him.

Going against his natural disposition, the tower officer ran forward and jumped up onto the burning biplane's lower wing. With all his might, he yanked the weakened pilot twice, trying to pull him out of the open-air cockpit. But at first his efforts were to no avail.

He yanked once more, and this time whatever was holding the pilot into his seat gave way. The tower officer fell off the wing and landed hard on his back, the Red pilot toppling down on top of him.

By this time a crowd of people—tower workers, sentries, Marines—had run up, and six of them rushed in and dragged the two injured men away from the airplane. No sooner were they a safe distance away than the smoldering PO-2 totally erupted in flames, its small fuel tanks exploding with the distinct crackling puff of gasoline being ignited. Within seconds, the biplane was reduced to a smoking wreck.

The tower officer got to his feet and shook off those who suggested he stay down. He had just risked his life to save a man and, damnit, he was going to make sure the bastard stayed alive.

Pushing his way through the crowd that had formed around the enemy pilot, the tower officer knelt down and stared into the man's face. His complexion was different from the North Koreans the tower officer had seen, indicating he was probably Chinese. Oddly, his left shoulder was already in bandages, and the scratches on his head and hands were already scabbed over, obviously results of a previous injury.

Amazingly, the man was conscious and apparently coherent. As the sound of the base's ambulance siren cut through the night, the tower officer grabbed someone's jacket and placed it under the man's head for a pillow.

That's when the Red Chinese pilot began to speak.

"I am Colonel Pei of the People's Liberation Army Air Defense Force," he said in halting, almost French-accented English. "I want to defect. . . ."

21

Tokyo

USAF COLONEL PAUL STANTON wasn't a superstitious man.

He had never put much credence in fate, luck, or the supposed import of so-called "meaningful coincidences." Yet this belief was shaken a bit when he arrived at his office in the UN General Command Building in Tokyo the following morning to find two bizarre field reports waiting for him.

As the chief intelligence officer for the Far East Air Force, it was Stanton's job to review mostly pedestrian reports on numbers, strengths, and dispositions of enemy forces. Still, mixed in with the mundane, he had seen accounts concerning everything from the supposed bulletproof properties of the uniforms worn by the Red Chinese troops to a sworn statement by an American soldier who claimed that the so-called Abominable Snowman had attacked him one night while on guard duty in the high mountains of central North Korea.

Stanton was accustomed to receiving these unusual communiques from the forward bases. In fact, before the war in Korea broke out, most of his military career had been devoted to wading through the sometimes murky undercurrents of covert operations where fact frequently mingled with the fantastic. In the last weeks of the war against Nazi Germany, for instance, Stanton had been in charge of a classified American intelligence unit that scoured the devastated European battlefield looking for German secret weapons. To the surprise of some, Stanton and his men had managed to find nine Nazi jet airplanes during one foray, and under his direction these were shipped to a secret U.S. air base in Mescalero, New Mexico, where they eventually made up America's first jet-aircraft squadron. As it turned out, data from testing these captured airplanes became the cornerstone for the aerodynamic advances incorporated into America's own early jet-aircraft designs.

His subsequent searches for Nazi superweapons—hydrogen bombs, intercontinental missiles, and rocketships capable of flying to the moon—were less successful. These, too, were based on relatively fantastic rumors, nine-tenths of which eventually ended up in a very deep "miscellaneous" file.

So up until this day, Stanton had considered himself somewhat of an expert in deciphering the fact from fiction. But the two reports that greeted him this morning were more than strange by the very fact that they were quite possibly true.

One concerned the defection of a high-ranking Red Chinese air-operations intelligence officer. The defector claimed to have information concerning a top-secret operation involving a new kind of American fighter. That was all he was saying until he met with top FEAF intelligence officials. As the defector held a rank as high as his own, Stanton knew he would be the one to interview the man first.

The report about a new kind of American fighter in Korea did not catch Stanton totally by surprise—he had been hearing the faintest murmurings of such a thing for the past week. But as a career intelligence veteran, he knew that any war zone was filled with rumors—working European intelligence in 1945 was like reading a science-fiction novel, so plentiful were the reports of secret weapons. So at first the edgy stories about a new American fighter seemed more fantasy than anything else.

Until now. With a similar report coming from the other side, Stanton knew he would have to give the "rumor" more credence.

The second report of that morning was even stranger, if that was possible. It concerned the somewhat mysterious crash of an Albatross seaplane out on the isolated part of the western Korean coastline. The British Royal Navy sailors who witnessed the crash not only recovered the bodies of two civilians from the wreck, they also found the equivalent of two million dollars in Russian currency near the crash site. The RN officer in charge had even sent a bag full of the Soviet money along with the report.

The physical evidence of the Russian money presented Stanton with a dilemma. He knew that in the past the best intelligence work was done with good, old-fashioned brainpower. Think it out, talk it out with colleagues, reach a conclusion, and follow it through. Nowadays computers were getting into the act—and an enormous one sat across the hall from his office. These machines were gradually taking over in the "brainpower" department. Information was typed in, collated facts were spit out. Input, output, conclusion, solution—sometimes it was as quick and simple as that. And if the machine couldn't figure it all out, the current thinking went, then it probably didn't happen.

Stanton was slowly nurturing a grudging respect for the machines. They had the ability to eliminate the obvious, and it was surprising how many things fell into place after that. His colleagues had come to rely on the machines almost totally. Some were even convinced that future wars would be won simply on the basis of who had the most and best computers.

Stanton wasn't that much of a convert—not quite yet. He felt that if he inputted the information on the defector's claim and the seaplane crash into the computer across the hall, it would most likely get chewed up beyond recognition. Despite their obvious advantages in time and volume, sometimes even the pure, concentrated rationalization of the machine came up empty. No, if there was one thing he'd learned from his years in the intelligence business, it was that the path to a human truth frequently came right from the gut. And for all their wonderment, computers had no gut. Events that defied explanation in their mechanical-cerebral terms sometimes made sense strictly in the realm of instinct.

And right now, something in Stanton's gut was telling him the defector's story and the doomed seaplane's mysterious cargo were somehow connected.

He punched his desk phone to life and called his adminstrative assistant, Lieutenant Tim Crayer.

"Pack your warm clothes," he told him. "We're leaving for Yokota immediately."

22

Mokpo Island

WALKING OUT OF THE fog that perpetually enveloped the beach, Choji Harakitsu reached one of his favorite tidal pools, out of breath and thirsty.

It had been a long day already, and still it was only early afternoon. The trip down to the cave for the rice and oil had taken longer than usual, but Choji didn't know why that was. Perhaps he was sick and didn't realize it yet. Or maybe he had let his mind wander and just didn't keep correct account of the time. Or maybe he was just getting old and tottering, and he could expect the weekly chore to take longer and longer each time.

He hunched down at the edge of the pool and unraveled his small net. The tide was still coming in—that much he had predicted correctly—and thus it was the best time to hunt for minnows. Normally he enjoyed being down off the cliff and on the beach—catching minnows, breathing the heavy salt air, and even splashing some of the cold sea water in his face. Had it been summer, he would have stripped naked and plunged right into the surf. Then he would not wash the salt from his body for six days, knowing as he did that few things in life were as good for the skin and the spirit as being immersed in salt water.

But for some reason the beach did not feel so very enjoyable today. Something was different; the usual tranquillity was missing. What could it be? he wondered. He looked around and slowly realized that the waves were crashing against the base of the nearby cliff with an increased ferocity. The water offshore was also very choppy. He turned toward the eastern horizon, trying to see the clouds off in the distance through the fog. It *was* dark out there. Perhaps there was a storm out to sea, he thought. Possibly a typhoon. After observing the conditions for five years, Choji knew the weather could change dramatically in this part of the Yellow Sea—sometimes in just a matter of minutes. With this in mind, he studied the fierce waves closely for a few moments and decided that if there were a storm coming, he would know soon. The swells would get bigger, there would be an increase of foam on the surface, and pieces of seaweed and debris would start to wash ashore.

And there would also be many minnows, racing in close to the beach to avoid the tempest. He began unraveling his net with increased urgency now, and after setting it just past the mouth of the pool, he turned and prayed to the Emperor that the dark clouds he saw through the mist out on the horizon were indeed the first signs of an approaching storm.

23

THE MAN AT THE helm of the Norwegian-registered Red Cross ship could feel the vessel tugging as the wind picked up dramatically.

"Where the hell is the latest weather report?" he called across the bridge to the ship's first mate. "This wind has gone up to thirty knots just in the past five minutes."

The first mate immediately got on to the radio and called down to the navigator's station, one deck below. After a terse conversation, he turned back to the helmsman.

"He says we've got a gale blowing up, sir," the first mate told him. "Coming our way."

The helmsman slammed his fist against the ship's wheel even as it began to shake.

"Christ, this is all we need!" he said. "Neilson will go absolutely nuts when he hears this."

The first mate looked off to the east. The cloudy sky was much darker out there and the sea much grayer.

"The weather can get real tough very quick around here," he said. "Any chance he'll want to turn back?"

"Not in a million years," came the helmsman's reply. "Cancel this meeting and all hell will break loose."

The sea was getting rougher by the minute as the helmsman plowed the ship on a north-by-northeast course. Already rain was splattering against the wheelhouse windows, hitting them so hard it could have easily been mistaken for hail.

The radio on the bridge suddenly crackled to life. The first mate answered the call, had another brief conversation, then hung up.

"Nav says we're here," he reported. "We're sitting right on the coordinate."

Still cursing, the helmsman called down to the engine room and ordered that the ship's speed be cut to one-third. Then he turned the wheel and gradually put the vessel into a wide circle pattern.

"These guys better be on time," he said.

Ten agonizing minutes dragged by as the Red Cross ship continued to circle.

Finally the radio buzzed again.

"We've got a sonar contact," the voice said through the static. "It's got to be them. . . ."

Both the helmsman and the first mate breathed a sigh of relief.

"Get Neilson on the blower," the helmsman ordered the first mate. "Tell him it's time to get this show on the road."

Olav Neilson, (AKA Olaf Nellison and Oliver Nelson) the actual captain of the Red Cross ship, celebrated the message from the bridge by pouring himself a quick shot of Scotch.

"Sorry, Karl," he said, turning to the only other person in his cabin. "I'm out of seltzer. . . ."

The other man waved away the explanation. He didn't drink alcohol and didn't fully trust anyone who did. It was for the exact *opposite* reason that Neilson didn't entirely have faith in Karl. Who could go through this life without seeking refuge in the spirits?

But they had to work together, so a truce on drinking had silently been drawn between them a long time before.

"Quite bad weather for sailing all of a sudden," Karl observed, noting the increased rocking of the ship.

"Yeah, for us," Neilson said. "Not so much for them. I'll bet they're used to this stuff."

"Do you think this will be the final meeting, then?" Karl asked.

Neilson drained his drink and poured another. "God-damn, I hope so," he said. "Our agreement is almost up. We've certainly done our part and worked damn hard at keeping it quiet. I just hope those bastards appreciate what we've done to keep this whole thing under wraps."

Karl inserted a cigarette into his holder and lit it.

"I've never known these people to appreciate anything," he replied.

Ten minutes later, Neilson and Karl were up on the bridge, wearing floor-length raincoats and woolen hats.

"Tell me something," Neilson said to the helmsman, noting the rapidly deteriorating weather conditions. "Do these guys feel this as bad as we do?"

The helmsman shook his head. Being the most experienced seaman on the Red Cross ship, Neilson frequently came to him with nautical questions.

"If they've got a good guy behind the wheel, they can sail right under all this," he answered.

Just then the first mate let out a yell.

"There they are!" he called out, pointing to a spot about fifty feet off the ship's port bow.

Neilson and Karl stepped up to the bridge's windows and turned their binoculars in the direction indicated by the first mate. Both of them immediately saw the periscope and radio vane moving slowly toward them.

Neilson slapped Karl on the back hard and yelled, "Just like the old days!"

"They're stopping, sir," the first mate called over to him. "Coming up to the surface . . ."

"Stop all engines!" Neilson cried out.

"Stop all engines!" the first mate repeated into his radio. Suddenly there was an abrupt shudder that ran through the ship as its propellers quickly ground to a halt.

"Get the boats out!" Neilson yelled to the first mate. "And be careful. I don't want any of these guys going into the drink at this point."

Three men emerged from the conning tower of the surfaced submarine and, by a system of three boats lashed together, they eventually climbed aboard the Red Cross vessel.

There were no handshakes, no exchanges of greeting between the men of the Red Cross ship and those coming over from the sub. Watching the transfer take place from the bridge, Neilson noticed that one of the submariners was armed. He quickly ordered his ship's first mate to strap a gun on and, with Karl in tow, then went below to his cabin.

Five minutes later, the three visitors were ushered in. With little fanfare, they took off their bad-weather gear and sat down at the small rectangular table set up in the middle of Neilson's cramped cabin.

"This weather is terrible!" the senior man of the three said. "The worst I've ever seen."

"Don't bullshit me, Tusk," Neilson said. "I know you guys can sail right underneath this weather."

Comrade Tusk was taken aback momentarily. He began to nervously pick lint off his uniform.

"No, we are too close to that island to go too deep," he said, his voice a little shaky. "Our vessel had very little room to maneuver. Plus we had to make sure no one on shore would spot us."

Neilson stared at him straight on. "There's no one on that island," he said sternly.

Tusk felt his teeth start to grind. "You could easily station a man at the top of those cliffs,' he said. "Just one gun could sink us and we'd have no defense."

Neilson laughed derisively, his large body shaking like jelly.

"One gun? On the cliffs? You've got to be kidding," he said, stroking his red beard.

"It is true," Tusk countered. "We could have walked right into your trap. . . ."

Neilson laughed again, then leaned so far across the table he was almost nose-to-nose with Tusk.

"Do you realize we could have a dozen UN antisub planes on your ass in a matter of minutes?" he sneered at him. "Or that I could make one radio call and have a squadron of F-80s or Panther jets tracking you like a wounded dog? You're in a war zone, comrade. You're fair game for anyone at this point."

Tusk was yanking at his uniform buttons now. His two companions were staring down at the table and shifting nervously in their seats.

"You would jeopardize everything now?" Tusk asked, his voice groveling.

Neilson smiled again. The man was sufficiently cowered. "No, not at all," he replied. "In fact, let us begin."

They got the lower-priority matters out of the way first. There was a question about late payment for an oil shipment arranged earlier that year for the French colonial government in Indochina. Then they discussed the whereabouts of a train filled with raw uranium ore that had somehow gotten waylaid in the Belgian Congo. Finally they exchanged updates on world wheat-growth projections for the years 1951 through 1954.

At last, they came to the real business at hand.

"We need more time," Tusk said matter-of-factly.

Neilson's face turned redder than usual. "What the hell are you talking about?"

Tusk shrugged and fidgeted with his tie clasp. "We need a few more days in addition to our original agreement," he said, trying to keep calm. "Is that such a big problem?"

"Damn right it is!" Neilson boomed, pounding the table. "The deal was ten days, and ten days it will be."

Tusk shifted uncomfortably in his chair.

"It was not long enough,' he said, pretending to consult his notebook. "We have compiled only about three-quarters of our data so far. . . ."

Neilson never stopped shaking his head. "I don't give a damn what you ain't got," he said. "We agreed on ten days."

Now Tusk was also shaking his head. "Why can't you be more flexible?" he asked. "We've had several unforeseen problems on our side."

"Like what?"

Tusk cleared his throat. "The weather, for one," he replied. "It's been very bad from here all the way back to Moscow. It has made the deployment of the newer models that much more difficult."

Neilson coughed out a sinister laugh. "Don't you dare sit there and complain about moving your aircraft," he said angrily. "You got it *damn easy* compared to us. Do you have any idea what it was like to get our planes over here, on time? Do you think we just walked into that manufacturing plant in Texas and said, crate up five of these babies and load 'em on that Mexican freighter anchored over in Galveston? No, it took time and it took money and it took finding the right people. All you guys had to do is fly the damn things right from the factory."

"But we've also had bad weather at our air bases, too," Tusk protested. "Our operations at Antung were cut in half the last week due to snow squalls."

Neilson pounded the table once again with all his might. "You *bastard*!" he roared. "I'm flying airplanes off a postage stamp in the middle of the worst weather in the world and you're going to bitch about a little wind and snow?"

Tusk was visibly sweating now.

"Another problem has been our pilots themselves," he contintued nervously. "They have taken longer than estimated to—shall we say?—find their valor."

"You mean, work up their guts!" Neilson interrupted. "Well, I'm not going to do you the favor of detailing what *my* guys have been going through. But I will tell you this: Four of them have back injuries so severe we have to pump them full of morphine. Yet they still rise to the call every goddamn night."

"That's because they are motivated," Tusk replied testily. "They are doing it for the money."

"The hell they are!" Neilson shouted back. "Don't throw any of that Marxist crap at me. These guys think they're doing this as part of a legit covert operation. It's all flag and apple pie for them. They know nothing about all this."

Suddenly Tusk's eyes brightened. "Ah hah!' he cried. "So now I have caught you in a lie!"

Even Karl laughed at this.

"What lie is that, comrade?" Neilson asked.

"The one where you want me to believe that your pilots are not being paid handsomely," Tusk answered. "At the beginning of this agreement, remember, you demanded extra money to be entered into your account specifically for these pilots."

Neilson shook his head and chuckled. "You've been eating too many beets," he told Tusk. "Sure, the flyboys are getting a little extra. But the rest of that money is set aside for an emergency."

"Such as?"

"Such as if anyone on our side ever catches on to this game," Neilson said. "When they go looking for fall guys, my people will leak that the flyboys have bulging Swiss bank accounts, opened by a secret note from the Central Bank of Russia. Get it?"

"Your plan still revolves around a swill of money," Tusk spit out, blind to his own contradiction. "And it's obvious we can't do the same thing on our side. It will take longer for our pilots to reach the right level of motivation."

"Jesus Christ, how hard can it be?" Neilson asked. "Your guys have been making mincement of those rinky-dink F-80s and F-84s for a month. Didn't they get some balls from that?"

"There is a vast difference between your F-80s and the Black Sabres," Tusk replied in a measured tone. "And these special pilots have seen several of their comrades go down in flames in front of the F-86s. This has made them, well, apprehensive. . . ."

Neilson shook his head and glanced over at Karl. "I don't believe this," he said. "This whole deal could be screwed up because they got a bunch of women flying their MiGs."

"We have, also, another problem," Tusk continued. "One officer at Antung saw too much. Found out too much."

Now Neilson glared at him. "You've never had any problem dealing with people like that before," he said grimly. "What are you worrying about? Too afraid to make it look like an accident?"

Tusk began to say something but thought better of it. He realized how foolish it would be to tell the American that the whereabouts of the man in question were at that moment unknown.

"Do you realize that we've got whole *squadrons* of guys who've seen too much on our side?" Neilson raged on. "You boys just don't know how hard it is for us to keep a lid on this. We've got war correspondents in the field. We've got intelligence guys nosing around everywhere. Regular infantrymen who see something strange in the sky and blab to their company commander about it. We're not like you. We just can't take these people out back and shoot them."

"Well, this is exactly my point," Tusk said. "Wouldn't more time help you also?"

"No," Neilson said. "We got our data, you should be getting yours, and we should be making the swap in three days. After all, you had a big head start on us on the technical stuff. You're the guys who first went with the swept-back wing."

Now it was Tusk's turn to get angry. "Don't throw that on us," he said. "We both know that that technology came right out of the Luftwaffe aerodrome at Lechfeld. And if your side hadn't have been so greedy . . ."

Neilson laughed, perfectly thwarting Tusk's rising anger. "Greedy?" he asked. "I don't think 'greedy' is quite the word you want to use there, comrade. It's not our fault that the Nazi eggheads all came running to us when the shooting stopped. You guys just raped too many nuns. . . ."

He turned and looked at Karl. "Ain't that right. *Obergruppenführer*?"

Karl blew out a stream of cigarette smoke so long it reached Tusk's nostrils.

"That is very true, my friend," he answered with a smile.

It took Choji more than half an hour to fashion the spear.

The fierce wind and rain of the on-coming storm had greatly hampered his efforts to find a sturdy tree branch to use as a shaft. Still, he'd located a piece of tall beach brush and hastily used his shoelaces to fasten his jackknife to its thicker end. Then he'd waded waist-deep into the tumbling surf and strained his eyes to see the calmer water below the turbulent surface.

It was the largest eel he'd ever seen—easily five feet in

length and very thick around. He'd been gathering in his minnows net, satisfied with his catch, when he saw the tell-tale splash of the moray about twenty feet out from the shore. He'd gone a little mad after that, dropping his net and jumping right into the rough surf, as if he could catch the eel with his bare hands.

Yet the first rush of cold water to his head had brought him back to reality. He knew the eel was looking for a place close to shore in an attempt to escape the storm and would therefore stay in the immediate area for a while. Choji had then run back to the tidal pool, retrieved his minnows (he had only lost a few), and then set off in search of the makings of a spear.

Now he was back in the water, the powerful waves smashing and tossing his diminutive body as if it were just another piece of driftwood. He knew the eel had the ability to swim just below the choppy surface, and it was on this region of the waist-deep water that he focused his attention.

There! he saw it. A long streak of gray and black, snaking its way about ten feet from him. Without hesitation, he launched the speer and missed. But not by much. He went deeper into the water, and now it was up to his nipples. Once again, the eel passed close by. Once again he hurled the spear. Once again he missed.

He took five more steps. Now the rough water was almost to his neck, and he was forced to jump for air every time a wave rolled in. The wind was getting worse and it was now raining very hard, but Choji had no intention of giving up. He had waited much too long for this moment.

Suddenly he felt a peculiar slithering near his feet. He looked down and was startled to see the eel making its way right between his legs! Quickly he thrust the spear into the water, and the corresponding resistance told him that the knife on the end had pierced the moray's skin. He yanked and thrust again, driving the spear deeper into the eel, all the while jumping and bobbing on the surface, trying his best not to be dragged out to sea by the fierce undertow.

He pushed the spear deeper into the eel a third time,

but at the same moment a large wave hit him broadside. He was suddenly underwater, the other end of the spear sticking into his stomach and the horrible face of the moray just inches from his own, its mouth open and rushing toward him as if to bite off his nose. Another wave hit and he was washed head over heels, the shaft of the spear shattering in the enormous wave break. Suddenly his mouth was full of sea water and he was choking in an effort not to swallow it.

Then a third wave hit him, one so powerful it picked him up and literally threw him up onto the shore. He vomited up a large amount of sea water even before he had stopped rolling and soon felt his legs burning from the wounds he'd received while being dragged across the rough beach. When he finally opened his eyes, he realized he was still holding the broken half of the spear shaft.

Feeling foolish, he crawled up the beach until he was past the highwater mark. The storm was blowing full gale now, and the rain that was hitting him felt like a blizzard of pebbles. He had failed miserably, losing his valuable jackknife in the process. This was not the way an officer of the Japanese Imperial Forces should act.

After he had thrown up more sea water, he finally felt strong enough to sit up and take normal breaths. He tried to rub the sand out of his eyes but soon gave up, as he was only making a bad situation worse. He would have to return to the water's edge and flush his eyes with handfuls of the sea that had nearly just killed him.

He made the trip on his hands and knees, quickly splashing two handfuls of water into his eyes. The salt stung him sharply, but through the pain he could feel most of the irritating sand wash away.

He then dabbed his pupils with his tattered shirt-sleeves and tried to blink away whatever sand was left. Finally he was able to open his eyes wide without too much discomfort.

That's when he saw the two ships.

The vessels were so close to him that for a moment he thought they were being swept to shore just as he had been. But then he saw they were both anchored—or, more accurately, one was anchored and the other was lashed to it.

Choji immediately went down on his hands and knees, not wanting those on the ships to see him. They were only a hundred yards away from him, maybe even closer. And he could see them clearly, despite the wind and the rain and the ever-present thick fog.

This was it, he told himself. This was what he'd been waiting for. . . .

He let his warrior instinct immediately take over. He studied the ships intently, committing to memory everything he would have to know.

The larger one was at least seventy-five feet long, was painted white, and had a large red cross displayed on its hull. Choji laughed for the first time in five years—he would not be fooled by this disguise. He knew the hated Americans frequently used hospital ships to carry out their dastardly military operations.

The vessel next to it was a submarine. Longer and somewhat sleeker than the ones he remembered seeing at the home ports in Japan at the beginning of the war, this one bore a large red star on its conning tower.

Russian pigs, he thought. *"Meeting with the Yankee dogs . . ."*

A bolt of excitement and terror ran through him. There was no question of what had happened. Five years ago, just before he'd arrived on the island cliffs, his squadron commander had told him that Russia was about to declare war on Japan, joining the Americans in an alliance of treachery and deceit unrivaled in history. In fact, part of his last mission was to seek out and destroy the lead element of a Russian task force that was reportedly making its way toward the Home Islands from the west. He had failed to fulfill his destiny that day. But now, by happening to see the brazen rendezvous so close to his island, he knew his moment of cowardice and shame could be avenged.

He deduced that the sub and the white ship were probably just part of a larger force—one that perhaps contained aircraft carriers, cruisers, possibly troop-carrying ships. In the next moment, he convinced himself that the two ships were actually part of an *invasion* force, probably heading out of the Yellow Sea and toward a landing on the northwest corner of the Homeland itself.

And he had discovered it.

Closing his eyes to check that he had absorbed all the facts correctly, he began to crawl back up the beach, hoping to reach the line of brush without being spotted. Once hidden in the prickly weeds, he looked back out to sea and was not surprised that the two ships had now disappeared back into the heavy mist.

But it made no difference to him—he had seen what he had seen. And as if to confirm this, he saw a great splash about ten feet from the shore. Straining his eyes, he was delighted to see the eel jump high out of the water, the broken half of his spear sticking right through him.

The Emperor could not have sent him a better omen. Crawling even deeper into the shore brush, Choji knew the time of planning had now passed and the time for action had arrived.

24

Yokota Air Base

THE MEETING WAS ONLY a few minutes old and already the conference room was becoming unbearably hot.

"This is, without a doubt, the most asinine idea I have ever heard!" Colonel Stanton fumed. "Do you realize that those responsible have unilaterally put the entire war effort at risk here?"

USAF Lt. Colonel Douglas "Hard-Ass" Harvey, the sole target of Stanton's wrath, shifted uneasily in his seat.

He had gotten the order to meet Stanton while eating his breakfast. Harvey had never met the senior officer before, although his name appeared on many documents that passed across his desk. Still, Harvey had no idea what Stanton wanted with him.

Now he felt his entire career going down the drain.

"I was under the impression that the president himself had authorized this mission," Harvey said by way of his own defense.

Stanton slammed his fist down on to the table. "Are you insane, man?" he half shouted. "The president would never permit this! Don't you think that he realizes the harm that could result?"

Harvey began to say something but couldn't. His mouth was so dry he couldn't speak. Stanton watched the color drain from the man's pumpkin face. It was a sure sign that Harvey knew the game was up.

It hadn't taken Stanton very long to track down the man they called Hard-Ass. Upon arriving at Yokota, Stanton had immediately met alone with the Red Chinese defector, Colonel Pei, and Pei had told him everything: the rumors at Antung that the Americans had deployed a new fighter; his superior's reluctance, then his strange turnaround in allowing him to proceed to Tsing Buk to look for evidence; his own witnessing of the strange air battle over the valley, this after a flight of MiGs had indiscriminately strafed his position on the valley floor.

Pei had told him about the incident involving the MiGs and the B-29s that had bombed the bridges over the Yalu, and it had taken only a few minutes of record checking for Stanton and his assistant, Crayer, to determine that the B-29s involved were those in Buster Force. The next step had been to find the intelligence officer connected with the nighttime mission, and that was what had led them to Harvey.

"Why were these reports covered up?" Stanton demanded of him. "You had a number of men in those B-29s who had seen something out of the ordinary, plus you had access to the POW named Baker. Why didn't you pass this information along to my office?"

Harvey was still having trouble speaking. "I was told to keep everything under wraps," he said finally, feeling the tiny beads of sweat on his forehead turning into a torrent. He didn't dare pull out his handkerchief and wipe them away.

Stanton reached over and turned on the large tape recorder in front of him.

"I'm going to take that as an admission that you were in on this from the beginning," Stanton told him sternly. "And your participation is tantamount to treason."

Harvey hung his head in silence. For a moment, he thought he was going to vomit.

"Did you ever stop to consider what would happen if those airplanes fail, Colonel?" Stanton asked him angrily. "Or if that secret base is discovered?"

"I was told that all the necessary precautions had been taken," Harvey blurted out. "I was told the chances of the Reds catching on were very, very slight. . . ."

Stanton stopped him in midbreath. His face, already creased with rage, was now turning an angry crimson.

"*Colonel*," he said, his teeth clamped together in anger. "It was a Red Chinese pilot who told *me* about all this. A defector who landed up at Kimpo two nights ago."

Harvey's eyes went wide in disbelief.

"I guess war is not fool-proof, sir," he stammered.

Stanton slammed his fist down on the conference table a second time. "Exactly!' he said angrily. "And were you told the ramifications if one of those airplanes is shot down? Or simply crashes?"

Harvey straightened in his chair and cleared his throat to speak.

"I was told that if one of them had to set down unexpectedly, let's say, the pilots were instructed to destroy the aircraft. There would not be a trace left. . . ."

Stanton stared straight at the officer, contempt burning in his eyes. He had been in the service of the U.S. government long enough to cultivate a strong mistrust of "Rear Area Heroes" like Harvey.

"Not a trace, eh?" Stanton asked him sarcastically. "And what about the pilots, Colonel? Were you told what would happen if *they* were captured? Will they self-destruct?"

"Yes, as a matter of face, they are," Harvey answered. "I was told that each pilot carries a revolver and two cyanide capsules. They are under orders to take their own lives should capture be imminent. . . ."

Stanton's mouth went wide in astonishment. "Are you actually telling me these pilots are under orders to commit suicide?" he asked incredulously.

Harvey nodded.

"I was told that they would automatically be awarded the Silver Star should it come to that," he added.

It was at that point that Stanton lost his temper completely.

"Colonel, pack your bags," he said through gritting teeth. "I'm sending you back to Washington for further interrogation. And I am going to personally recommend your court-martial to the president himself."

Harvey felt like he was going to faint.

Stanton continued: "Now, the only way—and I emphasize the word *only*—that you can hope not to spend the rest of your life at Leavenworth is for you to tell me right now who is behind all this and where the secret base is located."

In the flash of a moment, Harvey found himself wishing *he* had a poison pill between his teeth.

"I don't know the *exact* location of the base," he said. "I have only a rough idea. As for who is running the operation, I assumed you knew who was in charge."

"Don't ever assume anything, Colonel," Stanton said angrily. "Who gave the orders?"

Harvey unsuccessfully tried to summon up some saliva to wet his arid mouth.

"Well, sir," he croaked. "It was the CIA, of course. . . ."

25

Off the Coast of South Korea

LIEUTENANT TIM CRAYER WISHED he had packed a heavier sweater or, better yet, a parka or something warmer. For some reason he hadn't thought Korea would be so goddamn cold.

"How much farther?" he asked the Royal Navy captain next to him. "I think I'm getting frostbite."

The British officer checked his watch.

"I'd say another five, ten minutes, roughly," he replied. "Tell you the truth, it may be hard to tell for sure, with this blasted fog and all."

"Fog" didn't come even close to describing the thick-as-mud mist that had totally enveloped their small vessel. Crayer could see no more than ten feet in front of the bow, and even then the water looked pitch black, cold, and deadly. Turning to look over his shoulder, he could barely see the bright Union Jack flag that was fluttering in the breeze above the patrol boat's mast.

"Do the Red Chinese have submarines?" he asked the officer suddenly.

The Brit shook his head no. "Not that we've seen," he replied. "And you shouldn't worry anyhow. The Reds don't like to come near these parts anymore than we do. I'm sure you were briefed that the weather here is the most unpredictable in the world. Storms blow up out of nowhere. Ships go in, never come out."

"Yes, I heard that," Crayer lied. "Quite an unusual part of the sea."

"Aye, it is," the Brit went on. "There are at least four invasion fleets of ships on the bottom around here, dating all the way back to the khans and before. They were

115

all trying to invade someone, somewhere, but here is where they lie. And believe me, the Reds appreciate the history of this place as much as we do. So I don't expect we'll be running into any of them."

Crayer pulled up his thin-layered jacket and shook off a chill. As Colonel Stanton's administrative assistant, he had had his share of strange duties—but nothing like this. Shortly after their quick trip to Yokota, Crayer had been sent out to round up a small ship and crew—Royal Navy, by Stanton's orders. Only after Crayer had located the suitably British coastal patrol unit did Stanton partially explain why they had to use the allies for transport in their investigation: First off, the crisis at hand was so sensitive, one leak to the wrong person and the entire war could be lost—literally. Second, they couldn't trust any American outfit anywhere in Korea or Japan, for fear one person in thousands might not be kosher. Only the Brits could be trusted at this point.

And so, armed with information Stanton had drummed out of Hard-Ass Harvey, Crayer was sent out with the Royal Navy patrol boat to sail toward some undeterminable spot off the west coast of South Korea, looking for a sunken ship that wasn't really sunk.

"Listen," the British officer said suddenly. "That's an odd sound. Did you hear it?"

Crayer couldn't hear anything. "No, sir, I didn't," he answered.

"There it is again!" the officer called out. "I'd think it were waves if it didn't sound so strange. Hear it now?"

Once again Crayer strained his ears in an effort to cut through the sound-dampening fog. Still he heard nothing.

The captain yelled back to his crew to stop all engines on the small patrol boat. A few moments of dead silence followed.

"*Bloody hell*!" the British officer yelled. "Will you look at that!"

The captain had grabbed Crayer's arm and was now facing him toward the port side of the boat.

This time Crayer had no problem seeing or hearing the source of the officer's attention.

"*Jesus!* What is it?" Crayer heard himself yell.

Off the port bow, probably a mile and a half away, they could see a long stream of flame rising up into the sky. The fire was so bright it burned right through the fog and lit up the predawn skies. The noise accompanying it was a kind of echoing *whoosh*!

And then, as suddenly as it had come, it was gone, disappearing into the night sky overhead.

"Good Lord!" the Brit said. "That was the damnedest thing, wasn't it? What could it have been?"

"You're asking the wrong person," Crayer replied, still shaken by the strange sight.

"Do you want to get closer?" the captain asked Crayer as they consulted the crude map Stanton had drawn for them. "That flash must have something to do with what we are looking for."

Crayer checked his watch. Stanton's number-one priority was for the patrol boat to conduct their reconnaissance without being seen—by anyone, friend or foe. Yet he felt he was getting close to some of the answers that Stanton was looking for.

"We've got another fifteen minutes or so before it starts really getting light," Crayer said finally. "I think we should give it a go. . . ."

The captain yelled back to his crew to restart the engines but to proceed at the slowest possible speed.

"Better tell your men to break out some weapons, too, Captain," Crayer said soberly. "You never know who or what might be out there."

They cruised along in near silence for the next few minutes, their eyes and ears peeled for anything unusual. Yet all they heard was the gloomy lapping of the water and all they saw was the heavy blanket of fog.

But then, almost imperceptibly, the shade of fog off to the left became darker. After a few more seconds, Crayer saw a wavy outline of gray beginning to stand out from the rest of the gloom. Then, slowly, almost painfully, the outline turned into a silhouette, then a shadow of something big and black.

Then he saw it.

"Jesus Christ . . ." he whispered. "It really *is* an aircraft carrier. . . ."

*   *   *

The official United States Navy records listed the escort carrier USS *Holene Bay*, nicknamed "Holly One," as having been sunk on August 1, 1945, while on an antisubmarine patrol in the Yellow Sea. The small carrier—it carried no more than eleven airplanes and was a dwarf next to the giant carriers such as the *Lexington*—fell victim to an enemy kamikaze attack, the records claimed. It caught fire and went down near the deserted island of Mokpo, located 130 miles off the west coast of the Korean peninsula. Many of its survivors made it to Mokpo, but bad weather in the area prevented rescuers from reaching the island. Two days later, these survivors were captured by the Japanese, only to be released just a month later when the war ended.

Or at least that's what the official records said.

In reality, the ship *was* hit by a pair of Japanese suicide planes and severely damaged. But it did not sink. Instead, its captain ran her up on a sand reef that extended out from Mokpo Island and there it stayed—afloat though immobile, hidden in the perpetual fog and rain. As the war was all but over at the time, no one noticed when an unknown OSS officer intentionally entered the incorrect information on the relatively insignificant action into the Navy's massive war-records file.

And now Crayer was looking up at the *Holly One,* his mouth open in amazement. The smidgen of information that Harvey knew on the secret base's location had panned out.

"Look, another flash!" the British captain called out.

Crayer saw it too. It was exactly like the first one—a bright flame cutting through the dark fog, trailing smoke and a distinct *whooshing* sound.

But this time they heard an additional noise. It was that of a jet engine.

Crayer had his binoculars up to his eyes in an instant. Through the smoke and fog he could see the barest outline of a shape going directly over their heads. It stayed in his view for only a moment—but that was more than enough time. Crayer was an expert on aircraft identification—it was the main qualification for his job with Stanton—but he didn't have to be an expert to get the correct make on this plane.

It was an F-86A Sabre jet. It was painted all black, was carrying no insignia, and had a line of five red navigational lights on its tail. It was using Rocket-Assist Take-Off bottles to lift it off the deck of the small carrier, a dangerous procedure that he would have thought was impossible. Even odder was the fact that after the Sabre had gained enough altitude to stay airborne, its pilot did not jettison the RATO bottles, as would be normal procedure. Finally, Crayer noted that the airplane turned over on a northeasterly course before it finally faded from view.

"Okay, Captain," Crayer said to the Royal Navy officer after committing all he had seen to memory. "Let's get out of here."

26

CHOJI HAD STAYED UP all night, the thought of going to sleep never entering his mind.

He had so much to do and so little time—or so he thought. First of all, his rifle had to be cleaned and oiled. This alone took two and a half hours. Then he had to take apart his remaining bullets, carefully blow-dry the gunpowder, and reassemble them. This took another three hours.

Then he went to work on the troublesome fuel injector. This was his most frustrating task of all, as his meager supply of tools—his gun wrench, a small screwdriver, and his home-made hammer—all proved either too large or too small for the job. Still, he forged ahead, finally locating and disengaging the fuel injector's faulty spring trigger and rewinding it. At one point he found himself cursing his first cousin, Oka, simply because the man had worked at one time for the Nakajima Company, the people who had designed the infuriating device.

All the while, his combat uniform was hanging over his outside fire to dry, after the scrubbing he had given it shortly before sundown. Once an hour, he would set the fuel injector aside and go out to turn the uniform's wetter side toward the fire's heat. He would also take this time to drink a small cup of tea and let his eyesight clear up.

It was during one of these breaks that Choji saw his second omen in twenty-four hours.

It was an hour or so before dawn, and to celebrate his long night of fruitful work, Choji had decided to pour himself an extra ration of tea. Sitting crosswise next to the fire, he pretended that he could see the stars through the deadening fog, and suddenly his eyes caught sight of a flash out over the horizon.

Immediately, Choji was on all fours, crawling toward the edge of the cliff. The flash had been just like what he'd seen in a dream several nights before. Had he really seen it then? Or now? Or had it been just a mirage?

He was about to think that his mind was playing tricks on him again, when he saw another flash—this one much brighter and accompanied by a strange *whoosh*!

Both plumes of flame had shown up in the same area, a point he determined to be several miles off to his northeast. Instantly his mind was buzzing. That was the same direction in which he had seen the large American ship three years before, the one that he had been certain would land troops looking for him. But it hadn't, and he had the Emperor's mercy to thank for that. Three years before, he wasn't prepared to fight. Now he was.

He felt his body actually tingle when he saw two more flashes, just seconds apart, light up the same area. These two were brighter, louder, and their noise stayed in the misty air longer.

This was it, he told himself. This, and the fact that he had speared the eel the day before, all but confirmed it. His gun was ready—cleaned and oiled. His ammunition was ready, too, and his uniform was drying almost to a sharp crease. At that point, he returned to the fuel injector, his heart pounding with the knowledge that the climax was near.

Choji's third omen appeared thirty minutes after dawn.

He had just finished the fuel-injector repair and was out on the ledge, testing its spring action in the cool morning air. Suddenly it felt as if the whole cliff were shaking. Choji immediately felt his throat start to constrict —he had been in earthquakes before, and all his senses were telling him that another one was happening now.

But in the next moment, he knew it was not the earth that was shaking. Rather it was the air itself.

Looking up, he was completely astonished to see a strange aircraft flying right over his head. It was black and had swept-back wings of a style he'd never seen before. Most amazing of all, it had no propeller. Instead, a long tongue of flame was shooting out of its rear, making it seem like a dragon riding the morning sky.

Choji tried his best to stop trembling but couldn't. Unlike the eel and the flashes of light earlier that morning, he was convinced that what he saw above him was a specter, a haunted illusion sent by the Emperor's enemies to scare him.

And at that moment, they were doing a very able job.

27

Aboard Holly One

"HAS THERE EVER BEEN a day in your life that you haven't caused *some* amount of trouble?"

Gabe Evers answered the doctor's question with a long series of smoke rings, courtesy of his enormous cigar.

"That kind of behavior won't help you, Major," the doctor, a man named Spitz, continued. "I can't believe that you're allowed to stay in the service, never mind be a test pilot."

Evers ignored the man and continued blowing his smoke rings. "My eyes are beginning to hurt in this light," he said nonchalantly.

"Can you give me a reasonable explanation why you chose to deviate from the assigned landing pattern today?" Spitz asked him, waving away the smoke.

"Nope," Evers answered.

Spitz, a ratty little man with a strange accent, was getting more aggravated by the moment. "Why would you choose to fly over the island today?" he continued. "You know it's a completely undesignated approach."

Evers shrugged and puffed up another mighty cloud of cigar smoke. "Just had a whim, I guess, Doc," he said.

Spitz shook his head and made a notation in his notebook. Then he turned toward Hughes, who was slumped in a chair next to Evers.

"And you, Captain," the doctor said. "You were his wingman. Don't you have any concern at all about the lack of discipline?"

"There's that word again," Hughes said to Evers.

"Yeah, I'm starting to dream about it," Evers replied. "But I'm also starting to dream about growing a funny little mustache and changing my name to Adolf."

122

The last comment visibly stung the doctor.

"I am shocked at both of you," he said, having recovered somewhat. "I can't believe that you are so unconcerned about the importance of this operation. That you are both so . . . so . . ."

"Lackadaisical?" Hughes suggested.

The doctor's face turned red. Half from embarrassment, half from anger.

"I don't call icing four MiGs the other day lackadaisical, Doc," Evers said. "Add it on to our other scores and you got yourself twenty-two MiGs in nine days. . . ."

"So why don't you just leave us alone?" Hughes added, slumping lower into his seat. "Let us get some rest."

"Better yet, let us get off this tub," Evers said, knocking the loose embers off the end of his stogie. "Before someone in Washington figures out what you guys are doing."

There was a brief silence while Evers relit his cigar.

"You two don't have a clue as to who you are dealing with here," Spitz said, his voice suddenly becoming very dark.

"Yes, we do," Evers said, taking an extra-long drag from his reignited cigar. "You're all Spooks. You work for the Company. The CIA. What's the big deal?"

Spitz shook his head. "You're such a wise ass, Evers," he said. "You think you got all the frigging answers, don't you?"

Evers decided to let his smoke rings do the talking. A particularly well-formed one burst right on the doctor's nose.

"*I* don't have all the answers," Hughes interjected. "All I know is that you have had us locked up in that light-deprivation chamber for so long, I'm not sure what day it is."

"That cabin is a crucial part of our night-vision experiment," Spitz told him.

"Is it really?" Hughes countered. "Or maybe is it just so you guys can keep us under wraps, so we won't see anything we're not supposed to see?"

The doctor turned directly toward Hughes, hesitating for a moment as the ship itself rose and fell slightly.

"You're one to talk, Hughes," Spitz said. "I've seen your record. If you lose anymore stripes, your sleeves will fall off."

"That was a cheap shot, Doc," Evers said in the middle of a short burst of small rings. "This guy single-handedly saved our country's ass a few years ago."

"By punching a general in the face?" the doctor asked smugly.

"No," Evers shouted back, suddenly leaning almost on top of the doctor. "By stopping some Nazis from stealing an atomic bomb—*after* the war."

"Gabe, forget it," Hughes said, knowing they were getting into areas that even the highest level of the CIA didn't know about. Or so they thought.

"No, *I won't forget it,*" Evers continued, full steam ahead. "I'm sick of asses like this guy, questioning our integrity. Our ability. Our loyalty. Think I can't hear your accent, Doc? Where the hell did *you* go to school? Frankfurt? Dresden? *Berlin*?"

"You have no right . . ." Spitz sputtered, now absolutely red with anger.

"*Bullshit* I don't have the right!" Evers shot back. "Do you think we're fucking boy scouts? We spent the first year after the war flying with goddamn Nazis. *Real* Nazis. And we know there was a bunch of them living right over the hill from us. And more at Oak Ridge. And in Houston. And Los Angeles. You name it. And they all didn't decide to head for Paraguay in the middle of the night. Some of them got it too damned good!"

At this point Spitz was so flustered he couldn't talk.

"So don't talk to us about discipline, Doc," Evers said, staring the man right in the eyes. "In fact, I suggest you get some of your own first."

"Is that a threat, Major?"

Evers looked at him, then laughed right in his face.

"Hey, that's great, Doc," he said. "You're paranoid, too."

Spitz was silent for almost a full minute. Then he retrieved a single file from his desk drawer and leafed through it.

"At this moment, you two are earning exactly twelve

times more than a regular Air Force combat pilot," he
said, reading from one page. "That means you are pulling in as much money in one month as a top pilot will
earn in a year. Is that right?"

For once, Evers and Hughes had nothing to say.

"And you will continue earning that money at that rate
for the next year," Spitz went on. "That's what it says
right here in your contracts, doesn't it?"

Once again, Evers and Hughes could only remain silent.

Spitz smiled and slammed the file closed.

"So where the hell do you guys get off!" he asked, his
voice rising again in anger. "For that kind of money you
should be flying those goddamn missions blindfolded and
swabbing the decks of this ship, too."

"We earn that money, Doc," Evers said, but with only
about half a measure of his usual enthusiasm.

"So does a whore, Evers," Spitz spit back at him. "But
only when she follows the rules.

"Now get the hell out of here."

28

TWENTY MINUTES LATER, HUGHES and Evers were
back in the pitch-black pilots' quarters, burning their
fingertips as they split a pot of coffee with Kenneally and
Spencer.

Both men were somber, especially Evers.

"All kidding aside," he said, trying to pour a second
cup of the thick java, "I think it's time we started thinking about blowing this coop. These guys are really starting to give me the creeps."

"I second that motion," Kenneally said. "Special operations, I can understand. Psych Ops, coverts, black bags—

all this is not beyond me. But I get the feeling these boys are out there just a little bit too far.''

Hughes added his muffled agreement. The last nine days *had* been rather bizarre. Earlier in the war, he, Evers, and Spencer had flown missions for a CIA recon unit that seemed intent on provoking the Red Chinese into entering the war, and that had been strange enough. After the Inchon landings and the subsequent UN invasion of North Korea, Hughes and Evers were quietly shipped home, only to find they had orders—supposedly from the Air Force—to form a top-secret "Evaluation Unit" and return to the war zone almost immediately.

After being reunited with Kenneally, Spencer, and Ernst a week later, they found themselves on board the *Holly One*, sitting in the middle of the worst weather pocket in the world, being poked with needles filled with a variety of painkiller drugs and being made to stay inside a light-deprivation chamber in order to enhance their night-vision skills—all of this, they soon learned, not courtesy of the Air Force but of the CIA. In all, flying the Black Sabres seemed the least of their trials, though perfecting the dangerous short-deck carrier takeoffs and landings in such a short amount of time had been one of the hardest things they had ever been expected to accomplish.

At first they all just assumed the mission was part of a grander Black Ops scheme aimed at thwarting the onslaught of Red Chinese MiGs. They knew the Joint Chiefs had ordered standard-issue Sabres to Korea earlier in November; their job was to test fly the Black Sabres first, supposedly to see how well the F-86 design would do in actual combat conditions, thus sparing the regular Sabre pilots the potentially dangerous situation of getting their feet wet while dodging real bullets.

It all made sense to Hughes and the others: As they were recognized as the nation's best but least-known test pilots, they were used to operating under highly classified programs. Even while Hughes, Evers, and Spencer were carrying out armed recon missions against Red Chinese bases *before* China entered the war, they had assumed they were just part of a bigger plan, all nicely packaged and approved by everyone in Washington all the way up to Truman.

But for Hughes this "ours is not to question why" attitude began to break down soon after they had begun engaging the MiGs over the isolated valley of Tsing Buk.

Again, they assumed they were being fed incredibly accurate intelligence when they intercepted the MiGs over Tsing Buk for several nights in a row. In these encounters, the MiG pilots were fierce dogfighters, aggressive to no end and not at all shy about dying for Socialism. Still the Sabres, under the hands of the skilled test pilots, managed to best the communist jets on the first few encounters.

Then Ernst bought it, and everything seemed to change after that.

First of all, Ernst was not shot down—rather, he collided with one of the MiGs at the tail end of a particularly ferocious dogfight. Hughes and the other pilots saw him go down and watched as he stumbled from the cockpit of his burning plane. Once Evers, as the flight leader, determined that Ernst was clear of the airplane, he and the others strafed the wreckage of the Sabre, fulfilling one of their standing orders to prevent at all costs any part of the F-86 falling into enemy hands.

Quickly returning to the *Holly One*, the pilots beseeched the Spooks to send their on-board helicopter back to Tsing Buk to rescue Ernst. But the Spooks said no. Ernst's life was not important enough to risk the entire operation. Besides, they reasoned, he was probably seriously hurt in the crash, and his wounds, combined with the subfreezing temperatures, would kill him before the rescue chopper reached the area.

And should the enemy reach him first he was, like the others, under orders to take his own life.

The four pilots were appalled. Ernst had been their colleague and a damn good pilot. He was also a human being—that deserved at least an attempt at rescue. But the Spooks were adamant: Ernst would be left to die of his wounds or frostbite, or at his own hand should the Reds reach him. All in all, it left a bad taste in the pilots' mouths. Or as Evers so rightly put it, "This just ain't the American way."

Relations between the Spooks and the pilots began to deteriorate quickly after that. Their confinement in the darkened quarters seemed to amount to just so much hokum (although they had to admit it helped their night vision). The constant injection of painkillers—necessary because all four pilots suffered seriously wrenched backs due to the brutal RATO launchings—also took on a more sinister tone when they began to notice the injections becoming more frequent and the amount of painkiller more abundant. The combination of the morphine-based drugs and the dark quarters began to have a strange effect on them—Hughes especially. It was Kenneally who first pointed out that light deprivation and forced injections of morphine were tactics used by the Nazis during the war to get information out of high-ranking POWs.

When Evers happened to mention this fact to Spitz and two other CIA operatives aboard ship two days before, the Spooks became furious. When they had first arranged to use the test pilots for the operation, they had apparently been under the impression that the men would do as told, when they were told, and not ask questions. They just weren't prepared to deal with the free-thinking, free-wheeling pilots, especially the outrageously outspoken Gabe Evers.

"I say we break out," Evers was saying, wiping the hot spilled coffee from his hands.

"We've already talked about this," Spencer said, exasperated. "How are we going to do it? We just can't jump overboard."

Evers took a hearty slug of his coffee.

"We don't have to jump ship," he said anxiously. "We just fly away. Simple as that."

"Hold it," Kenneally said. "We've gone through all this before, too. Where the hell are we going to fly to?"

As always, Evers was making it up as he went along.

"To the nearest UN base, Mr. Harvard Yard," he said. "We got plenty to choose from. In fact, we could go all the way to Japan if we wanted."

Hughes looked at the faint form in the dark that he knew was Kenneally. He imagined he could see the man rolling his eyes, then shaking his head.

"What are you, nuts, Gabe?" Kenneally replied. "We just can't land those airplanes at some base unannounced. Despite what we think about the Spooks and whatever the hell game they are running here, we're still involved in a highly classified operation. There aren't supposed to be any Sabres in Korea. What would happen if all of a sudden four of them set down at Kimpo or Taegu?"

Evers shrugged. "Beats me," he said. "We'd probably get a party."

"We'd probably get a firing squad," Kenneally told him. "Or a one-way trip to Leavenworth."

"Or they'd find us floating out to sea," Spencer added grimly.

Evers began getting agitated. "What is it with you guys?" he asked. "Do you want to stay here? Do you want to see how this book turns out?"

"I don't," Hughes answered. "But I don't want to do anything stupid, either. If you go barging into some airfield in those Sabres, you'll open a can of worms that will never get closed."

"Not to mention that these Spooks could probably twist it so that we'd be charged with desertion," Kenneally added.

Evers threw up his hands in frustration. "Okay, you guys are the geniuses," he said. "You figure a way out of this mess. . . ."

"First thing we have to do is come up with a plan," Kenneally said.

"No, that's the second thing," Hughes replied. "The first thing we have to do is stop letting them inject us with those painkillers. If these guys start to get nervous, who knows what they'll put in those needles."

"Agreed?" Kenneally asked.

There was a mumble of consensus.

"No more painkillers?" Evers said sadly. "Damn, I was just getting to like them. . . ."

29

Yokota Air Force Base, Japan

NO ONE WAS SMILING as Colonel Stanton called the meeting to order.

Looking around the small conference table. Lieutenant Tim Crayer saw nothing but scowling, depressed faces. The mood was downright bleak—as it should be, Crayer thought. Each man in the room stood to lose something because of the rapidly unraveling, unauthorized secret Sabre program.

Sitting beside Crayer were the captain and executive officer of the USS *Cape Esperance*, the jeep carrier that had docked at Kisarazu, Japan, the night before, its insides holding the unit of salt-ravaged Sabres. Stanton had found out that the five Black Sabres had actually been shipped directly to Korea from the manufacturer's plant in Texas, via a fast-moving Mexican-registered freighter, even before the Joint Chiefs had ordered the first USAF Sabre squadron to the war zone. Stanton's investigators back in the states had cabled him that in all likelihood, the five Black Sabres had been procured with the flash of a legitimate CIA ID card and a substantial amount of money. However, a check of the official record back in Washington showed that five unidentified aircraft serial numbers had been mysteriously entered onto the secret orders of the USS *Cape Esperance*. This meant that not only had the persons who'd made the deal for the five Black Sabres covered their tracks but also that they were well connected—not many people could gain access to the "top drawer" that contained the Navy's missions and operations book.

Sitting next to the Navy men was the Air Force officer

130

named Doug Harvey. Crayer noticed that although the man was wearing a standard USAF dress uniform, it was devoid of any indication of rank. Of all the grim faces around the table, Harvey's looked the worst. His complexion was pallid and his eyes fully bloodshot. His hands trembled as he lit cigarette after cigarette. At one point, when he went to get a drink of water from the pitcher provided, he dropped the glass as he was filling it, soaking several documents Stanton had placed on the table.

Sitting two empty chairs away from Harvey was Stanton and, next to him, most unusual attendee of all. It was a Red Chinese pilot turned defector named Colonel Pei. As it turned out, Pei knew more about the *houng jung quay mut*—Chinese for, roughly, "strange things in the sky"—than any of the Americans. Now safely on the other side—and $100,000 richer due to a UN program that had just been instituted to entice Red pilots to defect with their aircraft—Pei was not reluctant to tell his story.

This, in fact, was the first order of business for the meeting.

Stanton introduced the communist pilot only by rank, not by name, and then explained that his job in the Red Chinese Air Force was roughly equivalent to that of Stanton's own—he was in charge of supply and refurbishment for all of the MiGs operating out of the base at Antung, plus he handled many of its intelligence duties. Speaking in halting English, Pei told of his own investigation after he had heard of mysterious dogfights between unmarked, all-black American airplanes and MiGs that came from no squadrons he was aware of. Then he recounted his near-disastrous trip to Tsing Buk, during which, he was now convinced, his own MiGs had tried to kill him.

He ended his testimony by briefly detailing how, after incurring the wrath of his superiors for asking too many questions and narrowly escaping death in Tsing Buk, he was able to steal a PO-2 biplane and make good his escape.

His story told, Pei was escorted from the room by two men dressed in civilian clothes who were actually mem-

bers of the elite British Special Air Services, a unit of
which Stanton had appropriated from the UN's General
War Command and which was quickly transferred to Korea from Malaysia. The FEAF intelligence officer was
still running his investigation on the premise that no
American units already in Korea could be trusted.

Once Pei was gone, Stanton harshly introduced Harvey as "a former officer in the U.S. Air Force." Harvey
then told his story: about being approached by the CIA's
Office of Special Operations; about agreeing to oversee the
secret supply flights for the small, clandestine air force;
about intentionally misleading another intelligence officer
who had been assigned to the case early in the investigation;
and about covering up the whole operation in general.

Throughout his story, Harvey repeated that he'd been
under the impression the rogue CIA operation was sanc-
tioned by Washington, but under tough questioning by
Stanton, he also admitted that the CIA had actually paid
him—$5,000 in cash—for his aid. That alone, Stanton
reminded him, made him a co-conspirator and was enough
for him to stand court-martial.

Harvey was likewise escorted from the room, his face
showing the realization that, for him, things were only
going to get worse. Once he had left, Stanton asked the
three men remaining to move their chairs closer to his.

Then, in low whispered tones, they discussed their
next course of action.

Many miles to the west, another meeting was taking
place aboard the disguised Red Cross ship.

"I think we'll finally have this baby wrapped up in
twenty-four hours, Karl," Neilson said, pouring himself a
tall glass of bourbon. "Then it will be on to bigger and
better things. . . ."

Karl looked around the tiny ship's cabin, then asked,
"Have you nothing that I can drink?"

Neilson quickly retrieved a bottle of spring water from
his small portable bar and handed it to the man.

"The guys on the *Holly* have a ton of data on those
Sabres," Neilson went on. "Stuff the Air Force wouldn't
know if it flew them night and day for two years."

Karl poured himself a glass of water and drank half of it in one gulp. "Don't you think that anyone will become suspicious that two swept-wing airplanes—one from each side—have been suddenly thrown into the theater?" he asked, in his worried, clipped voice. "Both within a month of each other?"

Neilson chuckled as he sipped his drink. "Who the hell would be smart enough to make the connection?" he asked. "Or stupid enough to blab about it?"

"How about your friends in the regular CIA?" Karl replied. "Surely some of them know this isn't just a spontaneous thing, that it is no mere coincidence."

"They've got enough of their own irons in the fire," Neilson told him. "Like I told you, we all have our own little schemes going. I'm not going to trespass on some other guy's turf, and they're not going to come wandering in here. That's the way old Wild Bill himself set it up. That's how you got your own fanny into Switzerland, isn't it?"

Karl didn't answer. He simply poured himself another glass of water.

"Cheer up, my friend," Neilson chided him. "You're going to have a bunch of money soon. And it's a great feeling, believe me. Damn, do you know I haven't cashed my government salary check in two years? Don't need to. I tell them to keep 'em, right there in my desk in Washington. Maybe someday I'll give it all back to them—as a gift."

"I feel you're letting this thing run away with you," Karl said, wiping the sweat from his forehead and feeling slightly claustrophobic inside the small cabin.

"You're probably right, but I just can't help it," Neilson replied. "I got such a sweet racket going here. Pretty soon I'll have a ton of data on the MiG, and Tusk and his boys will have all the dope on the Sabre. He sells his to the MiG bureau, I sell mine to the highest bidder, by way of my friends back home. The next day, you're rich. I'm rich. My friends are rich. And goddamnit, even that socialist bastard Tusk is rich. It's perfect. . . ."

Neilson gave himself a congratulatory slap on the chest and drained his drink.

"I'll tell you, Karl," he boomed, "I should write a book. The places I've seen, the things I've done . . ."

The dour man in black leather frowned. He hated this unnecessary talk.

"No one in his right mind would publish it," he replied, sipping his spring water.

"You never know," Neilson answered, moving about his cramped cabin with the delicacy of a bull. "Maybe someday there will be publishers beating down our door just to get us in print."

"Nonsense," Karl replied sourly. "What do we have that people would want to read about?"

"What do we have?" Neilson asked with fake astonishment. "We've got the world by the balls, Karl. *That's* what we have."

"You're letting yourself get too confident," Karl said, placing a cigarette in his pearl-handled holder. "The last grave error is usually one of ego. . . ."

Neilson took a swig of his bourbon and stroked his great red beard. "Karl, I'm surprised at you," he said. "I really thought you would be able to appreciate the position we've carved out for ourselves.

"Don't you realize that just two hundred miles that-a-way there's a war raging, up and down the lousiest piece of real estate on earth? And the stupid bastards fighting and dying in the mud and snow will make us millionaires? And after this operation, we got another pot brewing in Indochina and another in the Belgian Congo? These are opportunities, Karl—*capital* opportunities. War is business, and someone has to collect the money."

"War is honor!" Karl shouted, surprising himself with the volume of his voice. "War is an extension of the victor's philosophy."

Neilson was slowly shaking his head. "Don't kid yourself a second time, Karl," he said. "War is about money. I know you guys just loved dressing up pretty and rolling over every dink country you could get your hands on. But someone, somewhere, has to make the tanks and the guns and the airplanes and bombs. And no one does it for free."

"You are talking about an extension of war," Karl replied, "not war itself."

"No," Neilson said, "that's where you are wrong. *War* is an extension—of business. I know it because my old man knew it. He used to sell batteries to German subs out in the Atlantic during the First World War. He'd load up his yacht on Long Island with a hundred or so dry cells and have a customer waiting for him every time.

"Second World War rolls around, and he gets me out of the draft the day the Japs bomb Pearl. He puts me on a boat to the Azores and tells me to look up some of his buddies when I get there. The next thing I know, I'm running a refiller tanker under a Liberian flag, meeting German subs in the middle of the South Atlantic and selling them all the oil they can carry. And they're paying me in Yankee greenbacks!"

"Aberrations," Karl snorted.

"Aberrations *my ass!*" Neilson retorted, the bourbon getting the best of him. "Do you know the first thing Truman did when the war ended in Europe? He signed an executive order telling the U.S. Treasury to pay out close to fifty million dollars to Esso, Mobil, and a bunch of other big companies for damages to their European refineries caused by the Eighth Air Force bombing the shit out of everything. The goddamn peace treaty was still wet when companies like Krupp and BMW were toesies with Wall Street again.

"You know these things happen, Karl. How can you conclude that war is anything *but* business?"

Karl tapped out his depleted cigarette and inserted another into his holder.

"And so what?" he replied, carefully lighting it. "So you and your American intelligence-gathering friends trot around the globe starting wars and getting rich. To what end? You can only have so much money."

"Yes," Neilson answered. "But you can never have enough power. And that's the idea here, Karl. War is money; money is power."

"But power for what?" Karl asked.

Neilson was momentarily taken aback by the question. "To run things, of course," he said finally.

"Do you actually mean to rule the world?" the older man asked.

"Not rule it like your guys wanted to," Neilson answered, this time right away. "I mean behind the scenes. Once we get things cooking here in Asia, it's on to the Middle East. That's where one of the two most valuable commodities in the world sits, Karl. Right below the desert."

"Oil?"

"That's right," Neilson answered, pouring himself another drink. "And the other one is gold, and there's a lot of it right next door in Africa. That's all anyone will be fighting for in the next fifty years, Karl. Oil and gold. As we speak, I know guys who are working in Washington right now, planting the seeds for the U.S. to someday go on the gold standard. At the same time, I know of other guys in other places who are making sure that there will be more roads laid in California in the next ten years than in the rest of the U.S. combined. No trains and buses for Los Angeles, Karl. *Cars.* The people will drive cars. Because cars run on gasoline and gasoline is made from oil, and now we're back to those towelheads in the middle of the desert."

Karl let out an involuntary snort. "You'd better make sure you get rid of the Jews in Israel first!" he declared.

Neilson laughed and put his hand on the man's shoulder. "Old habits are hard to break, aren't they, Karl?" he asked. "Don't you see that the Jews will be doing us a favor? Just by plopping themselves down in the middle of the desert—the only part that doesn't have any oil, by the way—they'll get the Arabs so pissed off, they won't have time to concentrate on how to get rich. It will take years for them to stop fucking their camels and realize they're sitting on a bonanza."

"You and your friends seem to have it all worked out," Karl said, finally declaring a surrender.

"Anything that succeeds needs a master plan, Karl," Neilson said, quickly adding, "Of course, who am I to tell *you* that?"

30

ON A CLIFF LESS than three miles from the disguised
Red Cross ship, Choji Harakitsu climbed into his dress
uniform and strapped on his rifle.

Time was moving slowly, and he took that as a good
sign. The fuel injector was back in place and working,
and the thirty dry sticks of dynamite were in position. He
had cooked an extra-large batch of rice—more than three
times his daily ration—just in case he didn't have the
opportunity to do so later. The minnows he'd eaten earlier in the day had been very salty—again, another good
sign. Still, he had waited five years for this—he didn't
want to worry about cooking food when the time came.

Now he knew that all that was left was to wait and
pray, and this he would do on an hourly basis.

Returning to the hut, he knelt before the portrait of
his Emperor and began his first prayer. Rising, he then
walked to his lantern and carefully drew out twenty drops
of the precious burning oil and let them drip into his only
piece of china, a broken cup. This he placed in front of
his shrine as his offering. Then, after another prayer, he
took the gold chain his mother had given him years
before and put it in the cup, covering it with oil.

31

THERE WERE A TOTAL of thirty-five men on the *Holly One*.

Except for the four remaining Black Sabre pilots, all of the crew were civilian employees of the Central Intelligence Agency's Office of Special Operations, and most of them were Americans. Their duties ranged from working the deck during the brief, spectacular RATO launchings and recoveries, to maintaining the airplanes when they were safely hidden away below decks. Other men, these being more skilled, operated the sophisticated radar and communications equipment the CIA had placed aboard the ship. Still others, the less skilled, worked as cooks and maintenance men.

Except for the half-dozen men who worked directly with Neilson, very few of the *Holly One*'s crew knew the sinister details behind the secret Sabre program or even that its "official" name was Operation Stormcloud. Most of the crew were under the impression, shared by a few others in Japan and in Washington, that the secret project was an evaluation of the F-86 before the main force of Sabres went into action. And as most were veterans of the old OSS—the predecessor of the CIA—they knew their employers were not beyond securing the services of a ship that was reportedly sunk five years before, outfitting it to launch jet aircraft and keeping it secret from all but a handful of people. They simply did their jobs and didn't ask a lot questions.

However, they were not prepared to handle ghosts.

Of course, the *Holly One* was an ideal location for a haunting. The ship had sat abandoned in the gloom of the Yellow Sea for five years, long enough for the spirits of the men killed on board to roam her every deck, cabin, and compartment, wondering what had gone wrong. When the first team of CIA operatives landed on the *Holly One* just a few days before the North Koreans launched their invasion, they claimed (unofficially) to have heard screams, weeping, and the obligatory rattling of chains.

As the operation grew more ambitious and more operatives came aboard, there came a few reports of men actually *seeing* ghosts. In all cases, the person in question was working in an isolated part of the ship when they claimed to have seen someone walking down a passageway or disappearing into a cabin—someone they didn't recognize. Upon further investigation, these mysterious people could never be found. Not knowing what else to do, those in command of the ship would suggest the people involved pay a visit to Dr. Spitz, who would hand them a packet of tranquilizers, scribble a written report, and file it under "miscellaneous."

So it wasn't all that unusual when Spitz received a report from the ship's chief mechanic, saying that he and several others had seen "a ghost" standing at the far end of the deck just thirty minutes before. Spitz dismissed the report almost immediately, suspecting that it was just another attempt by members of the crew to obtain drugs.

But then, a quarter-hour later, one of the cooks claimed to have seen an unknown man "dressed all in black," creeping along a catwalk that projected out from the side of the ship just aft of the anchor chains. Spitz thought about this report only a little longer, but in the end, he simply issued the cook a pack of tranquilizers, theorizing that the crew was planning a clandestine pill-popping party for later on.

He began to get concerned when two more men came to his cabin within a minute of each other, each claiming to have seen two dark figures scurrying in the shadows below decks. Then another "ghost" was reported in the long-dormant engine room; then another was spotted just outside the ship's mess.

Startled, Spitz was just picking up his phone to call the

ship's command center when two "ghosts" burst into his office.

They were dressed all in black and carrying Sten machine guns.

"We're from the SAS," one of them said in a clipped British accent, "If you don't move, you won't get hurt."

32

"DAMNIT, I TOLD YOU guys we should have jumped ship!"

At that point Hughes couldn't have agreed with Evers more. The four pilots were sitting in a cabin, each of them tied to a bunk post by means of a length of heavy rope. Their boots had been taken from them, as had their belts. What was worse, as a last unintentional insult, the two British commandos who had "captured" them and left them in this state had also switched off the cabin's light before locking them in.

In the dark once again, the pilots were heatedly discussing their predicament, the conversation being interrupted every so often by the sounds of scattered gunfire.

"We should have smelled this one coming," Kenneally said. "Damn, we should have been smarter than this. . . ."

In addition to his present predicament, Kenneally was even more concerned about how the whole mess would affect his future, specifically his own hope-for political career—and that of his father. It probably wouldn't go over very well on Capitol Hill when it was discovered that the son of one of the nation's most powerful senators had been caught up in a very unauthorized CIA operation.

"We did smell it," Evers said, his voice echoing around the pitch-black room. "We just didn't do anything about it."

"Who the hell were those guys anyway?" Spencer asked. "They sounded English."

"They were SAS," Kenneally said, his Boston-accented voice sounding very low and gloomy in the dark. "Special Air Service. They're the best. And you can be sure that if it came to having to use them, then we are all in deep shit."

Two shots rang out close by.

"It must be serious if they're firing on the Spooks," Evers commented.

"I can't believe this," Spencer said. "I thought the British were our allies."

"They were . . ." Evers replied.

Most of the *Holly One* was secure by the time Stanton and Crayer were brought aboard by helicopter.

It was now close to dawn, the initial SAS assault having taken place around 0230. Flying in toward the ship, Stanton and Crayer were unable to see through the perpetual blanket of fog until they were barely a hundred feet above the deck. Only then were they able to pick out the five British ships—three patrol boats, a destroyer, and a mine sweeper—that now surrounded the *Holly One*. Barely lost in the distance was the mist-enshrouded island of Mokpo.

There were three other helicopters on the deck of the ship, and between them were two rows of the carrier's crewmen lying down on their stomachs, their hands tied behind their backs. They were being watched over by a small contingent of British commandos, who, in typical English fashion, had covered their prisoners with blankets to ward off the night cold.

Shots were still being fired when Stanton and Crayer climbed out of the helicopter, but the SAS officer who met them—a man of commander's rank named Salisbury—was full of assurances that his men were but minutes from mopping up. Stanton asked first about casualties, and the officer told him they were light: three wounded, one seriously.

"Most of them chose not to fight back," the officer reported.

Stanton and Crayer were immediately ushered to the aircraft compartment below decks, and it was here for the first time that they saw the infamous Black Sabres. The planes were now well lit and surrounded by heavily armed SAS commandos. Still, the jets looked menacing. It was obvious that the F-86s had seen a lot of action in a short amount of time. Their wings and fuselages were patched and scarred, and their gun ports were charcoal-gray from use. The officers noted with fascination the RATO bottles attached to the bellies of the airplanes, as well as the jury-rigged, strengthened undercarriage and the arrestor hook, both of which had been necessary to absorb the bone-crushing carrier landings.

Crayer thought the somewhat battered, somehow noble airplanes looked more like the product of a mad scientist's laboratory than a well-run assembly line in the states. Stanton saw them in a slightly different light. To him they looked exactly like some of the more experimental German aircraft he had uncovered during the last days of the Third Reich.

"There are about a dozen people back in D.C. who are never going to believe this," Stanton said to Crayer.

"I'm not sure I believe it myself, sir," Crayer replied.

SAS Commander Salisbury gave them a quick tour of the ship. At several points, they were passed in the corridors by SAS soldiers herding more prisoners up to the deck. For the most part, the captured men looked confused and sullen, as if they too had a hard time believing that soldiers belonging to America's closest ally had just shot their way aboard the secret floating base.

The two Americans were being led up to the command center of the ship when an SAS corporal came sliding down a hatchway, excitedly calling for the SAS detachment commander.

"Sir, the sergeant major needs you in the radio room right away," the young soldier told the SAS officer in the middle of a classic snap salute. "I think he caught someone sending out a message."

Three minutes later, Stanton, Crayer, and the SAS commander burst into the radio room to find three SAS commandos treating one of the crew for a gunshot wound to his neck.

"What happened, Sergeant?" Salisbury wanted to know.

"Caught him sending out a message, sir," the SAS noncom answered. "He was pushing this button here . . . Just jabbing it when we came in . . ."

The sergeant was pointing at a nondescript black button that was located at the bottom of a large radio set.

"We traced the wire right up to the transmitter, sir," the commando continued. "Figure it's a kind of telegraph or a panic button, sir."

" 'Panic button'?" Crayer asked.

"A simple device, sir," the sergeant explained. "We saw a lot of them in the Greek Civil War. Just a buzzer, really. It's only hit when there's trouble about. Whoever is listening on the other end gets the message right away. Get's a bit of a head start, you might say."

"Any way of telling who *is* on the other end?" Stanton asked.

"Not easily, sir," was the reply. "The buzzer goes out on a very high frequency, but really, anyone in the area who's privy to have that frequency tuned in would hear it."

"So someone out there knows the game is up?" Stanton said.

"If they were listening, yes, sir," the sergeant answered soberly.

Commander Salisbury turned toward the wounded man.

"And how was he shot?" he asked. "Was he resisting?"

The sergeant quickly shook his head. "He done it to himself, sir," he said. "Tried to off himself before we stopped him. He'll live. . . ."

Crayer stared hard at the man, trying to get a reading on someone who would actually commit suicide rather than be captured. He'd heard of it happening in rare instances and usually in connection with a very desperate covert operation. But why here?

The next hour proved very confusing for Salisbury and his SAS contingent.

First off, someone had hit the ship's on-board fire alarm and it took fifteen minutes for the SAS troopers to locate and disconnect the blaring klaxon. Then, after questioning one of the prisoners, Salisbury learned that there might be a store of explosives aboard, rigged to go off should the operation be compromised. For the next thirty nerve-racking minutes, Salisbury's men combed the ship—and found nothing.

Then another prisoner told Salisbury's second-in-command that right before the SAS seized the ship, they had been expecting an air raid by Red Chinese warplanes. Salisbury immediately called down to the destroyer and asked them to pump their radar up to maximum and be on the watch for a large formation of airplanes coming out of the north or west.

But when another prisoner told another interrogator that they had actually been expecting a *submarine* attack, Salisbury actually breathed a sigh of relief. He had seen the pattern before—separate stories, separate prisoners, all giving dire warnings that never materialize. It was an old trick, an instant disinformation campaign meant to confuse and agitate the dominant force.

Interspersed among these major events, Salisbury had to deal with a dozen smaller issues, such as how to lower the prisoners over the side of the carrier to the boats waiting below and whether or not he should feed them. Probably the most bizarre of the minor incidents had to do with the Norwegian Red Cross ship that pulled up next to the *Holly One* in the midst of the operation. Its captain, Salisbury was told, had just happened by on his way to Guam and stopped to see if he could be of assistance. Salisbury dismissed the offer curtly, telling his radioman to order the ship out of the area immediately.

All the while, Stanton and Crayer were hard pressed just to stay close to Salisbury's heels, watching him handle the barrage of crises. It was only after the last brushfire was put out that the British officer asked if they wanted to interview the pilots who were captured on board.

33

"**HOW COULD THIS HAVE** happened?" Karl asked, his voice finally betraying his concern. "Especially at this late juncture?"

"Someone blabbed," Neilson told him, mixing a bourbon and water with less than his usual flair. "Some crybaby got nervous and wet his pants."

Karl wiped his forehead with a ghastly black handkerchief. He'd been sweating profusely ever since they'd heard the panic button go off.

"You don't seem too concerned," he told Neilson. "Shouldn't we best just sail away?"

Neilson took a strong swig from his drink, raised his binoculars, and pointed them out the porthole. By squinting slightly, he could just barely penetrate the waning night and fog to see the outline of the *Holly One*, as well as the small fleet that now surrounded it.

"We can't bug out now," Neilson replied, double checking their current position just to be sure that his Red Cross ship was far enough away from the carrier to remain hidden in the mist. "We've got to make the switch, here and soon. If not, the whole deal will blow up."

"But can't you radio the submarine and divert them to a safer rendezvous point?" Karl asked. "Surely we can't meet them if the carrier is now in unfriendly hands . . ."

"Why not?" Neilson replied. "The guys on the carrier won't see us, because they're not looking for us."

"But what would you have done if they had accepted your offer of help?" Karl asked anxiously. "We have no doctors on board or medicine. We don't even have any bandages."

"Please relax, *Herr Obergruppenführer*," Neilson told him, in the voice of a man trying to calm his grandfather. "There was no chance they would have had us help them. This way at least we can hang around the area just a little longer."

"You play a dangerous game, my friend," Karl said, nervously lighting a cigarette—*sans* holder this time.

Neilson smiled. "Finally you recognize it for what it is, Karl—nothing more than a game," he said. "I admire you. You're making progress."

Neilson lowered the glasses and walked over to the bound package that was lying on his desk. Inside were reams of information on the combat performance of the F-86 Sabre jets.

"And all games have their prizes, their rewards," he said, tapping the package lightly. "Do you realize this package is worth twenty million dollars? And that's not to mention what I'll be able to sell *his* package for. That's why it's important that we make the switch at exactly the right time and place. As soon as we exchange packages, twenty million dollars will be deposited in a Swiss bank account in a matter of minutes."

"This is in addition to the gold we took on the other day?" Karl asked.

Neilson laughed. "That gold was simply good-faith money for Tusk—something to prime the pumps on both ends, if you will," he said. "He needed something to grease some palms, plus he had to hide some of his own money. So I told the bastard I'd fly some of his Russian currency to South America for safekeeping until he could get it back into Mother Russia. Now he owes me a big favor, which I have already called in. He should be happy, the sonofabitch—if everything went well, he has a ton of rubles on their way to his private bank vault in Brazil."

"And what is the favor he is to do for you?" Karl asked, his voice still jittery.

Neilson didn't answer right away. Instead he returned

to his porthole and refocused his glasses on the ships in the distance.

"I'm a student of history, Karl," he said with a properly mysterious tone. "And I know that if you run from a mistake, it will come back to haunt you, over and over. I don't need that kind of aggravation."

Neilson increased the power on his binoculars two steps.

"Look at them out there," he said. "They're like a bunch of sitting ducks. . . ."

Karl stared at him for a long moment. "What is it you plan to do then?" he asked finally.

Neilson sipped his drink again and took a deep breath.

"The same thing your guys tried to do at Bastogne," he said. "The call has already been made, Karl. It's time for me to go back on the offensive. . . ."

Stanton still couldn't believe it. Of the four pilots the SAS had found on board, he was close friends with three of them.

"I suppose I shouldn't be *this* surprised," he said to them, after the SAS men had untied them and left him alone in the cabin with them. "After all, who else would be crazy enough to fly those planes off of this deck?"

Stanton had known Hughes, Evers, and Kenneally from the old days at Mescalero Air Base. They made up three-fifths of the first contingent of American pilots tapped to test fly the captured German aircraft his own unit had uncovered at the end of the war.

They now explained their roles in the operation to him in detail: the orders from Washington, their deployment back to the war zone, their hustle aboard the *Holly One,* and their lucrative paychecks.

"Testing those airplanes before the authentic items came over made sense to me," Hughes told him. "It just seemed like something the Air Force would want to do. At first, anyway."

Stanton offered them cigarettes all around, and there was a brief orgy of matches being struck and furious puffing.

"The problem is that running around with suicide pills

might not wash when some congressional committee starts to pull this thing apart," Stanton said. "Signing on for all that money won't look good either."

"We've always worked for top money," Hughes said.

"I know that," Stanton replied. "But it ain't military. And if they can trace a money trail back to you, then it looks like you were doing it for personal gain. That's as bad as pulling the trigger."

"We've always been overpaid," Evers said scornfully.

"So you don't think there's any chance we can get out of this quietly, Colonel?" Kenneally asked him.

"It all depends on who wants to listen to your story," Stanton told them. "I can't say too much to you guys myself—technically, you're in it up to your eyeballs, just like the rest of the Spooks on this ship. And no one knows how deep it all goes: These guys were breaking into the Pentagon's most secure areas and changing secret orders, for Christ's sake. Why do you think we had to get the SAS blokes to do the dirty work?"

A very distinct chill came over the room.

"I'll tell you something else," Stanton continued. "Whoever engineered all this is a very powerful individual. He sounds like a Spook's Spook. It's almost scary. Not many people can sneak five brand-new Sabre jets halfway around the world, *then* arrange it so the Air Force's best pilots fly them for him."

Three of the four pilots let out a collective groan. As for Spencer, he said nothing. He was just happy that the lights were back on.

34

THERE WAS A CERTAIN amount of irony in the fact that the force of enemy bombers heading for the *Holly One* were actually former Luftwaffe aircraft, repainted dark green and bearing evidence of Soviet Air Force markings.

They were Heinkel 111s, twin-engined bombers that had been the workhorses of the German Air Force during the London Blitz. The squadron of airplanes—there were twelve of them in all—had been a dubious piece of booty claimed by the Red Army as it advanced into Germany in the last days of the war. Found locked away in a hangar at a small airfield just east of Berlin, it was long suspected that the Heinkels had been intended to carry the Führer and his entourage out of the Nazi capital just before it fell.

This historical footnote meant little to the Soviet soldiers who overran the airfield, though. Like everything else they came across that was deemed workable, they had disassembled the bombers, packed them in crates, and sent them back to the Motherland, where they were put back together and flown as trainers for the next five and a half years.

Had Comrade Tusk had more time, he would have been able to congratulate himself on his enormous foresight. It had been his idea to move the twelve bombers to Antung along with the first shipment of MiG-15s just before the Chinese intervention, feeling they might be helpful as transport craft, recon planes, or, in a pinch, troop carriers.

Though he would never admit it, the thought that they

would be used again to carry bombs had never crossed his mind.

The twelve airplanes left Antung less than two hours after Tusk had received the coded emergency message from Neilson.

It was to his credit that Tusk was able to order the dozen aging bombers loaded up with fuel, bombs, and men in such a short amount of time, all by way of sending coded messages of his own from the radio shack of the submarine to the command center at Antung. No one at Antung asked any questions, no one dared wonder where the airplanes were going or why. They just followed Tusk's orders and did so quickly, even down to his adamant decree that the red star emblem of the Soviet Air Force be covered over with paint—preferably black—before the squadron took to the air. Short of time and with no black paint about, the obedient ground crews hid the bright red Soviet star with hastily drawn balls of bright orange enamel.

The bombers headed south out of Antung, flying low above the water so as to avoid being detected by the UN radar net. Within two hours they had set down at Weihaiwe on the edge of the Shantung peninsula, which was part of mainland China itself. The Heinkels took on more fuel at the small air base and received their final orders: They were to proceed on a southeasterly direction to a point 130 miles off the South Korean coast, tuning their radios to a certain frequency and finding a radio-signal beacon that would help guide them to the target. Once there, they would find a small flotilla of ships that included a "disabled" aircraft carrier. They were to attack the ships, concentrating first on the carrier and then on the smaller vessels around it. The only target they should not attack was a Red Cross ship that might be in the general area.

Once the mission was completed, the bombers would turn due west and land on Laoyao or, if the weather were bad, Shanghai.

It was the radar operator aboard the British destroyer HMS *Sparkle* who first spotted the incoming force.

Alerted to keep an eye out for enemy planes, the ship's captain had ordered his radars to be put on long-range general sweep, a tracking system that was powerful enough to locate aircraft as far as forty miles away but not able to count them or identify their type.

The first report of the approaching aircraft reached SAS Commander Salisbury just as the first of the four Black Sabres had been brought up onto the deck of the *Holly One*. With most of those captured on board having been transferred to the smaller British ships, the plans now were to disassemble the airplane, lower it over the side, and place it aboard the HMS *Sparkle*, for transport back to Japan. The other three jets would remain aboard the *Holly One*, guarded by a contingent of SAS men, until a decision could be made as to their fate.

As soon as Salisbury heard that a large and unknown airborne force was bearing down on them, he immediately located the prisoner who had claimed that just such an attack was imminent. Now faced with the real possibility, the prisoner totally and convincingly recanted his story. At this point, Salisbury was certain the story *was* true, and he ordered his men to prepare for an attack.

Stanton had just passed his cigarette pack around to the pilots for the second time when Salisbury burst into the small cabin.

He was out of breath and excited, not the normal state of affairs for the stiff-upper-lipped SAS commander. Yet, typically, he got right to the point.

Turning to the pilots he asked bluntly, "How long before you chaps can get airborne?"

35

Mokpo Island

IT HAD BEEN A long cold night for Choji—one filled with vivid dreams of the war long ago, of his last mission, of his disgrace in not carrying it out.

He had slept in his uniform, rifle at his side, his belly filled with rice and cooked minnows. Waiting. Waiting for the Americans to invade. Waiting for his comrades to arrive. Waiting to end the five long years he had spent alone on the island, ready to spring back to life for his Emperor. Ready to wash himself of his humiliation.

But the attack never came. He had waited all that day, scanning the fog-shrouded sea for hours on end, searching for the American fleet he was certain the omens had told him would arrive. But it didn't. And as night fell and his uniform became wrinkled and dirty once more, he began to have more disturbing thoughts. Thoughts that told him he was nothing but a fool. The war was over—it had been over for years. He had seen the tremendous flash off on the eastern horizon that day soon after he'd chosen to land on the island instead of carrying out his kamikaze attack. Another flash came a few days later. A vision he had at the time told him that the Home Islands had been completely destroyed by these gigantic flashes, and now he was feeling that *these* were the omens he should have paid attention to.

Now as he rolled off his mat and onto the cold floor of the hut, his stomach was so upset he thought he might vomit. During the night the photo of the Emperor had fallen off one of its tacks and now was hanging off kilter. Choji felt tears come to his eyes. The photo looked old and faded and tattered—as if it had aged ten years overnight.

This was the real omen, Choji thought. All of his hard work, his sacrifice, his *doryoku*—his effort—had been a waste. All of it, nonsense.

For the first time since coming to the island, he actually considered not saying his prayers. But a creature of habit, Choji relented to the inner voice—dim and fading as it was—and knelt before the readjusted photo of the Emperor, mouthing the invocations, possibly for the last time.

Then he rose, retrieved the gold chain he had immersed in the cup of oil during the heady hours of the day before, and walked out to the ledge.

Suddenly he stopped in his tracks and looked out from the cliff with astonishment. For the first time ever, there was no fog, no wind, no raging seas in the distance. For the first time the morning was clear, and he could actually see the sun coming up over the horizon.

But it was what lay between him and the rising sun that shot bolts of excitement through his body. Five miles out from the island, he saw the American aircraft carrier—the same one his squadron mates had been ordered to attack five years before—at rest in shallow water, attended by a ring of protecting ships.

In a rush of indescribable exhilaration, Choji at once realized that by keeping faith, his prayers of redemption had come true. The Americans *were* here, and judging by the flurry of activity on board and around the carrier, they were preparing for action.

Choji was about to turn and run the half-mile back to the field where he had landed five years before, but a sound—a deep droning—kept him glued to the spot. Still unaccustomed to seeing his surroundings so clearly, he turned to the north just in time to see three dark specks emerging over the horizon.

They were airplanes, too big to be fighters. They had two engines apiece and were trailing twin plumes of dark smoke. As they drew closer, Choji realized they were bombers and of a design that he found faintly familiar.

Now three more specks appeared behind this vanguard and six more behind them. They were so low above the surface of the sea, he thought one of them would surely plunge in at any second. But they held their course and soon began to climb slightly, steering directly toward the small fleet of ships.

At that point Choji realized the airplanes were not coming to bomb the island. Rather, they were heading to bomb the ships.

Stuck in the throes between fascination and fear, Choji watched astounded as the first three bombers roared over the carrier, each one dropping a pair of bombs. He counted six explosions hard off the port side of the carrier—all near misses. As the first three attackers pulled up and into a wide circle, the second wave came in, they too dropping a total of six bombs.

The sounds of the first explosions were just reaching him when one bomb from the second wave landed squarely on one of the small patrol boats flanking the carrier. The boat exploded immediately, sending a large gush of smoke, water, and debris up against the side of the carrier. Choji felt a breath catch in his throat. It was the first combat he'd seen in five years, and now he felt it oddly chilling. One moment the boat was there—the next, it was gone. He couldn't imagine anyone surviving the direct hit.

The second wave of bombers pulled up and away just as the third trio of airplanes roared in. There was a scattering of gunfire coming now from the smaller ships around the carrier and apparently from the carrier itself. But at that precise moment, Choji saw a bright flash erupt from the stern of the American flat-top. Suddenly there was another airplane, roaring into the sky, flames pouring out of its tail as if it were already on fire.

With this he had another answer: The flashes he had seen in his dreams and in the fog, he was now watching in the best of visibility. And the black flaming airship that had gone over the island early the morning before had undoubtedly been an airplane from the American carrier. Five years had gone by, and it was obvious that the Americans had devised some kind of new fighter that needed no propeller and was rocket powered.

Choji was trembling with anticipation as he watched the strange black airplane rise nearly straight up from the carrier deck, the flame underneath its tail going out, to be replaced by a thin contrail of white smoke. Immediately the airplane turned over and found itself on the tail of one of the attackers. He heard a distant chattering and saw the front of the black plane light up. It was pouring gunfire into the slower, nearly helpless bomber. In a matter of seconds, the bomber caught fire. It began to spin out and, despite the efforts of its pilot, plunged into the sea with a fiery splash.

No sooner had this happened than the black airplane was racing head-on into a fourth wave of bombers that were bearing down on the ships. At the same time, the first wave had completed its circle and was approaching for a second bombing run. Choji had to close his eyes and open them again, making sure what he was seeing was not a dream or another vision. But it wasn't. Five years of nothing but fog and storms, and now on this first clear, bright, sunny morning, he was witnessing a fierce air and sea battle.

This is how dreams come true, he thought. This is how a destiny is fulfilled.

The headlong rush by the black airplane, combined with the increased antiaircraft fire coming from the ships, began to wreak havoc on the orderly fashion of the attacking airplanes. Now the bombers were scattered and coming in at the ships from all directions, heights, and speeds. Choji ran to the hut and retrieved his small telescope. Soon he was focusing on the deck of the carrier, just as another black airplane was lifting off, like a skyrocket, into the air.

Suddenly two bombers roared over the carrier's bow, dropping smaller bombs that just seemed to miss the flight deck. It was the first real close-up look Choji had of the airplanes, and what he saw startled him more than anything else in this astonishing morning.

Painted on the side of the airplanes were the unmistakable orange-ball emblems of the Imperial Forces of Japan.

36

NO AMOUNT OF PRODDING by SAS Commander Salisbury or Lieutenant Crayer could prevent Stanton from climbing to the bridge of the *Holly One*, a borrowed Sten machine gun in hand, and blasting away at the low-flying Heinkel bombers.

Crayer had no choice but to join him there—there would have been hell to pay if the colonel got killed while Crayer were hiding in some reinforced closet somewhere. So there they stood, alongside of six SAS troopers, firing at each bomber that came anywhere near the conning tower of the immobile carrier.

High above, they could see the first two Black Sabres screeching about the sky, igniting their RATO bottles at short intervals and blasting away at the mysterious bombers. They had already downed three of them and damaged at least two more. But still the remaining airplanes pressed the attack, their 250-pound bombs now slamming into the side of the *Holly One* with sickening frequency.

Down below, amidst the fire and smoke, the two remaining Sabres were on deck and ready for launch, their pilots yelling instructions down at the SAS men who had been pressed into service as flight mechanics.

Suddenly one of the Sabres took off, and even in the midst of the battle it seemed as if everyone had stopped shooting for a moment to watch the F-86, its RATO bottles firing at full blast, lift off almost vertically.

The second Black Sabre came right behind, its pilot rolling a bare hundred feet down the deck before hitting his rocket assist. Then he, like the three before, simply shot right off of the carrier and hung in midair for a

blood-curdling moment before its powerful jet engine
kicked in.

It was so unnatural, Crayer felt his hair stand on end.

"Good god!" he yelled above the incredible din. "How
do they do that?"

With all four Sabres aloft, the battle began to turn.
Two more bombers were splashed within the next minute
and it appeared as if the antiaircraft fire from the surrounding ships was starting to have some effect.

Still, Stanton and the SAS troopers on the bridge kept
firing away at the attackers. In between volleys, the
colonel was yelling at the top of his lungs, "Who are
they?"

His throat filled with gunpowder smoke, Crayer would
yell back, "I don't know, sir!" To him they looked like
old Luftwaffe Heinkels, painted with Japanese emblems
and being flown by standard Soviet Air Force attack
tactics.

The last pass by three of the bombers proved to be the
most devastating. All three managed to score direct hits
on the carrier, two on the stern, one on the bow. Suddenly both ends of the ship were burning, choking all
those caught in between with a cloud of black acrid
smoke.

Crayer felt himself on the verge of a rising panic. He
was an "office warrior," a paper pusher. Combat was
totally disagreeable to him. Then, through the fire and
smoke, he saw that the remaining attackers—some flying
low, others with engines smoking—were turning away to
the west.

In the middle of the terrifying confusion, Commander
Salisbury appeared out of nowhere, grabbed Stanton's
arm, and yelled, "Time to get going, sir!"

Stanton knew immediately what the British officer
meant. Turning to Crayer, he said, "Let's go, Lieutenant. We're abandoning ship."

The young officer offered no resistance. Moving quickly
down the gangways, they were soon on the burning
shrapnel-covered deck. SAS troopers were directing them
to the side of the ship, where lines had been placed.
Already some of the troopers and the few remaining

prisoners were shimmying down the lines to the British patrol boats waiting below. All the while the *Holly One* was being wracked by secondary explosions, the resulting heat and smoke nearly suffocating those still aboard.

Still, above it all, there was a tremendous, powerful noise. Crayer looked up and saw that the four Black Sabres had formed up into a finger-four formation. Then, as one, they turned off to the west and streaked away in hot pursuit of the fleeing bombers.

37

CHOJI WAS FURIOUS.

For the past half-hour he had been cursing every one of his ancestors for humiliating him this way. Off in the distance, over the small hill that separated him from the cliff and a view of the battle out at sea, Choji could see large plumes of black smoke rising into the morning sky. Up until ten minutes before, he could also hear the ferocious sounds of battle—the symphony he'd waited five years to hear again: the bomb bursts, the antiaircraft fire, the roar of airplane engines, the crashing sound of machines as they hit the water.

Now everything was getting very quiet. He had seen the bombers fly away toward the west, the four mysterious black rockets passing right overhead, giving chase. He had heard the various whistles and horns and sirens emanating from the ships under attack. And judging from the columns of smoke, he was sure the glorious two-engined bombers with the large orange balls on their sides had bested the American ships.

And he had missed it.

Was it the fuel injector? Was it his fuel? Was it his

battery? He couldn't tell. All he knew was that for five years he had religiously maintained his own secret weapon—the craft that had brought him to the island—and now, when he needed it the most, it wouldn't work.

The Nakajima Ki-44 was a better airplane than the more famous Mitsubishi A6M Zero, and this was something about which Choji was always proud. Most pilots in the Imperial Army Air Force resented the Zero pilots simply because they seemed to get more undue praise from their superiors. In fact, praising the Zero was a refuge for the ignorant in Choji's opinion. The Ki-44 could climb faster than the Zero, it carried more weapons, and it boasted a top speed of 373 mph, nearly 40 mph faster than the Mitsubishi airplane. The Ki-44 was also easier to handle, better to maintain, and built to last—unlike the Zero, which to Choji seemed to be built simply to throw away.

But now Choji was having a different opinion about the Ki-44. Looking out on the small field where he had landed in the airplane five years before, he saw it was now overgrown in some spots. Small trees and bushes had sprung up here and there in the intervening years. But these didn't bother him—he knew they would not unduly hamper his takeoff.

But he couldn't go into battle if his engine wouldn't start.

He felt tears come to his eyes as he rechecked his engine, rechecked his battery, rechecked his fuel supply. Everything seemed in order—just as it had been every time he'd made his way to the field during the past five years.

What was wrong? Choji stood before the dark green single-engine fighter plane, trying to conjure up some luck from the Cosmos. Were the natural forces really going to be this cruel to him? he wondered as the tears flowed freely down his face. He had been a coward five years before—that was why he was alive on the island and not beyond in the Greater Glory with his fellow pilots. But over these years he had told himself—or was it *fooled* himself?—that he was here for a reason, that his questionable actions back in 1945 would prove in the end to be justified.

But now, as the sounds of the dying battle became even more distant, he felt that his divine punishment had already begun.

There was only one recourse, Choji concluded.

He climbed back into the cockpit and drew together the two wires that connected to his auxiliary battery and ran to the back of the airplane, where he had placed the dynamite. Tearfully, he had settled on a final plan. He would beseech his ancestors one more time to start the airplane's engine and allow him some part in the battle. If they denied him, he would join the two wires, detonate the dynamite, and die here on the island in disgrace.

He bowed his head and tightly gripped the oily gold chain in his right hand. His mind flashed back to the relatives he had known in his life—his parents, his cousins, his uncles, aunts, and grandparents. Then he went further back, remembering the stories about *their* relatives and the ones before them. He was concentrating so intensely, his teeth bit his tongue, causing a trickle of blood to spot his lips. Horrified at the sight of his own blood, he quickly retrieved his uniform towel and wiped it away.

He said his final prayer to the Emperor, of course, telling him that he would abide by whatever plan the Divine Highness had for him but at the same time begging him for the last time to honor the requests of his ancestors and let him join the combat.

With the two wires dangling from one hand, Choji closed his eyes and pressed the Ki-44's battery-start switch.

The engine started almost immediately.

38

A RETURN TO FLIGHT was Choji's reward.

He found himself laughing hysterically as the Ki-44 lifted off from the bumpy, bush-obstructed field and, using the updraft caused by the cliff, leaped into the air with an almost effortless motion. His flying skills returned to him in a matter of moments—he had been waiting too long for this day to forget how to fly now.

But, almost as quickly, his heart sank again. Climbing to 5,000 feet, he looked out on the scene of the battle to find that, aside from the aircraft carrier, all the other surviving ships in the area had departed. Climbing higher, he thought he could faintly see what was left of the small flotilla, heading due east toward the Korean mainland.

He swung the Ki-44 back around and headed to overfly the carrier itself. It was burning fiercely at this point; flames were shooting out of every portal, and the conning tower itself was a mass of oily smoke.

This was no target, he told himself bitterly. Why strike a match next to a burning building? He felt the tears return, and once again he accidentally bit his tongue. *This* was his damnation. The gods were letting him suffer by allowing him to see what he had missed.

His heart sank lower as he noted his fuel-reserve needle. Very low due to the necessity of siphoning off the gasoline contaminated over the years, it had already reached the emergency-reserve level. Choji estimated he had ten minutes of flight time left—not nearly enough to pursue the withdrawing American ships.

Once again, he fingered the two battery wires in his right hand, taking little solace in the fact that by touching

them, he could become dust in the wind instead of dust
on the island. He whispered a final prayer and was about
to press the wires together . . .

But then, through the mist, something caught his eye.

It was the wake of a ship. He turned the Ki-44 and at
once saw that there *was* a ship still in the battle area.

Suddenly his heart was racing again. Somehow, some
departed ancestor somewhere had been jesting with him.
But through it all, Choji told himself, his spirit had only
been shaken, not destroyed. Now, as he concentrated on
the enemy ship moving slowly in the waters just off the
coast of the island 5,000 feet below him, he was certain
that at last, his destiny lay before him.

Filled with glee, Choji tied his ceremonial headband
around his flight helmet and put the Ki-44 into a steep
dive. . . .

39

"FEEL BETTER, KARL?"

For once, the elderly officer had to agree.

"I do," he answered Neilson. "I must say you have
skillfully covered every contingency."

Neilson mixed himself an extra-strong bourbon and
water and toasted himself.

"Covering contingencies is my profession, Karl," he
said, aiming his binoculars back at the ravaged, smoking
hulk of the *Holly One*. "And it's been my experience
that if you attend to details, you get lucky. Things just
seem to go your way."

Neilson certainly felt himself lucky at this point. With
the notable exception of the prisoners taken aboard the
aircraft carrier and the Black Sabres themselves, all di-

rect evidence of Operation Stormcloud was burning furiously about five miles away. He would leave no trail on this one—nothing that could be traced back to him. The Spooks caught aboard the ship would keep their mouths shut—of this he was certain—and the pilots themselves knew very little about the true purpose of the mission.

"In a way I feel bad for those flyboys," Neilson said. "They were really top-notch guys. Could fly the hell out of those Sabres, couldn't they? It's too bad, but knowing how the Air Force works, it will all probably come down on their heads, especially when we leak out that they have money in Switzerland. Court-martials, dishonorable discharges, maybe even prison time."

"They'd be shot back in my country in the old days," Karl said, triumphantly lighting a cigarette. "This is the best way to clean up unfortunate circumstances, plus their families would be told their sons had died in combat."

"You speak from experience, Karl," Neilson told him. "Was it your boy who said 'A man like me cares little about losing the lives of a million men'?"

Karl shook his head no. "That was Bonaparte," he replied. "The phrase you are thinking of says 'I can send the flower of our youth into the hell of war without the slightest pity.' "

"Two of a kind." Neilson almost sighed. "And damn me if I don't see them as being reasonable. In war, men *become* dispensable. They become machines. Parts, cogs, nuts, bolts. Some survive. Some have to be repaired. Some are thrown away."

"I agree, my friend," Karl said. "In fact, I believe that some day, all the fighting will be done by machines. All chance of human error will be factored out. Then we will see what my Leader used to refer to as 'perfect warfare.' "

Neilson took a sip of his drink and checked his watch.

"Karl, within ten minutes, there will be twenty million dollars deposited in a Swiss bank account in my name," he said, boastfully. "You're in for two million."

"*Two*?" Karl asked, his features creasing into a rare smile. "That is more than generous. And what did I do?"

"You were here, Karl," Neilson told him, stroking his

long red beard. "You were my confidant. I find that very essential in these types of operations."

Karl bowed his head deeply. "I am happy to have been of service," he said. "I hope we will be as successful in future ventures."

Neilson nodded and returned to his desk. Before him was a package sloppily wrapped in plastic and bound with black electrical tape. In the very midst of the battle, the hasty exchange of aircraft data had taken place, but only after Neilson had coaxed and threatened Tusk to bring his sub into the battle area. The switch had taken all of one minute, two lifeboats meeting halfway and exchanging packages, while the venerable Heinkels were bombing the aircraft carrier not five miles away.

Now as he examined the package before him, Neilson thought it so typical of Tusk to do a mish-mash job in securing the contents. Two thousand pages of valuable data, notes, calculations, and performance numbers of the MiG-15 in combat deserved more than a piece of plastic held together with tape. The package Neilson had given to Tusk—close to 2,500 pages of similar data on the F-86 Sabre—had been bound with wire and duct tape, wrapped in a waterproofed piece of tarpaulin, and then placed in a small steamer trunk that had its locks and hinges welded shut.

"These guys never do anything right." Neilson huffed, turning the package over in his hands. "They can't cook. They can't build an automobile, and they have a very hard time deciding what's valuable and what isn't."

"They have always been like that," Karl said, speaking from experience. "Have I told you what happened during our pact negotiations with them over Poland in 1939?"

"Another time, Karl," Neilson said, his mind concentrating on the bundle of data before him. Who would buy it? The U.S. Air Force? The French? Or a South American country with expansionist aspirations, perhaps? All of them were possible, Neilson knew, but unlikely. He saw himself selling it all not to a government but rather to an independent airplane manufacturer, most likely one in the states. Governments would muck up such valuable information, whereas a savvy aircraft builder—

such as the shadowy figure who owned the American Aircraft Company out of Las Vegas—would use the data to his advantage, building countermeasures to the MiG-15 into his next fighter design and then marketing the result as a verified "MiG-killer." Once Neilson had found a buyer, he knew he'd get the price he wanted: another $20 million, this time in gold, and this time with no questions asked.

Neilson returned to the porthole and sighted the burning *Holly One* through his glasses for the last time. The mist was starting to envelope the area once again and, mixing with the tremendous amount of smoke coming out of the burning carrier, made seeing over the distance of five miles fairly difficult.

He picked up his phone and placed a call to the bridge, instructing them to set a course for the open Pacific, on a heading of due south and at full speed ahead.

"On to bigger and better things, Karl," he said. "We've got a fuse to light in Indochina."

Karl smiled again. He couldn't remember a time when he felt more joy.

"We *will* rule the world, won't we?" he said quite suddenly.

Neilson had to laugh. "Yes, Karl, we will," he said. "Us and people like us, who realize that sentimentality is what separates a fool from power."

"And that war is business," Karl said, mimicking Neilson's earlier speech to him.

"Now you're talking," Neilson said. "Can I get you a glass of mineral water?"

Karl clapped his hands in delight. "No, today I think I'll actually have a little of your bourbon," he said, his ears just picking up an odd whining sound coming from above the ship. "I would like to toast to our brave new world. . . ."

Five seconds later, Choji's dynamite-laden Ki-44 slammed into the Red Cross ship, exploding on impact and killing all aboard.

40

Tokyo, Several Weeks Later

HUGHES HAD JUST DRAWN a king-high flush when Evers walked in with another can of beer.

"Who's winning?" the fireplug of a pilot asked, cigar permanently embedded in the left side of his mouth.

"Jesse James here is cleaning us out," Kenneally said, motioning to Hughes with an air of half-hearted disgust as the pilot pulled in twenty-seven dollars in winnings. "Where the hell did you learn to play cards, anyway?"

"You taught me," Hughes told Kenneally, stacking his dimes. "Don't you remember?"

The two MPs seated at the table retrieved what little money they had left and got up.

"Time to change the watch," one of them said. "While we still have some money left."

They gathered their helmets and gun belts and opened the hotel-room door.

"These guys need fresh meat," one of them said to the other pair of MPs standing guard outside. "They haven't stopped winning since breakfast."

Despite the warning, the newly relieved MPs took the two empty seats at the card table and cashed in. Evers passed out beer to everyone and dumped his own pile of change on the table. Spencer turned up the radio; everyone lit cigarettes. Another day of drinking and poker had begun.

It had been like this for nearly a month now. Hughes, Evers, Kenneally, and Spencer were confined to a hotel room in the Tokyo Hilton, being held under house arrest. The place was better than a brig anywhere—it had two beds and two couches, a large bathroom and sink, a small kitchenette, and one hell of a view of downtown Tokyo. Room service was prompt, and sometimes they were able to get American food like hamburgers and french fries. The only problem was that the beer was a stale-tasting Japanese brand that took some getting used to.

Stanton looked in on them every day, as his office was close by. He even sat in for a few rounds of jacks or better. The pilots were officially in his care, but knowing the men as he did, there was no reason to make their confinement punitive. In his eyes, they had done nothing wrong—quite the contrary, they had performed admirably during the attack on the *Holly One*. However, the Pentagon's secret investigation of the entire matter was still going on, and this necessitated the pilots being held in one place for reasons of the utmost security.

The only time Stanton insisted that the pilots appear "military" (that is, shaved, sober, and in uniform) was when one of the Pentagon investigative teams was due to call. When this happened, the pilots did their best to provide the Pentagon officials with as much information as possible on the bizarre Stormcloud affair. None of the CIA Spooks apprehended on board the *Holly One* had talked—yet. In fact, Stanton had told the pilots unofficially that most of the operatives were quietly being released and that some close to the investigation felt they would never unravel the true story of Stormcloud—what its ultimate purpose was, how the Albatross full of Russian rubles was connected, and, most important, who masterminded it and their present whereabouts.

But the story was about to take yet another unexpected twist this very morning.

Shortly after the MPs had changed the watch, one of them opened the door to reveal a venerable and totally unexpected visitor.

His name was Dr. Algis Litke. A Polish refugee from before World War II, Litke had joined the U.S. government in 1940 and become involved in a super-secret unit called the Aerospace Security Agency. The postwar testing of captured German aircraft at Mescalero had been initiated by the ASA under Litke's direction, and it was he who had made the final selection of pilots for the classified program—Hughes, Evers, and Kenneally among them.

Now, nearly six years later, Litke was a high-ranking member of Truman's staff and a trusted confidant of the president's inner circle. His White House office was only five doors away from the president's, and with proximity equaling power, Litke commanded more respect than a roomful of generals.

Instantly everyone at the card table froze. They hadn't seen the doctor in years, and though they had all been friendly with him back during the old Mescalero days, no one quite knew what to do at this moment.

Litke was not a military officer, so a snap to attention and a barrage of salutes would not be appropriate. It was Kenneally who first rose and greeted the man, trying with every ounce of his political charm to smooth over the appearance of the pilots and their comfortable surroundings.

Though effective, Kenneally's efforts weren't necessary— Litke wasn't the type of individual who demanded spit and polish. He knew all the pilots personally—especially Evers and Hughes—and he respected them. More important, he trusted them and, carrying the bad news that he did, he knew that trust was about to be tested to the limit.

"Please forgive me for dropping in unannounced," the diminutive doctor said in his whistling European accent after Evers had scrambled to get him a chair and the two MPs had discreetly left the room. "I would be happy to join you gentlemen in a game of bridge someday. But it will have to be a day that we all can relax. And frankly, I don't see that day as coming any time soon."

A bell went off in Hughes's head. He and Litke had had many long discussions around the time he first joined the Mescalero Test Pilot Program, and Hughes felt that he could read the doctor pretty well. As such, he had never seen the man look so apprehensive as he did now.

"One week ago, I was told very unofficially that the Pentagon investigation team was recommending that all of you be court-martialed for treason," Litke said in low, measured tones.

It was as if a bomb had gone off in the hotel room. No one could speak; their worst nightmares were apparently about to come true.

I'll never fly again, Hughes thought.

But then Litke cleared his throat and continued: "However, a matter of grave importance has come up since," he said. "And I fear we have yet to fully realize the effects of this Operation Stormcloud. Still, it might provide us with an opportunity to get you all out of your present predicament."

"Let's have it, Doc," Evers said, pulling his seat closer to Litke's. "We'll do anything. . . ."

The doctor took a long draw on his pipe and exhaled, instantly filling the room with the pungent smell of French tobacco.

"I know you men have been cooped up in here for quite a while," he began. "All very necessary, you understand. But I think it is fair to say that you are probably behind the times as to what has been going on over in Korea. So let me tell you.

"Our forces are in the midst of a tragic retreat. Many Marines have been killed up near the Chosin Reservoir, and many more had to be evacuated by sea at Wonsan. The Chinese have occupied Pyongyang and they have been moving on all fronts. The president has declared a state of national emergency, and the thinking is that by Christmas Day—only a week from today—the Chinese will be crossing the 38th Parallel."

All four pilots were ashen at hearing this report. Litke had been correct in saying they'd been out of touch with much of the news from the front, both when they were on the *Holly One* and during their stay at the Tokyo Hilton. When they were secretly flown to the *Holly One* in November, the Marines had been holding their own against the Red Chinese in the very northern reaches of North Korea. Now it appeared that in little more than a month, the Reds had gobbled up a lot of hard-won territory and were ready to launch another communist invasion of South Korea.

Litke wiped his eyes and continued: "But as terrible as the situation on the ground is, we are receiving even more disturbing news from the battle in the air.

"Simply put, gentlemen, our Sabres have been in the air just a week or so and they are getting the hell knocked out of them."

Now all four pilots reacted with shock.

"What?" Hughes said. "How? We proved that the Sabre could beat the MiGs. We've told every air operations officer who's come to talk to us how a guy in an F-86 can jack a guy in a MiG, despite their altitude and climb advantage."

"This we know, Captain," Litke replied. "And if it weren't for your information, I fear that our losses would be even greater than they are."

"So what's the problem, Doc?" Evers asked. "We thought we'd given those Sabres a hell of a work-out. Christ, they were actually *running* from us toward the end there."

"And that is why this is such a mystery," Litke said. "Apparently the Chinese know some things about the Sabres that we don't."

"But how could that be?" Kenneally asked. "We're the only guys who have ever flown them in combat, and the Spooks on board made a note of every time the engine so much as coughed."

Litke pulled out a handkerchief and dabbed his forehead.

"That's exactly the point," he said.

There was a brief yet somewhat frightening silence as the pilots looked at each other. Hughes was the first one to speak.

"Are you saying that Stormcloud was actually an *enemy* operation?" he asked.

Litke shrugged. "I don't know," he replied. "But maybe another possibility is that someone took the data you men collected on the Sabre and provided it to the enemy."

"I can't believe that!" Spencer exclaimed.

"These things are not uncommon," Litke explained. "We are certain that many of our country's atomic secrets were turned over to the Russians, and perhaps we have obtained many of the Soviet's secrets in turn. In fact, in the course of our investigation we've found that a substantial amount of gold was transferred to the *Holly*

One while you men were aboard. Plus, shortly before the operation was uncovered, an Albatross seaplane crashed about a hundred miles from your location. It killed both pilots but was later found to be carrying a substantial sum in Russian rubles."

"Rubles?" Evers repeated. "For who? For what?"

Litke could only shrug again. "We may never know," he said. "But I'm sure I don't have to tell you that there are individuals out there without any scruples in matters like this. Selling out one's country is actually easy for some people."

"There's not enough money in the world . . ." Spencer started to say.

Litke took several quick puffs on his pipe. "And then there are sometimes when it's not a question of selling it," he said thoughtfully. "Sometimes it's simply traded for, or given over by an individual who believes he can change the course of history. There's a power in that as well."

"So what can we do?" Kenneally asked.

Litke sighed and wiped his forehead again.

"The following remains classified, gentlemen," he said, his voice barely above a whisper. "Is that understood?"

All four pilots nodded.

"We suspect that the MiG operations are being run out of one central point," he began. "And if there is stolen data being used to give the Reds an advantage over our Sabres, then we believe that information is being disseminated from this central command point."

"Why just there?" Hughes asked. "How do we know it hasn't been copied and sent to Peking or Moscow by now?"

"Our intelligence indicates otherwise," Litke replied somewhat mysteriously. "Plus the data is more useful at this central point. And I'll show you why. . . ."

He reached into his briefcase and produced a grainy aerial photograph that showed an aircraft in its center.

"This was taken four days ago," he said. "Do you recognize the type of airplane?"

"Sure," Spencer said enthusiastically. "It's a Sabre."

The other three pilots nodded in agreement.

Litke produced another photograph that was actually a blow-up of the first.

"Look closely," he said. "What symbol is that on the wing?"

Hughes leaned in and squinted. "Is that . . ."

Litke nodded. "It's a star," he confirmed. "A red star."

"Goddamn," Evers swore softly. "You mean they got one of our Sabres, too?"

Litke nodded gravely. "Yes," he said. "But in this case, we know where they got it. It was shot down near the Yalu. The pilot lost his fuel pumps and brought it in for a landing on a frozen river, apparently with very little damage. Our fighters attempted to strafe the wreckage, but they had no idea as to the whereabouts of the pilot. . . ."

Each pilot thought back to the similar set of circumstances when their colleague Ernst crashed in the Tsing Buk Valley.

Litke went on: "When our recon boys flew over the spot the next day, the Sabre was gone."

"And now the commies are flying it," Spencer said.

"Exactly," Litke said somberly. "Not in combat but in aerial practices with their other pilots."

Everyone took a deep breath and let the news sink in.

"The combination of their having the data and an actual airplane to test it out on has become deadly for our pilots," Litke said.

"So what's the solution, Doctor?" Kenneally asked.

The little man shrugged, further wrinkling his dark gray three-piece suit. "We have to go in and destroy that airplane," he said matter-of-factly. "And their central command point."

The pilots were quick to get the implications of the statement. They knew that any base that held a captured Sabre and the valuable data would not be in North Korea. Rather it would more likely be located in Manchuria. Trouble was, Truman had forbidden any bases inside Red China to be attacked for fear that the relatively limited conflict in Korea would escalate into World War III.

At the same time, the pilots knew that there *had* been some covert attacks on Red China, both in Manchuria and the mainland's easternmost coast.

"Sounds like someone is planning a Black Op," Evers said.

The doctor replied in the affirmative. "It will be a very dangerous mission," he said. "And one that, if found out, will have worldwide implications. Should anyone get caught, they will be immediately disavowed and left to twist in the wind, as the saying goes."

Hughes was quick to catch on. "They want us to fly it, don't they?" he said.

Litke nodded. "Escort and bombers," he replied. "In return, the investigation into your role in Stormcloud will be forgotten, there will be no court-martials, and your commissions will be returned."

"Christ, these Pentagon guys are cute, aren't they?" Kenneally said angrily. "They'll absolve you of taking part in an unauthorized mission if you agree to fly another one that's just as risky."

"This is war, gentlemen," Litke said by way of explanation. "More wheels turn than one person can ever hope to learn about. Some of the things I've seen in my job I still can't believe, and I'm sure my office only sees a small part of what actually goes on."

Evers shrugged. Typically, he barged right to the point. "So we fly over Manchuria, flatten the base, make sure the Sabre goes up in flames, and scoot," he said. "Then we're heroes again."

"Correct except on one point, Major," Litke said. "The base isn't in Manchuria. Nor is it on the Chinese mainland itself.

"It's at Vladivostok, inside Soviet territory. . . ."

41

THE ATTACK ON THE air base at Vladivostok two nights later caught the Soviets completely by surprise.

Earlier in the evening, radar operators at the sprawling airfield just north of the Soviet-Manchurian border had picked up an unidentified aircraft flying fifty miles off the coast. Its large radar signature indicated it was an RB-36, a reconnaissance version of the U.S. Air Force's huge B-36 bomber.

This in itself was not unusual: Soviet intelligence had known that four RB-36s had been flown from Fairchild AFB in the U.S. to Yokota, Japan, early in December. Since then the enormous airplanes had been spotted at various times flying extremely high over the Yalu, over Manchuria, and, on at least two occasions, over the eastern coast of the Soviet Union itself. Despite picking up the RB-36s on their radar, there was little the Soviets could do about the big American recon bomber. By the time the recon planes were spotted and MiGs scrambled, the RB-36—with its sensitive radio-monitoring equipment able to detect any MiG activity at the base—would already be out of Soviet airspace and heading full speed toward Japan. Not wanting to cause a diplomatic incident that would definitely bear unwanted fruit, the Soviets chose not to send their interceptors anywhere near Japanese airspace.

On this particular night, when the RB-36 was first detected, the officer in charge of radar at the Vladivostok base told his operators to simply track the big plane and fill out a report on its behavior. Two radar operators were assigned to the task, and for the next thirty minutes they watched as the large radar blip went into a slightly oval flight pattern, circling out over the northern Sea of Japan.

At one point, the RB-36 dropped off the radar sets completely, at first leading the Soviet radar men to suppose it had finally turned for home. But when the large blip reappeared on their screens less than a minute later, the radar men concluded that the RB-36 had, for whatever reason, simply descended to a lower altitude for a few moments.

For the next five minutes, the blip zig-zagged back and forth across the radar screen, at times getting very close to the Soviet coast, and finally dropping off the radar screen completely. At this point, the radar operators summoned their officer, and after reporting the RB-36's odd behavior, all three theorized that the airplane might have crashed at sea.

They heard the first sounds of the attack several minutes later.

Two U.S. Marine F3D-2N Skynights were the first to roar in over the Soviet airfield, to the complete shock of the base personnel.

The Skyknights, as well as the other four aircraft in the strike force, had fooled the Soviet radar men by flying in close formation and thereby mimicking the large radar signature of the RB-36. Now, before the defenders could react, both of the night-fighters dropped a string of incendiary devices on the rows of MiGs stretched out on the Vladivostok flightline before streaking away into the night.

Next came two B-45C Tornado jet bombers, one piloted by Hughes, the other by Evers. Each airplane was carrying a pair of 1,000-pound Razon-100 radio-guided bombs. Hughes's target were two administrative buildings hard by the base's main runway. U.S. Air Force intelligence had pegged these buildings as the location for the stolen Sabre performance data. Evers's bomber was to strike at a large hangar on the outskirts of the base. A recon photo taken by a ground-based CIA operative two days before showed the captured Sabre to be housed in the isolated aircraft barn.

While these bombing attacks were taking place, Kenneally and Spencer would circle the base in F-86B Sabres, fighters especially adapted for long-range flight. Should any MiGs miss being caught up in the conflagration caused by the Skyknights' fire bombing and actually get airborne, it would be up to Kenneally and Spencer to deal with them.

The Razon-100 bombs were the latest in the Air Force's weapons and technology. Dubbed the first of the "smart bombs," the Razon-100 had a unique guidance mechanism in its tail section. Once the bomb was released, the bombardier could eyeball the weapon to its target by using radio signals to manipulate its fins. What differentiated the Razon-100 from the standard Razon guided bomb was that the 100 had a small but powerful lamp in its nose, thus allowing the bomb to be used at night.

As planned, Hughes came in on his target first. Holding the B-45C as steady as humanly possible, he signaled his nose-housed bombardier as soon as he spotted the first target building.

"Five seconds," he called to the bombardier, who, like the other three crewmen on the B-45C, was a volunteer. "Four . . . three . . . two . . . one . . . go!"

There was a corresponding jolt as the first half-ton bomb dropped from the bomb-bay and began its guided descent toward the target. Turning to the right just after the Razon-100 was released, Hughes watched as the bomb almost magically performed several maneuvers—two long, left-hand curves and a sharp jink to the right—its fins obeying the radio commands being sent by the bombardier. Then seconds after release, the bomb slammed into the side of the snow-covered red-brick building, its large high-explosive warhead detonating on impact.

Hughes was surprised that despite the scream of his jet engines, he was still able to hear the loud, sharp report resulting from the explosion.

"Good work!" he called down to his bombardier. "Looks like you put it right on the bull's eye."

Pulling up and to the right, Hughes had to do a quick climb in order to avoid Evers's B-45C, which was barreling in over the line of burning MiGs, heading toward the isolated hangar. Hughes watched as the first Razon-100 flew out from under Evers's Tornado, following a somewhat ragged course to its target. The bomb landed about ten feet from the front entrance to the aircraft barn, exploding in an instant and ripping the doors from the structure.

It was a good hit—but not quite good enough. No sooner had the Razon landed short of its target, than Evers had put the B-45C practically on its tail and into a turn to bring it back around for a second try.

Meanwhile, Hughes pressed in on his second target, a smaller admin building about a quarter-mile from the first. Bringing the B-45C down to 1,000 feet, he neatly dodged the flames and smoke from his first target and once again counted down the release point for the bombardier.

At the word "Go!" the bombardier let the second Razon-100 fly, this time putting it through a series of gyrations as a gust of wind played havoc with it in its first few seconds of flight.

The man in the nose finally regained control and flew the 1,000-pound smart bomb right into a second-story window. It exploded two seconds later with such force that the building immediately collapsed in on itself with a great rush of fire and smoke.

At this point, two MiGs had been able to get off the ground—but just barely. Kenneally and Spencer, watching the action from 5,000 feet, pounced on the Soviet jets before their pilots were even able to retract their wheels. First one, then the other were shredded by the concentrated fire from the night-equipped Sabres. Both MiGs smashed into the end of the runway, not ten feet from each other. No other Soviet planes attempted to take off after that.

By this time, Evers had steered his Tornado bomber back around and was screaming in toward his target. Once again, Hughes was able to watch as the second Razon-100 dropped out from the bottom of his friend's B-45C and made a beeline for the targeted hangar.

The drop was so accurate, Evers's bombardier hardly had to guide the weapon. It literally flew right into the opening of the aircraft barn caused by the detonation of the first bomb and exploded with a tremendous blast. As

Evers's jet pulled up through the smoke and fire it had created, Hughes could see its tail gunner firing his twin Browning machine guns into the instantly burning structure, just to make sure.

"Okay," Hughes heard Evers yell into his radio, "this party's over! Let's get the hell out of here!"

No one in the strike force needed further prompting. With the two Sabres in the lead, the four airplanes formed up and immediately headed for the open sea at full throttle.

As planned, Hughes set a prearranged radio signal back to the Yokota base, indicating the targets had been hit. Then as they approached international air space, he leaned back and relaxed for the first time in two days. He knew that if the administrative buildings had indeed housed the important Sabre data, then that data was now certainly destroyed. Likewise, if the captured F-86 was where the ground-intelligence people said it was, then it too was in all probability damaged beyond repair.

Reaching the coast and the relative safety of the open Sea of Japan, Hughes glanced back to see Evers's B-45C just fifty feet off his port wing. His mind flashed back to a conversation he had had with his friend the night before the mission. The normally rambunctious Evers had admitted over a few beers that he was thinking of settling down when he returned to the states. Get a pretty wife, buy a nice new house in a nice new tract neighborhood, and do some honest work for a change.

It had been an amazing revelation from a free-wheeling confirmed bachelor like Evers. Now, looking back at the second B-45C, Hughes was intrigued about how attractive that kind of life sounded. He watched as his fellow pilot snapped on his navigational lights and started blinking them madly. Hughes reached down and likewise snapped his nav lights off and on, returning the gesture.

But when he turned around to see Evers's reaction, he was shocked to see that his friend's jet was gone. . . .

Part Two

Men and Machines

42

Edwards Air Force Base, California
Five Years Later

"ARE YOU PACKED IN?" the voice in the headphones asked.

"Yes," Hughes answered, whispering to himself, *"Just light the goddamn thing . . ."*

"One moment," the voice told him. There was a short pause, then the voice said, "We've just been issued another wind delay."

"Damn!" Hughes muttered, realizing he'd spoken loud enough to be heard over the microphone. "How long?" he asked anxiously.

"Wind's back up to fifteen knots," the voice replied. "Specs say we can't light above thirteen-two."

"So, what should I do?" Hughes asked sternly. "I've been crammed in here for two and a half hours."

There was a burst of static, then the voice returned.

"Control says just sit tight. . . . Over."

It had already been a strange day for Hughes and it wasn't yet noon.

Originally the rocket-sled test had been scheduled for 0845, when the winds around Edwards Air Force Base were at their lowest and the temperature was a respectable 70°. But just as Hughes was being strapped into the contraption, an unexpected high front had blown in from the Pacific and delayed the test. First it was only supposed to be an hour wait. But then it became two hours, and now it was approaching three.

All this delay made Hughes uncomfortable. One of the most unpleasant side effects of his Korean service was that he now had a hard time tolerating dark, cramped spaces. And the rocket sled's compartment was a dark and cramped space.

Another burst of static snapped him out of his spell.

"Wind is at thirteen-nine and dropping," he was told. "Recheck pack . . ."

"Will you forget the frigging pack?" Hughes finally snapped at the young control officer. "The pack was secure when I climbed into this sardine can three god-damn hours ago."

"Roger," came the timid reply.

It was Hughes's fourth time on the high-speed rocket sled and the previous three rides had been as compli-cated and frustrating as this. This bothered him—he hated wasting time. Back in the old days, when he was just a simple test pilot, he would have flown a dozen aircraft prototype tests in the time it had taken just preparing him to ride the sled a handful of times.

Though he had to admit that once the damn thing was lit, it was one hell of a show.

The sled was designed to test a pilot's endurance to high-speed flight, velocities faster than any current jet aircraft could attain. As such, it was one of the first pieces of equipment located at the famous Edwards base that was tied *directly* to programs above and beyond those dealing with rocket- and jet-powered atmospheric flight. The data resulting from the sled's operation was not being evaluated for flight within Earth's cozy confines. It was, in fact, being studied for flights in outer space.

Hughes had always dreamed of one day flying in space, or at least being part of America's emerging space pro-gram. But never did the vision include his being assigned to Edwards. After all his years as part of the Experimen-tal Test Squadron at Mescalero Air Force Base, being transferred to Edwards was like being traded by the Brooklyn Dodgers to the crosstown rival Yankees. The animosity between the test pilots at the popularly known Edwards and those at super-secret Mescalero was so intense that fistfights broke out each and every time members of the two sides met, whether it was in their favorite off-base bar or in some neutral saloon elsewhere.

But now Hughes was working for the enemy.

After his service in Korea ended in late 1950, he had returned to Mescalero and went back to the fairly routine life of being a test pilot. Between 1951 and 1953, he had flown more than twenty experimental aircraft, some successful, some not. He had had some close calls, but that was his job: to get into perilous situations and then figure a way out of them.

As soon as the Korean War had finally dragged to a halt and the country returned to peace once again, Hughes began testing airplanes that were not totally for military design, something that pleased him to no end. He had never been comfortable with his role as a combination test pilot *and* a flier of secret missions. He had been in two wars now and had come to hate the entire concept. He had seen friends die; he had killed others himself. His service in Korea had left many scars—his lingering fear of dark places being one. He had also had more than his usual share of nightmares since the war, most of them centering around the last tragic mission to Vladivostok and the loss of his close friend Gabe Evers.

His service in Korea had also cost him his relationship with Molly, the only woman, he had convinced himself, that he could ever settle down with. He never saw her again after returning from Korea. She was five years gone now, living back in her native England and, at last report, married to a member of the British Foreign Service. There had been other women for him since— barmaids mostly—but none even coming close to Molly. So he felt himself suffering from several wounds that would not heal, and it seemed that war—or, more accurately, military actions—were the root cause. It had also aged him beyond his years. There were times when he felt like an old man before he had even reached the age of thirty.

But being assigned to Edwards had changed all that.

At last, here was a program that had nothing to do with faster and better ways to kill. Here was a program whose goals—no matter how far off in the future they may be—were aimed at discovery, knowledge, heightening man's awareness of the universe around him. By riding the high-g rocket sled, Hughes was able to tell himself that he was contributing to the day that the first man went into outer space; the day the first man went into orbit; the day the first man stepped on the moon. He would be part of it, and at least a small piece of his life's dream—to fly in space himself—would come true.

It was Jack Kenneally, his former colleague and now the junior senator from Massachusetts, who first informed Hughes about the small, incremental Edwards program, dubbed Project Libra. Through his Washington connections, Kenneally had learned that the National Advisory Committee on Aeronautics—NACA—needed one highly skilled pilot to work in Project Libra's initial phase, someone who was not part of Edwards's rocket-plane program. As the best test pilot at Mescalero, Hughes may have seemed the logical choice.

However, there was the matter of his court-martial in 1946 for assaulting an officer and his apparently permanent reduction in rank—he'd been a captain for nearly ten years. Then there was the stickiness of his involvement in the infamous Operation Stormcloud, though the daring yet tragic air raid of Vladivostok had officially wiped his record clean.

Although it was widely known that the NACA wanted its recruit to be squeaky-clean, Kenneally suggested that Hughes volunteer for Project Libra anyway, promising that he'd use his own influence and that of his powerful, recently retired father to get him in. Hughes agreed and began the long process of applying for the Project. So it was with great surprise that he learned via a telegram from Washington just several days after he'd applied that the Air Force had already assigned him to the project.

He'd been at it for nearly a year now.

There had been much classroom work at first, tortuous for someone like him who had just barely graduated high school. Then began two weeks of physical examinations, during which he'd been poked and prodded by a battalion of doctors and space-flight researchers. More classroom instruction followed. Then he underwent a series of endurance programs. There were splash tests, which recorded his endurance underwater. There were heat tests, during which he was put into a high-temperature steam chamber and cooked to well done. He spent time in a decompression chamber, which mercilessly sucked air out of its confines until the human guinea pig cried uncle. And there were the isolation tests, during which he was locked in a single-room cell for a week at a time, with nothing more than a wash basin and a toilet.

Only after these tests did his NACA handlers deem him ready to actually strap into some equipment.

The NACA had two whiz-bang gizmos at Edwards: the rocket sled and the Centron, which was a centrifugal-force machine. He hated the Centron. He hated how it looked (like a carnival ride gone mad), he hated how it felt (both greasy and sticky), he hated how it smelled (a combination of hydraulic fluid and vomit). A typical test would find him strapped into the machine's capsule and spun around and around at speeds so fast that the word *dizzy* didn't even come close to describing the state of his physical and mental condition. These sessions were murder on his ears, his jaws, and especially his stomach: Prior to each test, he had to go without food or water for twenty-four hours, a restriction he found annoying but one wisely instituted.

But the reason he preferred the more dangerous rocket sled to the safer but jarring whirly-bug centrifuge was that at least the sled *went* somewhere. He moved in it from one place to another. It was against his nature to just go round and round.

Still, despite all the twirling and sled riding, the strangest test that Hughes had to endure involved working with the NACA's food-testing workshop (FTW). Staffed by a crew of four, the FTW was a combination cafeteria and laboratory, where all kinds of bizarrely condensed foods were manufactured, the kinds that would eventually go into space with America's first space pilots. Every other day, after having his stomach stretched like a balloon and his lungs turned to leather, Hughes would dine on the likes of scrambled-egg cubes for breakfast, bacon-lettuce-and-tomato cubes for lunch, and steak-with-mushroom-gravy cubes for dinner. The odd thing was that the cubes—as weird and unappetizing as they appeared to the eye—actually tasted like the real thing. At least they did at first.

Despite the peculiarities, Hughes was excited about partaking in Project Libra. However, there was one other major sacrifice demanded in return. His flying time—the life blood of any test pilot—had been cut to nothing.

The reason the NACA and the Air Force had given Hughes for the cutback was that they now looked upon him as an investment. Time and money were being spent on him as part of Project Libra, and they did not want to risk having him plow into the desert floor during some routine jet flight. If that happened, they would have to find another "volunteer," spend more money, and start back at square one.

All of Project Libra's equipment installed at Edwards was new—in design and manufacture. Therefore during the initial phase, a lot of bugs had to be worked out. In NACA parlance, "debugging" was just another way of saying that intolerable delays, frustrating duplications of effort, and long periods of uncomfortable situations were forthcoming.

The rocket sled was particularly moody. Basically a chair with a liquid-fuel rocket engine on its back and attached to five miles of straight rails, the sled never seemed to want to work right the first time. It was always something: too much wind, too much sand in the air, too much heat. Fuel was too "wet"; fuel was too "dry"; fuel was leaking; fuel was giving off vapors—on and on, like the goddamn machine were inventing reasons on its own for not working. As a result, Hughes had spent more time sitting immobile in the rocket sled than he did sitting immobile at the officer's club and sitting immobile in front of his TV combined. He would occasionally convince himself that all this immobility, along with the lack of real flying, was turning his stomach into a bubbling cauldron of heartburn and nervous indigestion.

But then again, he would reason, maybe it was just the bad hamburger cubes.

"We've got a count," the control officer finally told Hughes at precisely noon. "We are at sixty seconds."

"It's about time," Hughes whispered, taking a deep breath and settling in to the sled's cramped, uncomfortable seat.

He lowered the visor on his helmet, and now the five miles of track that stretched out into the desert before him became dark and hard to see. If everything went all right, he would cover four-fifths of its full length—a distance of 21,840 feet—at full speed in a matter of seconds.

If something went wrong, he would be forced to pull his ejection cord and activate "the Pack," an explosive charge that would blast him clear of the malfunctioning sled (theoretically, at least) and carry him via a parachute to safety. Should that happen, it would be his first real flying in months.

"We are at fifteen seconds," the control officer said. "All check?"

"All check," Hughes called back.

"Ignition at ten seconds," the control officer continued as Hughes braced himself. "Mark now at one, two, three, four . . ."

At that moment, Hughes's mind for some reason flashed an image of the departed Gabe Evers. It was four years to the day that the Air Force had finally declared him KIA—killed in action—and so much had happened since he had been lost.

What would he have thought of all this? Hughes wondered.

"Five . . . six seconds . . ."

Hughes hunkered down further in his seat, ready for the blast, but then he happened to glance down at his feet. Was that a loose wire coming out of the bottom of the ejection package?

"Seven . . . eight . . ."

Jesus, I hope the Pack is okay, Hughes thought as the

control officer called out, "Nine . . . ten . . . we are at *ignition* . . ."

There was an ear-splitting explosion as the rocket engine erupted and the fuel lit off. Two seconds later, Hughes was hurtling down the rails in excess of 100 mph, his speed increasing exponentially. He felt his face instantly tighten back to a grotesque smile as the g-forces slammed against his body. His stomach began to deflate as his speed continued to increase. His chest started to ache, then his neck, then his butt, then his groin. The legs were next: They became heavy and leaden, cutting off all feeling from his toes.

As he passed the halfway mark, his teeth began to ache excruciatingly and his breathing became officially "labored." His eyes became teary, and he couldn't prevent a long stream of drool from involuntarily escaping through his lips. As always, he thought he was going to wet himself. But by working the muscles in that area he was able to hold it.

By this time he was traveling at 2,000 mph. The rails, the desert, the mountains beyond had disappeared by now—all that remained was a kind of purple blur and, oddly enough, stars before his eyes. Not just random patterns either—Hughes was convinced he could see definite constellations and stellar groupings in the split-second flash of stars that always seemed to hit his corneas near maximum velocity. When he mentioned it to one of the Project Libra physicians, the doctor told him the stars were a result of his increased blood pressure playing tricks with his eyes, nothing else.

But in this case, Hughes knew better.

Finally he heard the friendly click of the rocket motor shutting off and its parachute deploying. Gradually he began to slow down. Another half-mile and the sled was traveling at just 50 mph. His proper vision restored, he could see the gaggle of trucks and support vehicles waiting for him at the end of the test line. His neck, chest, stomach, legs, hands, fingers, toes, groin, jaw, teeth, kidneys, and bladder stopped aching more or less at the same time, and he had stopped drooling. The adrenaline was still pleasant pumping through his body, though, and by the time he'd slowed to a halt, he was vibrating with an energy that bordered on downright exhilaration.

"How'd it go, Captain?" the first man to reach him, a civilian NACA employee, asked.

"Great," Hughes replied. "I saw Pegasus, Orion, and the Little Dipper today."

43

Mescalero Air Force Base, New Mexico

MORE THAN 800 MILES to the east of Edwards, at the headquarters for Mescalero Air Base, a package wrapped in rotting electrical tape was placed on the base commander's desk.

"Just came in, sir," the commander's aide, a lieutenant, told him. "Looks like it's been in the water quite a while."

The base commander, General Dante Capote Xavier, ran his hand along the package and then squeezed the plastic fibers that came off between his fingers.

"It's amazing it held up so long," he said.

"The intelligence guys at Yokota made copies of a lot of the original stuff, sir," the lieutenant said, handing Xavier a crisper, drier package of documents. "They also included their analysis. It's printed on the blue paper."

Xavier checked his watch. He was a nervous and busy man and didn't have the time now to plow through the documents.

"I'm assuming you read the analysis, Lieutenant," he said. "What was their conclusion?"

"There's no doubt about it, sir," the aide replied. "It's a complete record of MiG-15 combat capabilities, compiled by persons unknown during a ten-day stretch sometime early in the Korean conflict."

"How early?"

The lieutenant shrugged. "The intelligence officers guess it was around November or December of 1950," he said. "Definitely early in the Chinese intervention . . ."

Xavier was out of his chair and putting on his uniform jacket. He had an important surprise briefing to conduct for the test pilots at the base. Still, he took a moment to flip through the copies of the documents that had been found in the semiwatertight package.

"This would have been very valuable information five years ago," he said. "My question is, will it help us out now?"

The lieutenant, a man aspiring to be a captain, nodded enthusiastically. "It will, sir," he said. "In my initial perusal, I identified several instances in which the 'human factor' was definitely a hindrance to the operation of the aircraft. Elements such as increased weight for life-support systems, load problems stemming from the ejection-seat mechanisms, large radio sets, extra weight for duplicated controls . . ."

Xavier held up his hand, indicating the man should stop.

"Don't ruin it for me," he said, his voice bordering on giddy. "I want to read it all myself. But right now, I have to skip."

"I understand, sir," the toady lieutenant interrupted. "Your car is waiting outside."

"Thank you, Lieutenant," Xavier said. "And while I'm gone, I want you to go over the copied text and underline every instance of 'human factor' troubles you can find. Is that clear?"

"Perfectly, sir," the lieutenant boomed.

Xavier walked over to the full-length mirror hanging on one of his walls and adjusted his jacket to his plump, almost girlish body. Then he placed his cap on his slightly balding head, tipping it slightly to the right as always. Finally, he slapped his face twice, hard, and smiled as the resulting red in his cheeks appeared. Deeming the crimson shade appropriately healthy looking, he turned to go.

"One more thing, Lieutenant," he said, momentarily stopping at the office door. "Slap a classified number on all that stuff. We don't want the wrong person reading it."

Captain Chas Spencer got word of Xavier's surprise briefing just as he was driving through Main Gate 3B at Mescalero. He had been off-duty for most of the morning and had used the time to make a long-overdue visit to the grave of General Cornelius Jones.

Jones had been the commander of the Mescalero test-pilot squadron until his sudden death—cause unknown—in 1950. A hero in the eyes of many during the 1940s, at the time of his command at Mescalero, Jones was the oldest and most experienced test pilot in the Air Force. He was also the most respected.

It was odd, then, that the country he had served so well had chosen to kill him.

It had happened just days after the sixty-five-year-old senior officer had returned from Washington, D.C., after appearing before the secret Congressional Committee on Subversive Activities. Despite his outstanding record of service to the country and to the advancement of its aeronautical technology, Jones had been labeled a communist by the heebie-jeebie politicians at the height of the Red Scare. His crime? He had flown for the Loyalists—and *against* the fascists—during the Spanish Civil War. And although many Americans had chosen this path in the late 1930s to combat the growing trend of authoritarianism around the world—a trend that would envelop the globe in fire and death just a few years later—the hysterical Red hunters in the U.S. government had paradoxically decided that fighting against fascism was akin to being a communist. For all intents and purposes, Jones had been convicted without trial, without a defense, without even knowing who all his accusers had been.

They found him slumped over in the cockpit of an F-80 jet early one morning, already cold and dead. (Oddly, several people would later swear they'd seen him take off and fly to the west, but they had obviously been mistaken.) The doctor who examined the body found no evidence of heart attack or stroke or any kind of seizure. He had simply died. Was it from a broken spirit? A broken heart? the doctor was asked by more than one friend of Jones. The doctor could only shake his head. He just didn't know.

Spencer had been on his way back to Korea when it happened, but between his involvement in the Operation Stormcloud affair and the isolation of the house arrest that followed, he didn't learn of the general's death until three days after the secret bombing of the MiG base at Vladivostok.

Ironically, it had been the same day that he, Kenneally, and Hughes had learned that the Air Force had given up looking for Gabe Evers and his B-45C crew. Because of the sensitive nature of the Vladivostok attack and Evers's last-reported position being so close to Soviet territory, the air-sea rescue operation had been ordered to perform only a rudimentary search. This they did for forty-eight hours, with one seaplane and one patrol boat. No wreckage was found, and the search was hastily called off on the morning of the third day.

That the air strike on the Soviet base had been a success did little to make up for the loss of the happy-go-lucky Evers, and in the ensuing years, Spencer and the others thought of him often. After being officially declared KIA, the Air Force had promised to erect a memorial stone on his behalf at the small combined-services military cemetery located about halfway between the Mescalero base and the city of Alamogordo, something it took them nearly four years to do.

Spencer had seen Evers's memorial for the first time that morning, surprised but happy that it had been placed so close to the tombstone of General Jones. But the visit to the cemetery had been too emotional for Spencer. He was the only original test pilot left at the Mescalero base and, as such, he felt like he alone carried the burden of the squadron's outstanding though controversial past. More than Evers or Kenneally or even Hughes, General Jones had been responsible for the unit's success, as well as Spencer's development as a test pilot. As such, the young pilot felt he should have known that the visit to the cemetery would have affected him as much as it did.

As it turned out, another person had chosen to visit

the graves that day. A person who, but by a quirk of the cosmos, should have been in a third grave.

The man was Grady "Bill" Curtiss, one of the original test pilots selected for the Mescalero squadron in the closing days of World War II. Curtiss, an English professor before the war, was such an unlikely candidate for the rigorous Mescalero program that many—maybe even including himself—believed the then-revolutionary UniVax computer that selected the original pilots had made a mistake in drawing his name. He had stuck with it, though, through a multitude of professional and emotional trials—problems compounded by those of his alcoholic, drug-addicted, frequently institutionalized wife, Maggie.

When Spencer happened upon Curtiss, sitting by the graves that morning, he didn't recognize the man at first. After a long ordeal in the desert following a near fatal crash back in the autumn of 1950, Curtiss had spent six months in the hospital recuperating from such maladies as sunstroke, kidney problems, serious dehydration, gangrene, septic poisoning, and numerous insect bites. Once released, Curtiss had been given a medical discharge from the Air Force and was awarded a full pension according to his last-held rank, which was that of a major.

Even before his airplane crash, Curtiss had been immersed in the culture of the Mescalero Apaches, many of whom lived on a reservation nearby and from which the air base got its name. Once recovered, Curtiss embraced the Mescaleros totally, moving to the depressing and bleak reservation, living in one of its shacks, and eventually being made an official member of the tribe.

So when he first saw the man wearing two long braids and typical Apache clothes, sitting crosslegged between Jones's tombstone and Gabe Evers's memorial, Spencer thought he was just another drunken Indian who had flopped in the graveyard the night before. Spencer's mistake was sad but understandable. Many of the Mescaleros were alcoholics, and it wasn't unusual to see them sleeping on the side of the road or foraging through garbage cans or panhandling in the streets of Bent, New Mexico, the nearest town to the air base and the reservation.

It was Curtiss who first recognized Spencer, even though they hadn't seen each other in years. There was an uncomfortable embrace—Spencer knew that Curtiss had never fully recovered from his tribulations, and his eyes were just as crazy as the last time he'd seen him—and their brief conversation was typically bizarre.

Spencer had little to ask the poor soul except about the health of his wife, Maggie. Curtiss told him she'd become a performer—a ballet dancer, in fact—and Spencer chose to believe him. He knew Maggie, who had been a college professor before she and Curtiss came to live at Mescalero, to be a very intelligent and cultured person, despite being a highly troubled one.

Feeling emotional and ill at ease, Spencer quickly paid his respects to the memories of both Jones and Evers and then decided to cut his visit short. He was very uncomfortable in the presence of Curtiss—the man was obviously unbalanced. Still, it was hard just to leave—Curtiss rambled on and on about some mystical Indian nonsense—and try as he might, the young pilot could not just break in, interrupt him, and walk away.

Finally, he saw his opportunity when, upon checking the time, he told Curtiss he had to return to the base. Curtiss hugged him again and bowed to him, chanting something in what Spencer could only guess was Apache.

Then Curtiss took up his position between the two graves and began laughing.

"I come here almost every day," he told Spencer. "And I laugh every time."

Spencer knew he should have left it at that—leave the crazy men to their ways and never ask questions—but he couldn't help but wonder why Curtiss found sitting on the graves of his two colleagues to be so amusing. So he asked him.

"I do it," Curtiss was happy to answer, "because neither one of them is really dead."

44

SPENCER SLID INTO A last-row seat just seconds before Xavier's surprise briefing was scheduled to begin.

Thankful that he'd made it in time, he stopped a moment to catch his breath, having double-timed it to the briefing building.

"You know, this really reminds me of high school," he said to the pilot next to him. "We had a real joker for a principal."

"Oh yeah?" the man replied. "What'd he smell like?"

"Can't remember exactly," Spencer told him. "Not as bad as the X-Man, though."

Suddenly Spencer straightened up in his seat and took two more deep sniffs. A few of the fifty or so pilots in the briefing room did the same thing.

"Here he comes," someone up front said.

No sooner were the words out than General Xavier— the X-Man—appeared at the room's side entrance. The assembled pilots immediately leapt to their feet, goaded on by a kiss-ass who yelled, *"Ten-shun!"*

Xavier walked in, stepped up onto the stage, and placed a handful of notes in its lectern, all the while virtually ignoring the roomful of ramrod-straight pilots.

"Would someone please light the candles?" he said, still not bothering to look up. "The official number is twenty-two. . . ."

Immediately, three front-row pilots had their cigarette lighters out and flaming. There was an almost comical rush toward the small candle stand located off to the right of the lectern, the men actually elbowing each other

195

out of the way. In a matter of seconds, twenty-two of the red novena candles were lit.

"All right," Xavier said, all but ignoring the display of self-promotion. "Now please, someone dim the lights. . . ."

The lights were dimmed drastically, and the pilots' briefing room took on the aura of a very small church.

Everyone knew that Xavier had taken the candle stand and several boxes of the small red novena candles from the base chapel, though the general would never admit to actually *stealing* the items. The base chaplain, a Catholic priest in a sea of mostly Protestant pilots, had discovered the candle stand and the candles missing one morning and had loudly notified the MPs of the theft. He was later humiliated to learn that the items had turned up in the pilots' briefing room, with Xavier claiming he'd sent a memo to the chaplain weeks before, informing him that he intended to "appropriate" the candle stand and suggesting that the chaplain requisition a new one.

The real reason for Xavier wanting the candle stand in the briefing room was, at best, as eccentric as the man himself. Each time a test pilot was killed at the base, Xavier would call a briefing and solemnly light another novena candle. That candle would then join all the others lit before every regular briefing "in memory of the departed souls." The more "dedicated" pilots believed the ceremony to be appropriate. Unofficially, the more cynical pilots believed the whole thing was a sham—just Xavier's cruel way of reminding them what a dangerous business they were all in. (As if they needed further reminders!) That fit more into the man's make-up than some kind of solemn remembrance for twenty-two pilots whom the General had never attempted to get to know while they were still alive.

But whatever the reason, in the three years of Xavier's command, the count was up to twenty-two candles. This was not really an unusually high number of deaths—in fact, Mescalero's safety record was among the best of any of the various services' test-pilot squadrons.

However the whole candle controversy had taken a strange turn several months before when Xavier started dimming the lights after lighting the candles. It was a stroke of genius on his part—the combination of the flickering flames and the darkened room really gave the place an authentic and weird atmosphere reminiscent of a church service. It also gave the base commander the undivided attention of most of those in attendance.

"At ease, gentlemen," Xavier finally told the pilots, many of them now going numb after standing at attention for so long. "Please be seated. . . ."

Once everyone had been settled, Xavier looked up for the first time. A wave of his obscenely overapplied Burma Shave cologne broke from the lectern at this point and, aided by the artificial wind created by the heat from the candles, wafted none too gently out into the room. As always, there were a few sneezes, a few coughs.

"Gentlemen, we've had what I call a reasonably good week," he began. "For the first time in quite a while, we do not have to light a candle for one of our departed colleagues. However, I want you all to gaze upon those twenty-two candles you see before you and remember that each one represents a human life. A soul, now moved on to Heaven.

"Exactly how they died is not important now—to them. But it is important to you. A few of them died as a result of accidents, malfunctions of the equipment. However, we all know that many more died because of what we like to call the 'human factor.' Human factor equals human *error*, gentlemen, the one incidental that cannot be factored out of the sophisticated and dangerous equipment it is our thankless duty to test."

Xavier looked out on the first row of pilots and counted a suitable number of dutifully impressed facial expressions.

"I believe it is an essential part of my command to remind everyone here of some gruesome numbers," Xavier intoned, his voice rising slightly in pitch. "Twenty-five percent of you will die some time during your tour of duty here. That's one in four.

"I ask you to look around you, gentlemen. Count the three people sitting next to you. In two years, only one of two things can happen: Either one of them will be dead or you'll be dead. It's that simple."

The hush that now descended on the room was like lead.

"More numbers, gentlemen," Xavier continued after the properly timed dramatic pause. "Fifty percent of you will have to eject from your aircraft at some point. Of that number, one out of three will suffer a serious injury, whether it be to your knees, elbows, shoulders . . . However, most injuries incurred during ejection involve the skull—be it a fracture or a serious concussion—or the spinal column, usually a complete snap. In the one of three who suffer the serious head or spinal-cord injury, more than half will be paralyzed for life or injured to the extent that their brain will not function beyond the level of a chimpanzee's. Either way, it's not a promising prospect.

"All this is to remind you gentlemen of what you must face every day. To that end, I hope you will join me in a prayer now. A prayer for the twenty-two men killed here in the last thirty-six months. A prayer that Our Lord will smile gentler on this place. A prayer that some day soon, our leaders will find the solution to all this needless death . . .

"So, gentlemen, let us pray. . . .

About half the pilots—the ass-kissers and "heroes" seated in the first few rows of seats—immediately bowed their heads. The remainder—the nonbelievers who were hidden in the middle-to-last rows of seats where Xavier could not possibly see them in the darkened room—were simply relieved that the morbid briefing was drawing to a close.

As for Spencer, being anchored in the very last row, he neither prayed nor hid. He had fallen asleep soon after the briefing had begun.

45

Clover Leaf, New Mexico

THE MAN THEY CALLED Snake was in his office counting the number of bottles in his latest shipment of bourbon when one of his waitresses yelled back to him from the bar.

"That broad you've been expecting is here, Snake."

"She ain't supposed to be here for another hour," Snake hollered back. "I'm busy. Tell her to cool her butt."

Snake went back to counting the whiskey bottles, upset that the woman had taken it upon herself to show up so early. What was it with dames these days? he wondered, discovering that his distributor had routinely shorted him one bottle in one of the bourbon cases. Broads were smoking now and drinking and wearing pants. And making demands! Give me this and give me that. *Me, me, me.*

Snake opened the last case and, once again, found only eleven bottles.

"Dames is getting uglier, too," he mumbled to himself, bold words from a man who'd come upon his nickname by way of his distinct reptilian features.

He sat back down at his dilapidated desk and scribbled out a misspelled note to his distributor, accusing him of shortchanging Snake's Cafe by four bottles of whiskey— twice the actual number. Then, as always, he tucked his Colt six-shooter inside his belt and went out front to the bar.

It was only eight in the morning, and the place was empty except for the waitress and the woman who was waiting at one of the corner tables. Her back was to him, so he was in for a surprise when he blustered over to her and she turned and he saw that she was absolutely gorgeous.

"You are Mr. Shagg?" she asked.

"The one and only," he answered quickly, using his pat line but this time just a few degrees below his usual level of haughtiness. He was simply thrown by her beauty. She had luxuriant red hair that was past her shoulders and lovely white skin. Her face was that of a movie star, and from what he could see of her figure, hidden as it was behind a rather heavy green jacket and skirt, it was right up there with the ones in his skin magazines.

"You were expecting me," she said.

"Yeah, I was," he said, sitting down and lighting a cigarette. Uncharacteristically, he offered her one and she took it.

"Was it Ronny who told you about me or Ken?" she asked, taking a deep puff from the cigarette.

"Ronny," Snake answered. "Ronny over at Alamogordo."

She smiled for the first time, and Snake actually felt a twinge of excitement go through him. "Did Ronny have good things to say about me?" she asked.

"Yeah, sure," Snake replied, dismissing the question. "But the only reason I called him in the first place was because I was desperate. That's when he gave me your number. . . . Said you put on a freak show or something."

Her smile disappeared in an instant. "It's not a freak show, Mr. Shagg," she said. "It's a performance."

"Yeah, well, all I want is a dancer," Snake replied. "Nothing fancy. Nothing freaky. I'm going to have a gang of people in here for a special party called Armadillo Christmas—"

She interrupted him with a beautifully sweet laugh. *"Armadillo Christmas?"* she asked. "Really?"

"It's an old cowboy tradition in these parts," Snake said, obviously upset that he had to explain it to her. "Goes back to the days of the big cattle drives when the cowhands weren't able to celebrate the real Christmas until the middle of the summer."

"So it's like a folk festival?" she asked.

"No," he grumbled. "It's like a couple hundred cowboys come in here and get rip-roaring drunk. My problem is that I need someone to entertain them."

"Don't worry," she giggled. "I'll do that."

Snake put up his hand. "Hold on," he said. "You ain't got the job yet. Ronny told me that you have some problems of your own. Personal problems. Like, what are they?"

"I don't have *any* problems," she said, her pretty face once again alternating back to sour. "None that Ronny should be talking about . . ."

Snake was starting to get upset. It was getting hot outside, and that meant that the dust on the only street in town was starting to rise up and get into his nostrils. To add to his discomfort, two jets from the Mescalero airfield fifty miles to the west had roared overhead, shaking the place to its dry-rot foundation. The combined racket of their engines stung Snake's ears.

"Look, lady," he said, while crudely twisting his finger into his right ear in an effort to clean it out, "I'll give it to you straight. It got so bad here last year that none of the regular girls will work the party. I know I'm going to have enough trouble on my hands without worrying about what you might do. So if you got any weirdo stuff in mind, then forget it."

She took a long drag of her cigarette and stared at him.

"Mr. Shagg," she began eloquently, "I have been staging my performance for six months now. I've worked for Ronny for the past three months. You trust Ronny, don't you? And I worked for Ken down in Santa Rita before that."

"I don't know anyone named Ken," Snake said, roughly blowing the hot dust out of his nose. "And I don't give a damn about what you did in Alamogordo or Santa Rita. You're almost in Texas now, lady. *West* Texas. There ain't none of those pansy airplane workers coming into this bar like you got over in Alamogordo. They're all cowboys in these parts, and they'd just as soon shoot you or me or each other if they think they ain't getting entertained."

She suddenly reached over and actually touched his

dirty hands. "Don't worry, Mr. Shagg," she said. "I promise you they'll be entertained like they've never been before."

"Well, it's either you, or I have to set up a movie projector and show the skinny movies," He said, his pulse quickening at the touch of her fingers.

"A machine? *Movies?*" she asked dramatically. "You can't compare what I do with a machine."

Snake felt her fingers tighten their grip on his hand. At that moment, two more jets screamed over the small town, once again the noise stinging Snake's ears.

"Well, what the hell is it that you do, exactly?" he asked, shouting over the fading din of the airplanes. "Ronny said it was . . . like, art stuff or something."

"It's ballet," she answered sweetly.

Snake immediately pulled his hand away from hers.

"Forget it, lady," he said, turning his slithering frame in the small chair and getting up to go. "You pull that stuff in here and those cowboys will rip this place apart. . . . And the next time I see Ronny, I'm going to punch him right in the nose for recommending you."

"No, this is special," she said, now grabbing his arm and digging in her nails, preventing him from leaving. "They'll love it. I guarantee it. . . ."

Snake shook his head and flicked his spent cigarette out through the authentic swinging saloon doors. "Lady, the only thing that is guaranteed in this world is that my exwife will make me miserable until the day I die," he said bitterly. "I'm sorry, but I'm just going to show skinny movies. . . ."

He got up and began walking away.

"Mr. Shagg," she called to him. "Please, at least give me a chance to . . . to audition. Let me show you part of the performance. Then you can decide . . ."

Snake stopped, turned, and looked back at her. From this angle he could see down the front of her jacket, just enough to determine she was wearing a black bra. That was all he needed to make him reconsider.

"Where?" he asked. "You can't just do it here."

She stood up, and for the first time he took full measure of her knock-out figure.

"You must have an office," she cooed seductively, standing so close to him he thought he could hear her heart beating. "And a record player . . ."

He nervously lit another cigarette. "Well, okay," he said. "But only because Ronny's a friend of mine . . ."

She quickly grabbed her bag of clothes and followed him to the back-room office. "You won't be disappointed," she told him.

The waitress behind the bar smiled when she heard Snake lock the door behind him. She knew the pattern. They'd be back out inside of twenty minutes. The girl would be putting her clothes back on and close to tears as she realized that she had exposed her privates to Snake and was still without a job. Then Snake would yell that he was going up to the attic to dig out the box of old dirty movies.

But this time the waitress was wrong. Snake didn't reappear for nearly an hour, during which time she could hear the strains of beautiful violin music coming from behind the closed door. When Snake finally did emerge, his face was beet-red flush and he was sweating more than usual. But, strangest of all, for a brief moment, the waitress actually saw him smiling, though in an odd kind of way.

"Get those Mexican carpenters over here, right now," he hollered at her. "We've got to build a stage."

The barmaid was so surprised, she almost asked him to repeat what he had said.

"And another thing," Snake went on, speaking faster than he had in years. "Put this woman on the payroll, right now. Give her a day's wages in advance."

"What!" the waitress exclaimed. "Pay her now?"

"I said *now*, didn't I?" Snake snapped at her. Then he turned back toward his office, where the woman was putting her clothes back on.

"Hey, honey, what's your name?" he yelled.

The voice that drifted out from the back room was sweet enough to melt even the waitress. "I go by the name of Jeannie, sometimes," she said. "Or Pamela . . ."

Two more jets went overhead, but Snake hardly heard them. He was positively beaming by this time, a confused state for him.

"No, I mean your *real* name," he called back to her. "I need it so's I can write you a check."

"Oh, in that case," the woman said, now appearing at the door, fully dressed and brushing her beautiful red hair, "it's Maggie. Maggie Curtiss."

46

THERE WAS JUST A single candle burning in Bunker 07, but it was larger and more ornate than the small novena lights in the pilots' briefing room.

"Five minutes to launch, General," the man behind the bunker's largest console said.

Xavier just nodded and, with a wave of his hand, indicated the man should continue. Sitting in his large chair up on the raised platform that looked out over the bunker control room, the general now felt a familiar excitement begin to creep up on him. This was the fourth launch in the past three and a half weeks, the eleventh launch in all. Each one felt better than the one before.

His thronelike chair was positioned in such a way that Xavier could see right out the narrow slits in the concrete bunker to the launch pad 500 feet away. Sitting on the pad next to the launch tower was Vehicle 11-98A, more commonly known as the F-98 Tomarc.

The missile—and it was a missile in the truest sense—was covered at the moment with a jungle of vinelike wires and hoses, some of which were emitting long jets of steam. The missile's long, slender fuselage was forty-seven feet tall, its deltalike wingspan just eighteen feet across. Painted shiny black, its welded stainless-steel construction reflected the blazing hot summer sunlight of the New Mexico afternoon.

The Tomarc was the Air Force's first true "unmanned interceptor" and the very term sometimes caused Xavier to very nearly lose control of some of his bodily functions. The aircraft was powered by not one but two means of propulsion. A huge LR59-AG-13 liquid-propellant motor would ignite at launch, sending the 15,500 pounds of pure missile screaming into the sky for the first 30,000 feet of its flight.

Then, once the Tomarc hit Mach 1—the magic 650 mph-plus number that shattered the sound barrier—its liquid-propellant rocket would die and its two enormously powerful RJ43-MA-3 ramjets would take over. Within minutes, the missile would be climbing upward of 70,000 feet and approaching speeds of Mach 3.

At around this point, control of the missile would revert back to the men currently scurrying around Xavier's bunker. The missile would be turned over to level flight and its engines locked on cruise. In real combat situations, data fed up from the ground-control station would direct the Tomarc to its target—which, in wartime, would be an approaching force of enemy bombers. A Buck Rogers-style target seeker in the missile's nose cone would lock onto the target, and once the missile—now going close to an astounding 1,800 mph—was in among the enemy aircraft, a proximity fuse would detonate its nuclear warhead. End of the enemy bomber force.

For Xavier, the Tomarc was a weapon made in heaven, and the candle he always kept burning in Bunker 07 was a reminder of its true value. As the first Air Force program-control officer assigned to the Tomarc project back in 1950, Xavier had fought hard for the missile's "F-98" designation. This way anyone in the know from congressmen to Air Force types would realize that the missile—like the F-94 or the F-86—was an interceptor in all respects except one: It didn't need a pilot to carry out its mission.

Though it went against his devout Catholicism, Xavier did not believe that God had made Man in His own image. Most men were far from being gods. His favorite quotation was from Pliny the Elder: "Man can learn nothing without being taught. He can neither speak nor walk nor eat, and in short he can do nothing at the prompting of nature, but weep."

Machines were different. Xavier was sure *they* were closer to the perfection the Almighty had intended. There was no long, extended learning process needed for them. You programmed them and they did what they were told. No opinions. No doubt about how much of the program was being absorbed and how much was being lost in a daydream. No opportunities for human failure. Machines meant total commitment. They were the perfect inhabitants for Xavier's fastidious world.

"Launch in one minute, sir," came the message Xavier had been waiting for. He gazed out at the beautiful missile, slumping in his seat slightly as the feeling of power and excitement began to pleasantly overwhelm him. God, how he loved that thing. If only it didn't carry so many unpleasant secrets . . .

"Everyone, take your places!" he called out in the tone of a lecherous king about to call in the concubines. His squad of twenty hand-picked technicians scrambled as told, taking up positions behind the battery of read-out screens and radio sets.

"Are the cameras in position?" Xavier boomed.

"Yes, sir!"

"Recorders on?"

"Yes, sir!"

"Flight path clear?"

"Clear to the maximum proximity range, sir!"

"Support systems on disconnect?"

"Support systems all clear, sir!"

Xavier rubbed his hands in delight, then loosened his belt buckle one notch.

"All right, gentlemen," he said, his voice now almost raspy. "On my command . . ."

The tension in the room was almost a tangible thing as the twenty technicians glued their eyes on the missile.

"Flight Officer, are you ready?" Xavier asked, his voice echoing throughout the bunker.

"Yes, sir!" was the reply.

Another belt notch loosened.

"Fire it!"

Seven buttons in all were pushed, and in one lightning-quick moment, the Tomarc's tail end ignited and the missile began to ascend.

"Clean off the pad!" came the flight officer's first report.

"We've got a ninety-percent burn," yelled the motor officer.

"Go to one hundred," Xavier called back, slumping lower in his seat as he followed the true vertical path of the missile.

"One hundred up, sir!"

"Guidance report?" Xavier yelled.

"Automatic program running normally, sir!"

"Velocity now?"

"At point-five Mach and climbing, sir!"

At this point, Xavier had to swivel around to watch the small black-and-white TV screen next to his chair. A TV crew situated on top of the bunker was shakily following the missile's ascent.

"Radio Officer!" Xavier boomed. "Tell those men to hold that camera steady!"

The radioman did as told, and the picture did improve somewhat a few seconds later. Still, with the residue of the blast clogging their lungs and its resulting wind buffeting their position, the cameramen were having a hard time keeping the picture level and focused.

'At point-eight Mach, sir!" came a shouted report. "Altitude now at fifteen . . ."

"Still at one-hundred-percent burn?" Xavier asked.

"Yes, sir!"

The video picture jumped once, causing Xavier to scream, "Switch over to second camera!"

In a burst of static, a new image came on the screen—this of a long thin trail of smoke rising up out of the desert—being shot by a camera crew stationed on a mesa twenty-five miles away.

"Beautiful!" Xavier yelled as he watched the missile

gain speed and shoot straight up and out of sight, at the same time feeling a familiar moisture between his flabby legs. "Did you see it, gentlemen? Wasn't it absolutely *gorgeous!*"

"*Yes, sir!*" came the assembled response.

47

Mescalero

"**CHRIST, IS THAT** *another* one?"

Chas Spencer lifted the flight cap from his eyes and saw a long trail of white smoke disappearing into the high clouds.

"Looks like one to me," he said, shading his brow with his hand. "That's number four this month."

"*Damn!*" the other pilot, a kid from Boston named Reilly, cursed. "I'm out of the pool."

There was close to a hundred dollars in the so-called X-pool, the game in which the pilots at Mescalero had bet how many Tomarcs Xavier would launch during the month of July.

"So, he's up to one a week now," Reilly moaned. "This is getting a little expensive, don't you think?"

Spencer took a sip of his beer, then settled back down under the shade of the tree.

"At a cool two million apiece?" he asked, with a note of spirited disgust in his voice. "I would say so. But the X-Man looks at them as his toys. His *very* expensive toys . . ."

They were relaxing in the back-yard of the Mescalero officers' club, a small patch of dry green grass that featured the tallest, and therefore the shadiest, trees on the entire base. Both pilots were officially off-duty. They had spent most of the morning testing out an experimental fighter called the YF-93. Now the brutal July heat was creeping over the base. And, as always, the hotter it became, the more pilots that came through the door of the officers' club. Hundred-degree temperatures made jet engines very disagreeable, and once the mercury hit that magic number, most of the flying at the base was curtailed.

But not so rocket-powered unmanned interceptors.

"I wonder just how many of those things he intends to light off," Reilly said as they watched the final wisps of the Tomarc's contrails finally blow away.

"I wonder if the damn thing even works," Spencer replied, pouring out another beer from their overly warm pitcher.

"I'm sure we'll be the last to know if it does," Reilly replied.

Unlike other similar projects at Mescalero over the years, the Tomarc testing program was so highly classified, none of the test pilots were privy to any of it. Aside from seeing several of the F-98 missiles trucked in under shrouds and watching the things flash up into the sky once a week, most of the squadron members could only speculate on the inner workings of the unmanned interceptor. Only Xavier and his hand-picked underlings—the "Shine Boys" because of their ridiculously spit-polished work boots—knew what the hell was actually going on.

However, this only increased the rumors floating around the base concerning the F-98. Some said the Tomarc could go as high as 100,000 feet—almost 18 miles up. Others claimed it could bust it at more than Mach 3, 4, or even 5, depending on who you wanted to listen to. Even the slowest estimates would make the F-98 twice as fast as the hottest jet airplane currently at Mescalero.

Now the hottest rumor of late had it that the F-98 used something called a "seek signal" in its warhead that helped it find its target automatically.

The biggest question, however, was, What happens when it gets there?

"It blows up," Spencer guessed, when Reilly asked the question again. "I heard it's designed to carry a small A-bomb in its nose."

Reilly nearly gagged on his warm beer. "An A-bomb!" he asked. "I thought it was an airborne interceptor."

"Well, it is," Spencer replied. "But picture this: Let's say its warhead finds an enemy bomber formation. Now, let's say it detonates a two-point-two kiloton bomb in the middle of it. Well, that would ice a lot of Russians. More than us and the entire squadron could shoot down."

"Damn," Reilly said, lighting a cigarette.

"Now, picture this," Spencer continued. "The Russians decide to bomb us—you know, just so all the bomb shelters won't go to waste. What would happen if American continental fighters had to go up against them? Let's say hundreds of them? How many would they get? How many would get through? Even if we shot down three out of every four, that could leave dozens of those bastards zipping in over the West Coast and dropping their A-bombs. Good-bye, Los Angeles. Good-bye, San Francisco. Good-bye, San Diego."

"Christ, it's like a science-fiction movie," the impressionable Reilly said, conjuring up visions of massive air battles.

"Yeah, a *bad* science-fiction movie," Spencer replied, lighting a cigarette. "But what's worse is Xavier and his gang thinking that these unmanned contraptions can do no wrong."

"It sounds like they can't," Reilly said.

"But of course they can," Spencer replied, a little testily. "Hasn't your airplane ever screwed up, just all of a sudden? No explanation? Damn, my airplane has! It had nothing to do with me. A seal or a pipe or a turbo joint or something just broke. Machines wear out. They're not perfect. They break down. Plus you can't eliminate the human factor, because humans are building the goddamn things."

"Somehow I get the feeling that the X-Man doesn't believe that," Reilly said.

"He doesn't," Spencer answered. "And all this happy crap with the candles and the prayers and reminding everyone that sooner or later you're going to plow in . . . Believe me, it's just his way of beating the drum for these frigging flying robots."

Reilly clapped his hands and laughed. Finally the beer and the hot sun were doing their job. "Jesus, that's what they could call the movie," he said. *"Attack of the X-Man and His Flying Robots!"*

Spencer took another swig of this beer. "Yeah," he said, feeling a bit drunk himself. "I like that."

They bought another pitcher and drank it as the back yard began filling up with pilots. The main topic of discussion was the latest Tomarc launch and its impact on everyone's standing in the pool. Then the subject changed to the latest rumors on just what miraculous things the F-98 could do.

In the midst of the chatter, Spencer shielded his eyes and stared off into the western horizon. All traces of the Tomarc were long gone by this time, but one question still nagged at him. One that no one seemed to ask.

I wonder where the goddamn things land, he whispered to himself.

The sergeant of the small Marine Corps shore detachment in San Diego was just finishing a cup of coffee when his corporal stuck his head into the guardhouse.

"They're coming in, sir," he said.

The Marine sergeant checked his watch. It was just 1400 hours. "That didn't take long," he said, retrieving his helmet and following the corporal out to the dock, where the rest of his detachment was waiting.

San Diego Bay was shimmering in the afternoon sun, the ocean breeze making the 92° temperature somewhat bearable. The sergeant raised his binoculars and immediately spotted the small ex-torpedo boat riding the calm surf and moving quickly toward the pier. Painted on its bow were the letters "USAF."

"Okay, you guys," the sergeant called out to his six-man detachment. "Get to your posts."

Immediately the Marines went into action. Two ran up to the small gate that anchored the two rows of barbed-wire-topped chain-link fencing that surrounded the access to the pier. Two more took up posts at either side of the small enclosure, their M-1 rifles in hand and loaded.

The remaining two hustled out to the end of the pier to help the boat's crew dock safely.

As always, the PT boat was towing a large, yellow-colored inflatable raft. On top of the raft was the shape of a long, cylindrical, winged object that was wrapped tightly in black canvas. Four armed men rode atop the object; four more were stationed on the boat's stern.

The boat docked without any difficulty, and as soon as its lines were tied, the man at the helm waved to the Marine sergeant.

"Okay, boys," the sergeant yelled out to his men in turn. "Let's get out of here."

The two Marines who had helped secure the boat did as told, running back up the dock and meeting their four colleagues. Behind them were four of the armed men from the boat, dressed in standard U.S. Army fatigues but bearing Air Force insignia.

A quick changing of the guard followed as the Marines exited the enclosure and the Air Force men took up their positions. Only when all the Marines had cleared out did the men on the boat start to untie the bindings around the canvas shape on the raft. This done, they maneuvered the raft into the pier's small, windowless boat port, being careful to close and lock the hangarlike doors behind them.

Meanwhile, the Marines watched the operation with diminishing interest from their truck across the street. This was a weekly event for them.

"You think that's the only boat that the Air Force has?" one asked the corporal.

"Probably," the man replied, stifling a yawn.

"Well, it looks like they caught what they were looking for again today," another Marine said, removing his hat and raising his head to get the best of the sunshine.

"They always do," the corporal said.

Although it was all supposed to be highly classified, each one of the Marines knew what was under the canvas on the raft. The Air Force guys had told them weeks before when the odd little operation first began. It was some kind of a top-secret missile, launched from somewhere in New Mexico, that had splashed down somewhere off the coast. Once a week, the Air Force guys would go out in their PT boat and come back anywhere from two to four hours later, towing the inflated raft and carrying the canvas-covered object. Later on that night, a tugboat leased by the Air Force would arrive at the small compound and the shrouded object would be floated away. The next morning, the USAF boat would also be gone, only to return exactly one week later at the exact same time.

Like all good members of the Corps, the Marines kept their mouths shut about the secret operation and their part in it. Yet there was just one strange aspect about the whole thing—one thing that seemed slightly baffling to the Marines.

Whenever the USAF boat would leave for a week, the Marines would use the empty boathouse as a cool, shaded place to eat their chow. But instead of smelling of oil and rubber and burnt rocket fuel, as one might expect, the boathouse always smelled like fish instead.

48

On the Road to Picardo

THE TWO F-94 STARFIRES were coming in so low the bus driver nearly slammed on his brakes.

"Goddamn . . ." he whispered as the two fighters rose just enough to clear the elevated desert highway and streak by, no more than a hundred feet in the front of the speeding bus. "Damn fools near gave me a heart attack. . . ."

He knew that fighters from nearby Mescalero Air Base had been buzzing vehicles on State Highway 32 for years. But for some reason they especially liked buses, and he traveled this lonely stretch of highway more than four times a week. This meant he was buzzed an average of once a day, and each time it appeared like the fighters were getting closer.

As usual, the bus going to Picardo, New Mexico, was nearly empty. There wasn't much to see or do at the end of the fifty-five-mile journey. Another bus station, a feed store, a bar room, a trailer park, and a car-repair shop—that was it. Still, the operators of the Cimarron-Pablo Bus Line made the trip every Wednesday and Friday, plus every other Sunday. Never were there enough people on board to make the run profitable.

The bus driver was particularly nervous on this day, and the harassing jets did nothing to calm him down. Of the four people scattered throughout the forty-four-seat bus, two were Mexicans who couldn't speak English and didn't have the correct fare; one was an old lady who made the trip every Wednesday because she had nothing else to do; and the last was a man who, the bus driver was convinced, had just gotten out of the loony bin.

Despite the large sign—printed in both English and Spanish—tacked up above his head that read "Please do not talk to driver while bus is in motion," the nut hadn't shut up since they'd left Alamogordo.

"I used to fly airplanes like that," he told the bus driver after the jets had passed over.

"Sure, pal," the driver replied, trying his best to brush the guy off. From the looks of him, the kook couldn't drive a nail with a hammer, never mind a fighter jet. He was dressed like an Apache, wore his hair long and in braids like an Apache, and spoke English in the clipped tones of an Apache. Yet the man was obviously white, right down to his tortoise-shell eyeglasses. He also walked with the aid of a cane.

"Used to be part of a top-secret operation over at the air base," he continued. "You wouldn't believe some of the things we did over there. Secret airplanes. Atomic bombs. Fighting Nazis. You name it, we were involved in it."

"I'm sure you were," the bus driver said, barely glancing back at the man who had lodged himself in Seat One, Row One.

"It's so strange," the kook continued, "because the spot we used to drop the A-bombs is called 'The place near Hell.' That's ironic, don't you think?"

The bus driver didn't know what *ironic* meant, nor did he care. All he wished was that the man would stop talking and leave him alone.

"Yep, sure had a lot of fun over there," the man continued, absolutely unaware of the driver's growing resentment. "You don't know what it's like to travel five, six hundred miles an hour. It's like living in a whole different world."

The bus driver nodded at the last statement—he believed the man could have come from another planet.

"But it's all over now," the kook went on, looking wistfully out at the desert speeding by. "Crashed up my airplane chasing a flying saucer. Got banged up real bad. Luckily this Apache brave—he was a ghost, by the way—found me out in the Flats. He walked fifty miles with me on his back. It killed him, finally. But he saved my life. I haven't been in an airplane since."

"Well, thank god for that," the bus driver blurted out.

"So here I am," the man said after a short pause. "Riding a bus. Picking up my car in Picardo. Then I'm going to see my wife."

The bus driver bit his tongue. He couldn't imagine this guy being married to a state-fair hog.

"Name's Maggie," the man said, pushing his specs back up onto his nose. "We've been married since the war. World War II, I mean. I'm going to see her perform. That is, if I can find her."

"Perform?" The bus driver couldn't resist. "Perform what?"

The kook blew his nose on his sleeve and readjusted his glasses.

"A ballet," he answered.

49

Mescalero

THE LONG LINE OF stockinged-feet Shine Boys snapped to attention when General Xavier walked into the base's little-used recreation room.

"At ease, gentlemen," the officer said in a tone that sounded more prissy than usual. "You may sit."

Like a troop of Boy Scouts, the twenty-four men—enlistees and junior-rank officers—sat down on the bare floor and formed a circle around the rec room's single desk. It was covered with twenty-four pairs of meticulously shined boots arranged, as always, in alphabetical order.

"Is everyone here?" the general asked, looking out on his team.

"Yes, sir!" several people replied at once.

"Good," Xavier said, smiling. He sat down behind the desk and began with a short nondenominational prayer.

Then he got to the real matter at hand.

"Aaronson?" Xavier called out, picking up the first pair of boots from his desk.

"Yes, sir."

"I see a scuff here," the general told him, closely examining the airman's right boot. "Get rid of it."

"Batty?" the senior officer continued, moving to the next pair of work boots. "Good . . . but not perfect."

"Coogan . . . excellent," Xavier droned on, getting to the third pair and moving from there. "Dugan . . . excellent. Faye . . . could be better. Finney . . . could be better. Goddard . . . getting better. Griswold . . . is that new shoe polish?"

On and on it went, the general inspecting each pair of

boots closely, while each man felt his heart in his mouth as the moment came closer for his footwear to face muster. The examination itself was quick. Xavier would run his right index finger over the boot's toe, along its sides, and up its back flap. Then, inserting the little finger on his left hand, he would quickly probe all the way up to the front and back again. A final quick sniff of the inside of the boot, and the inspection was completed.

Only then would the general pass judgment.

"Hardon . . . big improvement. Ingersoll . . . best yet. Kenney . . . you have to try harder."

Unlike most GI footwear, the boots did not have the names of their owners printed on the inside. It made no difference—Xavier needed no notes to tell which boots belonged to who. He simply knew—by touch and by smell—every man's boots individually.

"Yeoman . . . excellent," Xavier said, getting to the end of the line. "Zyminsky . . . better than last time."

The general looked up, at the same time wiping a smidgen of dirt from his finger.

"Overall, very good, gentlemen," he pronounced, to the profound relief of all those in the room. "There's always room for improvement, but I must say I'm very pleased."

It was smiles all round for the Shine Boys. When Xavier was happy, they were happy.

Xavier produced a notebook and opened it up to a precisely marked page.

"I'm glad to report that our latest launch was the best so far," he told them.

They responded with a spontaneous cheer.

"According to our instrument calculations," Xavier continued, once the room had quieted down, "we reached our highest altitude and our highest velocity, and the splashdown was successful."

Another cheer.

"Your performance in the bunker was excellent," he said. "However, you men on the cameras need more practice, I'm afraid. More *self-control*."

A murmur went through the group, followed by some angry stares directed at the men operating the TV cameras.

Xavier's hand went up, and there was an immediate silence.

"Nevertheless," he went on. "With this latest launch, I think we can count it as our *coup de maître*. I have been informed that a directive is circulating in Washington today that will affect our program exponentially. If this happens, we will then be completely inexpugnable. . . ."

Xavier expected a cheer; instead, the news was greeted with a stunned silence.

"This is all *good* news, gentlemen," he said, quickly realizing a translation was in order. "This means we have our goal well within our grasp. That we are closer to our dream of the future."

The expected cheer now erupted.

"However, this does not mean that we can let our guard down," Xavier warned them. "There are many that will still oppose us. But remember, when we do triumph—and we will—every man in this room will taste the fruits of our reward.

"Now, let us pray . . ."

All heads bowed, but a knock on the door preempted the prayer.

"Come," Xavier yelled exasperatedly.

A second lieutenant entered the room and quizzically glanced first at the ring of crosslegged airmen, then at the table full of shiny boots. He quickly handed a note to Xavier.

"Message just in from Luke Air Base, General," the man said. "Marked urgent for you."

Xavier took the note and dismissed the man with a curt salute. Opening it, he saw it bore a single, enigmatic sentence: "Weather has deteriorated since last launch."

Xavier's mood changed in an instant. He crushed the message in his soft but powerful hand until it was small and sweaty.

"*Everyone dismissed!*" he shouted at the men. "And take these dirty boots off my desk!"

50

Washington, D.C.

THE SECRETARY'S PHONE RANG eleven times before she was able to pick it up.

"Senator Kenneally's office," she said, flustered and out of breath. "This is Betty."

"Is the boy there?" the raspy, familiar voice on the other end asked.

Betty's hand unconsciously went to her unbuttoned blouse, wrapping it around her breasts as if the man on the other end could see her.

"Yes, he is, sir," she stuttered. "One moment, please . . ."

She quickly pushed the hold button and then took a breath of relief.

"It's your father," she called back into the larger office. "He's on line one."

"Thanks, Betty."

Jack Kenneally was also buttoning up his shirt when he picked up the phone and punched line one.

"Da? We still on for lunch today?"

"I'll be late, and it will be a quick one," was the senior Kenneally's reply. "I just had a little bombshell drop on me, and I'm going to drop it on you."

Jack Jr. sat straight up in his chair. "Is it serious?"

"At the moment, it's just bothersome," his father replied. "But you never know—it could explode. See you in the Senate Dining Room in thirty minutes."

The luncheon special was corn beef and cabbage, a strange selection for such a hot day in July, but Jack Jr. ordered it anyway.

He was taking his second bite when his father walked in. It wasn't easy for the recently retired, long-time senator—a powerhouse on Capitol Hill for more than thirty-five years—to make his way across the crowded dining room. He couldn't pass a table without someone rising to shake his hand, pat his back, or whisper something in his ear.

Finally he made it to Jack's corner table, arriving just as his usual double bourbon did.

"Read this quick," he told his son, handing him an unmarked manila envelope and readjusting his impeccable seersucker suit. "And hide it if any of these Republican monkeys come around."

Jack Jr. did as told, removing a two-page document from the envelope and quickly studying it.

"Oh, brother!" he said several times as he skimmed the single-space typed paragraphs. "Unmanned interceptors? Unreliable human factors? Budget savings? What does all this mean?"

Jack Sr. had half-finished his drink by this time and was hand-ordering another.

"For one thing, it could mean the unemployment line for your old friends down in Mescalero," the older man said. "If this cockamamy unmanned air defense force proposal flies, they'll be the first to go—and a lot of other pilots will go right after them."

"Do you really think it will come to that?" Jack Jr. asked, almost laughing. "I mean, this thing is so ludicrous, I can't imagine the Joint Chiefs passing on it."

"Don't be so sure," the older Kenneally replied. "There are underlying forces at work here, boy. People who know what they're doing."

Jack Jr. took a sip of his own drink, shaking his head as he did so. "But Dad, if I read this right, the entire U.S. Air Force would be just about dismantled. That's got to be a violation of the National Security Act or something."

"It isn't," Jack Sr. answered. "And even if it was, these guys could overturn it. And there isn't enough sympathy for the Air Force up here to put up a half-decent fight.

"You've got to remember that the Air Force is only eight years old, Jack. That puts them behind the Army and the Navy by about a hundred and seventy-five years. Lot of tradition, lot of horseshit packed into all those years. Now, if this thing went through, it could start a trend that would certainly cut down the Air Force, probably to such a size that it would revert back to being controlled by the Army. And *that's* what I think is behind all this."

Jack Jr. knew what his old man was talking about. The Air Force was established in 1948—officially separating all the old Air Corps elements from the Army. The paring off left some old Army commanders bitter, as it decreased their power drastically. The poor coordination between the Army ground troops and the Air Force during the Korean War only worsened the already poor relations between the rivals, leaving more than a few of the grunts dreaming of the day the upstart Air Force was put in its place, if not eliminated altogether.

"You see, the people behind this are working it well," Kenneally Sr. continued. "They know Ike would like to cut back on the defense budget without being branded a softie on the commies, so they're presenting these unmanned warplanes as cost-cutting measures as well as new technologies. I mean, this Tomarc contraption looks great on paper."

"But it's so crazy," Jack Jr. replied. "Planes without pilots? It's such a radical idea. Will anyone up here even support it?"

"Oh, it will stick to the wall, believe me," the older man said. "On *both* sides of the aisle. And I'll tell you why: Machines don't need uniforms, they don't have to be fed, or trained, or paid, or pensioned, or housed. Plus they're expendable—which alleviates the sticky situation of these one-way bombing missions and this kamikaze factor that everyone's been so worried about. So that proposal you're holding might sound stupid and, on first examination, unworkable. But to repeat myself, whoever put it together knew what they were doing."

The younger man reread the last paragraph and noted the one name that stood out.

"I'm surprised to see this General Xavier's name all over this thing," he said. "He's the guy who took over down at Mescalero."

"All I know about him is he used to lead the Catholic Officers' Club at the Pentagon," the senior Kenneally replied. "He was in the Army back then. When the Air Corps went Air Force, he went with them, right into the New Weapons' Office. Then he got his first command smack dab in the middle of your buddies down in that New Mexican hell hole and wiggled enough to get the top spot for the Tomarc tests."

"But why is he advocating this crap?" Jack asked. "Isn't he cutting his own throat?"

"No, not really," Jack Sr. said, taking one of the biscuits from the bread basket and meticulously buttering it. "As the honcho for the Tomarc tests, he knows that if this whole unmanned concept goes through, he'll be the guy carrying the ball. Plus, like I said, he was Army before, he can be Army again."

"I seem to recall the guys telling me he was kind of flaky," Jack said. "But that was a few years ago."

"Whatever he is, he's probably in bed with the Tomarc contractors," the father replied. "I mean, they've got to be in on this thing, too, in order to make it spin. I'm sure they see dollar signs building an entirely new weapons system that doesn't have to carry a pilot along for the ride."

Jack Jr. returned the directive to the envelope and sealed it tightly. Then he looked up at his father.

"This not only seems stupid, Dad, it's seems wrong, almost unpatriotic," he said sheepishly. "Doesn't it?"

"Son, it doesn't make a damn bit of difference up here if it seems 'wrong' or not," the elder man replied. "But if that's your way of asking my opinion, then my answer is yes, it *is* wrong. I believe this country needs all three services. But second, these guys scare me because they're so weird. They're not old school, but they're playing the old-school game. People like that can be dangerous. And apparently, that missile can be dangerous, too."

"How so?"

Kenneally Sr. motioned for another drink.

"I did some checking before coming over here," he

said, lowering his voice a notch. "Turns out some people believe the margin for error with one for these F-98 missiles is high."

"Why?"

"Well, you won't see it in that report," the older man said, recieving his third drink. "But these Tomarcs are being designed to carry atomic warheads. It's really the only way they'd be able to work effectively. Now, if you had thousands of them stationed around the country like this Xavier and his gang want, the chances of one or two or more going off accidentally—because the wrong button was pushed or whatever—are very, very high, especially in such a new-fangled technology. And as their plan calls for them to be placed around major cities, well, we might just be doing the Russians the biggest favor ever— accidentally A-bombing our own people."

"So we could posture this as a *serious* threat," Jack said. "Something that could harm the population of this country."

"It could be done that way, I suppose," his father replied. "And I think this may be a good issue for you to cut your teeth on. But remember, there are some minefields here. If this first series of tests they've been conducting down in New Mexico is going as well as they say, then you'll see a stampede of our distinguished colleagues rushing to vote for weapons that don't risk the lives of our servicemen—*cheaper*, futuristic weapons at that."

"Well, these guys have to be cut down before that happens," Jack Jr. said, sitting straight up in his chair. "What should I do?"

"You can start by warning your friends down in Mescalero," his father answered. "I'm sure they've seen the Tomarc test shots, but they're probably being kept in the dark about the details of the program, which isn't surprising when you think of it.

"After that, call in some favors and get your friends to pressure the Tomarc manufacturers to back off. I imagine these companies must be wining and dining Xavier and his guys like crazy. Probably getting them all laid, too. Tell your friends to tell them you know of someone who'll pass a secret memo to the *Post* saying these Tomarcs are being designed to carry atomic warheads, and if they're unstable, no one will want them in their back yard. It won't stop them cold, but it will at least get their attention."

Jack was writing it all down. "I agree, but how can we pull the plug on the whole program?"

The senior Kenneally shook his head. "It's not going to be easy, not with the accuracy numbers these guys are projecting," he said. "But somewhere along the line I think you'll have to catch this Xavier character with his pants down. All of those test numbers can't be *that* good. There's got to be a hole in there somewhere. Why not talk to someone down at the base. Like what's his name, the big hero."

"Hughes?"

"That's the guy," Jack Sr. said. "He's a character. Maybe he can come up with something."

"Normally, he would," Jack answered. "But he's not there anymore. He's been in that new NACA program for a year."

"Project Libra?" the senior Kenneally asked. "The one where they get spun around and eat strange food?"

"That's the one," Jack Jr. said. "I got him in because the guy's always wanted to fly in space. But after all the crap we went through in Korea, well, that probably ain't going to happen. So he believes this is as close as he's ever going to get.

"In fact, I don't think he's even doing any flying these days."

"Well, he'd better start," Jack Sr. said, ordering his fourth drink.

The young senator turned the sealed directive over in his hands, pondering the Air Force without pilots that it advocated. He ran his finger over the stamp that said, "Top Secret."

"Where the hell did you get this, anyway, Da?" he asked.

The older man took a sip of his bourbon, then reached for the menu.

"I'll tell you when you get elected to your second term," he replied. "Now, you tell me: How's the cabbage?"

51

Clover Leaf, New Mexico

CURTISS HEARD LAUGHTER COMING from the end of
the dusty street.

He turned around to look for its source but could only
see the four men he'd just walked past after parking his
Oldsmobile on the edge of the small town. The men had
been playing cards and drinking rye when he approached
them to ask for directions—but they had ignored him.

Now they were laughing at him.

He used his ability to shut out all unwanted external
distractions, then walked across the street and into the
dilipated boardinghouse. The lobby, if it could be called
that, was dirty, smelly, and empty. Nothing more than an old
couch, surrounded by a scattering of threadbare chairs—
it looked as if no one had sat in any of them for years.

He walked over to the front desk and knocked his cane
against it twice in an effort to summon somebody. Above
the desk was a sign that read "Rita's Rooms."

He had to knock four more times before a large,
sweaty woman—Rita herself—appeared from a back
room. She took one look at him and said harshly, "No
Indians."

"I'm not an Indian, ma'am," he calmly replied as she
was turning to go. "I'm a veteran."

She turned back and gave him a longer look. The
braided hair, the Apache shirt and pants, the necklace,
the moccasins.

"You sure look like an Indian to me," she said.

Curtiss pulled out his license and VA card and showed
them to the woman. "I am not an Indian," he repeated.
"But I'd be proud to be one if I was. . . ."

She gave him a look that bore ample evidence of years of prejudice, then reluctantly retrieved her register from behind the desk. "Five-fifty a night," she said. "Read the rules."

She pointed at a small sign to the left of the check-in desk. It read "No Cooking. No Singing. No Wild Drinking. Check-Out Time Is Noon."

Curtiss memorized it, then drew five dollars and fifty cents from his waist satchel and placed it on the desk.

"Any sights to see?" he asked her as he scribbled his name on the register.

"Here?" She laughed cruelly. "Sure, Cochise, if you like trailer parks and bungalows."

She deposited the money inside her blouse, threw the room key at him, and waddled away.

The room was just a smaller version of the lobby: dirty, musty, and little used. The iron bed posts were rusty with age, the floor was stained and it creaked with every step, and the backing on the wall mirror had deteriorated to the point that a reflected image was little more than a shadow.

Curtiss pulled the sheets back and spent a minute brushing off the jumping spiders that had claimed the place as their home. Then he dragged the room's rotting wicker chair over to the window and drew back the ripped curtains.

Across from Rita's was a small cafe. In its largest window a man was installing a neon sign that read "Tonight—Saloon Ballet."

Curtiss felt a familiar jolt of excitement run through him.

"Well, at least I'm in the right place," he thought aloud.

52

SPENCER HADN'T BEEN TO Alamogordo Municipal Air Field in five years, and he was surprised how much the place had changed.

The last time he'd been there was back in early 1951, when he'd returned from Korea via a commercial flight. At that time the place was little more than a glorified bus station with a cracked and bumpy landing strip. Now the field boasted five runways—all of smooth, almost shiny black asphalt—a large passenger terminal with a dozen gates and departure stations, and a control tower that matched the ones at Mescalero in size and sophistication.

The airport also had a rather luxurious bar, and that's where Spencer had been sitting for the past two hours, drinking whiskey and smoking Chesterfields, waiting for an unusual flight to arrive.

It was all very mysterious at first: First a call to his house earlier in the evening from a woman named Betty, whom he didn't know. Go to the airport, dressed in civilian clothes, and wait to be paged, she had told him. And, above all, don't tell anyone.

Strange as it may have seemed, Spencer followed her instructions. After spending so much time in his seven-year career working on military covert programs, phone calls from out of the blue such as this one didn't phase him much anymore. And although he hadn't been contacted in such a manner since the Operation Stormcloud mess in Korea, he was still technically an employee of the super-secret Aerospace Security Agency, the people who usually came calling when some Spooks had to be flown somewhere on the QT. They were paying him more money than an average USAF test pilot—a *lot* more—and therefore he was obligated to at least answer the phone when it rang at unusual hours.

However, this time it would be different—actually, he had it all wrong. The call wasn't the beginning of some secret ASA operation, though there would be times in the coming days that he wished it were.

He was on his third drink when he heard his name boomed out of the terminal's public-address system, instructing him to go to Gate 3. He did so and found a young man sitting in the otherwise empty waiting area. The man seemed to know Spencer, as he walked right up to him and introduced himself as "Jerry."

Then he turned and pointed to a small airliner that was parked out on the darkened runway, the airport's blue landing lights reflecting on its silver fuselage.

"Senator Kenneally would like to talk to you," Jerry said.

The meeting was all too brief.

Spencer hadn't seen Kenneally in three years—ever since his former colleague had been elected to the Senate from Massachusetts. They'd spoken on the phone a few times and occasionally exchanged letters and postcards, but for the most part, their careers had gone on divergent paths since the end of their service in Korea.

So it was with some dismay that Spencer learned the surprise visit was for less than festive reasons.

"That's the whole nugget," Kenneally told him as they sat in the lounge of the Kenneally family's airliner. He had just told Spencer the gist of the report his father had shown him earlier. "Your General Xavier is part of a small but growing movement to dismantle a large portion of the Air Force. No more manned fighters. No more manned bombers. No more human pilots. If they get their way, everything will be done by machines—robots and stuff."

Spencer was equally surprised and embarrassed. Although he had suspected as much, he felt he should have seen the pieces of the puzzle coming together long before this. Xavier's ritualistic snap briefings, the morbid statistics, the memorial candles—all were just a way of brainwashing the "dirty minds" at the base into thinking that manned flight was too dangerous and something that was rapidly becoming obsolete.

His only question was, How could it all happen so quickly?

"Xavier and his gang have really covered the bases in Washington," Kenneally explained. "First of all, most of them are old Army Air Corps vets who have never gotten over the fact that their means of air support was pulled away from them. For all we know, they've probably been planning all this for years.

"The second thing they did was play kissy face with the contractors, and they with them. I've seen the numbers, and there's more money to be made by manufacturing unmanned weapons than manned ones—there's just no question about it. So the Tomarc people welcomed them with open arms—and, from what I hear, open legs, too.

"Third, these guys are operating in an atmosphere in Washington that still stinks of McCarthy paranoia, yet one that wants to move on, you know, into the next era. Combine all this with the happy-horseshit Buck Rogers attitude going around the country that every machine that comes off the assembly line is better than the human who made it and you start to see their strategy. These guys are actually telling people that by 1960, robots will be doing everything from vacuuming your floors to blasting the Russians. And people are starting to believe them."

"But there's a big problem there," Spencer said. "Don't they realize that by eliminating the man from the machine, they'll eliminate innovation? I mean, improvements come from errors—trials and errors. There hasn't been a machine built yet that can figure out a better way of doing what it was built to do."

Kenneally was given pause at this point. "Why, Mr. Spencer," he said, with a smile that was worth at least a couple of thousand votes, "that's the first time I've heard you say anything that could be described as eloquent."

"Is that what they call it?" Spencer asked.

Kenneally reached over and shook his hand. "Yes, Chas," he said. "That's *exactly* what they call it."

The young senator poured out two more drinks and then continued the discussion.

"I was able to do some snooping around before I flew out of D.C.," Kenneally told him. "And although Xavier's people have dazzled a lot of guys on Capitol Hill with their preliminary data, there are some who believe this Tomarc isn't all it's cracked up to be. They feel there's a chink in the armor. The question is, where?"

Spencer took a moment to think. "I don't know," he said finally. "The grapevine at the base is usually pretty reliable—after you cut through all the crap, that is. From what we hear, the thing can almost bust Mach 3, it can go up to at least ninety thousand feet, and it can be directed to the target by radio."

"Damn, that's better than what the brochure says," Kenneally said.

"We see them launch," Spencer told him. "Goddamn thing is up into the clouds in a snap, over our heads and gone, baby, *gone*! It's quite a show."

"I know," Kenneally nodded. "There's a film making the rounds at the Pentagon showing a Tomarc launch. My god, it looks like they hired Cecil B. DeMille to make the damn thing. Slow motion. Lots of smoke and fire. 'America the Beautiful' playing in the background. That's what makes it so hard to resist. It's so frigging *pretty*."

Suddenly a thought came to Spencer.

"Maybe that's it," he said. "It looks good on launch. But you know something—I've never heard anyone bragging about seeing one come down."

Kenneally's eyes lit up, and his hands went to his mouth as if in prayer.

"Maybe you've got something there," he said.

The meeting broke up shortly afterward, Kenneally's plane taking off and heading west, Spencer just about clicking his heels with the knowledge that they had uncovered Xavier's plans in time.

He was in the mood for a good fight, and if the Air

Force needed saving, well then they were just the guys to do it. Besides, things around the base had been pretty dull since Hughes jumped over to NACA, and he needed a little excitement in his life. But the boredom was soon to end—of this he was sure.

In fact, Spencer was so enthused when he left the airport terminal that he didn't notice the two men sitting in the main lobby area who were watching him from behind open newspapers.

Both were wearing superbly shined boots.

53

Mescalero

GENERAL XAVIER HAD BEEN in his office since dawn, studying the summaries his lieutenant had prepared from the slightly water-damaged MiG-15 combat data.

It had been three hours of pure bliss for Xavier. Just about everything in the report—from the design of the bulky ejection seat to the drawings of the overly heavy oxygen pump and support systems—fit right into his antihuman-factor scenario. This evidence would be more than his *coup de grace*—it would be his secret weapon. For when the time came for him to present all of the evidence in favor of unmanned interceptors, he would be able to compare his data not only to the best American fighters but also to one of the best *Soviet* fighters as well. Being able to beat the Air Force's manned-flight advocates was one thing. Beating the Russians was quite another.

His glee was interrupted by a knock on his door. A sergeant, one of the Shine Boys, was granted permission to enter.

"I have two pieces of disturbing news, General," the man began, his voice shaky.

Xavier looked up from his summary for the first time.

"You are going to ruin my morning?" he asked crossly. "Is that what you are saying?"

"I think it's information you should know, sir," the man continued, though hesitantly. "It may affect the overall F-98 program."

Xavier closed the MiG-15 report and leaned forward in his chair. "Speak."

The sergeant came closer to the desk and lowered his voice.

"First of all, sir," he began, "two of the guys followed Captain Spencer to the Alamogordo airport last night. They saw him go aboard an airliner—a *private* airliner—that was parked out on the runway. He stayed for about an hour, then went home."

"Whose airplane was it?" Xavier asked, knowing full well that as an employee of the ASA, Spencer was no stranger to hastily arranged meetings at odd hours.

"It belongs to a company called the New England Bay Corporation," the sergeant replied. "It came in from Washington and stopped in Little Rock for fuel."

"And this New England Bay Corporation," Xavier asked, "it's owned by who?"

The sergeant lowered his voice even more. "The Kenneally family."

Xavier felt his heart plunge to the bottom of his stomach. He wasn't quite sure why, but he knew that Spencer meeting with someone connected with the Kenneallys could only mean bad news.

"What else?"

The sergeant cleared his throat. "We've got a new aircraft coming in—from California," he said. "A flight plan was radioed ahead about a half-hour ago. You'll be getting it any minute now."

Xavier was bewildered. "New airplane?" he asked. "I knew nothing about this."

"The flight plan requested is typical for a new-model ingress," the sergeant said, still speaking in measured, hushed tones. "Confidential takeoff time, avoiding populated areas on overflight, security asked for on landing."

Xavier pounded his fist on his desk three times in quick succession.

"*Damn them!*" he mumbled through clenched teeth. "I've spent the last six months trying to keep new manned models *out* of this place. And now someone is sending one in and not letting me know about it?"

"That appears to be the case, sir," the sergeant answered. "Apparently the pilot will be carrying further orders with him."

Xavier tried to think quickly, but he couldn't. His mind was too full of plots, counterplots and *counter-counterplots* to deal with this new entanglement. But when his stomach began to rumble, he feared it was telling him that the new airplane's arrival had something to do with Spencer's mysterious meeting the night before.

Typically, he decided to kill the messenger.

"*Well, do you even know what kind of an airplane it is?*" he screamed at the noncom.

The startled sergeant could barely shake his head. "No, sir," he answered. "All we know is that it's coming in from Burbank. . . ."

Now Xavier's expression turned from one of anger to one of horror.

"Oh, God," he said. "That can only mean one thing."

The sergeant nodded numbly. "Whatever kind of airplane it is, it's coming in from Lockheed's Skunkworks."

54

THOUGH TECHNICALLY A HIGHLY classified operation, it didn't take long for word to spread around the Mescalero base that a new aircraft prototype was coming in.

The event, once almost a weekly occurrence, was now so rare in the days of Xavier that the flight line was actually crowded and abuzz with anticipation of the new arrival.

The jet appeared out on the western horizon at precisely high noon. First a tiny gleaming speck, it grew and grew until it looked frighteningly like a mighty silver dagger, rocketing through the sky, pointing directly at those on the ground. In no time at all, the new airplane had flashed over the flight line, its pilot performing a perfect roll, followed by a steep bank to the north. Another bank around back to the east put the new jet into a final approach for landing.

Those assembled on the flight line were open jawed and unanimous: Pilots and paper pushers alike, they had never seen anything like it before. Even the business-as-usual crew chiefs and hangar types were impressed.

"What the hell is it?" several people asked at once.

No one knew—including Xavier. Due to the security surrounding the arrival of some of the most advanced, and therefore more secret, aircraft prototypes, no one at the base—not even its commander—was ever aware of what was coming in until it landed.

In this case it was a Lockheed XF-104A Starfighter, the absolute latest interceptor being built by the Air Force. Long at fifty-four feet and sleek with stubby wings and a high tail, the Starfighter looked like a flying stiletto. It was powered by a General Electric J79-GE-3 afterburning jet engine that could deliver almost Mach 2.6 on demand and could carry the needle-nosed airplane up to 80,000 feet. The XF-104A could lug up to 4,000 pounds of weapons under its wings and fuselage, including deadly air-to-air missiles on its wingtips. For good measure, the designers had added a 20-millimeter Vulcan cannon on its left-side fuselage, a powerful gun capable of firing 6,000 rounds a minute.

One look would tell even the most cynical observer that the Starfighter was advanced far beyond any other airplane the United States had ever built. It was also probably the only airplane ever manufactured that carried a piece of felt cloth as part of its standard equipment. This was because the Starfighter was so sleek, and its wings so exceptionally thin and sharp, that a felt cap was needed to cover their razor-sharp edges. If not for the covering, the jet's ground crew could slice themselves to pieces during servicing.

As the XF-104A glided in for a landing, the assembled at Mescalero gave it a greeting reserved only for the most impressive arrivals. They applauded—everyone except Xavier and his entourage. The last thing the general wanted to do at that moment was cheer. He had heard about the development of the XF-104. It was a product of the Skunkworks, the semisecret Lockheed facility in Burbank that turned out a radical aeronautical surprise every year like clockwork. Lockheed was the arch rival of the makers of his beloved Tomarc. More disturbing for Xavier was that although he had never actually seen a Starfighter until now, its design was not entirely foreign to him.

In fact is was very familiar, because the XF-104 looked more like a rocket than an airplane. And for good reason. Its design had actually come from a rocket, a Lockheed-developed research missile called the X-7—the exact same design that had given birth to the F-98 Tomarc.

The crowd surrounded the Starfighter as it taxied up to a special hard stand, its pilot warning the attending ground crew of the dangers of the straight-razor-type wings. Shutting down the powerful engine, the pilot, a civilian employee of Lockheed, climbed out of the airplane and was met by Xavier.

He introduced himself and handed a sealed packet to Xavier. "Here are the orders, General," he said.

Xavier took the pouch and handed it to his lieutenant, who dutifully opened it and retrieved a single-spaced typed letter and a specifications booklet. He handed the letter to Xavier and stepped back, theorizing that the general was not going to like what he was about to read.

The lieutenant was right: The farther Xavier's eyes scanned down the letter, the redder his face became.

"This is preposterous!" he said, crumpling the missive and tossing it away.

The Lockheed pilot just shrugged as he watched the ball of paper blow away in the wind. "I'm just the delivery boy, General," he said. "Sorry . . ."

Xavier had nothing more to say to him. He simply turned on his heels and headed full steam back toward his office, his entourage of admirers in tow.

With the general gone from the scene, the Starfighter, its felt covering in place, became the sole object of attention. The Lockheed pilot, a cup of steaming coffee in one hand, gave a thumbs-up to the other pilots, who wanted to study the engine, take a look inside the cockpit, inquire about the air-to-air missiles, and gawk at the awesome Vulcan cannon. Others in the crowd were simply content just to touch the side of the sleek fighter as if it were a religious relic.

Amid the hubbub, only Spencer chose to chase down the letter Xavier had tossed away. In fact, it took him several minutes to catch up to the highly classified memo as it blew across the tarmac, several times coming tantalizingly close to his grasp. Finally he cornered it, pinned it with his boot, and retrieved it. Then, breaking at least four government security regulations, he smoothed it out and read it.

Moments later, some of those gathered around the Starfighter heard Spencer howl with delight, even though he was almost a quarter-mile away.

55

Clover Leaf, New Mexico

CURTISS AWOKE TO FIND that he was still sitting at the window, his lanky frame crunched into the old wicker chair, a fine layer of sand dust coating his eyes, mouth, and throat.

He stumbled to his feet and immediately doubled over. The ever-present pain in his back, a constant reminder of his near-fatal plane crash five years before, was now excruciating due to his awkward sleeping position that night. He reached for a dirty glass and barely managed to half fill it with warm water before his arm gave out, and he had to put the pitcher down before he dropped it. Immediately his head began to spin. He wobbled to the bed and fell on it with a loud squeak.

For him, another day had begun.

Still he was in high spirits. His physical being was painful beyond belief, but his heart and mind were alternately soaring and vibrating. He had *seen* her, by god. Right across the narrow street from the boardinghouse. He had seen her walking into the cafe, a bag in hand, her red hair flowing long and beautiful. She had been wearing a green dress, with black-seamed stockings and extra-high heels.

The dusty town had no streetlights, of course. Just about all of the illumination at night came from the garish red neon lights of the cafe, offset by the dull, pale pulse from the dim bulbs surrounding Rita's ancient sign. Even through this electric murk, he had seen her, walking proudly as she always had, carrying herself like a member of royalty.

He'd stayed awake all night, his eyes never leaving the front doors of the cafe. Though many men went in—cowboys mostly—she never did come out. He remembered shutting his eyes just as the sun was coming up, and still she had not left by then. Perhaps she was sleeping there, in a back room or on the second floor. Wasn't it natural for an establishment to provide lodging for its hired performers? Where else would a ballet dancer sleep in a town like Clover Leaf? Certainly not at Rita's Rooms.

He realized now that it had been a jet airplane passing overhead that had awakened him, and even this seemed appropriate. For while he was sleeping, crunched over the rotting window sill, he had dreamed again of his old friend Gabe Evers. He had seen him, plain as the light of day, first sitting at his breakfast table, reading the newspaper and sipping coffee, and then standing in his vegetable garden, tending his crops, watching the sky. Curtiss had called out to him, but just as before, Evers had been too busy to talk. He'd waved Curtiss away—shooing him lest someone see him. Curtiss had called back to him, saying he understood, and then he'd left. For Curtiss, it had been a nice trip.

His heart was *really* pounding now. Seeing her and dreaming of Evers was each quite an occasion. The next step would be for him to touch them both.

He climbed off the bed, all the pain in his body long since disappeared, and retrieved his waist satchel. Carefully counting out five and a half dollars in change, he headed downstairs to pay Rita for use of the room for another night.

56

Edwards Air Force Base

IT HAD TAKEN MORE than twenty minutes for the room to stop spinning before Hughes could get up off his bunk and go to wash his face.

He had done battle with the Centron again that day and the mechanical tornado had won. He should have seen it coming: The night before, one of the NACA employees had stopped by his quarters and warned Hughes that he shouldn't eat at all because of the upcoming test in the centrifuge. When Hughes told the man, thanks, but he had already gotten the memo on it, the man had shook his head and said worriedly, "No, I really mean, don't eat a *thing*." Then he'd quickly left.

What the good-hearted man had tried so clumsily to warn Hughes about was that the Centron test for this day was not one of speed but of endurance. Basically, they locked Hughes up inside the capsule and told him to scream—loudly—when he had had enough.

It was a hell of a position to be put into. His longest ride on the hated centrifuge had lasted one second longer than twelve minutes, and at a speed equivalent to four gs, it had been murder. But it had also established the benchmark—the established threshold of pain, a record

that Hughes knew he'd have to try and break. Climbing
into the capsule, his head had been full of questions:
Should he cry out at twelve minutes and *two* seconds? Or
twelve and ten? Or even thirteen minutes or more? How
would he know how long to last? The Centron compartment did not come equipped with a clock.

As it turned out, he'd simply strapped himself in and
told his torturers to flip the switch and blink the lights
every five minutes. At first they had resisted—it was not
regulation to blink the lights. But Hughes was nothing if
not persuasive. A promise of a bottle of Scotch later, he
was twirling around the centrifugal chamber at five gs,
his eyeballs cemented to the tops of their sockets, so far
up he couldn't have seen an atomic flash, never mind a
blinking light.

In the end it made no difference: He had stuck it out
for eighteen minutes and thirty-seven seconds, the last
five of which he had spent composing a jangling letter to
the head of NACA, telling him that this was definitely
his last trip to the Centron.

Later, when he returned to his quarters, he had actually tried to write this letter, but, strangely, his pen kept
running off the side of the notepaper. When he closed his
eyes and thought he saw the outline of Ursa Major on
the inside of his eyelids, he knew it was time to lie down.

Now as the room slowly came to a halt, Hughes was
suddenly awash in a wave of melancholy. Did he really
like this all that much? Was all this outright torture
worth it, just so some other joker could finally get rocketed into outer space? What made him any different
from a guinea pig? They stuck the needles in *him*, twirled
him around, sent *him* roaring down five miles of track,
and if it all didn't kill him, then that meant it was safe for
a *real* spaceman to try it out.

It was not the first time he had had this feeling—many
times since coming to Edwards he had wondered if it
were really all for naught. He was paying a big price
either way. He couldn't fly. Half the time he couldn't eat
for twenty-four hours at a stretch, and the times he
could, it usually turned out to be a repast of disgusting-
looking turkey-and-mashed-potato cubes.

All this didn't leave much time for his other pursuits, those involving wine and women. But even this didn't make much difference: There *were* no women to speak of at Edwards, and the Glory Boys who flew the X-planes at the other end of the base were experts at making him feel like an outsider any time he went to the OC for a drink. Like elephants, they had perfect recall that in the long-standing war between Edwards and Mescalero, the pilots from New Mexico had won the greater share of brawls.

The departed General Jones had once told him that there were two ways to go crazy in the service: by drinking and by *not* drinking. Yet Hughes was never one to drink much alone. What was the point? Besides, to drink or not to drink was not the question here. Something else was eating at him—something he couldn't put his finger on exactly.

It was just that he felt that somehow, somewhere, something big was about to happen—and he was going to miss out on it.

57

Mescalero

"I DON'T KNOW HOW they were able to do it," the voice on the other end of the telephone was telling General Xavier. "The Kenneallys can really pull strings when they want to."

"They're nothing but a bunch of goddamn Irish hoods!" Xavier boomed so loudly that the six aides huddled on the other side of his closed office door could actually feel it vibrate with each syllable. "The grandfather ran more booze than Capone, and the kid has been mixed up in every Black-Op-gone-wrong since V-J Day!"

The phone line to Washington, D.C., was thick with static and it kept fading in and out. But this had no affect on Xavier's ire.

"What about the Tomarc people?" he asked his counterpart, a General Lee, who, along with ten other former Army Air Corps officers, made up the nucleus of Xavier's allies in the Pentagon. "What about all their promises that something like this wouldn't happen?"

"They say their hands are tied," Lee responded. "The guys at the Skunkworks were in on the development of the X-7 rocket out at Edwards, and Tomarc had to beg them to transfer some of the technology, even though it was all paid for with tax money. So not only did the Skunks know that the Tomarc was going to be built, they developed the initial tech stuff. And at the same time, they were very tight-lipped about this damn Starfighter of theirs. In fact, the Tomarc guys thought it was going to be an unmanned fighter, too."

"Then we've been double-crossed," Xavier replied, his voice so angry it could barely get past a whisper. "And those frigging Mick politicians from Boston are sticking their noses into it just to make trouble."

"Well, they're still trying to make the kid a hero," Lee agreed.

There was an uncomfortable silence between the two, broken only by the occasional bursts of static on the line.

"So what should we do?" Lee finally asked. "I'm meeting with the others in twenty minutes, and they'll want to know."

"*What the hell can we do?*" Xavier fumed as he reread the telexed confirmation of the directive the Lockheed pilot had handed him. It was the words "competitive analysis flight" that upset him the most. "We can't buck these orders."

"You mean you're going to go through with it?"

"We *have* to," Xavier replied, his voice back to an angry mumble. "If we don't, it will open up a Pandora's box, with the procurement people, the defense-appropriations committee . . . God, we've got so many things hidden under the covers on this thing now, if those camera-happy Kenneallys get wind of it, they'll go right to the press with the whole ball of wax."

"But we can't send up an F-98 to *race* against that Starfighter," Lee protested. "Not now. Not yet."

"We have no choice is what I'm telling you," Xavier replied harshly. "Besides, if we stick to the usual procedure, we'll be all right. They'll never be able to figure out what's going on. Now, go and tell the others to keep quiet until you hear from me."

"All right, if you say so," Lee answered weakly.

"And another thing," Xavier said, before hanging up. "Stop calling it 'a race.' "

"A *race?*" the young pilot named Reilly asked. "I can't believe the Air Force would actually make them *race.*"

Spencer couldn't stop smiling. Just like the cat who ate the canary, he knew more than the other eleven pilots sitting around the beer-soaked table at the Mescalero OC. The talent would be in not saying too much.

"We shouldn't be calling it a race," he replied. "It's actually called a 'competitive analysis flight'—at least that's what the Lockheed pilot's orders to Xavier said. When two weapons systems with similar missions are built simultaneously, like the Tomarc and the Starfighter were, then the defense-appropriations people in Congress want to know which one performs better. Why build two aircraft that will, in effect, do the same job, which is to stop the Red bombers before they reach the continent?"

Another pilot, a guy from Georgia named Ash, screwed up his face and looked sideways at Spencer. "That sounds like you've been reading up on the topic," he said suspiciously. "Or talking with someone who has. Are you sure you don't know more than you're telling us?"

The question went right to Spencer's gut, but he managed to keep a straight face.

"Hey, this is important to me," he replied, trying to emphasize the protest in his voice. "And it should be important to you guys, too. If this Tomarc program gets the go-ahead funding, we could be looking for other employment inside of three or four years. Do you want a robot taking your job? Do you want to be unemployed?

What kind of job can a fighter test pilot find if machines are doing all the work by 1960?"

"I still say he knows more than he's telling us," Ash said. "Look at him—he's got that same funny look on his mug like when we ask him what the hell he was doing during Korea."

Spencer felt the crowd turning, but he just couldn't stop grinning. "You guys are watching too many war movies," he said. "I told you, I wasn't even *in* Korea during the war."

"Well, goddang, isn't that a smart answer!" Ash said, to a chorus of agreement from the others.

Spencer was about to continue his protest when two more pilots— Apple and Gunston—came into the OC and headed straight for the table.

"Well, it's all set," Apple said, breaking into a broad smile himself.

"What's all set?" Spencer asked.

"The pool, of course," Gunston replied. "We've just telexed every base from here to the Coast and back. We got guys begging to get in."

Now the smile came off of Spencer's face quite easily.

"Pool on what?"

The two men looked at him like he'd just fallen off the hay wagon. "The pool on the *race*," they both answered at the same time. "You know, as in 'who's going to win it?" Gunston added.

"Right now it looks to be dead even," Apple continued as both newcomers sat down. "Half say the Starfighter; half say the X-Man's big missile."

Spencer was astonished. He hadn't expected this.

"You guys started a pool on a classified program?" he asked, bewildered.

"You bet your ass we did," Gunston answered proudly. "We even got some Navy guys out in San Diego involved. We might have to take action from guys back East, too, the way things are going. In fact, a bunch of guys are driving down here just for the show."

"I don't believe this," Spencer said, fumbling for a cigarette and going pale.

Ash turned back to him. "What's the problem?" he

asked. "You've been in all the other pools before. It's our main form of recreation."

"Yeah, but none of us are supposed to know anything about this," Spencer said, finally getting his butt lit. "When Xavier finds out you guys started a pool, he'll go nuts."

"He's *already* nuts," Apple pointed out. "Besides, everyone already knows about the race."

"But it's not really a race," Spencer said, the protest in his voice now very authentic. "It's a 'competitive analysis flight.' "

Apple leaned over the table toward Spencer. "Look, Chas," he began. "Yes or no? Are they going to send up the Starfighter and the Tomarc at the same time?"

"Yes . . ." Spencer barely mumbled.

"And are they going to point them in the same direction? Yes or no?"

"Yes . . ."

"And are they going to give them identical-distance intercept points out over the Pacific?"

"Yes . . ."

"And whichever one passes the point first with their goodies still intact wins this 'competitive analysis flight'?"

"Yes . . ."

"Well then," Apple said, spreading his huge hands out to the others at the table. "That's a goddamn *race*."

The others at the table let out a long and boisterous cheer. All except Spencer, of course. He and Kenneally had agreed that it would be best for all concerned if the competitive analysis flight were kept relatively quiet, lest anyone find out that it was only through Kenneally's influence on the Senate defense-appropriations committee —and the backing of his powerful father—that got the program pushed through in lightning-quick time in the first place.

"So, Captain," Gunston said, taking out a small but well-worn notebook and pointing to Spencer, "who are you picking and how much are you in for?"

58

Edwards Air Force Base

HUGHES WAS ABOUT TO bite into a huge hamburger when the two men walked into the base messhall and approached his table.

"What the hell are you doing, Captain?" one of them, a civilian NACA employee named Rand, asked him harshly.

"I'm eating chow," Hughes answered, his teeth just inches away from the burger and bun.

"But that's not approved chow," the other, an NACA nutritionist named Rooney, said, "You're supposed to be eating the second part of Program Six today."

Hughes took a quick bite of the sandwich, more in protest than anything else. "I can't eat that crap today," he said with his mouth full. "It's making me sick."

"It's *supposed* to make you sick," Rand said. "If it didn't, how would we know how to improve it?"

The explanation may have made sense to the two civilians but not to Hughes. He took another huge bite of the burger.

"Stop that!" Rand screamed, now attracting the attention of everyone in the crowded mess.

"Hit the road," Hughes told them, turning his back on them and protecting the three quarters that were left of the sandwich.

Rand leapt across the table and tried to wrestle the hamburger from him. Hughes retaliated by hitting the man on the chin with his elbow. In the next instant, pandemonium broke out. Hughes found himself in a shoving match with both men, the half-eaten burger crumpling into gristle and crumbs somewhere in the middle.

"You're ruining the program!" Rooney was screaming

245

at the top of his squeaky little voice as he attempted to
pull Hughes down by the shoulders.

"This is ridiculous!" Hughes heard himself shout to the
crowd that had now gathered around the strange scene.

If either one of the NACA tweets had been a pilot—or
another man of equal value—Hughes would have simply
punched him and they would have had a standard brawl
on their hands. But as it was, he was mortified that he'd
been drawn into the tussle at all.

Someone yelled, and two Air Force MPs showed up.
Through quick work and night sticks, they were able to
separate the warring parties. If they hadn't, Hughes feared
it might have degenerated into hair-pulling or even
face-scratching.

"You'll pay for this, Hughes!" Rand sneered at him.
"You'll be busted out of this program before this is
through!"

Hughes turned and looked at the astonished crowd.

"For eating a hamburger?" he asked them helplessly.

Two hours later, Hughes was sitting in the outer office
of the NACA's program administrator.

He felt like a schoolboy who had just gotten caught
smoking in the bathroom. He couldn't imagine what the
administrator would say to him, though he was sure that
it was well within the man's power to get him drummed
right out of the program.

The question on Hughes's mind at that moment was
this: Would that necessarily be a bad thing?

"Is all this really worth it?" he whispered to the otherwise empty room, at once startled that he had now begun
talking to himself. It seemed that he deserved better than
this, especially with everything he'd gone through since
joining the service nearly eleven years before. He became one of the youngest combat aces ever during his
tour in Europe; he thwarted an attempt by ex-Nazis to
steal atomic-bomb secrets just a year later; he had performed some dangerous yet crucial aerial reconnaissance
just prior to the Inchon landings in Korea; and, despite
the unsavoriness surrounding Operation Stormcloud, he
and the others *did* shoot down a ton of MiGs, while

proving the worth of the F-86 Sabre. And—*damn it!*
—they had pulled everyone's asses out of the fire by
conducting the raid on Vladivostok at the expense of the
life of his close friend Gabe Evers.

And now he was about to get busted for eating a
hamburger?

"This *is* ridiculous . . ." he mumbled, this time less
upset that he was carrying on a conversation with himself. If it weren't for the fact that he'd already been
court-martialed once, busted down once, and part of
several unseemly covert operations, he'd probably be a
colonel by now, wearing a chest full of ribbons that
would make even the most skeptical dame wet.

As if to underscore his resentment, two fighters
screeched overhead, the sound waves from their powerful engines shaking the building.

He shook his head wearily and lit a cigarette. Someone
in his past had once told him, "The worst thing God can
do to you is have your dreams come true." His dream
had always been to fly in outer space. True, he had
adjusted that dream somewhat by jumping into Project
Libra, which, after all, was still quite a bit short of
blasting off into outer space. But he had convinced himself that this was what he wanted—being spun around like
a human top, being rocketed almost into oblivion, being
made to eat a strict cubist diet. And, worst of all, *not*
being able to fly.

Well, if this were the dream and God had made it come
true, he thought, then score another one for the atheists.

He took a long drag on his cigarette and checked his
watch. He'd been waiting for almost half an hour now,
and it was beginning to get to him. He toyed with the
idea of just walking out, collecting his things, and leaving
the base. Trouble was, it would probably amount to
going AWOL. Plus he had no transportation, and Edwards, up in the high California desert, was miles away
from anywhere.

Just then the administrator's door opened and a secretary slipped out. She carefully closed the door behind her
and then did her best to ignore Hughes as she hurried by.

But Hughes was not going to let her get off so easily.

"Hey, lady," he called after her. "What's going on? I've been here for a half-hour. How much longer do I have to wait before your boss gets around to me?"

She turned and immediately froze on the spot, seemingly terrified that he, the well-known ruffian from that awful Mescalero place, had even chosen to speak to her.

"He's meeting with a very important person from Washington right now," she said in that tone reserved for all secretaries who, though flustered, still knew they had you by the balls. "You'll just have to wait. . . ."

She was gone in a snap, her step quick and confident after zapping Hughes. Two more jets screamed overhead, once again running him through with a feeling that he should have stayed up there—flying—rather than come down here to eat cubes and deal with prissy technicians and snitty secretaries.

Just then the administrator's door opened again and the man himself came out.

Hughes stood up and involuntarily grimaced as the top NACA man grimly walked toward him, a nasty-looking envelope in hand.

"Captain Hughes," he said, handing him the envelope. "Those are your discharge papers."

Hughes was stunned.

"You realize we had no other choice, considering the circumstances," the administrator told him. "It had to be done this way."

Hughes couldn't speak. He'd been in the military since 1944. What would he do now?

"What will I do now?" he said aloud.

The NACA man looked at him quizzically. "You mean, you don't know?" he asked.

Hughes looked up at him and shrugged. "Know what?"

"About your new job?"

"What new job?"

The man scratched his chin, then put his hand on Hughes's shoulder. "Come into my office," he said, his voice an absolute monotone. "We've just been discussing your situation. . . ."

Hughes was walking through the door before he could

register the ramifications of the administrator's state-ment. *Talking about my situation?* he thought. *With a VIP?*

The first thing he saw as he walked into the large, ornate office was that one wall was covered with photos of the many aircraft—rockets mostly—that had been tested at Edwards over the years. Then he noticed the huge bank of phones to the right of the administrator's gargantuan desk, which, due to the size of the room, appeared to be about half a football field away. Last, he noticed just the legs and right arm of the man sitting in the high-backed leather chair, facing away from him.

"You've been talking about me?" Hughes asked the administrator.

"That's right," the man answered. "I guess our wires got crossed somewhere along the line—happens all the time around here. I thought you were privy to all this."

Hughes felt a spark go off inside him. "Privy to what?"

The NACA man bit his lip for a moment, then said, "Well, we've got a unique problem here, Hughes—but we think we've come up with a unique solution. . . ."

By this time they had slowly walked about halfway toward the desk.

"But first," the administrator continued, "let me intro-duce you to my guest."

At that point, the man in the chair sat up and turned around. Hughes saw the smile and the teeth first, the long shock of brown hair second.

"Captain Hughes," the administrator began, "this is—"

His guest cut him short. "Mr. Hughes and I know each other," he said, smiling. "Don't we?"

Hughes suddenly felt like the world had just tilted back in his favor.

It was Kenneally.

59

Clover Leaf, New Mexico

NIGHT HAD FALLEN AND Curtiss had taken up his position at the window of his dumpy room.

There was an undeniable excitement in the air—and it wasn't just due to the crowds of men and women who had been filing into the cafe for the past half-hour. Curtiss could see a distinct greenish-yellow aura off to the west, rising from an area in the desert that he could only imagine was the Mescalero Air Base.

Must be big doings at the field tonight, he found himself thinking absently.

The thought passed quickly from his mind, though, as he returned his attention to the hubbub at the saloon across the street. He couldn't imagine this type of thing happening very often in Clover Leaf: There were only eight buildings total, on the one and only street, the rest of the town being made up of a rusted grain tower, a broken-down corral turned parking lot and a gaggle of house trailers and adobe bungalows.

The street itself was more illuminated than ever before. This was due to the stream of headlights heading toward the town, plus the fact that the neon sign in the cafe's window—the one that read "Tonight—Saloon Ballet"—was blinking brighter and more furiously than before.

It's almost a command performance, Curtiss thought, imagining that he saw two large spotlights outside the door of the cafe, the same kind used at Hollywood galas. *So, this is what it's like to be in love with a celebrity.* . . .

He checked his watch and saw it was almost eight o'clock. Now, for the first time since coming to the small town, he actually felt the anxiety begin to build up inside him.

"You have to go through with it," he heard one of the many voices inside his head tell him. "It's been five years and it's been five million miles. . . ."

He took several deep breaths and then retrieved his bag of clothes. *Only the best,* he thought, as he laid out a pair of dark gray pants, a white shirt, and a smallish sombrero. He had bought of the clothes new, just waiting for this occasion. In all, they had cost him $7.98.

One of the cars streaming into the small town was an official vehicle belonging to the U.S. Air Force.

However, its three occupants were not on official business, nor had they wanted to come to Clover Leaf in the first place. They were lost and had simply followed the crowd.

"I can't believe we've made it this far," one of them said, as they drove the brand-new, all-black Plymouth through the center of the town. "My ass is killing me."

"And we're almost out of gas," the driver added.

The three men, Air Force officers all, agreed that they should stop in the town and hopefully get gas, food, and directions before pressing on to their ultimate destination. They parked the Plymouth next to a battered Oldsmobile in the corral lot just off the main street and walked back to the crowded and dusty thoroughfare.

"I'll tell you, these people down here know how to have a good time," one officer said, taking in all the activity. "It must be the chili. . . ."

They strolled down the wooden sidewalk and into the place marked "Rita's Rooms." Rita herself—all 355 pounds of her—was stationed behind the check-in desk. She took one look at the three uniformed men and especially the suitcase one of them was carrying and cried out, "No rooms left!"

The men looked at each other, then back at Rita.

"We're not looking for a room," one of them said, adding as an aside, "Though I can't believe *this* place is full up."

"Well it will be," Rita replied rudely. "You blind? You see what's going on across the street? Happens every year. Once that show is let out, these rooms will be filled with every cowboy lucky enough to find a living, breathing girl to hump."

All three Air Force officers were taken aback by the large woman's crudeness.

"We need some information, that's all," the spokesman said, "Like, where's the nearest filling station?"

Rita lit her pipe and gave a cruel laugh. "You missed it about forty miles back on the highway," she said. "What else you want to know?"

"How about food?" the man asked.

"Only place is the joint across the street," she replied. "And as you can see, it's filling up mighty fast."

"How about some directions?" the officer persisted.

"To where?"

"To Mescalero Air Force Base," he replied.

Rita shrugged her shoulders, causing a massive ripple effect to run down her grotesquely flabby arms. "Don't know where the hell that is."

Another officer stepped forward. "C'mon, lady," he said. "You must see the airplanes going over here every day, don't you?"

"Damn sure I do," she half-shouted back. "But that don't mean I know where the hell they're going. . . ."

All three men had reached their limit with her by this point.

"Don't you have any idea at all?" the third officer asked.

"Nope," Rita snapped, clearly loving the fact that she was being difficult with the men. "But if you boys want to find this Mescalero place, then I suggest you wait for one of those damn jets to come over and then follow it."

The three Air Force officers found themselves jammed into the absolutely last available table in the small cafe.

The place was filled with authentic cowboys, with a

meager mix of cowgirls thrown in. The jukebox was blaring what seemed to be the same three country-and-western songs over and over, and, most distressing, the officers were told they would have to wait up to an hour for a bowl of chili and a side order of chicken-fried steak.

However, their waitress was able to bring them a pitcher of cold beer.

"What the hell is going on here?" one of the officers asked her. "This doesn't go on every night, does it?"

"In this town?" She laughed. "You've got to be joking."

She went on to explain that it was the annual Armadillo Christmas party, an event that began back in the 1830s when gold miners and *real* cowboys roamed these parts. The occasion called for a blow-up at the saloon, and this year its owner, Snake, had decided to bring in some live talent instead of the usual fare of mostly old, grainy, black-and-white skin films.

The officers didn't bother asking her for directions to the Mescalero air base—they had decided to eat first and ask questions later. With their carefully handled suitcase placed on the table before them, they divided the pitcher of beer three ways and sat back to relax and watch the goings-on around them. They talked about the hot weather, about their paying for their instant three-day passes, and about the long, last-minute drive down from Louisiana. Then they discussed the meager ratio of one cowgirl for every twenty cowboys stuffed into the saloon.

Still, after a while, they couldn't help bringing the conversation back to their reason for coming to New Mexico and the contents of their suitcase.

"I know this is stupid," one of them said, "but just check the damn thing. Make sure it's all there."

"That *is* stupid," another replied. "You want these shitkickers to see what we're carrying? They'll shoot us and no one will ever find our bodies."

"Relax, will you guys?" the third officer, and the man designated to actually carry the suitcase, said. "I've been doing this longer than both of you."

Then, in one deft motion, he clicked open the suitcase's snaps, lifted the lid, took a quick survey of its contents, then slammed it shut and locked it again.

"It's all there," he said confidently. "All three grand . . ."

The other two men visibly relaxed. "It's a lot of money," one of them said, his voice noticeably relieved.

The other one nodded, his manner almost giddy.

"Lot of money to bet on a missile," he said.

60

THE THREE AIR FORCE officers got their chili right on time—exactly one hour after they had arrived. But the wait was not as bad as they had feared.

The cafe was now literally overflowing with people—at least three dozen patrons were forced to take their seats outside the establishment, close to the big picture window, which allowed them to look in. At various times, chants of "Start the show!" would spring up, build in intensity, and reach a crescendo so dramatic the place was literally shaking. Then they would die down, only to be revived several minutes later.

The officers were also getting drunk on the powerful Mexican beer, and they gradually felt themselves slipping into the spirit of the occasion. The tacky red and green decorations, the near-dead Christmas tree, the never-ending Christmas carols that had replaced the worn-out C&W tunes—all of it began to fit. Even the red-hot chili tasted festive, though they didn't realize that the sweet-tasting if slightly dry and chewy meat within was authentic armadillo.

They had just wiped their bowls clean and ordered another pitcher of beer when suddenly the lights of the cafe dimmed. A roar came up from the crowd as two spotlights—one white, one pale blue—were switched on and directed by a versatile waitress toward the small square stage in the middle of the dance floor.

Snake, the owner of the establishment, then jumped up on the platform and was met with a chorus of drunken boos.

"Kill those fucking Christmas carols!" he yelled, his order instantly accomplished with one kick from the cowboy sitting next to the record player.

"Okay," Snake continued. "Tonight, it's my pleasure to present to you the finest dancer you will ever see!"

"Guaranteed?" someone yelled from the audience, to the laughs of the crowd.

"You bet!" Snake yelled back. "All I ask is that you keeping a-drinkin' while she's on."

He jumped off the stage and over the bar, taking over control of the spotlights from his already overworked waitress. Suddenly another kind of music rose up in the now-hushed room. It was Debussy's *Afternoon of a Faun.*

The three Air Force officers were totally mesmerized. The combination of the strong beer, the chili, and the lush if scratchy strings suddenly seemed to expand the room to three times its size. A gasp came over them and the rest of the crowd as the door to the back room opened and they saw, standing in the silhouette of its pale light, what looked like a vision.

With an elegance not seen very often in many parts of New Mexico, the woman dancer seemed to glide through the crowd and up to the stage. She looked absolutely beautiful—long red hair flowing, her pearl-white, skin-tight outfit covered only by see-through multi-colored veils and her delicate ballet slippers.

Then she began to dance. . . .

For the next five minutes, the room was absolutely silent as the waves of Debussy's classic work washed over the crowd. Slowly, one by one, she removed her veils, each time revealing more of her perfectly curved body. Soon the outlines of her breasts were in clear view. Another veil was removed, and her delicate nipples could be seen. Then her lovely thighs, her gorgeous buttocks, her outstanding legs. Through it all, no one spoke, no one moved, no one dared to even drink their beer. They were spellbound—transfixed by the music and the movements of the woman slowly removing her clothes.

At a predesignated point, Snake switched off the white spotlight, and now the dancer was bathed only in hypnotic blue. A titter went through the crowd as she slowly lowered the straps of her ballet gown, throwing back her red hair to let the audience see the full beauty of her bare white shoulders. Still gracefully moving to the strains of *Afternoon of a Faun,* she pulled the skin-tight fabric away from her chest and dramatically ripped it—causing a gasp to come up from the crowd. Bending down into a *porte-à-bras,* she pulled back the fabric completely, and when she arose, her bare breasts were revealed for all to see.

"Oh, my God!" one of the Air Force officers moaned. "This is unbelievable. . . ."

"Keep quiet!" another snapped. "You'll ruin her show."

"No, I don't mean her," the officer said. "I mean *that* . . ."

He tugged his companion's sleeve and pointed to the table next to them. Sitting there was half a dozen of the biggest, toughest, dirtiest-looking cowboys. They had a candle going on their table, and one of them was holding the end of a long metal bar over the flame.

"What the hell . . . ?" one of the officers began.

The other leaned over to the cowboys and, in his best horseshit voice, whispered, "What you doing, partner?"

The man turned back toward him and laughed drunkenly. "We like her so much, we're going to brand her," he said with a whispered slur.

As proof, he removed the end of the bar from the flame and held it close to the officer's nose. It was white hot, and its design was that of an *R* with a circle around it.

The officer looked back at his two friends, his eyes the size of silver dollars. Then all three looked up at the dancer, who was now just removing the last of her clothing.

In the next instant, all hell broke loose. The drunken cowboy was just rising from his seat, the white-hot branding iron in hand, when suddenly, an oddly dressed man jumped up onto the stage and screamed, *"No! No more!"*

The man looked somehow familiar to the Air Force officers. He was dressed in dark pants and a white shirt and was wearing a sombrero. But just seconds after taking over the stage, he stripped off these clothes to reveal a full Apache garb—poncho, long shirt, stitched pants, and moccasins—underneath. He was also wearing tortoise-shell glasses, and despite his costume and long braided hair, the pasty-white color of his skin revealed him to be very much a paleface.

The woman dancer, now all but naked, was astonished to see the man fly up to the stage with her. She turned toward him and in a split second seemed to recognize him. It was almost as if she were about to raise her hand to strike him when a voice boomed, "Get away from her! She's mine!"

The voice belonged to the cowboy with the branding iron, and he was now angrily moving toward the stage, hot metal in hand, and tossing people out of his way like they were weightless.

In the next instant, the blue spotlight went out. Then someone threw a bottle at the stage, missing it and knocking out an unsuspecting cowboy standing near the swinging door. This prompted a return bottle, thrown by the unconscious cowpoke's friend, and the fight was on.

"Get the money!" one of the Air Force officers screamed.

"I got the goddamn money!" he was told. "Let's get the hell out of here!"

The three officers started for the door, trying their best to duck the bottles, chairs, and other missiles that were flying through the air in all directions. Somehow the candle the cowboys were using to heat their branding iron fell over, and a clump of tacky Christmas decorations next to their table quickly ignited.

Now screams of "Fire!" were added to the shouting and grunting as the brawl reached a new height of savagery. Their route of escape brought the three officers right next to the stage, now the center of all the fisticuffs. Though their common purpose was to get out of the burning cafe, the three officers couldn't help but notice that the man who had so dramatically leaped onto the stage was now getting pummeled unmercifully by the cowhands. Meanwhile, the drunken cowboy with the branding iron had thrown the dancer over his shoulder and was running out of the cafe by the back door, intent on finding the small town's Justice of the Peace.

Whether it was their military training or just plain human nature, the three officers paused in their flight just long enough to pull off the cowboys who were beating the bespectacled man and drag him out through the front door with them.

"I can't believe this is happening!" one of the officers yelled, his voice a mixture of terror at what he saw and relief that they were finally out of the burning, brawling structure.

To no one's surprise, the fight went right on without them. Smoke was now pouring out of the swinging front doors. A chair came crashing through the window close to them, demolishing the neon "Saloon Ballet" sign in the process. All the while, the strains of Debussy were still very much in evidence, providing a surrealistic soundtrack for the scene.

"Let's go before the state cops get here!" the officer hugging the suitcase full of money yelled.

His companions needed no further prodding, but there was the question of the man they'd pulled out of the battle.

"Shit, let's bring him," one said. "They'll kill him if we don't."

Again there was no time to argue. The cafe was smoking even more heavily now, and the massive fistfight was spilling out into the street.

Dragging the man between them, the three officers reached their car just as a detachment from the brawl spotted them. In seconds, they saw about twenty-five crazed cowboys running their way.

"Jesus, start the fucking car!" one of them yelled to the driver as all four piled in.

The Plymouth kicked once, then finally turned over. The driver put the car into gear and squealed up a few pounds of gravel as they roared away, literally leaving the enraged cowboys in the dust.

"Lord, please get me back to Louisiana in one piece!" one of the officers yelled as the Plymouth quickly roared past the town limits and onto a barely paved desert roadway.

Their hands and voices still shaky from the narrow escape, the officers turned to look at the battered man who was now riding with them.

"Close call there, bub," one of the men said.

The man, suffering from what looked like a multitude of small cuts and abrasions, adjusted his glasses and wiped his face with his hands.

"I just can't believe she would do such a thing," he mumbled. "She was taking her clothes off so that everyone could see her. . . ."

"Don't feel bad, pal," the officer driving said. "Lots of dames dream about doing the exact same thing."

"So where you going, anyway?" another officer asked him. "You can't go back there."

"I don't know," he said. "I feel like my whole life has just come crashing down."

"Well, where do you live?" he was asked.

"I can't remember," the man replied tearfully. "I used to be in the Air Force. But I don't think I am anymore."

The men looked at his clothes, and all nodded in agreement. Still, the man's statement gave the driver an idea.

"Air Force, eh?" he said, pushing the car past 70 mph. "We're looking for an air base around here. It's called Mescalero. You wouldn't know where it is, do you?"

The man wiped his eyes with his grimy hands. "I used to be stationed there," he said, the words choking in his throat.

"Are we close?" the driver asked, excitedly. "Can you tell us how to get there?"

"It's easy," the man said, painfully rolling down his door window and pointing to the bright greenish aura that was lighting up the night sky off to the west.

"See that light in the sky over there?" he said. "Just follow it."

61

Mescalero

FOR THE FIRST TIME in five years, Chas Spencer actually wished he were back in Korea.

Spending days on end in the light-deprivation chamber aboard the *Holly One*, during the painful takeoffs and landings and being charged with treason almost seemed like a pleasant diversion compared to what he'd gone through in the past twenty-four hours.

The whole impetus behind the plan to stage a competitive analysis flight between the Tomarc and the Starfighter had been Kenneally's. The young senator had contacted the appropriate allies in Congress and told them about Xavier and his clique; he had arranged to have the XF-104A flown immediately to Mescalero and had even arranged to have the defense-appropriations staff order Xavier to hold the competition in the first place. But as he told Spencer the night of their meeting aboard the Kenneally family's private airplane, the key to the plan's success was to limit the number of people who knew about the competition to the absolute minimum.

This was now impossible. Spencer had let the genie out of the bottle when he told the other Mescalero pilots exactly what was written on the orders Xavier had so foolishly thrown away. At the time, he thought it was a good idea. After all, wasn't the effort to defeat Xavier and his admirers important to all pilots, everywhere in the Air Force? Little did he know that his colleagues would turn the news of the competition into a wagered event that would make even the most cynical Kentucky Derby bookmaker take notice. Word of the "Mescalero Pool" had simply spread like wildfire, and for the past day the base had been besieged with requests from pilots stationed at other air bases *around the world,* wanting to get in on the action.

The phone lines into the base had been hopelessly jammed since noon the day before, and the nonsecure radio lines were even worse. Pilots were even exchanging bets via air-to-air radios, which was a direct violation of Air Force regulations.

But radio chatter Spencer could have dealt with—it was the larger problem of the pilots who showed up in person to see the race that made him long for those relatively peaceful nights in the dark aboard the *Holly One.*

He first became aware of the problem when, at 0800 that morning, he heard a symphony of blaring car horns. The racket was coming from Gate 3B, the base's main gate, and for a while it sounded like a wedding party leaving a ceremony. But when it persisted, Spencer hopped into a jeep and sped to the gate, only to find a traffic jam of Air Force sedans and jeeps outside the entrance.

He asked the MPs what was going on and was horrified to learn that the vehicles were filled with Air Force personnel—pilots, mostly—who had heard about the competition, collected hundreds of dollars in bets, and driven, sometimes hundreds of miles, to Mescalero to get in on the action, as well as to see the start of the race.

The first few carloads had arrived during the night and gained access to the base with a simple flash of their ID pass and an excuse that they were visiting someone. But as dawn arrived and more cars showed up, the MPs called their superior and he called Xavier. Now the MPs were not only closely questioning each member of each car, they were searching the vehicles themselves. And any vehicle attempting to leave the area was stopped by the MPs, its occupants identified and, in some cases, detained.

Spencer had an 0930 test-out in an F-93, and after completing the forty-five-minute exercise, he came around on his landing approach and overflew the main gate. To his dismay, the traffic jam had grown even larger, as had the MPs' presence. It was beyond him how so many servicemen could get so many three-days passes on such short notice.

After he had landed and filled out his report, an MP delivered a message that he was wanted in Xavier's office immediately.

This is it, he thought glumly. *I'll be out of my wings by sundown. . . .*

The five-minute walk to Xavier's office was pure torture for Spencer. First, he found himself wondering what airline would hire a pilot who had been drummed out of the Air Force for gambling. Then, as he drew closer to the base's administration building, he began to think that being charged with gambling might be the least of his problems. Possessing and passing on classified information—crumpled by a general or not—was an offense that could send him to Leavenworth.

But as was so typical of everything in Xavier's orbit, reality was far removed from what Spencer had anticipated.

He entered the general's office to find it crowded with happy, talkative pilots—some from Mescalero, some he didn't recognize. A couple of secretaries were filling in as waitresses and were distributing cheese and crackers. There was even a bottle of champagne making the rounds.

"Welcome, Captain Spencer!" Xavier boomed. "Come in and join us. . . ."

While Xavier busied himself with other things, Spencer slipped around the back of the crowded office and grabbed the young pilot named Reilly by the arm.

"What the hell is going on here?"

Reilly just shrugged and took a sip of champagne. "The X-Man went nuts when he found out about all these guys headed here for the race," he said.

Spencer looked back to the fastidious senior officer, who, it appeared, was actually getting drunk.

"He doesn't look too upset to me," Spencer said, declining a secretary's offer of a glass of pink bubbly.

Reilly laughed. "Well, he's not," he said. "Not since they told him they were here to bet on the race."

"You mean he's *happy* that they're here?" Spencer asked, dumbfounded.

"No," Reilly said, getting a refill of champagne. "He's happy because they're all betting on the Tomarc to win."

Spencer left the party early and trudged back to the flight line to finish up some postflight work on the F-93.

He knew he had to contact Kenneally to tell him of this latest unexpected development, but his heart wasn't really in it right now. That a majority of Air Force pilots believed the unmanned Tomarc would beat the Starfighter was gloomy enough. But the fact that he had learned Xavier was actually matching their bets, dollar for dollar, was especially disheartening. To Spencer, this meant that Xavier was so sure that the Tomarc was going to win, he was willing to *lose* money on the Starfighter just to see his "unmanned vision" pay off.

Suddenly the thought of a job flying for some two-bit airline seemed pretty appealing.

It took him about twenty minutes to wrap up his work on the F-93, and then he began the long walk back to the main part of the base. Finished for the day, he was intent on getting a good seat at the officers' club and drinking himself into oblivion. Then he might call Kenneally. . . .

Walking across the tarmac, he noticed the Starfighter had been wheeled out of its protective hangar and was now sitting at a special hard stand, one that was surrounded with small floodlights. There was a battery of public-information photographers circling the new airplane, taking pictures of it from every imaginable angle. There was even a 16mm film crew on hand, taking footage of the futuristic airplane.

Spencer morosely drifted on by and was caught up in the action. A drawing of the Tomarc—depicted at about one-twentieth its actual size—had been placed next to the XF-104A, to give the lensmen some comparison. A set of larger floodlights was being installed around this illustration, these no doubt brighter than those around the Starfighter.

Xavier had really outdone himself this time, Spencer thought. It was one thing to turn what was supposed to be a classified project into a three-ring circus. It was quite another to jump in late in the game and declare oneself ringmaster. Yet that was exactly what the X-Man was doing. He realized that if the Tomarc beat the Starfighter, the more people who knew about it—both officially and unofficially—the more powerful the un-manned-fighter lobby would be. And that meant that Xavier was damn sure the missile was going to win.

Spencer was even more in need of a beer at this point, and he quickened his steps toward the OC. As he reached for the door to go in, the Lockheed pilot who had flown the XF-104A to Mescalero was just coming out. Oddly, he was dressed in casual clothes and was carrying an overnight bag with him.

They had never been introduced, but Spencer stuck out his hand, told him who he was, then got right to the point: He asked the pilot if he thought he'd be able to beat the Tomarc.

"In that Starfighter, you mean?" the man asked.

Spencer nodded. "You must know that airplane better than anyone," he said. "Can you do it?"

The man just shrugged. "It ain't my call," he said. "I'm not involved in the competition. In fact, I'm on my way to meet my transit flight back to California right now."

Spencer looked down at the man's overnight bag and finally made the connection.

"Well, if you're not flying the 104," he asked. "Who the hell is?"

The Lockheed pilot picked up the bag, threw it over his shoulder, and grinned.

"Beats me," he said.

62

THE DAY OF THE race dawned hot and sunny.

There were scattered high clouds up at 55,000 feet and the wind stream above Mescalero was blowing southwest to northeast, as always. It being a Saturday, most of the base was "dark," meaning little or no regular work was scheduled. This coincidence insured a large turnout of personnel on the flight line, waiting for the beginning of the event. Their number included not only those assigned to the base but also the several dozen visiting "speculators" who had first been detained by the Mescalero MPs, only to be granted clemency and eventually entertained by Xavier later on.

By this time, many on hand realized that a close reading of the specifications of the competition proved that the word "race" *was* fairly inaccurate. There would be no starting gun, nor an imaginary point in the sky that would serve as a starting point. All that was required for the commencement was for both aircraft to be at 60,000 feet at approximately the same time.

From then on, the only real race would be against the clock.

For safety reasons, there would be two finish lines— Intercept Points A and B—both the exact same distance in miles from Mescalero but a hundred miles apart on a north-south plane. For the first leg of the flight, both aircraft would follow what was called a one-third tracking path. This was a course that would carry them in parallel directions due west of Mescalero and over into Arizona. During this portion of their flight, both aircrafts would be tracked by ground stations at Mescalero and later by those located near the Luke Air Force Range, which was located in rugged desert country just to the southwest of Phoenix.

Once the aircraft had passed over the first third of Arizona, their courses would diverge. The Tomarc would be steered to the south; the XF-104A would turn slightly toward the north. From then on, the Starfighter pilot would lose visual contact with the F-98. The tracking duties would also be divided at this point. Two California Air National Guard C-119s would pick up the XF-104A's radio transmissions and, monitoring these signals, they would determine the exact time the Starfighter reached its intercept point, Point A. Meanwhile the Tomarc program recovery team would be positioned on the waters a hundred miles to the south, monitoring the radio signals from the F-98. They would determine the exact time the missile passed through its intercept point, labeled Point B. By comparing the radio-tracking and time-of-flight data from the two sets of observers, it would quickly be determined which aircraft had "won" the race.

The establishment of the two intercept points was necessary by Air Force safety regulations. It was standard operating procedure to clear a hundred-mile radius area for any supersonic missile test—a zone from which all commercial and private aircraft were strictly forbidden. By dividing the end points for the competition, the Air Force was avoiding the nasty possibility of the F-98 crashing through the flightpath of one of the C-119s or even the XF-104A itself. Indeed, the missile would be traveling so fast—at close to 1,800 mph, it would cover nearly a mile every two seconds—that even a near miss would be enough to disrupt the airflow around the pokey C-119s and quite possibly cause a crash.

These unorthodox rules had no effect at all on the frenzy of wagering, which was still going strong. To the dismay of the Mescalero pilots, just about all the smart money was being bet on the F-98, even though, rumors of Mach 3 speed aside, on paper, both aircraft were pretty evenly matched. It was only because of Xavier's promise to match each bet that the Tomarc was the runaway favorite.

Plus there was the question of who was going to fly the Starfighter. The original Lockheed pilot was long gone, and none of the Mescalero pilots had been tapped. And even if one of them were, it would have taken the designated man at least a day to become familiar with the XF-104A.

Anticipation built as the hour approached, and still no pilot for the Starfighter had appeared. A rumor swept through the base around 0930 that another Lockheed pilot was being flown in to do the job. Several Air Force cargo planes landed at Mescalero during the morning, and with each one the crowd would speculate that the civilian Starfighter pilot was aboard. But in each instance, these airplanes carried only military bigwigs from other bases—"invited" guests who had come to watch the start of the competition.

As it turned out, Spencer was the first one to learn who would be behind the controls of the XF-104A.

He had received a call at 0945 from an old friend named Peter McDoogle, the man who ran the Mescalero squadron's favorite off-base bar, which was located in nearby Bent, New Mexico. McDoogle, no stranger to intrigue, simply told Spencer to get over to his place, the Bum Dummy, as quickly as possible. Spencer did so and found the big red-headed Irishman grinning from ear to ear when he arrived.

"This better be good, Pete," Spencer told him. "Big doings at the base today . . ."

"I know all about it," McDoogle replied, leading Spencer over to the bar and pouring him an orange juice and vodka pick-me-up. "We even got a pool going here. Hate to say it, but the big missile is about a four-to-one favorite."

Spencer took a long chug of his drink. "I'm not surprised," he said, gloomily. "People want to believe that the future is here. Robots, computers, wars between machines. Maybe they're right—maybe guys like me *are* becoming obsolete. . . ."

"Jonesie would kick your butt if he heard you talking like that. . . ."

Spencer looked up from his glass and right at McDoogle. "Who the hell said that?" he asked.

At that moment a figure stepped out from the bar's back room.

Spencer couldn't believe his eyes.

"How you doin', Chas?" Hurricane Hughes asked.

Somehow it all made sense to Spencer—after a while, anyway. Hughes explained how he'd been discharged from the NACA's Libra Project only to find out that Kenneally had already made a deal with Lockheed. The agreement allowed him to sign on with the Starfighter's manufacturer for the competitive analysis flight under a one-day contract.

He had been studying the XF-104A flight manual ever since.

What better way, Spencer reasoned, for the manned-flight advocates to have a chance at success than by having one of the best test pilots in the Air Force fly the XF-104A?

"Could affect the whole betting scheme," McDoogle said just after Hughes and Spencer had exchanged a hearty bearhug. "That's why the senator suggested that Mr. Hurricane get here quietly and hide out until the last possible moment."

Spencer was getting excited again—he'd been in the doldrums since witnessing Xavier's champagne party the day before. But now he was beginning to realize that he'd been mistaking the senior officer's arrogance for confidence.

Still, he had to put the question to Hughes: "Can you do it, 'Cane? Can you beat that goddamn missile?"

Never one for overconfidence, Hughes just shrugged and said, "We'll give it one hell of a try."

A half-hour later they were back at the base, and Hughes was presenting his formal orders to Xavier.

It was an uneasy reunion for the two men: Xavier had been Hughes's commander before the pilot left for the Libra Project, and although Xavier had been relatively low key during that time, he and Hughes had consciously avoided each other whenever possible. Xavier knew of

Hughes's war record, his thwarting of the ex-Nazi atomic theft, his involvement in Operation Stormcloud. The senior officer was also well aware of Hughes's reputation as a test pilot. As such, he was the last person Xavier wanted to be flying the Starfighter.

Hughes knew only a handful of the other Mescalero pilots, so his return to his old base was actually sedate. To most of the personnel, he was just a famous name—like Patton or Tibbets or Yeager. And while a few of the men assembled—senior officers down to airmen alike—may have been tempted to change their bet from the missile to the fighter, for many it was too late. The base bookmakers had declared 1030 to be post time, and as such, very few new bets were taken after Hughes's arrival.

Despite the crowds and the assembled dignitaries, the "start" of the race went off with surprisingly little fanfare.

A radio set up on the tarmac near the XF-104A's hard stand was in direct contact with the Tomarc launch twenty miles away. When all was in readiness for the F-98 launch, Hughes climbed into the Starfighter and started up its powerful engine. Another call to the Tomarc control confirmed the missile was ten minutes from launch. At this point Hughes taxied the XF-104A out to the end of the runway. A third call revealed the Tomarc was seven minutes from launch. Once that information was confirmed, Hughes was given the clearance to take off.

Once the competition began there would be very few "rules" for him to ponder. Hughes's preflight briefing summary stated that he should "fly the XF-104A as if on a normal intercept mission, following the most 'expedient' flight path to the assigned point over the Pacific, at the same time making all efforts to preserve the integrity of the aircraft and crew."

In other words, get to the intercept point as quickly as possible without tearing up the aircraft or killing himself in the process.

Hughes did one last check of his flight instruments, at the same time getting himself into the right frame of mind for the mission ahead. During the last twenty-four hours he had come to greatly dislike Xavier, the Tomarc, and everything connected with them. Unlike Spencer and the others, who were only gradually made aware that the unmanned-fighter conspiracy was creeping up on them, Hughes had gotten a burst of education on the subject from Kenneally and a couple of inside sources had contacted from the Skunkworks.

In one respect Hughes was glad he hadn't been in on the first skirmishes of this philosophical battle—if he had remained at Mescalero, he knew that he would have probably run afoul of Xavier a long time ago and thus have been deprived of the opportunity to do him in now, if only symbolically. But he was also thankful that Kenneally had rescued him from Project Libra when he did, because Hughes had come to realize something else: that his involvement in the NACA program was not the stepping stone into space he had convinced himself it was. Rather, it was a step back from what he was best trained to do—flying high-performance jet aircraft. He had no idea what lay ahead for him after this competitive analysis flight; as he was signed on to Lockheed for just one day, it was anyone's guess whether the contractor would keep him on or not. But in many ways, Hughes didn't care. All he knew was that he wanted to fly, and be it the latest supersonic air buggy or a prop-grinder for some small airline, he'd be happy as long as he was behind the controls.

A message from the Mescalero tower concerning the wind conditions snapped him out of his daydreams.

"You are go for takeoff,' the flight controller told him. "Good luck."

Hughes took a deep breath and then ran the Starfighter's engine up to full power. Staring down the same runway he had lifted off from many times before, he felt a renewed surge of energy run through him.

Just like the old days, he thought.

He took one more deep gulp of oxygen, then popped the brakes on the Starfighter. He was instantly slammed back against his seat as the needle-nosed aircraft with the razor-sharp wings began to roar down the runway.

Ahead of him, the open, nearly cloudless blue sky seemed to symbolize the Big Question before him: Who or what would predominate the future of the Air Force, men or machines?

He was about to find out.

Seven miles away, sitting atop a mesa and looking out over the Mescalero airfield, Grady Curtiss watched as the Starfighter took off in a flash of fire and exhaust and roared into the sky.

Despite being five years out of the service, Curtiss could still appreciate the power and the beauty of the aircraft as it gained altitude, turned up on its tail, and streaked straight up into the heavens. He watched it until it was just a tiny silver speck disappearing into the high clouds, a pang of regret pinching his chest because he knew he could no longer soar as the pilot of this radically designed airplane could.

His attention turned back to the suitcase in front of him. He had been wracking his brain since early that morning, trying to remember exactly why he had it and what the money inside was for. All memory of the bizarre night in Clover Leaf lay hidden within him now—stored away in his subconscious, possibly never to be revived again.

What he *did* remember about that night started with the breakneck drive toward Mescalero and the long discussions about gambling and money and making the odds. At one point along the way, they had stopped for gas and met several other Air Force officers who were also enroute to Mescalero. These officers had told those in his car that the "odds were changing and to bet the plane."

Curtiss had then directed both cars to the front gate of the base, only to find a small traffic jam had formed there. He recalled the horror on the three officers' faces when they saw the Mescalero MPs searching the cars, questioning the people inside and apparently confiscating betting money.

Then he remembered the driver of the car trying to pull away from the gate, but a jeep full of MPs had screeched up and told him to stay put. At that point, the officers told Curtiss to get out and to take the suitcase with him.

Curtiss had done as they asked, walking past the MPs, who, after looking at his shabby dress and his ruffled condition, asked him what he was up to. Curtiss had told them he was a hitchhiker and the three men had given him a lift. The MPs had bought the story and let him go.

He had walked quite a ways down Route 32 before he recalled what had been said inside the car before the officers had told him to get out. Just before the MPs appeared, he seemed to recall hasty plans being made—something about all of them meeting again later, at which point Curtiss would return their suitcase to them.

The problem was that Curtiss couldn't remember where they were all supposed to meet.

He had slept in the brush that night and dined on some desert quail eggs that morning. Something had told him to climb the mesa—possibly something that the three men had said to him, but there was no way to know for sure. All he did know was that the suitcase contained three thousand dollars and he didn't know what to do with it.

He lay back and focused on the clouds moving slowly high above. His life had taken so many strange turns in the past five years—nothing was ever the same after his plane crash. But even though he had learned much since becoming a member of the Mescaleros, there was a nagging within that he would like to rejoin the whites. Even to fly again.

Or at least give it a chance.

In days past he would have dismissed such a thought as ridiculous, a judgment that one glance down at his hobbled and twisted body would confirm. But now, on this morning of high clouds and little wind, the thoughts didn't seem so preposterous. Did it have something to do with that jet that had just taken off? Or the suitcase of money now placed at his feet?

He didn't know. So he closed his eyes and immediately began to dream again about his old friend Gabe Evers.

Hughes leveled off the XF-104A Starfighter at 60,000 feet and throttled back to 600 knots.

He rechecked his position and then scanned the horizon, looking for the tell-tale plume of smoke. At first he saw nothing.

Maybe the goddamn thing blew up on the pad, he thought, at the same time knowing that he wasn't that lucky.

He took a deep gulp of oxygen from his mask and then he saw it—the long white trail of fire and smoke rising out of the morning clouds about twenty miles west of his position.

At the head of the blazing cyclone was the unmanned F-98 Tomarc missile, black and ominous—a direct contrast to his sleek, spaceshiplike Starfighter. He watched with unintentional awe as the missile reached 60,000 feet, effortlessly turned over, and streaked toward its predetermined intercept point out over the Pacific.

Suddenly everything that Hughes had endured in the last ten years as a test pilot—all of the flight testing, the tragedies, the loss of friends, the combat in Korea—was at stake. Had it all really been in vain? Was the unmanned Tomarc really the wave of the future? Would it make pilots like him obsolete?

It was up to him to find out.

He took another deep gulp of oxygen, then slammed the Starfighter's throttle forward. He instantly felt the resounding kick as the XF-104A's powerful engine opened up and hurtled him through the sound barrier in pursuit of the Tomarc.

The race was on. . . .

63

Beverly Hills

THE PHONE RANG TWENTY times at the mansion on Waverly Drive before the butler, awoken from his late-afternoon nap, finally answered it.

The man on the other end didn't identify himself—he didn't have to. All he said was "I'm calling about the football game . . ."

The butler was an old pro at these things by now. He checked a small brown notebook that he always kept next to this, the so-called "guest phone," and confirmed the code words. This meant that his employer's visitor would want to be disturbed with news about the "football game."

"Please hold on one moment, sir," the butler told the caller, gently laying the phone down on the table. Then he walked across the room to another phone and dialed a three-digit number.

I'll let this ring five times, he thought. *Anything more might be excessive. . . .*

Far at the opposite end of the twenty-five-room house, another phone, this one colored in shocking pink, began to ring.

"Don't you dare answer that," the naked woman said, spilling a few drops of her champagne glass as it touched her lips. "It might be the studio or my agent."

She was at the foot of a mammoth-size heart-shaped bed, dancing to a light bossa-nova tune that was being pumped into the room via the house's intercom system. Moments earlier she had stripped off her two-piece bathing suit, and covered her breasts with baby oil.

The last thing she wanted to do was be disturbed by a call from the outside.

"I have to," the man on the bed replied. "It's probably for me—I've got a few important things going on today."

Nearly naked himself, Jack Kenneally reached over and picked up the pink phone just as it was in the middle of its fifth ring.

"A gentleman with news on the football game would like a word with you, sir," the butler told him in a perfect, but phony, British accent.

"Put him through," Kenneally replied, motioning for the woman to climb up onto the bed with him. "This is the good news I've been waiting for," he told her.

"What's it all about?" she asked, seductively rubbing his hairy chest.

He chuckled and took a sip of champagne from her glass.

"Can't tell you, darling," he whispered in her ear. "National security matter . . ."

At that moment, the outside caller came on the line.

"Just heard from our people in San Diego," the man told Kenneally. "The missile won. . . ."

64

Bent, New Mexico

HUGHES WAS DRUNK.

He'd been at it for two days now, holding down the bar at Pete McDoogle's Bum Dummy and subsisting on little more than bourbon, beer, and the house specialty, grilled bacon and cheese sandwiches.

"You can't let this get to you, 'Cane," McDoogle told him for the thirty-sixth time. "It has nothing to do with you as a pilot."

"It has everything to do with it," Hughes replied, slurring every other word. "I had a chance to beat the goddamn thing, didn't I?"

Even in his inebriated state, Hughes could not help reliving what had turned into the most disastrous flight of his career.

"The damn thing was right ahead of me, Pete," he told McDoogle despondently. "God, one moment it was neck and neck. And then the sonofabitch just disappeared, and my plane went . . ."

McDoogle had heard the story so many times by now that he could have mouthed the words along with Hughes. From all reports, the competitive flight had started off well. Hughes had picked up the Tomarc launch immediately and virtually pulled even with the missile for the first ten minutes, flying slightly above and just a quarter-mile behind the F-98, to avoid the potentially damaging rocket wash.

They passed out of New Mexico and into Arizona, maintaining the strange formation at about 1,500 mph, the only unusual aspect being that a large weather front, complete with thunderheads, had rolled right into their flight path.

Hughes had taken the first sight of the storm as a good omen. Although according to a strict interpretation of the "rules"—especially the one about preserving the plane and its crew—he should have flown around or above the weather, he never once considered it, even though any other pilot probably would have. The loss of time and speed would have been too great. Besides, he was convinced that the XF-104A would do better in bad weather than the radio-controlled missile.

That's when he made what he believed was a critical mistake.

Convinced that he would pass through the clouds more cleanly than the Tomarc, he reduced his speed to 1,100 knots, rightly figuring that it would conserve fuel that he could expend at a higher velocity once he was out of the soup.

But no sooner was he inside the cloud bank than the Starfighter suddenly started to lose control.

"I'll tell you, Peter," Hughes slurred out for the tenth time in two hours, "it was the damnedest thing. One moment I was in the thick of the weather—flying level, being bucked around some, but nothing to get concerned about. Then, in the next second, I'm inverted and the damn airplane wouldn't stop spinning. . . ."

It took Hughes about half a minute to recover controlled flight, and he ran through several tricks in the test pilot's book to right the Starfighter. The trouble was, when he broke clear of the cloud bank, the Tomarc was nowhere to be seen.

"It's obvious what happened," he told McDoogle, who was now sitting across the bar from him, reading the sports page and simply nodding at all the pertinent parts of his story. "They jumped the missile when it was in the weather, figuring I'd throttle back like all good fly boys do."

"Error in judgment," McDoogle said, not taking his eyes off a story about the Chicago Cubs. "That's all . . ."

"Well, that's enough," Hughes said bitterly.

Once he had emerged from the cloud bank and couldn't find the F-98, he supposed it had already diverged from the one-third tracking path and begun its turn to the south. Still confident that he could make up the time lost in the storm, Hughes had proceeded at full throttle to the point where his own "divergent airborne monitor track" began. He made radio contact with the lead aircraft of the two C-119s circling out of the Pacific, and they started monitoring him from then on out.

He reached the intercept point less than a quarter-hour later.

He felt he had reason to celebrate as he approached the end of the race. The time he'd spent in the storm had accounted for barely thirty-five seconds, and he had made excellent time throughout the rest of the flight, maintaining an outstanding 1,690 mph until he was out over the Pacific. Knowing that the Tomarc's top speed was close to his own and that the missile had had to battle the turbulence of the storm too, Hughes was certain the difference between first and second place would be due to his flying skills. Unlike the missile, which was de-

signed to blindly plow through the atmosphere toward its
target, he had been able to steer the XF-104A with and
against the roguish air currents, making the wind pockets
and turbulence work for him and not against him. It was
this touch-and-feel system that had allowed him to shave
full minutes off his projected time—human instinct, accu-
mulated through his experience, that could not be factored into a machine's guidance system.

Even as he hit the home stretch, he had one more
trump card to play. At thirty miles to the intercept point,
he booted the 104's throttle and put the jet into a slight
dive. Using the increased velocity and the gravity of the
shallow dive, he rocketed through the intercept point at
1721.45 mph and let out a victory whoop, convinced
he'd won the race.

By his rough calculations he'd beaten the unmanned
interceptor by a good three minutes.

So it was with complete astonishment that he heard
from the C-119 pilots that not only had the Tomarc hit its
mark several minutes earlier but that its recovery team
had already located the spent missile in the water and
was hauling it in.

Flying the XF-104A back to Mescalero was the dreari-
est flight of his career. There was no crowd to greet him
upon landing—most of the ones who had bet on the F-98
were already in the officers' club celebrating. Only Spencer and a skeleton ground crew were on hand when he
taxied up to the hard stand, and the normally exuberant
young pilot was gloomier than Hughes—he and a very
few others had bet heavily on the XF-104A.

He spent that night in Spencer's quarters, writing a
report for Lockheed in which he suggested they reevalu-
ate the Starfighter's razor-sharp wing design, as he believed this had been the cause of the XF-104A's sudden
departure from the flight envelope in the middle of the
storm. He took a condolence phone call from Kenneally
around midnight, the senator telling him that, put in
perspective, the "race" didn't mean a whole lot anyway.
But Hughes was buying none of it. The race had meant
everything to him. It was supposed to have been his
resurgence into the test-pilot arena, his own personal

reenactment of the Phoenix, rising out of the ashes. He suffered through bad dreams until dawn, only to find out via a 0700 phone call that Lockheed wasn't going to pick up his option to stay on with them.

"I'm out of the Air Force," Hughes was saying to McDoogle. "I can't go back to the NACA, and Lockheed doesn't want me. I just can't believe it—I've never been unemployed before."

At this point, McDoogle did look up. "I told you, you've always got a home here," he said sincerely. "Pour beers for me every other night and I'll pay you wage and lodging."

Hughes ran his hand through his long, ruffled hair. He'd been staying in one of McDoogle's spare rooms for the past two nights, even bedding one of his pretty waitresses in the process. But he still felt a lost, empty feeling inside him. He didn't regret taking part in the race—he regretted losing the damn thing.

The machines had won.

"I just can't figure out what went wrong," he began mumbling again, pouring another beer from the bottomless pitcher in front of him. "Maybe I lost more time than I thought? Or maybe I went off course somehow? Or maybe the damn missile *should* replace us?"

At that moment, McDoogle reached over and took the beer glass away from him.

"I've got a suggestion for you," he said, pouring the despondent pilot a cup of thick black coffee instead. "Drink this and another cup."

"Why?" Hughes moaned. "It'll just sober me up."

"Exactly," McDoogle said, pulling out the keys to his jeep and handing them to Hughes. "Because as soon as you're seeing straight, I'll tell you about a place where you can go and think about all this and get it out of your system."

65

NOT ONLY HADN'T HUGHES seen Grady Curtiss in almost five years, he had thought he'd never see him again.

So he was startled when he drove up to the small military cemetery McDoogle had suggested he visit and found Curtiss sitting crosslegged between the memorial stones of General Jones and Gabe Evers.

Despite his perpetually confused state, Curtiss recognized Hughes right away, clamping a bearhug on him so tight that Hughes gasped for breath.

"I meet all my old friends here," Curtiss told him, pointing out the two tombstones and reading every word inscribed on them to him from memory.

Hughes was at first apprehensive even to stay and talk with Curtiss—the man was in a fairly deranged state when he saw him last in 1950, and that was *before* his crippling air crash. Now he looked like a white ghost in Indian clothing—bent over, skin blotchy and thin beyond belief. If it weren't for the trademark tortoise-shell glasses and the distinctive high, whiny voice, Hughes would have passed his old friend on the street without a second look.

But, oddly enough, after recounting the old times for about a quarter-hour, Hughes began to feel a strange kinship with Curtiss. To him it seemed like they were both in a similar situation—a couple of struggling vets, banished from flying and not knowing what lay ahead. It was partially due to this frame of mind—combined with the accumulative effects of the past forty-eight hours of drinking—that Hughes eventually relaxed and settled down next to Curtiss in the grassy area between the two tombstones.

And then there was the matter of the suitcase.

"It has three thousand dollars in it," Curtiss told him, eventually opening the valise and fingering the rubber-banded piles of fives and tens. "And for the life of me, I don't know who it belongs to."

Hughes asked Curtiss to recount how the suitcase had come into his possession, but the man had to admit that he remembered even less about it than he had the day before.

"All I know is that I woke up one morning and it was there," Curtiss said. "And my right hand was callused, so I must have been carrying it for some time."

Hughes examined the money and, judging from its fairly crumpled and disorderly condition, determined that it probably wasn't the result of a bank heist or some kind of hold-up.

Then a thought came to him out of the blue: Could the money have been meant for a bet on the Starfighter-Tomarc race?

"Did you get this from servicemen?" he asked Curtiss. "Maybe guys you met on their way to Mescalero?"

Curtiss closed his eyes tightly and nearly grunted from the intense thought. Still, all he could do was shake his head. "I just can't remember . . ."

Time passed, and they were silent for a while. The cemetery *was* a peaceful place—an island of cool trees in the middle of the scorched desert and a total flip-flop from the boozy recesses of the Bum Dummy. Yet the fact that Curtiss was nonchalantly walking around with the case of money intrigued Hughes to no end.

"So what are you going to do with it?" Hughes asked him finally.

Instead of answering the question directly, Curtiss launched into a half-hour explanation on the difference between dreams and visions. After about five minutes of the intense mumbo-jumbo, Hughes was totally confused. Still, he got the initial gist of Curtiss's spiel, which was that if a person were trained properly—as he had been by the Mescaleros—then they could turn their ordinary nighttime dreams into "important" visions. Then, again with proper training, these visions could be used like signposts, giving directions on what to do with one's life.

"I've been working on a dream I've been having lately," Curtiss told him. "It's quite nearly evolved into a vision."

"And where does the money come in?" Hughes was almost afraid to ask.

"Well," Curtiss answered, "in order to fulfill the vision, I'm going to have to double it, maybe even *triple* it."

"And then?"

"And then," Curtiss replied somewhat casually, "I'm going to use it to rescue Gabe. . . ."

66

"LAS VEGAS?" McDoogle exclaimed, nearly spitting out a mouthful of grilled cheese and bacon. "You've got to be kidding!"

Hughes and Curtiss sat down at the Irishman's private table located in the deepest corner of the Bum Dummy. "Do we look like we're kidding?" Hughes asked him.

McDoogle finally swallowed and took a large swig of beer. Unlike the others, he had seen Curtiss off and on over the years, feeding him occasionally and even letting him sleep in the back room on cold or wet nights.

McDoogle expected the deranged expilot to come up with crazy ideas. It was Hughes he was beginning to worry about.

"You're letting all the booze from the last three days affect your thinking," he said directly to Hughes. "You don't actually think you can *make* money in Vegas. It's impossible. The Mob makes sure of that."

"That's only if you stay at one table and play over a period of time," Curtiss interrupted. "My plan is to bet it all on just one thing—one shot, that's all."

The suitcase full of money was up on the table in front of McDoogle. He had already counted it with his eyes and determined that the figure of $3,000 was accurate.

He turned to Curtiss.

"Bill, think about this," he said. "This is as good as found money—no one's coming back for it. Now, you're not in the best of shape, and I know you spent a lot of your savings on your wife's hospitalization way back when. With this dough, you could get a good place to live. You could eat well every day. Maybe even put some in the bank and get interest. You wouldn't have to be a hobo anymore. . . ."

A pained expression washed across Curtiss's face.

"I look at this money not as a gift," he said, his voice clearer than it had been in years, "but as a sign, a vision. I *have* to put this money to good use. I have a mission that's been coming to me in my dreams for a long time. You know a lot about the Mescaleros. You know how powerful they consider dreams to be and how they can lead them to better lives. My dreams have already turned into visions, and I have been given a special quest. I have to fulfill it or I *cannot* live like a man. That means that I have to double or triple this money and then carry out my mission to rescue Gabe."

McDoogle was getting so upset he was unable to finish his lunch.

"But for god's sake, man, Gabe is five years dead," he said, his irritation coming through loud and clear. "He was killed—"

"No he wasn't," Curtiss said matter-of-factly. "I've seen him. I've talked to him."

McDoogle rubbed the cool condensation from his beer glass over his forehead. Then he turned back to Hughes.

"I sent you over to the cemetery because I thought you'd get some solace after seeing the resting place of the general and Gabe," he said. "I never expected you'd come back as party to some nutty scheme."

Hughes just shrugged. He wasn't buying any of Curtiss's dreams and visions malarkey. He just wanted to go to Las Vegas.

"So does this mean we can't borrow your jeep for a couple of weeks?" he asked McDoogle sheepishly.

The Irishman's face turned a deeper shade of crimson.

"Are you crazy?" McDoogle scolded him. "Or are you still drunk?"

"A little of both," Hughes replied. "Plus I got all the time in the world on my hands."

"Time you should be putting to better use," McDoogle told him, his tone still severe.

Hughes just shrugged again. "The bus it is," he said to Curtiss. At that, both of them got up to leave.

"Does this mean I'm not going to talk you out of this?" McDoogle called after them.

Both Hughes and Curtiss shook their heads no.

At that point, the Irishman stood up and crankily stretched out to his full frame.

"Hold on, then," he said, walking to his quarters in the back. "I'll pack my bag."

"Your bag?" Hughes asked. "What for?"

McDoogle turned back to him, his face still red but not as angry. "You don't think I'd let you two go alone, do you?"

67

THE TRIP to Las Vegas turned out to be a long, grueling, bumpy affair—one that stretched McDoogle's war-surplus Willys jeep to the limits of its considerable endurance.

More than once did Hughes ask himself if he had gone nuts for embarking on the journey. McDoogle had been

right—things *did* look different after he had sobered up.
What the hell did he want to go to Las Vegas for? To see
a mentally unstable man lose three thousand dollars?

The trouble was, they had been on the road more than
half a day before Hughes's hangover struck with eye-
opening vengeance. By that time it was too late to turn
back. So Hughes simply took his turns driving and gagging on the horrible roadside food they were forced to
eat.

Oddly enough, the farther they went, the more McDoogle
became entranced with the whole idea. It began the first
night, when he started regaling Hughes and Curtiss with
tales of various Irish heroes who had gone off on quests,
successfully completing them each time. With each passing mile, McDoogle came to believe that he was now
part of a noble mission—"the last of me life," he kept
repeating. By the time they saw the glow of Vegas lights
on their fourth night of travel, McDoogle was beside
himself with glee at the adventure of it all.

The famous Las Vegas Strip was everything Hughes
had heard it would be.

The larger casinos looked like something out of 1001
Arabian Nights, by way of Buck Rogers; the smaller
establishments looked like glorified Bum Dummys. They
found a cheap motel just off the Strip and an even
cheaper restaurant close by. Thus fortified with their first
solid meal in days, the trio set out for the Flamingo
Hotel, Curtiss carrying his $3,000 booty in the same,
now-worn suitcase.

They had stopped in a small New Mexico town about
halfway in their journey to buy cheap slacks and sports
shirts, all of the same garish colors. Now as they walked
through the front door of the ornate hotel, they received
more than their share of sideways glances. McDoogle—
large, red headed, bulging stomach with a prospector's
beard—led the way. Curtiss—anemic, long hair in Apache
braids, walking with a splintered, battered cane—was
close behind. Hughes—unshaven, eyes drooping, stomach still churning—brought up the rear. They looked so
odd, even in a town used to odd, that the casino's plain-

clothes security forces put them under surveillance even before they'd gotten past the lobby.

Curtiss had to be reminded that he'd have to convert the $3,000 into players' chips, something that took a while, as the man behind the money desk insisted on counting the small fortune twice. Finally, armed with 600 five-dollar chips, Curtiss made a beeline for the nearest roulette table and settled down on the first open stool.

"Do you think it's still wise to bet it all on just one spin?" McDoogle asked, his vision of adventure now being colored a bit by good old Irish pragmatism. "Might win more if you break it up a bit . . ."

Curtiss was already shaking his head.

"The mission is to triple the money on one turn," he said. "Don't worry. Apache dreams are strong. We'll win."

At that moment, Curtiss dramatically shoved all six hundred of the blue chips onto the double 00 space in front of him, this to the collective gasp of the other players.

"Do you know how to play, sir?" the man behind the wheel asked.

Curtiss nodded. "I want to bet it all on this spin," he said evenly.

The croupier looked at all three of them nervously.

"This is an unusually large bet to start off with, sir," he said. "Perhaps you'd like to see a few games played before wagering?"

Curtiss shook his head so hard his braids made a snapping sound as they whacked his neck and shoulders.

"No," he said defiantly. *"I want it all on this spin."*

The croupier gave a quick nod to the two security guards hovering nearby. One of them came right up in back of Curtiss, the other went to get the floor manager.

"Drinks are on the house," the security man said to Curtiss.

Curtiss turned back toward the man and somehow immediately tagged him as a casino employee.

"I don't drink," he said with an air of dismissal.

"I do," Hughes said quickly.

"And I," McDoogle added.

A waitress appeared out of nowhere with three shots of Scotch. Hughes and McDoogle helped themselves.

By this time the all-powerful floor manager had appeared and was surveying the situation.

"You realize that you could lose all this?" he calmly told Curtiss, pointing to the stacks of chips.

Curtiss nodded.

"And that there are no refunds, no arguments, once it's gone?"

Again Curtiss nodded, not realizing that should he win, he'd collect $108,000, *thirty-six* times the original bet.

The man then turned to McDoogle. "He's your friend?" he asked the Irishman.

"And I'm proud of it!" McDoogle boomed, his throat moistened by the shot of fine Scotch.

"Is he responsible enough to play this much money on one bet?"

"He is," McDoogle declared.

The floor manager shrugged and nodded to the croupier.

"Play it," he said.

The man took in the other patrons' bets and then gave the wheel a mighty spin. By this time the incident had caused a small commotion on the floor and a crowd had gathered. Together they all watched as the ball went round and round, Curtiss's large pile of blue chips almost gleaming at the center of the table.

To Hughes's battered senses, it seemed as if it took forever for the wheel to slow down. He was actually getting dizzy trying to keep his eyes on the little silver ball that was traveling clockwise on the counterclockwise-spinning wheel.

Finally everything seemed to go into slow motion. McDoogle was leaning in over Curtiss's left shoulder, Hughes was hanging on his right. The crowd held its collective breath, as did the croupier and the security men. If the ball rested on 00, the casino would lose quite a bit of money. If it didn't, then the three strangers could get nasty. Either way, the casino employees were prepared for a possibly volatile situation.

At last, the wheel squeaked its way into its final revolutions. The silver ball lost its centrifugal force and began bouncing in and out of the numbered slots. Cheers and groans rose up from the crowd as the sphere tantalizingly hopped around. For his part, Curtiss was sitting perfectly still, his eyes closed, his lips murmuring some unheard Apache chant. Hughes, too, found he was forced to close his eyes until the very last second.

Finally the ball fell into a final slot and stayed there. When Hughes opened his eyes, he saw it was resting in Red 17, not even close to 00.

It was a good thing the security people had stationed themselves so close to Curtiss, because when he saw he had lost, his first reaction was to leap across the wheel at the croupier, screeching a violent Apache war whoop as he went. The two burly security men caught him in midflight and yanked him back, first slamming him to the stool and then all the way down to the floor.

In the next instant, one of the guards turned and sucker-punched Hughes in the right eye for no good reason. Reeling back from the blow, Hughes collided with a woman and her date who were trying to escape the brawl and ended up in a tangle on the floor. From this vantage point he saw McDoogle lift up one of the security men by the scruff of his neck and hurl him, one-handed, across the casino floor. At almost the same time, he saw Curtiss down at floor level, viciously biting the other guard on the ankle.

More security men arrived, and as patrons scattered, Hughes, McDoogle, and Curtiss found themselves lifted up and carried toward the main door, their bodies being punched and kicked the entire way. With the aplomb of people who had done this sort of thing before, the security guards triggered the automatic doors to open and, in one smooth motion, tossed all three men out of the casino and onto the hard asphalt of the driveway beyond.

"You'll lose your kneecaps if you try to get in again!" one of the security men yelled, reciting the line as if he were crying out a passage from *King Lear*.

Hughes was almost run over by a limousine as he hit the pavement hard and tried to roll to cushion the blow. There was a screech of brakes and a small cloud of smoke as the car's massive chrome bumper stopped barely half a foot from his chin. When he opened his eyes, the first thing he saw was the word "CADILLAC," inscribed in small shiny metal letters across the car's grill. Six inches more and the letters "I-L-L" would have been imbedded in his forehead.

He was barely to his feet before he found himself and the others surrounded by yet another contingent of plain-clothesmen, these being better dressed than the ones who had just bounced him from the casino. Another difference: These men were not concealing their weapons.

"This disagreement does not call for gunplay," Hughes heard McDoogle boom as two men grabbed him from behind.

"Just calm down, sir," someone yelled.

Hughes struggled to get away from the two men hold-ing him—unsuccessfully, as it turned out. But in the midst of the grappling, he saw that Curtiss wasn't being manhandled at all. In fact, he was leaning over toward the back window of the stretch limousine, talking to some unseen presence in the back seat.

Hughes finally agreed to stop resisting, and the two men let go of him. McDoogle had negotiated a similar deal, and now he too was brushing himself off and push-ing back his ruffled hair. It was at this point that both men saw their friend Curtiss climbing into the back seat of the Cadillac.

"What the hell is going on here?" Hughes asked.

The security men on either side of him were similarly perplexed. "Our boss wants to talk to your friend, I guess," one of them finally said.

The strange scene—the waiting limo, its engine run-ning, McDoogle and Hughes bracketed by the nicely dressed bodyguards—continued for about a minute, all the while Curtiss being inside the car, carrying on a conversation with god knows who.

Finally he reemerged, wearing a broad smile.

"Yes, sir," he called back to the occupant of the big Caddy's back seat. "See you tomorrow."

With that, the limo driver honked his horn once, and the bodyguards disappeared into the enormous Cadillac. A second later it roared away, down the circular drive and out onto the Strip.

"What the hell was that all about?" McDoogle asked Curtiss, who was smiling so much it appeared that he was having trouble breathing.

"That guy recognized my Mescalero fertility necklace," he replied, jangling the string of beads he always wore around his neck. "He wanted to know where he could get one. Then I told him why we were here and what had just happened, and he said we should go up to his place tomorrow for lunch. . . ."

Hughes and McDoogle looked at each other in disbelief.

"Lunch?" Hughes asked. "I'm not going to some gangster's pad for lunch."

"He's not a gangster," Curtiss replied. "He's a millionaire. No, wait—I mean, a *billionaire*. And he says he'll help us find Gabe. . . ."

68

San Diego

THE MARINES SNAPPED TO attention as soon as the black Air Force staff car pulled up.

Their sergeant graciously opened the back door and waited a few moments for the man inside to step out. When he did so, the first thing the Marine sergeant recognized was the long brown shock of hair and then the smile.

"Welcome, Senator Kenneally," he said. "It's an honor to meet you."

Kenneally pushed his hair back against the early morning coastal wind and then shook hands with the man.

"Where you from, Sergeant?"

"Delaware, sir," the Marine answered. "Just outside of Wilmington."

"Nice country," Kenneally replied easily. "I've got a lot of friends down there. . . ."

Accompanied by two Air Force MPs and the driver of the staff car, the men moved over to the gate that led to the dock entrance. Two more Marines, a corporal and a private, were waiting there, still frozen at attention.

"Corporal Webster and Private Franklin," the sergeant said by way of introduction.

Kenneally shook hands with both, then asked, "Either one of you boys from Massachusetts?"

"My aunt lives in Lowell, sir," Webster answered.

"Lowell, you say?" Kenneally replied. "I've got a lot of friends in Lowell. . . ."

He took a look around the fenced-in dock, especially eyeing the attached sealed-up boathouse.

"I want to thank you men for getting up so early to give me this tour," he said, once again pushing back his hair. It was barely six in the morning, and except for the Marines and his own small entourage, the waterfront was deserted.

"Our pleasure, sir," the sergeant replied.

He opened up the gate and escorted Kenneally and one of the Air Force MPs down the ramp to the dock itself.

"Very useful program, this missile system," Kenneally said to the sergeant. "You must have a lot of activity here."

The Marine shrugged. "It's been busy about once a week for the past month or so," he said. "When things are jumping, we get out of the way and let the Air Force boys do their job."

Kenneally noted a slight tone of resentment in the Marine's voice.

"You mean you never get to go out and recover the missiles?" he asked.

The Marine shook his head. "No, sir," he replied. "We're trained in small-boat operation, sea-rescue-type stuff. That's why they assigned us here originally. But we haven't been out on the water yet, sir."

"Interesting," Kenneally said, walking toward the

closed-up boathouse. "You do see the missiles when they come in though, don't you?"

"Sure do, sir," the Marine replied enthusiastically. "Hard to miss something that big. Still smoking sometimes when they bring it in."

Kenneally nodded. "I believe it," he said. "What happens when they're recovered and towed to the dock?"

The sergeant shrugged. "Well, like I said, we just step back and let the Air Force guys do their work. We help them tie up their boat, of course, then they drag the missile around into the boathouse."

"Then what?"

"Then a tug comes down from the Navy base," the Marine went on. "The Tomarc recovery team loads the missile onto it, and then they take it away."

Kenneally smiled. "Boy, oh boy," he said. "We've got the Marines helping the Air Force, the Navy helping the Marines. I'm glad to see so much interservice cooperation. . . ."

"Just following orders, sir," the Marine said smiling, adding a half-salute for good measure.

They walked to the boathouse, and the sergeant let them inside. But upon entering the small structure, the Marine was appalled to see his men had left some sandwich wrappings behind the last time they'd taken their lunch inside the shaded building.

The senator didn't seem to notice, though. "How long does the missile stay in here?" he asked.

"Usually until nightfall the day of the launch," the Marine answered. "Though occasionally they leave it in here for an extra day or so."

Kenneally took a deep sniff and chuckled. "Did this place used to be a fish-packing house?" he asked good-naturedly.

The Marine laughed along with him. "Smells it, doesn't it, sir?" he replied. "I don't know whether it's the missile fuel or the fact that it stays in the water or what. But this place stinks to high heaven anytime they haul one in."

"Well," Kenneally said with mock seriousness, "we'll have to make sure our missiles start smelling better. . . ."

They all laughed and walked out of the boathouse and back onto the dock.

Kenneally took one more look around, then turned back to the sergeant. "You and your men are an important part of this mission," he said. "And you're all doing a great job. Keep up the good work."

Once again the Marine half-saluted. "Thank you, Senator," he said. "We'll try."

They walked back up the ramp and to the staff car.

"Just one more thing, Sergeant," Kenneally said, before climbing into the back seat. "You or your men ever catch a glimpse of one of these missiles going overhead?"

The Marine stared at him, then pulled his chin in thought. "Now that you mention it, sir, we haven't," he replied. "Guess they fly too high . . ."

Kenneally nodded and shook the man's hand. "Yes, I'm sure it's something like that," he said.

69

Las Vegas

HUGHES HAD JUST TAKEN his last bite of salmon supreme when the two menservants appeared and began clearing the dishes.

He, Curtiss, and McDoogle had been sitting in the penthouse dining room for nearly two hours at this point, and its opulence was still overwhelming them. Everything from the table settings to the chandelier to the picture frames to the tiles in the floor appeared to be made of either silver or gold. This particular room was filled with pictures—all of them depicting, oddly enough, 1930s aircraft.

From his seat, Hughes could see out the huge picture window and down onto the Strip below. The penthouse, being on the top floor of the World International Casino Hotel, was the highest point in Las Vegas—so said the assistant who had picked them up earlier in the same limo from the night before.

Trouble was, he didn't tell them much else.

By piecing together parts of Curtiss's conversation with the Mystery Man and what the man who came with the limo had told them, all that Hughes and McDoogle could fathom was that their host was incredibly wealthy, had an interest in aviation, owned most of Las Vegas, and was obsessively reclusive. This was confirmed by the fact that although they'd been at the penthouse since noon, they had not yet seen or heard from their host.

That was about to change.

With the lunch dishes cleared away and the coffee and after-meal drinks served, two men appeared from behind the room's large foldaway doors, carrying a small speaker with them. Without much fanfare, they plugged the speaker wire into a wall receptacle and turned it on.

"All set, sir," one of them called into it.

There was a five-second burst of static, and then a high, thin, reedy voice came on.

"Your lunch was satisfactory, gentlemen?" the voice asked.

"Just great," Curtiss replied enthusiastically.

"That's good," the voice replied. "You know, I have a new chef flown in from New York City every month. I like a good change of pace."

"So do I," Curtiss shouted back toward the speaker.

"Good. Well, let's get down to business, gentlemen," the electronic voice intoned. "I'm a busy man and I can give you only about five minutes."

"Where should we start?" McDoogle asked. "We're in your town solely by chance. On a whim, you might say."

"Nothing is done by pure chance," the man replied. "Believe me, after owning six casinos for the past few years, I know what I'm talking about.

"But when I saw your friend's, Mr. Curtiss's, necklet last night, I was very surprised. The Mescalero people are a fascinating study, and they have been a favorite of mine for years."

"Mine, too," Curtiss beamed.

"And then," the voice continued, "when Mr. Curtiss

told me the reason you three came to Las Vegas, I was very intrigued. I thought men like you died out with Cervantes."

"Tilting at windmills, you mean," Curtiss called back.

"No, believing in dreams," came the reply. "Like the Apaches, I've always tried to follow my own dreams or what I consider to be the interpretations of my dreams. And I admire anyone who does the same. My astrologer tells me that my dreams have brought me many things—my property, my airline, my movie studios. But what I like about dreams is that they're endless. Not just for me but for people like yourselves."

"I've been believing in my dreams since I was a boy!" Curtiss yelled out.

"So have I, Mr. Curtiss," the voice replied, a hint of happiness in its dour tone. "So have I . . ."

There was a brief silence. Hughes and McDoogle glanced at each other, not knowing whether to laugh or speak or just sit there and keep quiet.

"So, Mr. Curtiss," the voice began again, "just where is it that you believe your friend is being held by the communists?"

Curtiss sat straight up in his chair and leaned forward toward the speaker. "I believe it is somewhere in Southeast Asia," he said. "In my earlier visions, I saw the aftermath of a great battle. Destroyed military equipment. Bombed-out countryside. Even skeletons still stuck in the mud and dirt. All the while I have a sense of great heat, like the sun is shining twenty-four hours a day."

"Could you be talking about Tonkin in Indochina?" the voice asked. "Somewhere around a French battle-field, perhaps?"

"Perhaps," Curtiss replied.

"That big battle of last year . . ." McDoogle added.

"Dien Bien Phu," the voice answered. "Ah yes, the end of the line for the French colonialists. I have seen moviereels of the final days of the battle and indeed it was like a nightmare. Fanatical bastards. The communists tunneled right into the French compound and then blew themselves up, just to kill the French commanders. Then they came at them in human waves until there was just about no one left. And did you know that Ike had a bomber in the air with an atomic bomb aboard and orders to drop it if the French were being overrun? It's true. . . . But someone talked him out of it and the airplane was recalled. I believe they would have been better off dropping the darn thing! Solve a problem that's just going to come back to haunt us. Those native people— the Tonkinese—have a long history of warfare. If they're all turned into Reds, well, they won't be happy unless they're fighting someone. . . ."

At that point, Hughes (never a geography buff) wasn't even sure where the hell Tonkin or even Indochina was. He would learn later that up until the French surrender to the communist Viet Minh forces the year before, the place had been known as *French* Indo-China. It was next to Laos and old Siam, now Thailand, and just below China.

Now some people called it Viet Nam.

"But anyway, we're not here for me to tell you how I would run this world," the voice crackled. "Let's get on to this other part of your dream. Something to do with your friend planting flowers or some such things? What do you suppose all that means?"

"I believe they're actually crops," Curtiss replied. "Every time I see him, he's working very hard, weeding and hoeing and taking care of this garden of some kind. I can't see what kinds of things he's growing. Not clearly, anyway. Some are very bright green. Some are very dark, almost olive in color."

There was another short silence, then the voice returned.

"All right, gentlemen," he said. "Our time is up. Thank you for coming. Good-bye and good luck . . ."

The two assistants had disconnected the speaker phone before Hughes had a chance to say a word.

"That's it?" he asked the two men. "Good-bye, good luck—just like that?"

The two men stared back at him icily.

"A car will bring you back to your hotel," one of them said.

The next two days were pure hell for Hughes.

Between the three of them they had only forty-four dollars, enough for gas and food for the ride back to Mescalero with about ten bucks to spare. Las Vegas was the last city in the world in which to be stranded with no money. There was nothing to see but sand and desert and casinos. And the way the three of them were dressed, it was apparent they were not big spenders and thus were entitled to no freebies.

So they stayed holed up in the tiny hotel room, Hughes and Curtiss arguing nonstop about taking the trip in the first place, losing the money, having the strange conversation with the unseen, eccentric billionaire, and whether or not dreams and/or visions can come true.

Not surprisingly, with his already minimal enthusiasm for the adventure now completely sapped, Hughes had become the champion of the antidream contingent.

"Look at it this way," he argued dozens of times. "There are almost two billion people on this planet. Every one of them dreams something almost every night. That's billions of dreams every year. With numbers like that, of course *some* of them are going to come true—and those are the ones you hear about. Like 'I dreamed I found a million dollars and my dream came true.' Well shit, man, I've dreamed I gave a good roasting to Marilyn Monroe and it ain't happened yet."

"And it won't unless you *believe* it will," Curtiss would always reply. "Like I keep telling you, we're not talking about ordinary go-to-sleep dreams. These dreams are special. And you have to be trained in the art of recognizing them as being special and then turning them into visions."

At that point, Hughes would usually retreat under a pillow.

The only reason they remained in Vegas at all was because someone had paid for their hotel room for two further days. The benefactor could only have been the Mystery Man, and this was what kept Curtiss ardently believing in his mission.

"He wants us to stay," he argued over and over. "He's doing something, behind the scenes . . ."

"What the hell could he be doing?" Hughes would

counter. "Dropping in on Viet Nam and seeing if there any Americans there growing corn?"

McDoogle kept silent most of the time, uncomfortably cast in the role of referee.

"We've got a free roof over our heads for two days," the big Irishman would say. "Let's take advantage of it. If nothing happens in that amount of time, we'll leave."

In the end it was McDoogle's car, so he had the final say. But waiting around for forty-eight hours, with little money, in brutal heat, and with nothing to do but stare at four walls and listen to Curtiss's ramblings was enough to drive a person like Hughes off the deep end. For him it was all too reminiscent of the days he spent locked up on the *Holly One*.

Finally the last day of their free lodging arrived and the phone hadn't rung once.

"Happy now?" Hughes taunted Curtiss that fateful morning. "That guy was just a crazy rich ass who gets his kicks talking to some little people, that's all."

At this point even Curtiss appeared to give in. "It's too bad," he said as he joined McDoogle and Hughes in packing up their meager belongings. "I was working on another dream about Gabe last night."

"Yeah, well, I had a dream last night too," Hughes said, hurriedly stuffing his extra change of socks and underwear into his duffel bag. "I dreamed that I was unemployed and standing in the dole line. Trouble is, I woke up and realized that this is one dream that *will* come true."

Although the cutting remark had been aimed straight at him, Curtiss hadn't heard it. Instead, he was trying to explain his latest nocturnal vision.

"This one was really odd," he said sincerely to McDoogle, who patiently pretended to listen. "For the first time Gabe was actually trying to tell me something. Usually he just tries to shush me away."

"What was he telling you?" McDoogle asked.

"I'm not sure," Curtiss replied. "Something about a duck . . ."

Hughes rolled his eyes and continued packing stolen towels into his bag. "Great, he's dreaming about ducks!"

"Yeah," Curtiss continued, oblivious to Hughes's insulting attitude. "But he wasn't saying it. He was . . . was tapping it out to me . . ."

"What do you mean, 'tapping'?" McDoogle asked.

"You know, Pete, like on tom-toms," Hughes said with a cruel laugh. "Or is it a drum telegraph?"

"No, not that," Curtiss replied earnestly. "It's just that it's so hard to explain."

"I'm not surprised to hear that," Hughes said to McDoogle, finally tying off his duffel bag.

Curtiss then turned to Hughes and asked, "Did you and Gabe ever communicate by Morse Code?"

Hughes stopped in mid-gasp.

"What did you say?"

"Morse Code," Curtiss replied. "Was there a time when you guys used to speak to each other in Morse Code?"

Suddenly Hughes's mind flashed back five years, to the secret missions over Korea when he and Gabe Evers used to carry on a conversation by blinking their cockpit lights on and off, thereby sending messages in Morse Code.

"Just knock off all this talk and pack so we can get out of here," Hughes told Curtiss angrily. "You're really beginning to get on my nerves."

Curtiss shrugged. "Just telling you what I saw, that's all," he replied.

They were ready to go within ten minutes. McDoogle courteously returned the room key to the front desk, at the same time checking to see if their anonymous benefactor had re-upped them for some more free nights at the hotel. He hadn't.

Returning to his jeep, the big Irishman climbed behind the wheel and let out a long, tired breath.

"Maybe some day this will all make sense," he said.

He put the jeep into gear and started to move out of the dusty, unpaved parking lot. But just at that moment a limo appeared, so quickly they nearly collided with it.

The two familiar-looking assistants emerged from the back seat and sauntered over to the jeep.

"I told you!" Curtiss yelled, waving enthusiastically to the men.

"Maybe they just want their rent money back," McDoogle said.

The men were carrying an envelope, and by the time they'd reached Curtiss's side of the jeep, they had it opened and were pulling out a photograph.

"Our boss wanted us to show this to you," one of the men said in a distinctly Mormon accent. "He wants to know if it looks familiar to you."

McDoogle and Hughes crowded around Curtiss's shoulders as he studied the photo. It was an aerial shot depicting what looked to be dense jungle below.

But the closer Hughes studied the photo, the more chills ran up his spine.

"Good god!" he said, pointing to a patch of land in the upper right-hand corner of the photo. "Look at that. The way those bushes or whatever are arranged."

It took McDoogle and Curtiss a moment to see what Hughes was talking about. But then they saw it, too. There was a flat portion of the landscape that was dotted with patches of light and dark vegetation.

"Look at them!" Hughes just about yelled. "Those dark patches. They're dashes. And dots. They're . . ."

"Morse Code," the assistant finished for him. "Our boss saw them, too."

"But what does it say?" McDoogle asked.

"It says two things," the suitcoat-and-tie assistant replied, checking with a small notebook. "One is a variation on 'have intercourse with a duck.' The other is 'U.S.A.' "

" 'Have intercourse with a duck'?" Hughes asked excitedly. "You mean 'fuck a duck'? That was Gabe's favorite expression! You guys remember—it was the name of his airplane in World War II!"

McDoogle looked at Hughes in disbelief, then made the sign of the cross. "Jesus, Mary and Joseph," he whispered. "Maybe, he *is* alive . . ."

70

Burbank, California

THE TWO LOCKHEED DESIGN engineers were so nervous, they'd already smoked nearly half a pack of cigarettes between them in just a little more than an hour.

They had never met a senator before—or any politician of high repute, for that matter. What's more, their bosses had been ordered not to reveal exactly what Senator Kenneally wanted to discuss with them. They were told only to bring their current files on the X-7 rocket to an out-of-the-way room located at the back end of the huge Lockheed plant and wait for the senator to arrive.

Thus they had been waiting now since seven in the morning. It was nearly eight-thirty when Kenneally and two assistants finally came in, accompanied by the aircraft plant's chief security officer.

The senator instantly put the pair at ease with a wide grin and two hearty handshakes.

"Where you from?" he asked both men. As it happened, both men were from Texas.

"Great country," the senator replied. "I've got a lot of friends down there."

Then they got down to business. Kenneally requested and received a complete briefing on the X-7, the missile that had given birth to both the Tomarc and the XF-104A. The two engineers reviewed the history of the X-7—how its engines, though faulty at first, proved to be adaptable for the needs of the Tomarc, while its stiletto shape helped in the design of the Starfighter. At times, the conversation got too involved, even for someone like Kenneally, who, as a test pilot for nearly seven years, knew his way around the guts of an experimental aircraft.

After the hour-long review, Kenneally then asked the first of the two most critical questions.

"In your opinion, what is the most serious drawback of the Starfighter?"

The engineers immediately became anxious again. The senator was asking them to reveal negative aspects about the product of one of their company's biggest contracts. But a quick nod from the Lockheed security chief let them off the hook. They discussed the question in whispers between themselves for a few moments, then came up with a frank answer.

"Besides the fact that the ejection seat blows down, which would be tricky at low altitudes, overall the airplane would tend to be unstable under certain flight conditions," one said. "Probably not the best aircraft in less than ideal weather. The engines have always been slightly bothersome. And the wings are of a radical design—possibly a little *too* radical."

Kenneally made a few notes on the back of an envelope, then asked his second questions: "What's the biggest drawback of the Tomarc?"

Immediately both men answered at once: "Range," they said. "It's very limited in that area," one added.

Kenneally's eyebrows perked up. "Range?" he asked. "Why?"

"Engines are too big," one engineer replied.

"Can't carry enough fuel to feed 'em for a long time," the other added.

Kenneally scratched his chin in thought. "What kind of range are we talking about?" he asked.

The security chief interrupted at this point. "I'm sorry, Senator, but that *is* proprietary information. We really can't talk about it. . . ."

"I understand," Kenneally replied. "But just let me ask you this: Can that missile go as far as a Starfighter?"

Uncharacteristically, for engineers, both men actually laughed.

"No, sir," one said. "Not even close . . ."

"The F-98 can fly high," the other continued. "And it can fly fast. But it can't fly very far."

71

One Week Later

"MY GUESS IS THAT we're in Colorado," McDoogle was saying, surveying the landscape around him. "East Colorado has terrain like this."

Hughes shaded his eyes and took a slow 360° turn.

"Naw, the sun's not right," he concluded. "I'll say Utah. The high desert . . ."

Curtiss didn't even bother to look up. "How do you even know we're still in the United States?" he asked.

Hughes and McDoogle looked at each other and shrugged. Considering the events of the past few days, they had to agree with their strange friend. They *could* be anywhere.

After seeing the remarkable aerial photos, they had abandoned McDoogle's jeep in the motel parking lot and ridden back to the World International Casino in the Mystery Man's limo. Once there, they were introduced to a character simply known as Bull, who made it quite clear to them that he was the best soldier of fortune in the Western world.

He was also the highest paid—and Bull was about to become even richer. He announced that the Mystery Man had hired him to find Gabe Evers and a dozen other Korean War POWs who were believed to be held in what was being called communist North Viet Nam. He wanted Hughes, McDoogle, and Curtiss to go along on the rescue mission.

That had been seven days ago. In the time since, the three men had been outfitted with three changes of camouflage uniforms (including socks and underwear), two pairs of specially sealed jungle boots, a feather-light pith helmet, a special waterproof M-1 rifle, and a survival kit packed with the exact same type of cube food that Hughes had consumed during his NACA days.

It was the cube food that convinced Hughes that the Mystery Man and Bull were serious.

The photo they had been shown by the two assistants had been taken the day after their first "meeting" with the Mystery Man. It had been developed and rushed to the U.S. in less than twenty-four hours. Though they were never told exactly how he had been able to get a photo-recon unit over communist Viet Nam, Bull had informed them later that through a series of blind companies and dummy corporations, the Mystery Man had employees and aircraft "everywhere, except the North Pole, and he's working on that."

After spending three more days at the penthouse, Hughes, Curtiss, and McDoogle accompanied Bull and ten of his men on a late-night C-47 flight to nowhere— literally. The C-47 crew had blackened the windows and followed a very long and circuitous flight plan. When they landed early the next morning, Hughes was convinced that even Bull himself didn't know where they were.

The terrain was high desert, and they were close to a mountain that boasted several manmade caves. Hidden inside one of these caves was the unusual aircraft that would be their means of transportation to Southeast Asia.

At first glance, the airplane looked like an enormous flying luxury liner. Much larger than a B-29, its dimensions actually approached that of the behemoth B-36. Like the B-36, it had six propellers, supplemented with four smaller jet engines, the powerplants being placed on a long, wide wing running atop the fuselage. The body of the aircraft itself was wide and squat and seemed to have an inordinate amount of doors and hatches. Although six separate sets of foldaway wheels provided the massive craft with the ability to land on hard ground, its curved, boatlike underbelly was proof enough that it was designed to land on water.

But it was what was inside the aircraft that made it most unusual. Bull explained that the Mystery Man—who was, among other things, an aeronautical designer—had literally dreamed about the aircraft one night shortly after the Japanese had attacked Pearl Harbor. Knowing that any U.S. Pacific campaign would have to be fought island by island, the Mystery Man proposed that the Army Air Corps build a fleet of the huge amphibious aircraft. The airplanes would be large enough to carry hundreds of soldiers and many large guns, some of which could be attached to the insides of the airplane and used for added protection in flight.

In theory, these enormous airplanes would swoop down on the island to be invaded without warning. Landing just off shore, the airplanes would pull in close to the beach, disgorge the troops and equipment, pull out, and return to their base to pick up another load. Besides the obvious features of surprise, the flexibility in which the airplanes could be used was outstanding—they could ferry soldiers to trouble spots on the invasion beaches instead of being locked into set plans such as transporting troops ashore via landing craft from large naval vessels.

The concept was a good one, and the Army secretly gave the go-ahead to have one of the airplanes built. This was completed in record time. But somewhere along the way, the U.S. Navy got into the act and, seeing the aircraft as a threat to its power and surface fleet, persuaded key legislators to cut off funding for the secret project. They did, and with little else but one airplane to go on, the Army scrapped the whole project. Hurt and feeling a little betrayed, the Mystery Man locked the single aircraft up in the cave and let it sit for nearly fifteen years.

Until now.

"I guess you're on for twenty dollars," Hughes said, shaking hands with McDoogle. "I say Utah, you say Colorado."

They walked back inside the cave and, passing the small army of mechanics who were working industriously to get the airplane airworthy, they wound up as requested in Bull's makeshift office, deep in the back of the hidden hangar.

Bull was a huge specimen, aptly named and dwarfing even the mighty McDoogle. He was nails-for-breakfast tough, crude spoken and pockmarked with scars and burns from previous engagements. He also knew how to keep a secret.

No sooner had the trio walked in than Bull revealed a large map of Indochina as well as a smaller one of North Viet Nam.

"We've pinpointed the area where that photo was taken as being up in Conkin Province," Bull said, indicating a point on the map that was toward the far western reaches of the country, close to the border of Laos. "We've got an operative on the ground nearby. He's a Swedish guy and, as you probably know, the commies love kissing up to those Swedes.

"Anyway, he did some snooping around and he was able to pay off a few people. Remember, commies are the easiest people in the world to bribe because they ain't got but a few pennies in their pocket for most of their lives.

"In any case, for a couple bucks, our guy learns that for some reason, the communist Viet Minh made a deal with the Red Chinese a while back to loan 'em some of their Korean POWs and MIAs—guys that the Reds didn't include in the prisoner exchanges after the Korean ceasefire. Our man thinks it has something to do with the Viet Minh using new ways of indoctrination and brainwashing.

"So, some time last year, the Chinese shipped a bunch of captured GIs down to North Viet Nam. Put them all to work in the fields during the day, apparently. Just what they do to them at night is anyone's guess. Apparently they've got some very unusual living arrangements for them—very strange stuff.

"Anyway, we figure your buddy—or someone who knew of him—has got to be one of these prisoners. If it *is* him, we're just lucky he kept his wits about him."

"That sounds like Gabe all right," Hughes said, equal parts excited and hopeful at the thought that his friend might still be alive.

"Well, he must be a character," Bull said, with a rare

grin. "*Growing* a message in Morse Code is way out there. It's a good thing that the Reds have *nada* aircraft. He'd be skewered and eaten if they figured it out."

"I have a question," Curtiss piped up. "You said that the Red Chinese didn't return all their prisoners after the war. How come?"

Bull sat down behind his desk and lit a cigarette.

"That's the joker in the deck," he said after taking a series of mighty puffs. "They told us—officially, anyway—that all of the POWs who *wanted* to come back were repatriated."

"What the hell are you saying?" Hughes asked, getting angry at what he thought Bull might be suggesting.

"I'm saying that we've got to assume that these POWs are guys that didn't *want* to come back," Bull stated bluntly. "Guys who either were brainwashed into idiots by the commies or who actually liked communism. You've heard about them. They made radio broadcasts during the war."

"Well then, that ain't Gabe down there," Hughes shot back. "He would never have turned sides."

"I agree," McDoogle added. "Not Gabe . . ."

Bull just shrugged. "Let me tell you fellows something," he said from behind a cloud of cigarette smoke. "You probably have no idea what the Reds did to some of our guys. I do. They had ways of making our guys think that they were already home in Illinois or Ohio or whatever, and that China had already won the war and taken over America!"

"How could they possibly do that?" Hughes asked, somewhat doubting Bull's claim.

The man looked down at his desk and shook his head. "I'm sorry," he said. "I can't tell you."

"Why not?" McDoogle wanted to know. "Military secret?"

"Worse," Bull replied. "It's a *company* secret. My employer's company. He knows things that presidents would lose their cookies for if they ever found out. So take my word for it. It happens—whether it be through drugs, or beatings, or just wearing down a man's resistance, the Reds could break your buddy, no matter how strong his will is. . . ."

*   *   *

They took off forty-eight hours later, the big airplane—known before the mission simply as the XSA-57—having been christened the *Dreamer* on orders from the Mystery Man himself.

No sooner were they airborne and en route to their first stop—a small island off the coast of the California Baja—than Bull was giving the first of many briefings to the rescue force, the dozen and a half mercenaries of many different nationalities that the commander forever bragged about hand-picking himself. Hughes, McDoogle, and Curtiss also sat in on these meetings, as the three of them had been asked by Bull to go in on the ground with the rescue force.

The plan was to fly hopscotch over the Pacific, receiving fuel and stores along the way via a series of midocean rendezvous stops with supply ships. Once they were close to the Gulf of Tonkin, the waterway that bordered Viet Nam's eastern coast, they would set down and drift westward to wait for what Bull kept referring to as "attack weather." In reality he meant a monsoon—an Asian downpour that would give the *Dreamer* and its passengers the cover they needed to fly over North Viet Nam without being detected.

Once they were over Conkin Province, the *Dreamer* pilots would be on the look-out for Ban Cai Giang Lake—also known as "Liberation Lake"—a large body of water that emptied into the northern part of the Mekong River. Bull was confident that the huge seaplane could safely set down on the lake and come within twenty-five feet of its shoreline. From there, the rescue force would disembark and travel the five miles to Bac Ha, the town near Dien Bien Phu, where the strange Morse Code message had been spotted.

Traveling on the large seaplane turned out to be a pleasant, even leisurely experience for Hughes and the others.

Despite its size and its ungainly appearance, the aircraft flew true and smooth, its massive bulk cutting through the roughest turbulence with not so much as a hiccup. Their accommodations could only be described as luxurious

—Hughes and McDoogle shared a state room that had been intended for the airplane's commander, and Curtiss had taken up residence in the even larger "guest cabin." Bull insisted on bunking in with his men, their quarters being the comfortable middle deck, with its fold-down couches, flight trays, and large porthole-style windows. Even the flight crew had it good. Made up of six individuals in all, they flew the airplane in two shifts and relaxed in the airplane's crew quarters—the most spacious compartment of all—when they were off-duty.

Still the comforts of the flight did nothing to ease Hughes's anxiety over the whole mission. In his mind, there were a lot of potential minefields between them and the mysterious camp at Bac Ha. Could they actually fly right across a communist country without being seen? Could the big airplane stay airborne during a monsoon? Could it stay on course? Would the lake be big enough to land the giant? Would they be spotted coming in? What lay in the five miles between the lake and the camp? Wouldn't the monsoon make the roads muddy and maybe impassable? How many guards would be on-duty around the prison camp? More than twenty-one? Could the Reds call for reinforcements to be dispatched quickly?

And even if the mission went well and they were able to get the POWs back to the airplane, then what? The plan called for them to continue flying westward, over neutral Laos and then down to friendly Thailand. Would the MiGs that they knew to be stationed in the communist capital of Hanoi give up pursuit just because they were flying over neutral territory? Probably not.

But still, Hughes knew from experience that unanswerable questions were part and parcel of any dangerous covert operation. What bothered him the most was the never-ending stream of dreams that Curtiss claimed to be having throughout the entire flight. Unlike all his other visions about which he would speak until Doomsday, Curtiss steadfastly refused to discuss these recent dreams.

"They're too frightening," he told Hughes over and over, speaking more clearly and more authoritatively than at any time since Hughes had known him. "I don't want to jinx the mission. . . ."

72

Hollywood

THE CLACKING FILM PROJECTOR came to a sudden halt just as the actress on the screen was removing the last piece of her clothing.

"This better be good," Kenneally muttered as the lights went on in the otherwise empty screening room. "*Damn* good . . ."

"There's a man from your office here to see you, Senator," an amplified voice from the projection room told him.

Kenneally turned around just as the congressional assistant hurried in.

"Sorry to bother you, sir," the man, a young Harvard graduate student named McNally, said. "But we've just gotten two pieces of information from Betty back in D.C."

Kenneally sat up in his seat and stretched. "Well, let's have them," he said.

McNally produced a notebook and lowered his voice to a whisper. "They've found a guy who worked on the Tomarc who's willing to talk," he said. "For a price . . ."

"How much?"

McNally bit his lip. "Two thousand," he replied.

Kenneally rolled his eyes. "God, are there any honest men left?" he wondered, adding, "How close was he to the project?"

"*Very* close," McNally answered. "He was on the original design team that took over the technology transfer from the X-7. Stayed with the project up until six months ago. Then he was fired."

Kenneally took out a small thin cigar and lit it. "Fired?" he asked. "Why?"

"He claims he saw Air Force people fooling with the numbers," McNally replied. "He reported it to his boss, and the both of them were gone the next day."

Kenneally smiled and blew a long stream of blue smoke toward the ceiling. "So he's a man with a fish to fry," he said, his Boston accent thick and nasal.

"It would appear that way," McNally confirmed. "He took some documents home with him when he cleaned out his desk, so he claims he can back up what he tells us."

Kenneally thought for a moment, then asked, "Where's he working now?"

"He's not," McNally answered, checking his notes. "He says that since Tomarc gave him the gate, he can't get another job."

"I'm not surprised," the senator replied. "Okay, you can draw the two grand out of the Chowder Club reserves. Get Betty to turn it over twice—once as a money order and then as a cashier's check from the First National in Boston. Then you, Sammy, and Al meet with this guy and pump him for everything he's got. And I mean *everything*. For that money I want names, dates, and numbers, especially the ones he claims the Air Force boys were queering. Got it?"

"Got it," McNally confirmed.

Kenneally took another long drag from the cigarillo, then asked, "What else?"

"Well, we were able to track down your friend Captain Hughes," McNally said.

"'That *is* good news," Kenneally replied, relieved that the Hurricane—whom no one had seen for two weeks—had been found. The senator had tried to get in touch with Hughes after the revealing conversations with the Lockheed engineers, but neither Chas Spencer nor anyone at the base knew of his whereabouts. He had left the base shortly after the unsuccessful competition against the Tomarc and simply disappeared. That's when Kenneally put two of his men on the case.

"Holed up in a cathouse, was he?" he asked.

McNally frowned slightly. "Well, I don't believe he's having *that* much fun," he said. "Our guys tracked him to a bar called the Bum Dummy. I believe you know its owner, Peter McDoogle? Anyway, we talked to the workers at McDoogle's bar and it seems that Hughes and McDoogle and another gentleman—an Indian named Curtiss, could that be right?—left for Las Vegas almost two weeks ago."

"Las Vegas!" Kenneally exclaimed. "I can't picture those guys at the blackjack table. . . ."

"There's more," McNally said. "We found out they were in an altercation with the security people at the Flamingo Hotel. Apparently one of your friends dropped about three thousand dollars in one game of roulette. When he didn't win, a fight broke out. . . ."

Kenneally was looking up at McNally in astonishment. "Well, at least they're fighting in better places," he said.

"It gets stranger," McNally said. "One of the Flamingo goons told us that they saw your friends talking to people connected with the American Aircraft Corporation."

Now Kenneally felt a chill run down his back. He knew all about American Aircraft Corporation and its wealthy, mysterious owner.

"People from American Aircraft paid your friends' hotel bill for two days—in cash—and then all three vanished again," McNally concluded. "End of report . . ."

"God damn," Kenneally exhaled worriedly, snuffing out his cigarillo. "What have they gotten themselves into now?"

73

GABE EVERS LOOKED UP from the morning newspaper and took a sip of coffee.

"How did you sleep last night, darling?" his wife asked as she prepared a breakfast of fried eggs.

"Fine," he answered. "No bad dreams . . ."

"And how did you enjoy dinner last night?"

"Fine," he repeated. "That steak was very lean."

"Did you enjoy the children's school poetry recital?"

"Yes, I did," Evers replied. "They are very talented, as are their schoolmates."

"And where will we be going tonight?"

Evers had to think for a moment. "I believe we have a PTA meeting," he finally answered.

"That's right," the woman replied, lifting the two cooked eggs off the frying pan and throwing them into the garbage pail.

"Are you happy, my darling?" she asked him.

He looked up from the newspaper and surveyed the brightly lit kitchen. Everything sparkled so—the stove, the refrigerator, the sink, the walls and the windows. Even his wife seemed to sparkle—from her Toni-Perm blond hair to her blue checkerboard-pattern dress to her frilly apron to her seamed stockings and black high heels. Everything looked perfect.

"Yes," he replied. "I am very happy. I love you. I love our kids. I love our house and this neighborhood. I love my job, growing the corn and the alfalfa. . . ."

"That's good," she replied. "But you know that we owe the banker our mortgage payment today. . . ."

Evers suddenly cast his eyes downward. "Yes, I realize that."

"And we don't have the money," she said. "Do we?"

"No, we don't," he replied.

"And why is that?"

Evers cleared his throat. "The corn hasn't grown in as I had hoped," he said. "We won't have enough to sell to pay the bank."

"This is the third time it's happened, isn't it?"

"Yes," he said somberly. "The third time . . ."

The woman glanced out of the small kitchen window and nodded to the man waiting outside.

"Here's the banker now," she said. "He is here to collect his money. What will we do?"

"I don't know," he replied. "We have no choice."

A man dressed entirely in black appeared at the ranch-style door and stared at Evers.

"Money is what got us into this trouble," his wife said. "Bankers always mistreat their customers. . . ."

The man in black walked into the kitchen. "Now the banker has to take away something that you love," the wife said. "Doesn't he?"

Evers nodded slowly.

"Follow us," the wife said, leading the man in black through the small cozy house to its main bedroom.

Evers did as he was told, and soon he was sitting in a hard, splintered chair, watching the man in black take off his pants.

The wife, too, was slowly removing her clothes. "Because some of the people have more money than others," she said, taking down her nylons and removing her bra, "those without money are deprived. You *do* know that, don't you?"

"Yes," Evers answered, his voice just barely a whisper.

At that point, both the man and the wife were naked. Without so much as a kiss or a caress, the man climbed on top of the woman, penetrated her, and began furiously pumping.

"This is how it has always been," the woman called out, her voice a monotone despite what was happening to her. "This is how it will always be. . . ."

But at the moment, Evers was not watching the two on the bed. Rather, he was looking out the bedroom window's lace curtains, his eyes fixed on a point out beyond the other cozy houses in his neighborhood, beyond the muddy river, beyond the hot, dense jungle. Out on the western horizon, he saw a gathering storm.

Looks like a monsoon, he thought.

74

Mescalero

GENERAL XAVIER CHECKED HIS watch. It was just a quarter to midnight, and yet he was already very anxious.

"They should have been here by now," he said to his lieutenant as they scanned the long stretch of desolate highway in front of them, looking for any sign of headlights. "Perhaps they were recalled. . . ."

"If I may, sir," the lieutenant replied. "Our last contact with them was just an hour ago, and they were close to the Alamogordo city limits. Surely they won't be recalled at this late hour. Everyone is asleep in Washington. . . ."

Xavier rubbed his weary eyes and turned his coat collar up against the desert chill.

"It's strange," he said, more to himself than to the junior officer. "I slept better before our missile beat that damn jet. . . ."

The lieutenant, amazed and a little bit frightened that the senior officer would confide in him so, nevertheless seized the opportunity.

"Napoleon rarely slept, General," he said carefully. "Neither did Patton nor even Alexander the Great."

"It's because so many people have heard about us," Xavier continued, not even hearing the lieutenant. "Suddenly everyone wants to get into the act. Everyone wants a piece of my machine. . . ."

"There are always drawbacks to success," the lieutenant tried again. "Your program is the talk of the Pentagon, sir. Your name is on the lips of very important people. What could be better than that?"

"The more people know about you, the more reasons they have to destroy you," Xavier continued to mumble, carrying on a parallel conversation with himself. "Jealousy is the problem. Having a good idea is one thing. Letting everyone know about it is another. Suddenly everyone wants a piece of the praise, and the original idea gets watered down in the process."

"Your idea wasn't just a 'good idea,' General," the lieutenant tried for a third time. "It was a *brilliant* one."

Xavier's mind flashed back to the pile of letters, telexes, and telegrams sitting on his desk. Their subjects ranged from asking his opinion on robotic battleships and aircraft carriers (which would launch unmanned carrier-attack craft) to preliminary drawings on a division of robotic tanks. There was even a proposal from the Army War College on building and programming an army of robot soldiers.

"This dream has turned into a nightmare," he rambled. "We went too far. . . ."

Suddenly the lieutenant was grabbing him by the arm.

"There they are, sir!" he cried. "See the headlights?"

Xavier strained his eyes and sure enough saw the dull beam of an approaching set of lights. Behind it appeared two more and then two more.

He was not surprised that no sigh of relief came to him. In fact, upon spotting the headlights of the approaching convoy, he felt every nerve and fiber in his body tighten up an additional notch.

"I did my job too well," he whispered bitterly. "Now they want to take it all away from me. . . ."

The convoy was carrying two more Tomarcs from their assembly plant in Michigan. These were the last of the F-98As, the missile type that Xavier had been testing for the past six months. Data from that testing was being incorporated in a newer, faster Tomarc, the advanced F-98B, which was scheduled to fly in eight weeks.

The problem was that Xavier would not be acting as the launch command officer for the new Tomarc flights. By the time they were ready to go, he will have been promoted to two-star general and recalled to Washington to run the Air Force's new study on a complete integration of unmanned aircraft into the service. It was a promotion most service officers only dreamed of—but not Xavier. He knew the post would not last long, not when the new launch command officer took over and looked into the numbers behind the first series of F-98A test flights.

"We moved too fast too soon," he continued, as the convoy reached their location and rumbled on past toward the Tomarc launching-pad facility, a quarter of a mile away. "Our secrets will no longer be ours. . . ."

The lieutenant counted the trucks as they went by, checking their serial numbers against the ones he'd written down on his clipboard sheet.

"All transports accounted for, sir," he said. "I'll have the men fed and rested and tell them to begin work in the morning in setting the first missile into launch position.

"With any luck, we'll be able to launch in three days."

"*No!*" Xavier exclaimed suddenly. "Have them begin launch preparations immediately. I want to go in two days, maximum . . ."

The lieutenant was stunned at the order. "Sir, if I may," he began. "These men have been driving for four days. I don't think—"

"You are not being called upon to *think*," Xavier snapped at him. "You're being called upon to carry out my orders. Now do so."

The lieutenant did a quick salute and began running down the dirt road after the convoy.

"And another thing, Lieutenant!" Xavier called out, stopping the young officer in his tracks. "Make sure every one of those men has a shine on his boots that I can see myself in!"

75

Indochina

FOR HUGHES, THE FIRST indication that something was wrong with the giant seaplane came when he was thrown across his cabin. He slammed right into McDoogle, who had also been tossed out of his bunk and was heading in the opposite direction.

"Christ! Are we going down!" McDoogle yelled as they tried to disentangle themselves from a heap on the cabin floor.

Their cabin lights were blinking, some kind of warning klaxon was blaring, and outside, Hughes could hear the painful screeching of the *Dreamer* engines as they tried to keep the huge airplane airborne.

They were flying right in the middle of Bull's "attack weather," what he thought was the monsoon that would give them the cover they needed to penetrate North Viet Nam's airspace undetected. The only problem was that the monsoon Bull had selected after drifting in the Gulf of Tonkin for hours had turned out to be a full-fledged typhoon.

It had been bumpy right away—the last clear thing Hughes had seen out of his cabin window was the irregular coastline of Viet Nam, just barely visible through the fast-moving dark rain clouds. At that point, and upon the recommendation of the on-duty flight crew, Bull had ordered everyone on board to strap in and be prepared to ride out some turbulence. Hughes and McDoogle had complied, but now the gyrations of the *Dreamer* were so intense they had actually snapped free of their safety harnesses.

"God, they'll be finding us in little pieces all over the

318

ground!" McDoogle said anxiously as they stayed down on the cabin floor and groped for something solid to hang onto. As a test pilot who had gone on some very rough aerial rides, Hughes was a little calmer—but not much. The large seaplane was bucking so violently that for several brief but frightening moments, he and McDoogle found themselves nearly standing upright on the cabin walls.

"These guys are good!" Hughes yelled over to his friend, trying to calm himself as much as the big Irishman. "They can hold it together. . . ."

It went on like this for almost half an hour, each minute seeming worse than the last. Almost as bad as suffering through the chaos inside their cabin was having to listen to the cacophony of sounds coming from other places in the airplane: violent creaks and groans, the crashing of what they could only assume was thunder, the sizzling of the electrical wires behind the cabin walls, the distinctively shrill shouts of men caught in a crisis.

And then, almost in a matter of seconds, it ended. Suddenly everything was calm, almost serene. The ship leveled off, its engines regained some of their comforting resonant hum, and the electricity started blinking.

"Good Lord!" McDoogle said to Hughes, as both men stayed in place and held on. "Could it be over, or are we just in the eye of the storm?"

Hughes closed his eyes and just listened for a few moments. "I think we're through it," he finally said.

The shouts coming from the decks below—no less urgent but in more hopeful tones—were encouraging, as was the fact that the electricity blinked twice again and this time stayed on.

"Let's get out of here," Hughes said, tugging McDoogle. In seconds they were out of their cabin and running along the catwalk that looked out into the vast second level of the airplane. They met Curtiss staggering out of his cabin, and the three of them leaned over the railing to get a look at the situation below. There was equipment strewn about down below them, and they could see several of the mercenaries being treated for what looked like minor wounds. Other than that, everything looked to be in relatively good shape, considering the battering the plane had taken.

Bull spotted them and immediately yelled, "Hughes, get up to the flight deck. The pilots had a bad time and the reserve crew is injured. See if you can help out up there! You other two come down and help with the injured."

When Bull talked, people listened. Hughes immediately turned on his heels and ran up toward the flight deck, while Curtiss and McDoogle scampered down the passageway's spiral staircase to get to the level below.

Hughes burst into the flight cabin to see that the chaos had not ended with the turbulence. Several of the plane's cockpit windshields had been cracked and the air was screeching in. Worse still, both pilots had received cuts about the head and face when a fire extinguisher had come loose during the height of the storm and ricocheted around the cabin, injuring the men.

Still, despite their bloody condition, both fliers had remained at their controls and gotten the airplane through the worst of the typhoon. For that, they had earned Hughes's unqualified admiration.

At that moment, the navigator was trying to treat both men and keep the airplane on course at the same time.

"Where the hell are we?" Hughes yelled to him.

"We're just ten miles out from the lake," the navigator yelled back, trying to be heard above the howl of the wind. "But we've got to set this thing down now or abort the mission and go on to Thailand."

"We ain't giving up nothing," Hughes replied with determination. He moved through the clutter of broken glass and, with the help of the navigator, gingerly lifted the brave and bleeding pilot out of his seat. Then Hughes slipped behind the controls of the seaplane and, after a moment of orientation, took a glance out through the cracked windshield.

Right off the port side, clearly visible through the few remaining clouds, was what the navigator assured him was Liberation Lake.

Hughes felt a rush of adrenaline run through his body as he quickly checked the wind speed, engine trim, and altitude.

Then he yelled back to the navigator, "Go tell Bull to get everyone strapped in as best they can. We're going in . . ."

For Nguyen Phan Dong, the typhoonlike storm was devastating.

His small fishing boat, the one he had used for the past twenty-two years to fish the meager waters of Liberation Lake, had been destroyed—dashed against the rocks in the violent winds. He had seen the dark storm clouds blowing in but, like everyone else, thought it was simply another monsoon and that he had enough time to pull in his nets and head for shore. But no sooner had he retrieved one net than the waters of the lake suddenly began to swell. The rain began, and then came the wind—so strong it blew him toward the jagged boulders on the lake's southern end.

He had had no choice but to jump out of the boat and swim to a smaller outcrop of rock that lay about a hundred feet from the shore. He had just barely made it to the small island, his lungs filling with water and the rain being whipped against his body so hard it produced painful welts. Just as he was climbing onto the rock with his last ounce of strength, his small pram was crushed against the rocky shore. He cried as he watched his boat break up into dozens of pieces. It was like seeing a friend of twenty-two years suddenly get killed.

So it was understandable that after Nguyen had finally coughed up most of the water from his stomach, while at the same time watching the storm move on, he thought he was hallucinating when the large black shape appeared overhead.

The thing was so large and moving so slowly, it appeared as if it were too heavy to stay up in the air. Yet, as he was able to focus on it, he saw the propellers and jets and the long thick wings and realized it was man-made. It moved right overhead, then went into a gentle spiral, getting lower with each turn. Nguyen was seized with a mixture of fear and awe as he realized that the gigantic aircraft was going to land on the lake.

There was no place to hide on the small rock, so he

was forced to slip back down into the lake and hold on to a small ledge, just barely keeping his head above the lapping water. From this vantage point he watched the aircraft circle once again, then level out and come in for a landing, not more than fifty yards from his position.

The huge seaplane hit the surface once, bounced up, and then settled down for good, leaving waves so big in its enormous wake that Nguyen was nearly washed off his rock when they hit him. Once the aircraft was down, he could see the propellers suddenly slow down and almost stop completely. The machine then turned into a tight circle, further dissipating its landing area. Within thirty seconds of its landing, the airplane had stopped and was settling into the water.

Nguyen's fear increased when he saw men inside the airplane toss out a series of anchor lines. They were Caucasians, dressed in green suits and wearing combat gear and helmets. He had seen such uniforms before— and this was the reason that he was overcome with a feeling of dread. Up until that moment he had hoped that the huge airplane was from China or Russia or some other friendly socialist country. Now, seeing the white men and their uniforms, he was sure that it was an airplane sent from France, to gain revenge for their defeat on the battlefield at Dien Bien Phu, not ten miles away.

But what could he do about it? He knew that the commander of the small military garrison in his village nearby had to be warned about this mysterious aircraft. But the sun was going down and it was getting darker by the second. And despite his years as a fisherman, he was not a good swimmer. In his depleted condition, the hundred feet to shore might be too far for him to attempt. After a few minutes of sheer panic, he came to the realization that he would have to stay clinging to the rock until he could regain his strength and attempt the swim to shore.

In the meantime, he told himself that watching the airplane and its crew was the best he could do.

76

Luke Air Force Range, Arizona

THE SUN WAS JUST coming up when the small civilian aircraft crossed over the tallest peak of the Sand Tank Mountains and turned southwest.

The tiny Cessna-15 had taken off from the Scottsdale airport at four o'-clock, exactly one hour before, and had circled the outskirts of nearby Phoenix briefly before steering toward the Sand Tanks. Now heading southwest, it crossed over the Quiotosa Wash and hopped over a second series of mountains known as the Saucedas.

Three minutes later, the airplane entered restricted airspace.

The pair of USAF F-94 Starfires appeared behind the Cessna just ten minutes later.

Scrambled from nearby Luke Air Force Base, the F-94s were sent to intercept the unauthorized airplane, their pilots having been ordered to take all necessary actions to prevent the Cessna from flying over the very sensitive "middle division" of the vast Luke Air Force Weapons Range.

Pulling up on either side of the Cessna, the huge Starfires dwarfed the single-engined civilian craft. Dropping their landing gear and throttling back to the lowest possible power, the F-94s were barely able to match the Cessna's 145-mph speed. With just enough light now from the rising sun, the Air Force pilots peered into the small plane's cockpit. They were mildly surprised to see a woman at the controls.

"Luke Control, this is Tango Delta Leader," the pilot of the lead jet called back to his base. "We have intercepted the bogie at 3,500 feet. Read it is a civilian Cessna, female at the controls. Present speed about one-four-five. On a south-southwest heading . . .''

"You are cleared to contact and attempt ID," came the Luke tower's reply.

Moving his airplane slightly up and ahead of the Cessna, the lead F-94 pilot blinked his navigational lights twice, hoping for a similar response from the Cessna. Although it appeared that the female at the controls was well aware of the presence of the two fighters, no reply was received.

Next he attempted waving his hands, but still there was no response from the woman at the controls. She simply kept facing straight ahead.

"Try radio contact," the F-94 pilot called back to his rear-seat radar officer.

"Cessna-One-Five, Cessna-One-Five," the radar man called into his helmet microphone after punching in the standard area civilian radio frequency. "This is the Air Force F-94 off your port wing. You are flying in a restricted zone. You must turn north 90° and leave this area immediately."

"I can't . . ." came the weak reply.

"Say again, Cessna?" the radar man requested.

"*I can't fly this airplane!*" the woman in the Cessna said. "I'm so scared my hands are frozen to the controls. I can just barely speak to you on this radio. . . ."

"What is your condition, Cessna?" the F-94 pilot asked.

"My husband is unconscious in the back," the woman told them. "He's sick. . . . He passed out just after we took off from Scottsdale. We were heading for Yuma and he just closed his eyes and fell backward."

"Can you tell us what his condition is?" the F-94 pilot asked.

"He is still breathing," the woman answered. "But I don't know exactly what's wrong with him. I just can't wake him up."

"Are you a pilot?" the F-94 commander asked.

"No," came the frightened reply. "I only know a little from watching my husband fly. I can just barely keep it level as it is."

By this time the strange formation of the two F-94s and the small civilian airplane was approaching the highly restricted middle division of the Luke range. Under normal circumstances, the Starfires were bound by standing orders to shoot down any airplane that passed over the sensitive area.

However, a quick conversation with Luke AFB control confirmed that the Starfires shouldn't take such a drastic action—yet.

"Cessna pilot, we will attempt to instruct you to turn your aircraft," the F-94 flight commander called over to the woman. "Just stay calm and follow my instructions.

"Do you understand?"

There was a burst of static, then the woman's frail voice came over: "Yes, I understand . . ." she said.

"Okay," the F-94 commander replied. "Now, first I want you to relax. You can start off by telling me your name."

There was a short pause before the radio crackled to life again.

"It's Betty," came the woman's reply.

There was an ambulance waiting when the Cessna came in for a bumpy landing at the small airfield near Aztec, Arizona.

Located ten miles north of the outermost perimeter of the Luke Air Force Range, the field at Aztec was the nearest airport available for the Air Force pilots to direct the woman to. Once they were assured by the airfield's control tower that they had been successful in talking the woman down, the pair of F-94s circled the base once, then roared off back to Luke AFB, their unexpected Good Samaritan mission accomplished.

The man in the back of the Cessna was barely conscious when the ambulance drivers and a pair of Arizona Highway Patrol officers lifted him out of the cockpit and into the ambulance. One of the officers checked the man's pulse, then leaned over and sniffed his breath. It reeked of alcohol.

The officer told the man's wife that they would have to come to the state-police barracks after her husband was sobered up and released from the hospital. Once there, the man would have to answer charges of flying while intoxicated. The FAA would also be contacted, as would the Air Force, should they decide to press charges. Seemingly relieved that she was still alive and on the ground, the woman said she understood.

Then, with the help of the two policemen, she unloaded her belongings—several suitcases and a camera with a rather large telescopic lens—from the back of the Cessna and joined her husband in the back of the ambulance for the trip to the hospital.

Three hundred miles to the west, on the northern rim of San Diego Bay, two men approached each other from opposite sides of an otherwise deserted fishing pier.

"Where's Frankie?" one of the men, a USAF lieutenant and a member of the Tomarc recovery team, asked the other.

"He's busy," the man replied. "Sent me in his place."

"Okay," the officer replied. "No big deal if you have the cash."

"I got the cash," the other man answered.

They walked silently to the end of the pier, below which a twenty-foot launch was tied. In its hold were seven wooden boxes. Both men climbed down to the boat, where the lieutenant pried the lid off one of the containers.

The other man reached inside and came up with a large, clawless Pacific lobster.

"Looks good," the man told the officer. "How many you got?"

"Five dozen," was the reply. "Also got ten pounds of oysters, three boxes of salmon, and an eel."

"How much for the whole lot?"

"My boss says a buck apiece for the lobsters," the officer replied. "Twelve dollars a pound for the oysters and forty bucks for the salmon. You can have the eel for free."

The man pulled out a roll of bills and counted out two hundred and twenty dollars.

"When again?" he asked the lieutenant, handing him the money.

"Figure another week," the officer said, climbing into the boat and lifting the boxes onto the dock. "We'll let Frankie know."

With that, the lieutenant revved his engine and took off. No sooner had the launch moved away than the other man pulled a walkie-talkie from underneath his coat.

"There he goes," he called into the radio set. "You got him?"

"We got him," came the reply.

The man on the dock then retrieved a pair of binoculars from his pocket and followed the launch as it headed straight out to sea. He watched it until it shrank to just a speck. At that point a tugboat appeared out of the morning fog and the launch headed straight for it.

He keyed his walkie-talkie again.

"Do you see the tug?" he asked.

"We see the tug," was the reply.

Within half a minute, the small boat had pulled alongside the larger vessel and was lifted up onto its deck.

"I can't make out the letters on the side of the tug from here," the man on the dock continued. "How about you?"

"We can see them," came the answer. "They are *U* . . . *S* . . . *A* . . . *F* . . ."

The man on the dock smiled and yelled into the walkie-talkie: "We got 'em, boys. . . . You taking pictures?"

"We're taking pictures," was the answer. "See you back at the truck."

The man folded up the walkie-talkie's antenna and moved the boxes of fish and lobsters up and under a holding shed at the end of the pier.

Then he opened the smallest box of the lot and gingerly lifted out the squirming, five-foot-long eel.

"You got a reprieve," he said, noticing the eel had a long healed-over scar, as if made by a jackknife, running down its back. "This is your lucky day. . . ."

With that, the man tossed the eel back into the water, then turned and walked back to the beach to meet his associates.

77

Phoenix

THE THREE RAPS ON the door were followed by a low-pitched wolf whistle.

Jack Kenneally, stretched out on a chaise longue located on the small porch of his twenty-second-story hotel room, checked his watch. It was just ten in the morning.

"Let him in," he instructed his congressional assistant.

The young man did as he was told, and as soon as the door was opened, Chas Spencer bounded in.

"We hit the bull's eye, Jack," he told the senator.

Kenneally clapped his hands in delight. "Good, clear stuff?" he asked, jumping up from the lounge.

"Clear enough," Spencer answered.

He unzipped the black portfolio bag he was carrying and dumped several dozen photographs onto the massive bed. With the help of Kenneally and his assistant, he positioned the still-damp photos into three groups.

"No problems with the camera?" Kenneally asked.

"None at all," Spencer replied. "The lens was great. The film was clear, and they had no trouble at all shooting through the bottom of the airplane."

"Where's the plane now?"

"It's still at Aztec," Spencer said. "It's been impounded, but I doubt that anyone's going to be looking at it very closely."

"How's Betty and Sam?" Kenneally asked, pouring each a tall glass of orange juice.

"They'll be tied up with the highway patrol for a while, I'm afraid," Spencer replied.

"Don't worry about them," the senator said. "I've

already got my pals in Scottsdale working on it. And the FAA has already been called off."

"They did a great job, especially Betty," Spencer said. "When I met her at the hospital she played the part of concerned wife to the limit. And poor Sam was in the other room getting himself drowned in coffee. You should give them both a big raise."

"Anyone nosy as to who the hell you were?" Kenneally asked, sipping his orange juice.

"Nope," Spencer replied. "Just a concerned friend from nearby, taking care of their belongings."

At this point Spencer picked up the first batch of photos.

"Okay, here's the clearest shots of our first objective," he said, showing the first photo to Kenneally. "See the scorch marks?"

The photo was of the desert just inside the middle division of the Luke Air Force Range. It showed a small mountain range on its left and what looked to be a dry river bed on its right. In the middle was a long black line of varying widths and color intensity.

"It looks like it ripped up almost half a mile," Kenneally said.

"Look at this one," Spencer said, handing him another photo. It too showed a long black scar carved out of the desert floor, this one seemingly surrounded by some debris at its base.

"That doesn't look like a smooth landing," Kenneally said with a chuckle.

"None of them were," Spencer said, handing him two more similar photos. "My guess is that they just radio-controlled them down as far as they could, put them horizontal, and then hoped for the best. . . ."

Kenneally picked up a photo from the second grouping. It showed what looked to be about two dozen tractor-trailer trucks parked in four neat rows next to the side of a fair-sized mountain.

"Oh, boy, the Teamsters wouldn't like this," Kenneally joked. "I've got a feeling this local isn't organized."

"You can be sure of that," Spencer replied. "There's only one reason those trucks are out in the middle of nowhere."

"They're recovery vehicles," Kenneally replied with a nod of his head. "They didn't bother to hide them very well."

"Why should they?" Spencer said. "No one's supposed to be flying over there. They don't even let the aircraft from Luke into that region unless absolutely necessary."

He picked up the third set of photos.

"These are the bombshells," Spencer said. "The smoking guns . . ."

He handed the top photograph to Kenneally, and even the normally unflappable senator felt his jaw drop with amazement.

The photo depicted a large pit that was squeezed in between two mountains. Sticking out of the pit, clear as day, were the tail ends of six depleted Tomarc missiles.

78

Indochina, Outside Bac Ha Village

THE FIVE-MILE TREK to the suspected POW camp at Bac Ha was a painful, grueling affair.

Just as Hughes had feared, the road leading from Liberation Lake to the outskirts of the village had been nearly washed out by the typhoon. This meant that the twenty-two-man rescue force—comprised of the eighteen mercenaries, Hughes, McDoogle, Curtiss, and Bull himself—had to pull, push, and sometimes just about carry the five heavily armed jeeps they had off-loaded from the large seaplane.

Finally, just after three in the morning, the mud-soaked soldiers reached the outer perimeter of Bac Ha and took cover in a line of trees that bordered the hamlet's northern reaches. All that could be seen of the village were the tops of some houses and two sets of towers, only one of which was employing a searchlight.

But that was enough for Bull.

"No doubt about it—this is the place," he told the rescue force, checking his map and explaining that electricity and electrical generators were so scarce in the Asian country that only the highest-priority locations were illuminated. "They wouldn't waste the juice lighting up an ordinary village."

Off to the east, they could see the outer edge of the valley known as Dien Bien Phu, the site of the historic battle fought between the French and the communist Viet Minh just a year before. Hughes noted a strange mist rising from above the place, which sent a chill down his spine. He knew that should anything go wrong with the rescue mission and the primary means of retreat become blocked, Bull's plan called for anyone separated from the main force to cross right through the northern rim of the infamous valley.

Bull then instructed six of the soldiers to set up a defensive perimeter and suggested everyone else take fifteen minutes to rest up and clean the mud from their ears, eyes, and throats.

Then he darkened his face with charcoal and crawled off into the night.

The sun was just coming up when Bull rolled back into the encampment, his blackened face now streaked with patches of red mud.

He called Hughes, McDoogle, Curtiss, and the mercenary second-in-command—a Scotsman named MacNee—together and gave them a quick briefing.

"This place is the goddamn weirdest thing I've ever seen," Bull told them, his voice pitching way above its usual deep, cool, collected timbre. "You've got to see it to believe it."

"What are we up against?" the mercenary officer asked.

"I spotted two perimeter outposts with three guys apiece in 'em," Bull replied, pulling out his map. "Light weapons and no radios. We can take them easy.

"After that, they got a trenchworks around the village itself with a sentry every fifty feet or so. There's a small bridge going over this ditch that leads into the place. If we grease two sentries on either side of the road, that will give us the opening we need to drive the jeeps through."

"Then what?" Hughes asked.

"Then there's only one way to do it, Hughes," Bull told him. "Send in a couple of advance parties and hope they can locate where the POWs are being kept. Once we know where to look, then we plow through in the jeeps and roust the whole village. Surprise them. Tear the fucking place to the ground."

"And hope the advance guys get the POWs out in the confusion?" McDoogle asked.

"That's right, Paddy," Bull answered.

A tense quiet fell over the group as the potential consequences of the mission ahead began to sink in.

"Who's going in first?" Hughes asked.

"You three in one party; MacNee and two grunts in the other," Bull said, indicating several points on his map at once. "MacNee will take out the first string of guards. In the meantime, I want you three to circle around to here—the place where those crazy Morse Code plants are growing. If you're real lucky, you might see your buddy out there. Now, if he's brainwashed or drugged, he might be so screwed up he'll pull an alarm. But if he sees someone he recognizes, it might shock him long enough for us to move."

Hughes turned to Curtiss. "Can you make it, Bill?" he asked, glancing at the man's ever-present cane.

At that moment, a strange look came over Curtiss's face. He closed his eyes tightly, so much so that several long streams of water began running out from under his lids. As the others watched in mild astonishment, Curtiss began murmuring something in a low and moaning voice. Then he dramatically stood up, took his cane, and snapped it over his knee—not once but twice.

Throwing the four splintered pieces away, he pulled himself up to his full lanky height and said, "Let's go."

Gabe Evers put his hoe down for a moment and wiped away the sweat that was already pouring off his forehead.

It was only six in the morning but he'd been out in the field for a half-hour already. Some kind of animal had gotten in among the crops the night before, pulling about a dozen corn stalks up by their roots and gnawing at the kernels. Exasperated, Evers had cleared away the broken stalks and dug new holes in which to replant them, all the while knowing that the chances of the corn regrowing in time were next to nothing.

Retrieving his hoe, he walked the short distance over to his first alfalfa patch and fingered one of the stems. It glistened at his touch, pinching out a single drop of moisture that felt extremely cool on his finger. The alfalfa was almost a luminescent shade of green—so bright it looked artificial. He raised his head and looked over to the next separate patch, this one a "dash," and then to the one below it, which was a "dot."

Then he looked up at the sky and shook his head.

He returned to the corn patch and, anticipating the usual visit from his wife at any moment, quickly went back to work. Suddenly he was hit square on the back of his head by a rock.

He swung around, his hoe up and ready—the monkeys in the area were known to throw objects at humans on occasion, if they felt their territory was about to be infringed upon. The monkeys could be dangerous: Some were rabid, others would clamp their powerful jaws on a victim's throat and stay there until either the victim died or the monkey itself was killed.

In his present state of mind, Evers was looking to lop off the head of the troublesome simian and stake it on the edge of his field. This was a foolproof way of insuring that the rest of the troop would scatter.

But as he turned toward the tree line some thirty feet away, he saw not the gangly shape of a monkey but that of a man.

· The man was standing on the edge of the tall grass that led up to the corn rows, beckoning to him. He was a white man, outfitted in a camouflage outfit and pith helmet and carrying a rifle and sidearm. He was also wearing his long hair in braids, and he sported a pair of glasses.

"Gabe! *Gabe!*" the man called to him in a kind of loud whisper.

Evers tried to shake away the hallucination—he had had them several times before, and now they were starting to frighten him.

"Gabe!"

"Go away!" Evers called back, his voice thick as he desperately tried to make the ghost vanish.

"Gabe, do you know who I am?" the man called to him.

"*I said, leave me alone!*" Evers yelled back, putting his hands to his ears and shutting his eyes tight.

When he finally opened his eyes again, the figure was gone.

On the other side of the village, MacNee, Bull's second-in-command, was leading a small patrol of Gurkha mercenaries to the outskirts of the village, after having just silently eliminated the guards at two outer-perimeter Viet Minh outposts.

"Good God, the Bull was right!" he whispered as he and his men hunkered down in the tall grass near the village's main gate. "This place *is* weird! . . ."

Even the Gurkhas were amazed. Instead of the typical Southeast Asian thatched huts they'd expected, they saw that the town was actually comprised of strictly American houses.

"It looks like a ruddy movie set," MacNee said to himself.

It was an apt description. The houses were laid out in typical small-town pattern, with straight-as-arrow streets and perfectly squared-off intersections, complete with street signs. There were also streetlamps, telephone poles, fire hydrants, mailboxes, white picket fences, and a few elm and oak trees lining the streets. There were even a few late-model American cars parked about.

If it weren't for the thick jungle surrounding the place, MacNee would have guessed he was peering in on a small town in Illinois.

No wonder the POWs went daft, he thought, waving to his men that it was time to fall back and rejoin the others.

*   *   *

"What's the matter, darling?"

Evers could only shake his head. "I don't know," he said. "I don't feel well today. . . ."

The woman in the blue print dress and the blond Toni perm looked around the cornfield.

"You can't be ill from doing too much work," she said. "From what I can see, you haven't yet started your daily tasks."

"I said I'm feeling sick, my darling," Evers repeated. "My eyes and my head are aching. . . ."

The woman nodded to the three Viet Minh soldiers who were waiting in the 1952 Buick Special parked nearby.

"You know the consequences of not doing your work today," she said, turning back to Evers, who was leaning heavily on his hoe. "We will not have enough corn to sell and the banker will not be paid. Do you know what happens then?"

"Yes," Evers murmured, the ghostly vision of the man at the edge of the field still burned into his retinas. He had looked so familiar. "I think so . . ."

"And do you still insist on taking a day off because you are sick?"

"Yes, I can't work. . . ."

"And do you know that the banker will come to visit us if you do?"

"I tell you I can't help it!" Evers cried, feeling something in the back of his brain start to snap.

The woman motioned for the three soldiers to come forward, which they did. But then, suddenly, two figures walked right out of the cornfield off to the left.

"Who . . . what?" was all the woman was able to say.

In the next instant, the two men in the corn rows had raised their weapons and mowed down the three astonished Viet Minh soldiers.

Evers had looked up just in time to see the chests of the soldiers explode. He spun around and saw that the man who had beckoned him earlier had reappeared at the edge of the field and was walking toward him.

"Gabe! Do you know who I am?" the man shouted as he made his way through the tall grass.

Evers squinted so hard his eyes became teary.

By this time the two men from the cornfield had stepped forward and joined the man at the edge of the field. Now all three of them were calling to him.

"Gabe! We've come to rescue you!"

Evers looked more closely at the men.

"Come on, run!"

"Hurry!"

At that instant, the woman pulled a pistol from her apron and put the barrel right to Evers's chest. At the same time, the two men raised their rifles again and aimed them at her.

"*No!*" Evers screamed. "She's my wife! . . ."

Suddenly two shots rang out. The pair of bullets hit the woman squarely in the chest. She stood absolutely still for one long moment, contemplating her wounds. Then she fell back over, dead.

The next thing Evers knew, he was running.

Running over the field, breaking down the rows of his carefully planted corn. He reached the three strange white men in camouflaged uniforms and then was literally dragged along by them.

"It's us!" one kept repeating. "Don't you recognize us?"

Evers felt his head start to swim. He was dizzy from all the running, and he felt like he was about to throw up. Then, like a man about to die, parts of his life began flashing before his eyes. Suddenly he was back in the pilot's seat of the B-45C Tornado, returning from the mission over Vladivostok. One moment everything was going along fine—the next, all of the jet bomber's hydraulic and electrical control had vanished. A one-in-a-million shot from a Red AA shore battery had caught him in the tail without anyone even realizing it—until it was too late. The airplane spun out of control. There were no lights, no power, no way to send out a Mayday. The Tornado hit the water hard and everyone onboard was killed—except him. Three days later, he woke up in a Red Chinese POW camp.

"Gabe, my friend," the large man with red hair and a beard yelled back to him as they ran through the dense undergrowth. "You must recognize *me.*"

Evers wasn't sure. He'd been tricked and fooled and poked and beaten and hypnotized and drugged so many times over the past five years, he had lost track of what was real and what wasn't. He remembered the day the war in Korea officially ended. His Chinese captors had told him all about it—they even showed him some English-language newspapers from Japan that blared the truce in their twenty-point headlines. But the Chinese did not release him with the other Korean POWs because they claimed he'd been caught fighting some other war. He'd been shot down bombing the Soviet Union, not Korea or China. Therefore he was not eligible to be repatriated.

Only when the United States had admitted that they had bombed Soviet territory and apologized for the act would Evers be released. Not before.

"Gabe, it's me," the man who looked like a cowboy yelled to him, even as he dragged him across a small stream and into another patch of thick jungle. "God, man, you must know it's me!"

Five years, moving from one prison camp to another. Different indoctrination methods, different drugs, different ways to be tortured. Finally, his captors had sent him "home"—to Chinese-controlled America, or so he had been told. The place *looked* like America, but it was hot all the time and he wasn't sure exactly what small town in the U.S. was surrounded by tropical jungle and had snakes and rats and rock-throwing rabid monkeys.

They continued running, along the edge of the forest and close to the main gate of the village. There were sounds of gunfire everywhere now. Jeeps were skidding up and down the main road, and several of the houses inside the village were burning. Out of breath and exhausted, the men finally stopped running and plopped Evers down beside the trenchworks that ran near the front gate of the hamlet. More white men in green camouflage appeared, and there was a hurried, confused conversation.

Just at that moment, a huge explosion went off no more than twenty feet away. Evers found himself face down in the mud of the trench when another explosion went off, this one closer. Suddenly he was jerked up and around and was running again, with the same three men who claimed to know him so well. Looking back toward the village, he saw that literally hundreds of soldiers—the small Asian soldiers who had been brutalizing him for the past five years—had appeared out of the forest behind them, bristling with weapons and riding on several tanks.

Another pair of explosions went off very close by, and the three men were now practically dragging Evers away. Still trying to keep one eye back on the village, he saw two jeeps get blown off the road near the camp entrance while another was blasted into a ditch. The Asian soldiers were swarming all over the trenchworks now, chasing the men in the camouflage uniforms, who were scattering in all directions.

Evers felt like he was going to pass out, and he found himself gagging on the thick mucus that had built up in his throat. His vision suddenly went hazy and his legs turned to rubber. The huge man with the red beard picked him up, tossed him over his shoulder, and began carrying him, all the while not missing a step in their attempt to escape the Asian soldiers.

Still, as they ran along, Evers was able to reach out to the man who looked like a cowboy and yell to him, "Where's my wife?"

It was the relief pilot of the big seaplane who saw the survivors of the rescue force first.

Sitting in the cockpit of the huge aircraft anchored forty-five feet from the southwestern edge of the lake, the pilot spotted the dimmed headlights of a single vehicle racing toward him out of the jungle. It was one of the rescue team's jeeps, with at least twelve people hanging onto it, careening wildly on the muddy approach road.

It reached the shore of the lake and kept right on going, its driver plunging it into the rocky shallows off the beach, the sudden impact catapulting several hangers-on up and over the vehicle's hood and into deeper water.

"Get the rafts out now!" the pilot yelled into the airplane's intercom.

Just a few seconds later, two other members of the

flight crew were in the water and madly paddling two
rafts toward the partially submerged smoking jeep. Already men were swimming out toward them, and within
minutes, fourteen individuals, including Bull, had crowded
onto the pair of rafts.

Turning back toward the seaplane, one of the relief
crew asked Bull: "Where are the others?"

"There are no others," the man answered quickly.
"We got four POWs with us. Nine of our guys were
killed."

"How about the cowboy, Hughes, and his guys?"

Bull could only shrug. "They found their friend," he
explained. "But just as we were all linking up, we were
jumped by a bunch of commies and two tanks. We went
one way, and Hughes and his guys went the other."

They had reached the seaplane by this time, and the
next few minutes were devoted to getting everyone—the
rescue-force survivors and the liberated POWs—safely
aboard.

The first pilot of the airplane then pulled Bull aside.

"What's our status?" he asked.

"We lost the commies about two miles back," the
mercenary leader said. "But it will be just a matter of
time before they figure out where we are if we don't get
the hell out of here damn quick."

"How about Hughes and the others?" the pilot asked.

"If they ain't already dead, they know the procedure,"
Bull replied. "We've got to take off and land somewhere
over in Laos. We'll circle back at dawn tomorrow.

"If they ain't here, then we've got to go for good. . . ."

79

Mescalero

THE SUN WAS JUST starting to drop behind the mountains to the west of the Tomarc launch facility when a sergeant handed General Xavier a message.

"Just came in over the secure telex, sir," the man told him.

Xavier took the message and held it in his hand unread for a moment. There was an undeniable excitement in the air of the launch bunker—a hubbub mixed with melancholy. This would be the first night test of a Tomarc—and quite possibly the last launch of any kind that Xavier would command. He was due to fly out to Washington in two days to begin his new assignment as head of the Air Force's study on further unmanned weapons. From that point on, a grand future lay ahead for him—but only if he were able to keep the lid on several Pandoras at once.

Still, he hated to leave his little empire at Mescalero. For this final occasion, he had made sure that every man within the bunker was wearing his best dress uniform—and that each one had perfectly shined boots. He was even wearing a new uniform for the occasion, the first time ever that he dared to wear his new general's stars.

He even invited a special guest for the launch: Danforth Walker, former head of the then-sizable Atomic Energy Commission contingent at Mescalero, now a top executive in the consortium of companies that produced the Tomarc. It was Walker and his staff who had put together the first lobbying efforts on behalf of the unmanned programs, who wined and dined the appropriate politicians, who provided prostitutes for the appropriate Pentagon procurement officers.

Walker probably knew more about the Tomarc concept than anyone else—except for Xavier.

What will happen after tonight? Xavier thought wistfully, finally opening the message. *What does the future hold?*

The words typed on the telex sheet hit him like a twenty-pound sledgehammer in the gut.

It was from the commander of Luke Air Force Base, a secret ally in the unmanned-weapons campaign:

Weather is worse than ever. Not expected to improve.

The message had nothing to do with the weather conditions—it was actually in code. Translated, it meant that someone, somewhere, had figured out the shell game Xavier and his allies had been running during the first series of Tomarc tests.

Xavier immediately called Luke AFB and demanded to speak with its commander. He wound up talking to a series of low-level staff officers at Luke. One told him the commander was not on the base. Another claimed that he *was* there but unable to come to the phone. A third swore the man was actually in his quarters yet could not be reached.

Xavier hung up after five minutes of this frustration—he knew a dodge when he saw one. The Luke commander was already distancing himself from Xavier and the Tomarc, like a rat scurrying off a doomed ship.

"So this is how it will begin," Xavier said, crushing the telex message in his plump, sweaty hands.

Xavier was still flushed with anger when Danforth Walker arrived at the launch complex.

The general had actually been relieved when he first saw the man. At least here was an ally with whom he could discuss the message from Luke AFB in confidence.

But one look at Walker and Xavier knew that he, too, was carrying bad news.

"They're on to us," Walker whispered to him urgently as they retreated to a quiet corner of the facility. "They've spotted the missiles out at Luke, they've got pictures of the scar marks. Everything."

"Who does?"

"The Kenneallys," Walker said with a spit of disgust.

Xavier went numb with shock. "Those frigging Mick gangsters!" he shouted, loud enough for several of the enlisted men nearby to hear.

Xavier quickly began to think of ways to cushion the blow, his mind going in a hundred different directions at once.

"We can't panic," he told Walker. "We still might be able to smooth this over. We got our team out in San Diego. Surely they're still intact—they're our best and most loyal men. . . ."

Walker laughed in his face—a long, cruel cackle.

"Are you kidding?" he said derisively. "Kenneally's guys have been on to them for at least a week. Do you have any idea what your loyal subjects were doing while they were bobbing out in the Pacific, pretending to be recovering those missiles?"

Xavier could only shake his head no.

"They were fishing," Walker told him angrily. "And not only were they fishing—they were selling the damn things to a Mafia fishing co-op up in North Bay."

"Fishing?" Xavier couldn't believe it. "Mafia?"

"You better believe it," Walker said. "The Kenneallys not only have pictures of the whole thing, your boys sold one of them a bunch of salmon and lobsters."

"I'll *kill* them!" Xavier exploded, at that point quite capable of following through with the threat.

"It's too late," Walker said. "They've already sung to Kenneally's people."

Xavier was beginning to tremble now. "They know everything?"

Walker nodded, nervously dabbing his own forehead with a handkerchief.

"Kenneally talked to some big mouths at Lockheed," he said. "Then he paid off a guy we'd fired from Tomarc manufacturing. That was enough for him to figure out that we were screwing with the launch distance numbers and that your boys in San Diego were doing *everything but* retrieving missiles."

"But how do they know about Luke?" Xavier asked, his voice panicky. "It's a restricted area—even Kenneally couldn't get in. . . ."

"No, but his guys got over it," Walker replied. "They faked an off-course airplane stunt late last night. Pretended that some broad's husband had passed out at the stick and that she had wandered over the range—exactly where we had these babies landing. The bastards must have had the Lockheed guys calculate just how far they'd fly from here to Luke, and that's the point they entered the restricted airspace. Christ, Luke sent up two intercept airplanes and they led them to an airfield. All the while someone was taking pictures out of the bottom of the fucking airplane. . . ."

Xavier felt his head start to do a slow spin.

The problem all along with the first series of Tomarc missiles was the weapon's embarrassing short range. Instead of flying more than a thousand miles out to reach a target, the missile—with its bulky dual-propulsion engines and the literally tons of fuel needed to make them work—could barely fly half the advertised distance.

It was the Tomarc consortium itself that had proposed a solution to get through the first series of tests while they worked to improve the range of the newer F-98B. They had simply provided one dummy missile to the San Diego recovery team and had them continuously haul it around with them, making everyone from the Marines guarding the small missile hangar to the new weapons-procurement people in Washington think that all was going well with the tests.

"It was that damn competitive analysis flight that screwed us up," Walker was saying. "And we thought that storm was a stroke of luck for us. . . ."

"It was because Kenneally had his friend flying the Starfighter," Xavier said, his lips quivering uncontrollably at this point. "Any other guy wouldn't have crossed that intercept point in anywhere near the time he'd put in."

"You're right—that's what set off the bells and whistles." Walker nodded glumly. "Here we were, whooping it up, and Kenneally had his guys calculating that there was no way the missile could have beaten someone flying that airplane like that. When we queered those numbers, that was the beginning of the end."

"God, now what do we do?" Xavier asked.

"I've already sent in my resignation," Walker told him plainly. "Wrote it out just after Kenneally's goons left my office, Kenneally himself has already been to Luke. And now they're on their way here."

"Here?" Xavier was appalled.

"Yes, *here*," Walker hissed at him. "What makes you think they wouldn't pay you a visit? They're tripping around the country, pretending like they're a congressional investigation committee, and you're the last stop before they fly back to D.C."

At that moment, one of Xavier's Shine Boys interrupted the tense conversation.

"We're one hour from launch, General," he reported.

Xavier felt a sharp pain rip across his temples. Suddenly he was talking, but it sounded like another voice entirely.

"Just where is Kenneally flying out of?" he asked Walker.

"Phoenix," came the reply.

"When?"

Walker shrugged. "My guess is tomorrow some time. Check with your office. I'm sure they've called looking for you by this time. . . ."

With that Xavier turned back to the enlisted man. "Tell the launch officer to get here on the double," he said, his voice strangely serene. "We're delaying the launch. . . ."

80

Indochina

IT WAS DARK AND musty inside the bunker and the place smelled of death—literally.

"God, I've gone to hell" is how McDoogle so aptly put it as he and the three others dove into the crumbling concrete structure.

"This may be worse," Hughes told him.

The bunker was filled with insects, rat droppings, pools of stagnant red water—and skeletons.

Fleeing the Viet Minh soldiers out beyond the outskirts of Bac Ha, the three men and Evers, still slung over McDoogle's mighty shoulders, had had no choice but to attempt escape across the edge of the battlefield at Dien Bien Phu. Even a year later, the evidence of war—rusting gun barrels, vehicles, tanks, and even dried, leather-skinned bodies—was everywhere. They'd found the bunker—probably a French Army observation post—next to a tangle of twisted burned metal and overgrown jungle vines and knew it was their only hope of refuge.

"French or Viet Minh?" McDoogle asked as they surveyed the half-dozen skeletons scattered about on the bunker floor by the light of his cigarette lighter.

"Both," Hughes answered, pointing to the pair of ghastly cadavers who looked as if they were still locked in combat.

"No one bothered to bury the dead," Curtiss said, wrapping a kerchief around his nose and mouth to cut down on the inhalation of the gruesome stench. "These souls cannot rest without proper burial. . . ."

It was only about five minutes later that they heard the communist troops approaching. Upon dousing their cigarette lighters, the bunker was plunged into absolute darkness, and the four men hunkered down and became very still. For the next ten heart-stopping minutes they didn't dare breathe, as they could hear the Viet Minh troops searching for them nearby.

"They'll never come in here," Evers muttered under his breath after a while. "They don't have the balls. . . ."

The comment, coming as it did out of the pitch-black dark and in Evers's usual flippant tone, was so reminiscent of the time he had spent in dark isolation aboard the *Holly One* that for an instant, Hughes thought he was back aboard the grounded carrier.

It also gave him hope that his friend was slowly coming around to understanding what was happening.

As soon as it sounded as if the Viet Minh had moved away, Hughes crawled over to Evers.

"It was the message you made out of the plants," he whispered to him. "That's how we knew where you were. . . ."

Evers didn't answer right away. Instead, the sounds of sniffing and maybe even weeping came out of the dark.

"It's almost too impossible to believe." Evers said, his voice thick and raspy. "I've been through so much. . . . You have no idea what they've done to me. . . ."

"Shut yer yap for now," McDoogle hissed at him, hearing the sounds of the soldiers returning. "Or we'll all wind up in some commie stew."

"I told you, those guys don't have the guts to come down here," Evers repeated, his voice getting stronger with every word. "I've been in that village for almost two years, and none of those guys ever came anywhere near this place. That's why all these bodies are around here. They're too afraid to come near them. These Reds are all superstitious bastards."

"If you don't keep quiet they'll hear us!" McDoogle whispered urgently across the completely dark chamber.

"Let 'em!" Evers suddenly half yelled. "I've been kicked around by those assholes for five years. They can't do much more to me. . . ."

Hughes was both heartened and horrified by the exchange. On the one hand, it sounded as if Evers were returning to his old self—and at post-Mach speed. On the other hand, he *was* talking loudly enough to attract the Viet Minh soldiers, whom they could now hear chattering just outside the bunker.

"Keep it down, Gabe," Hughes told him urgently.

"Oh *bullshit!*" Evers replied. "I've been shut up for five years!"

"Do I have to punch you?" McDoogle whispered angrily.

"You know, you owe me money," was Evers's reply.

"Fer what?" McDoogle replied, his voice now reaching the same dangerous volume as his friend's.

"For the goddamn World Series," Evers told him. "I had fifty bucks on the Nationals, and you never paid up."

"He's recovered," McDoogle declared. "Now I won't feel bad socking him. . . ."

Both men quieted down as the sounds of the Viet Minh soldiers alternately got louder and then, finally, more distant.

In the few hours of relative safety that followed, Hughes and McDoogle took turns explaining to Evers what had happened in America over the past five years and how the rather incredible set of circumstances had brought them to the point where they'd been able to attempt his rescue.

Even in the complete darkness, Hughes could see Evers nodding his head, rubbing his hands together, and nervously squinting, just like he used to do during their weird days inside the light-deprivation chamber.

At one point he turned to Hughes and asked if he had married Molly after all. Hughes nearly choked up while explaining that Molly was long gone by the time he'd returned from Korea.

All the while, Curtiss sat in one corner of the bunker, chanting softly under his breath: "We have to become invisible . . ."

It was close to midnight when they finally moved out of the bunker.

They had no choice but to abandon their hiding place,

even though they could still hear the rustlings of the enemy soldiers nearby. Bull's original plan called for any stragglers to rendezvous back at the lake by dawn the following day. Anyone not there would be left behind.

Evers was nearly fully recovered from the shock of the ordeal by this time. He and McDoogle had spent much of the time in the pitch-black bunker arguing about old, unpaid baseball bets. As for Hughes, he was happy just to sit by the entrance of the bunker, acting as the lookout and listening to his two friends squabble. Throughout it all, Curtiss hardly said a word, beyond his chanting about becoming invisible.

Now, stepping out into the dark, moonless night, they got their bearings from the stars and began moving northeast, toward Liberation Lake. Hughes estimated they were about seven miles away, with most of the terrain in between being heavy jungle. However, according to his map, there was a road a mile and a half from their position that would carry them close to the seaplane's original landing point.

They agreed that their best chance of being rescued was to reach the road and then double-time it to the lake.

Curtiss led the way as they battled their way through the dense vegetation that bordered Dien Bien Phu and separated them from the road. Even Evers was surprised by the man's remarkable skills in finding the path of least resistance through the hellish forest. It had taken Hughes more than an hour back at the bunker to explain to Evers how Curtiss had become a full-fledged Mescalero Apache as well as the impetus behind the rescue mission. But as they snaked their way through the jungle, Hughes could see that the strange man was reaching new heights of skill and daring, a far cry from the shell of a human being he had encountered in the military cemetery just a few weeks before.

"Faith," Hughes heard himself thinking. "The man has faith in what he's doing. . . ."

The first sign of trouble appeared just as they came up on the road.

Curtiss instantly froze, the others quickly following suit. Coming right for them was a patrol of twenty Viet Minh soldiers.

"God, this is it," McDoogle whispered, knowing as they all did that there was no route of escape.

Hughes dejectedly loaded the first round into his M-1's chamber, realizing that it would be a quick firefight when the shooting broke out.

Is this how my life ends, he thought, *killed in the middle of the jungle by a commie?* After the many death-defying test flights he'd taken, it seemed ironic that he should meet his end at the hands of some ignorant, sandal-clad bastard who had probably never even seen an airplane up close.

"Let's take as many of them as possible," Evers said as the enemy soldiers approached to within fifteen feet of them.

"No!" Curtiss urgently whispered to them. "We're not going to fight them. Put down your guns. . . ."

"Are you crazy?" Hughes growled at him. "These guys aren't going to take prisoners."

"Just do what I tell you," Curtiss replied sharply.

Moving quickly and silently, Curtiss had the three other men crowd together, each one facing a different direction. Then he added his own body to form a tight square.

"We will be *invisible* to them," he whispered. "If we just stay tight, keep our elbows touching, and think it . . . *think it* as hard as you can. . . ."

The enemy soldiers were so close no one had any time to argue with him. Hughes felt his body freeze into the position, his right elbow tight against McDoogle, his left against Evers, his finger still on the trigger of his rifle.

"Think it!" Curtiss urged them in a desperate whisper. "We are invisible. . . . They can't see us. . . . Don't stop thinking it. . . ."

At that moment, the first two soldiers entered the small patch of open ground where the four Americans were standing. Hughes did his best not to tremble but found it difficult. He was prepared to hear the first crack of gunfire that would cut the four of them down like a sickle through weeds.

But then the strangest thing in his already unusual life happened. *The first two enemy soldiers walked right by them.* Hughes felt completely spooked. He didn't know if it was the lack of light, or the shadows, or what, but it did appear as if the Reds couldn't see what was right in front of them.

Suddenly Hughes's mind was racing: "I *am* invisible. . . ."

Slowly, more of the enemy patrol came toward them. Again, to the utter astonishment of Hughes, Evers, and McDoogle, the communist soldiers just walked right on by.

Hughes felt like he was going to lose his bodily functions. The communist soldiers were passing by so close, one man's face was no more than half a foot away from his. The soldier even looked directly at him—into his eyes!—and then looked away and continued walking.

The incredible terror of the moment passed as the last of the Viet Minh soldiers walked by and kept right on going, deeper into the forest. Still the four men stayed frozen in place for the next five minutes—not one of them wanting to move, less they break the spell and reveal their position.

Finally Curtiss spoke: "Okay, very slowly move your elbows down and let your arms hang at your sides."

The three others unquestioningly did this, confused as to why they were still alive. Had it been a miracle? Or a fluke? Or had Curtiss somehow tapped into an incredible supernatural power?

They would never know.

"And now breathe," Curtiss told them.

Again, they followed his instructions. A second later, Hughes felt as if he'd woken from a trance.

Curtiss rubbed his eyes hard and took a deep breath himself. "Now," he said, "let's get out of here. . . ."

They reached the edge of Liberation Lake just as the long strange night was coming to an end.

They had trotted most of the way down the road to the lake, not seeing a single Viet Minh soldier after their bizarre encounter in the middle of the jungle. No one talked about the strange experience—no one dared.

They were alive, and for the moment, that's all that mattered.

Hughes was not surprised or disappointed to see that the seaplane was not on the lake. Quite the opposite, he was heartened that it was *not* there. All their efforts to reach the lake would have been for naught if they had arrived to see the burning hulk of the seaplane drifting out on the water, its passengers and crew slaughtered. Now the very fact that it was not there meant that someone had survived the raid on Bac Ha and that if they stuck to Bull's plan, then they would return for them.

They hid in the foliage about a quarter-mile from the original landing spot and waited. Fifteen minutes later, Curtiss was the first to hear the whine of the approaching airplane.

"Here it comes," he said, almost to himself.

The others had to strain their ears for a few moments before they too heard the unmistakable sounds of the six propellers and four jet engines of the *Dreamer*.

"Okay, everyone," Hughes said. "Time to take off your pants."

They did as they were told. Following Hughes into the shallow water, they mimicked his method of creating a flotation device by tying off the bottom of each pants leg, then capturing air in the rest of each leg itself. Then, by fastening the top of the pants with their belt, each had an improvised set of water wings.

The seaplane overflew the lake once and, with a quick blink of its taillights, indicated that the four men had been spotted. Slowly the huge aircraft circled, spiraled down, and finally landed with a great splash.

"Almost home, Gabe," Hughes yelled over to his friend. "We're almost there. . . ."

Nguyen Phan Dong watched the big seaplane circle the lake, and this time he was prepared to act.

He had clung to the rock all of the night before the last, petrified at what horrors the men in the airplane might be bringing back to the area around Dien Bien Phu. Finally, that next morning, after he had watched soldiers and equipment be loaded off the great airship and onto the beach, he summoned enough courage inside to attempt the swim to shore. He had made it—but just barely.

Running at full speed back to his village, he had been disappointed to learn that the small garrison of soldiers usually stationed there had moved out. There had been a battle of some kind going on at nearby Bac Ha, and the soldiers had been sent to help the prison guards. With only children and old women to tell his story to, Nguyen had collapsed from exhaustion and gone to sleep.

He had been awoken later on by the sounds of gunfire and the terrifying roar of the airplane's engines. Rushing back to the lake, he'd arrived just in time to see the seaplane take off and disappear over the horizon to the west. Again he had returned to his village to find that some of the garrison had returned. With pleading tones he had told his story to the garrison's commander, who, although he'd just fought against the mysterious raiders at Bac Ha, refused to believe that they had arrived on Liberation Lake by an airplane of such enormous proportions.

"They had jeeps," the officer had told Nguyen harshly. "They drove here in them and they escaped in them. We checked the lake and saw no airplane."

Nguyen was appalled that the officer would not believe him. Returning to his hut, he had fallen into a fitful sleep, only to be awakened early in the morning by the far-off sounds that he thought were of the airplane engines. Knowing the garrison commander would probably shoot him on the spot if he dared to wake the officer at that early hour, Nguyen had retrieved an old French rifle he had surreptitiously taken from the Dien Bien Phu battlefield a year before. He had then set out for the lake once again.

Now hidden on the beach, Nguyen loaded his only bullet into the rifle and looked out toward the taxiing airplane. The rifle, probably once used by a French Army sniper, was equipped with a telescopic lens, which is why Nguyen had taken it in the first place. Although the scope was cracked and loose, it had still aided him in bringing down birds and small game, meat with which to supplement his family's meager food ration.

Sighting through the scope, Nguyen watched as the huge airplane slowed down and approached the four men who were floating out toward it. His original intention was to shoot the pilot of the huge airplane, thinking this would disable the whole aircraft and that he would thus have proof of its existence. But to his dismay, the windows of the cockpit were dark and fogged, meaning that he could not be certain with one shot that the pilot would be killed. Knowing he had to change his plan, he watched the four men swim toward the open hatchway at the rear of the airplane.

One of them would have to be his victim, he thought.

He propped the rifle up on a shore rock and sighted the first man being pulled up into the airplane. Cocking the gun, he took a deep breath and then pulled the trigger.

The bullet hit Evers behind his right ear.

81

Mescalero

"SIR, WE HAVE TO launch within twenty minutes or the fuel load will be unstable."

Xavier grabbed the nearest microphone and switched it to send a message throughout the Tomarc launch bunker.

"Attention," he roared. "As of this moment, any man who questions my judgment concerning this launch will be court-martialed."

Shaking, tired, and mentally depleted, Xavier threw the microphone away from him, hitting a small TV screen on his command console and cracking the glass slightly. The men in the bunker had been at their stations all night and into the afternoon of this day, the launch of the Tomarc waiting for Xavier's orders.

The men could see that Xavier was acting irrationally—his half-dozen outbursts during the night seemingly confirmed their most hidden-away suspicions. For many it was the senior officer's orders around midnight to disconnect all the outside phone lines except one that proved he'd gone off the deep end. Without contact with the various tracking stations that stretched from the bunker to the Mescalero base itself, the missile could not be launched safely. Others were convinced that Xavier was losing his grip when he led them in a long, rambling prayer session around four that morning, the only illumination being the single prayer candle Xavier always kept lit when the bunker was occupied. During the fifty-five-minute ordeal, the general mumbled and coughed frequently, repeated himself often, lost track of his thoughts on several occasions, and overall appeared to be very confused. For many of those in the bunker, it was a frightening display to watch. Up until then, Xavier had been their hero—a quixotic leader, true, but still someone cut in the mold of a Patton or Pershing or Billy Mitchell.

The day dawned in the stuffy bunker and there was no morning chow. The only refreshment for the men was a rusty water bubbler, and this too seemed to be running low. Many began to feel trapped inside the bunker, forced to listen to Xavier's frequent outbursts as well as his meandering, all too sentimental reminiscences. Although deserting their posts may have meant a court-martial, most men would have bolted for the door. The Shine Boys stayed, however, and listened as their commander apparently went insane.

It was close to four in the afternoon when the only phone line into the bunker rang twice. Xavier casually picked up the phone, listened intently for a few moments, then asked the caller to repeat the information: "You say it just took off from Phoenix? What's its heading? Speed? Altitude? Okay, two-engine Starcruiser. ETA Mescalero one hour, twelve minutes . . . Thank you and God bless . . ."

The call seemed to pump new life into the officer, though he became even more twisted.

"Okay, boys, we are finally ready for launch!" he declared, standing up on his console to address the men as if he were a Roman emperor addressing his people. "Launch Officer, get up here and I'll give you the new flight coordinates. . . . Pad crews, get the hell out there and do your preflights, double-time, now!"

Only one voice chose to question the madness. It was the fuel-consignment officer.

"Sir, the fuel may be unstable by now," he called out as calmly as possible. "We may have to void it and refuel. . . ."

Xavier's complexion went through six shades of crimson before he climbed down off the console and walked up to confront the man.

"For what reason do you choose this moment to defy me?" he asked.

"Sir, the fuel has been in the missile's tank for nearly twenty-four hours," the extremely nervous man began. "It has been alternately exposed to the heat of yesterday afternoon, the coolness of last night, and now the heat of today. That's enough to make the mixture unstable."

Xavier scratched his chin in thought, like a schoolmaster contemplating the punishment for an unruly pupil.

"You will do anything to postpone this launch, won't you?" he asked the man. "Anything to make it less of a success? Can you please tell me what our mission is here today?"

Somehow the man found some more nerve at this point.

"Sir, our original mission was to actuate the first night launch of the missile," he said. "But due to the delays, I can't imagine that happening now."

"Launching at night was simply a cover for our actual mission," Xavier suddenly declared with an absolutely frightening smile. "We will launch in fifteen minutes."

"General!" the fuel officer surprised everyone by shouting. "It's now ninety-nine degrees outside, sir. That fuel has gone through three serious temperature fluctuations. You know that's dangerous."

"You are hereby relieved of your duties," Xavier told the man quickly. "You are to lock yourself up inside the lavatory and stay there until further orders. When we return to the base, you will be put in the brig until I convene a court-martial. *Now move!*"

Xavier turned and stared defiantly at the rest of the men.

"Is there anyone else here who would like to question my authority?" he asked.

There were no takers.

"Fine," he continued. "Now, let me at last tell you the *real* mission we are here to accomplish."

Xavier retook his position atop his command console and spread his arms out like a priest addressing his flock.

"This exercise has actually been part of a secret project all along," he began. "Because of security reasons, I had to withhold this information from you all until now. My recent disciplinary action will be more understandable once I explain to you the purpose of this rather unusual mission."

Xavier took a deep breath and continued.

"What we have been simulating here is a situation as close as we will ever get to an actual wartime condition without war actually being declared. We have been locked up here, gentlemen, for almost twenty-four hours. We have not been fed. We have not gotten our proper rest. We have begun fighting amongst ourselves. Now, I ask you, what would happen if our country were really under attack and we, the holders of the sword of defense for the entire country, were cut off from our command? Wouldn't it be exactly like this?"

There was a smattering of nods.

"Then you see, men, we have accomplished the first part of this very unique exercise.

"I apologize if I frightened or confused any of you during the course of this exercise. But you must realize that my orders—which came straight from the Pentagon—explicitly stated that I be responsible to imitate every condition of a state of war as possible. I think we have all done that very well. I congratulate all of you and will issue a unit citation as soon as we return to the base."

One man started clapping, and suddenly the room was filled with loud, if still somewhat uncertain, applause.

"Now it is on to the second part of the exercise!" Xavier yelled. "For the first time we have been given an actual target to shoot at. A drone has just been launched from Luke Air Force Base and it is heading this way, simulating a rogue Soviet bomber. It is our mission to shoot it down. So, everyone to their posts!"

There was a scramble for positions, some of the men fully buying the "wartime conditions" explanation. It would not be the first military exercise they'd participated in that came with that label. As for the others, they being the doubters of the group, they too returned to their posts and began working with gusto, sensing, if anything, that they would not leave the bunker until the damn missile was launched.

However, the overall launch officer—the man who actually pushed the button that ignited the Tomarc's engines—had one question.

"Who is going to handle the fuel-consignment officer's duties?" he asked Xavier.

The general didn't pause for even a split second.

"I will," he said.

82

THE CELEBRATION WAS IN progress as soon as the airplane owned by the New England Bay Corporation took off from the Phoenix Municipal Airport.

Jack Kenneally himself popped the cork from the first bottle of champagne while his pretty secretary, Betty, passed out plastic cups to the five congressional aides and to Chas Spencer.

"We beat the bastards!" Kenneally yelled as those assembled clicked their filled glasses in a toast. "Now it's on to bigger and better things. . . ."

"Your father will want a full report," Betty told him, her voice just slightly more familiar in tone than a secretary would normally use to address her boss. "Are you going to tell him all of it?"

Jack Jr. looked at Spencer and laughed. "How can I not?" he asked. "He probably knows as much about it now as I do."

"Maybe more." Betty giggled.

Spencer gulped his champagne and then stuck his cup up for more. He was having more fun than he had ever had on a three-day pass.

"When you think of it, Xavier and his guys turned out to be kind of dumb," he said. "All they had to do was come clean that the F-98A was lacking in range and then go from there. We all know that range is usually a function of weight, and weight can usually be reduced over time. We see it all the time in our tests."

"They got arrogant," Kenneally told him. "Too ballsy and too greedy at the same time. Plus they were like a bunch of religious zealots. You couldn't reason with them—it was their way or no way. That's a dangerous way to think in these times.

"But you have to give them credit for something: Shooting those missiles into the desert and pretending like they were splashing down in the Pacific—that took a certain finesse to pull off."

The bottle was passed around a second time, and Kenneally proposed another toast.

"To manned flight," he said. "Always and forever."

"Amen!" Spencer replied.

Five minutes later, the Starcruiser airliner passed over the Arizona border and into New Mexico.

Kenneally picked up a white telephone and called ahead to the flight crew.

"How long before we set down at Mescalero?" he asked the pilot.

"About another hour, sir," came the reply.

83

Mescalero

"LAUNCH IN FIVE MINUTES . . ."

General Xavier leaned over his tracking map and drew a straight line from the point indicating Mescalero to a point close to the Arizona-New Mexico border.

"I want a radar-track confirmation on that bogie now!" he yelled to his tracking crew.

"Bogie just over Black Mountain, sir," was the reply. "Approximately one hundred and fifty miles out and closing."

"Shall I confirm that track with Luke, sir?" Xavier's radio officer asked.

"No!" the general exploded. "We are under wartime conditions here. Would you expect it to be so easy to pick up a phone and call Arizona if our country had just sustained an atomic attack?"

'No, sir," came the sheepish reply.

Xavier spent the next few minutes fiddling with the missile's fuel-feed-system dials. Instead of emptying its tanks and refilling them, he'd simply been purging the Tomarc's fuel through its pumps and back into its tanks again, theorizing that this would cool off the volatile mixture of ethene and kerosene.

"Launch in four minutes . . ."

Xavier clapped his hands in delight as he leaned over the control board's radar-tracking screen and fixed his gaze on the small blip that was moving slowly across the green screen.

"Launch in three minutes . . ."

"Begin active tracking system!" Xavier called out.

"Yes, sir!"

"Input update controls to the guidance system!"

"Done, sir!"

"What is the target's present position?"

"We read bogie at one hundred and twenty miles, due west, sir," the tracking officer reported. "Speed at two hundred knots. Altitude seventeen thousand feet, descending slightly . . ."

"Lock those coordinates into the targeting system," Xavier ordered.

"Done, sir."

Xavier reached down and loosened his belt all the way. A familiar sensation was starting to well up between his legs. *The last one is always the best,* he thought.

"Two minutes to launch . . ."

Xavier took a long deep breath and said a quick prayer. "God forgive me for what I am about to do," he whispered.

"One minute to launch . . ."

At that point the launch officer nervously approached Xavier as the man continued to twist the dials on the fuel-consignment control board.

"General, that bogie is tracking very large for a drone," he said. "Any chance that Luke may not have cleared the area of civilian aircraft?"

Xavier didn't even look up at the man. "We are under wartime conditions," he told the man. "We can't cross every *t* and dot every *i*."

"Thirty seconds to launch . . ."

The launch officer sighed and checked his clipboard.

"Fuel systems up and on line, sir?" he asked, putting the same question to Xavier that he would normally have asked the fuel-consignment officer.

"Roger," Xavier said, strangely sounding like a young boy.

"Twenty seconds . . ."

"Arm the warhead!" Xavier called out.

"Warhead armed, sir."

"Fifteen seconds . . ."

Xavier sat back and relaxed for the first time in days. Squinting slightly, he could see the huge Tomarc out on the pad, waiting to leap into the air at his command.

Well, Mr. Kenneally, he thought. *Your son is finally going to become a hero. . . .*

"Ten seconds . . ."

At that moment, Xavier casually swung his feet up onto the control desk, pushing his hands down past his opened belt buckle and close to his crotch.

"Five seconds . . ."

In an instant, Xavier looked at his boots and was horrified to see a large smudge on his left toe.

Just as he leaned forward to rub the imperfection away, the launch officer cried out, *"Fire!"*

The missile exploded on the pad. At the moment of ignition, vapors remaining in the fuel purge lines were sparked off and instantaneously blew up one of the missile's main fuel tanks. The Tomarc, instantly engulfed in smoke and flames, actually lifted off from the pad but went no higher than ten feet before it slowly lost power and began to sway. In the meantime, fuel from its other tank gushed out of several perforations and streamed right into the launch bunker.

When the missile came crashing back down onto the pad just six seconds after the launch officer had pushed its ignition button, it sparked off the hundreds of gallons of fuel that had flooded into the bunker, obliterating it and instantly incinerating all inside.

EPILOGUE

Mescalero, Two Months Later

THE TWO YOUNG PILOTS saw the senior officer coming down the flight line from almost a quarter-mile away.

"That's him," one said to the other. "I hear he can be okay, but if he asks you any questions about your aircraft, you'd better have the right answer."

This being only their second day at Mescalero, the two pilots awaited the arrival of the base commander with a somewhat nervous anticipation. As they watched him walk past the long line of jets on the tarmac, they saw that he was dressed in a full flight suit and carrying his own helmet. The man accompanying him was also dressed in a flight suit, though with his rather longish hair and glasses he didn't appear to fit the usual military-pilot profile.

The pilots snapped to attention and cracked off crisp salutes as the commander reached them.

"New here?" Hughes asked them.

"Just in last night, sir," one of the pilots answered. "I'm Captain Simms. This is Lieutenant Orly. . . ."

"Well, at ease, men," Hughes said. "I'm new here myself, at least in this capacity. No sense in all this saluting and ceremony if we're just out here on the flight line. Understood?"

"Yes, sir," both men answered.

Hughes returned their habitual salute, and he and Curtiss continued walking down the flight line until they'd reached the two-seat F-89 Scorpion.

"I can't tell you how much I appreciate this, 'Cane," Curtiss told him, his eyes misty as he regarded the big F-89, the first fighter he'd been this close to in years. "It must have taken a few strings being pulled to get clearance for a civilian. . . ."

"It was actually no problem at all," Hughes replied as they both climbed up into the fighter. "Besides, all the strings were snapped when they reactivated me and made me commander of this place."

"Stranger things have happened. . . ." Curtiss said.

It was late afternoon, and the hot New Mexico sun was just beginning to dip behind the mountains to their west. With minimal help from a three-man ground crew, Hughes got the F-89's big engines up and running quickly, and within ten minutes he was taxiing toward Mescalero's main runway.

"I've waited five years for this," Curtiss called to him over the plane's interphone. "I just never thought it would happen again."

"Relax and enjoy it," Hughes told him, pulling out onto the runway. "I owe you much more than this. We all do."

A minute later they were streaking down the runway. In one swift motion, Hughes pulled back on the big jet's controls and they were airborne.

He steered the F-89 due east, over the base's main hangars, over the base-personnel housing project nearby, and out beyond the Main Gate, 3B.

Within two minutes they were flying over the burned-out shell of the Tomarc launch center. There were about half a dozen yellow jeeps parked around the place, vehicles belonging to the Air Force team investigating the accident that destroyed the facility.

Turning north, they cruised over the outer reaches of the place known as the Flats, the location of Curtiss's near-fatal airplane crash five years before. Curtiss had specifically asked Hughes to overfly the area, knowing that if he saw it from this vantage point again, it would help dispel the demons that had haunted him since.

Hughes circled the area three times, then banked sharply and headed south toward the small town of Bent, New Mexico.

On the ground, inside the Bum Dummy saloon, Peter McDoogle looked up from his grilled cheese and bacon sandwich, his ears detecting the first sounds of the approaching jet.

He knew it was probably Hughes taking Curtiss up for his long-awaited "joy ride," and he smiled just for a second, the first time he'd been able to do so since returning from the harrowing rescue mission in Indochina.

Some are saved, he thought, shaking his head at the thought of how Curtiss had changed—how he had rejoined the living, so to speak.

Then he thought of the person sitting in the small apartment on the second floor of the saloon and the smile quickly vanished. *From five weeks in a hospital to this,* he thought.

The jet passed overhead about half a minute later,

flying low enough to shake the ancient wooden barroom to its rafters.

Upstairs, sitting motionless in a rickety rocking chair, his body permanently paralyzed, his brain damaged beyond repair, Gabe Evers could not hear the airplane.

About the Author

Brian Kelleher has worked as a sportswriter and editor as well as in the press-relations field. He is a graduate of Emerson College in Boston and a native of Newburyport, Massachusetts. He currently writes on aviation topics full-time.